Praise for the novels of Rick Mofina

"*The Panic Zone* is a headlong rush
toward Armageddon. Its bri[...]
remind me of ear[...]
—*New York Times* bests[...]

"*Vengeance Road* is a t[...]
It's a gr[...]
—Michael Connelly, *New Yo[...]

"A gripping no-holds-barred mystery...
lightning paced...with enough twists to
keep you turning pages well into the wee hours.
Vengeance Road is masterful suspense."
—Allison Brennan, *New York Times* bestselling author

"*Six Seconds* should be Rick Mofina's
breakout thriller. It moves like a tornado."
—James Patterson, *New York Times* bestselling author

"*Six Seconds*...grabs your gut—and your heart—
in the opening scenes and never lets go."
—Jeffery Deaver, *New York Times* bestselling author

"A great thriller."
—Lee Child, *New York Times* bestselling author,
on *Six Seconds*

"One of the leading thriller writers of the day."
—*Penthouse* magazine

"A lightning-paced thriller with lean, tense writing...
Mofina really knows how to make the story fly."
—Tess Gerritsen, *New York Times* bestselling author,
on *A Perfect Grave*

"*No Way Back* is my kind of novel—a tough, taut thriller."
—Michael Connelly, *New York Times* bestselling author

"*The Dying Hour* starts scary and ends scary.
You'll be craving Mofina's next novel."
—Sandra Brown, *New York Times* bestselling author

RICK MOFINA

THE PANIC ZONE

MIRA®

ISBN-13: 978-0-7783-2794-3

Recycling programs for this product may not exist in your area.

THE PANIC ZONE

For questions and comments about the quality of this book please contact us at Customer_eCare@Harlequin.ca.

www.MIRABooks.com

Printed in U.S.A.

**This book is for
Laura and Michael**

And I looked, and behold a pale horse:
and his name that sat on him was Death,
and Hell followed with him.
                    —*Revelation* 6:8

1

Big Cloud, Wyoming

Emma Lane whispered a prayer for her baby son, Tyler, cooing in his car seat behind her.

Her miracle.

Over the past few days, he'd been pale and had run a fever.

"Just a little cold. Give it another twenty-four hours," the doctor had told Emma, who had succumbed to the anxieties of being a new mother until Tyler's illness had passed.

Now, with her worries eased, Emma smiled and reached back to adjust her son's straps as their SUV cut across Wyoming's rolling plains.

"Everything good?" her husband, Joe, asked as he drove.

"Everything's good." Emma caressed Joe's firm shoulder, then kissed his cheek.

"What's that for?"

"For putting up with me."

"Do I have a choice?" He chuckled.

They gazed at the Rockies before them, a majestic reminder that some things stood forever, while others lasted no longer than a shooting star. And after what they had gone through to have Tyler, Emma took nothing for granted. Life did not come with guarantees. It was as indifferent to you as those mountains out there.

Emma thought it was funny how the things she'd

dreamed of had come to her in ways she never expected. She was thankful for the blessings she could touch, hold and love forever: her son and her husband.

Today, they were headed to a pretty spot north of town, for a picnic beside the Grizzly Tooth River. This would be a break for Joe, who had been putting in twelve-hour days for the past three weeks straight, building houses in Big Cloud's new subdivision.

Lord knows they needed the overtime cash, but fretting over Joe's long hours and Tyler had kept Emma on edge lately.

On Monday, her two-week break ended and she would return to Rocky Ridge Elementary School where she taught children in the first and second grades. They were little sweethearts and Emma loved teaching, but she hated being apart from Tyler.

Joe guided the SUV along the empty highway, a meandering back route few people took. With the exception of a couple of cars that had passed them earlier, the road belonged to them. It was soothing. As the wheels hummed, Emma thought of other matters, like the spate of wrong number calls to their house over the past month. They had come at all hours—in the afternoon, when Emma was home alone with Tyler, and in the middle of the night. The callers never said anything. They were quick hang-ups and the number was always blocked.

Like someone was checking in on them, she thought.

But Joe shrugged it off. "Just people who can't dial," he assured her.

Eventually, Emma stopped worrying about it, too. Until the episode with the mystery car.

One day last week, after she had finished shopping downtown and was leaving her parking spot, she noticed a white sedan that had arrived at the same time she had.

It was a few cars back and it seemed to be following her.

When she pulled in to the mall, it was still a few spots

behind her. After Emma parked and got Tyler into his carriage, she saw it again, parked off in a far corner. It was still there when she returned to her car and left the mall's parking lot. Emma was not certain if the sedan left when she did because she had lost sight of it in the drive-home traffic.

A day later when she took Tyler out for a stroll to the park, Emma saw the same white sedan at the end of their street.

"Do you think maybe you're being a little paranoid?" Joe had said when she told him about it later. "It's the mama grizzly syndrome kicking in."

When she didn't smile at his teasing, he got up from the kitchen table, left his receipts and job estimates, and put his arms around her.

"Em," Joe said, "Big Cloud has nine thousand people. We bump into most of them every other day. You're likely seeing someone new."

She pressed her cheek to his hard chest and nodded.

"Besides," he added, "you're one of the most fearless people I know. Woe to anyone or anything that comes between you and Tyler. If it was a mama griz, I would fear for the bear."

Emma smiled at the memory and turned to her husband. He was her rock, her protector, her hero because of what he'd gone through for her.

Tyler did not come to them the usual way.

Joe was a proud man and what he did for her was not easy. But he had put her happiness before his own and, no matter what happened, Emma would always love him for that.

Always.

She studied Joe's strong jaw stubbled just the way she liked. She looked at the tiny lines at the corners of his eyes that crinkled when he laughed, or searched the horizon as he did now.

Emma was about to tell him that she loved him but the

words never left her mouth. A sharp blast of their horn jolted her. Joe's expression switched to one of surprise. An oncoming car had veered onto their side of the road, leaving them no escape from a head-on crash.

"Hang on, Em!"

Joe twisted the wheel, swerving to miss the collision.

"Joe!"

The SUV was airborne with the world churning, glass breaking, metal crunching, sparks flying, as it rolled and rolled before everything went black.

When Emma came to, she was outside their vehicle, facedown on the ground. Her vision was blurred. Something was ringing in her ears. Their horn was blaring.

Tyler was screaming somewhere, but Emma couldn't see him.

She saw Joe.

He'd gone halfway through the windshield. Emma crawled to him, reached for him and took his hand.

"Stay with me, Joe. Don't leave me."

Emma passed out, came to, then did it again and again.

Time stopped.

She could smell gas, burning rubber. Something was hissing, she heard car doors, people running, someone shouting. Someone was checking the wreckage. Everything was hazy.

Emma's heartbeat thundered in her ears.

"Hurry!" she screamed.

An engine raced.

"Find my baby!"

Emma felt Joe's pulse stop as people carried her away.

"Get my husband out! Find my baby!"

The air around them spasmed as if hammered by an invisible fist that delivered the heat flash and fireball as the SUV ignited.

Someone rescued Tyler. Emma saw them carry him to safety.

Or she thought she did.

Where was her baby?

Oh, God! Tyler had to be safe. He had to be, because he wasn't screaming anymore.

Emma was.

2

Rio de Janeiro, Brazil

The next day, Gabriela Rosa, a reporter at the Rio Bureau of the World Press Alliance, reached across her desk to answer her phone.

"*Alo,* Gabriela Rosa, WPA."

"*Eu tenho que falar a—*" The female caller's voice was overtaken by street noise. She was likely using a pay phone.

"Please speak louder."

"I have to talk to a reporter with your news agency about a big story."

"I am a reporter," Rosa said. "What's the story?"

"Not over the phone, we have to meet."

"Give me your name, please?"

"I can't."

"Perhaps you could come to our office?"

"No. I want to meet you somewhere public. I have documents. This has to get out as soon as possible."

The woman's voice betrayed fear and desperation, as if she'd had trouble summoning the courage to make this call, forcing Rosa to make a quick decision. She had nearly finished a feature on crime on the metro. Then she'd planned to visit a detective, but she could skip it.

A good reporter never turned a tipster away.

Rosa would meet the caller but she would be careful.

"Fine," Rosa said. "We are in the Centro on Rua do Riachuelo near *O Dia's* offices. Do you know it?"

"Yes."

"Five blocks west of us on Rua do Riachuelo there is the Café Amaldo. Meet me there at 2:00 p.m. sharp. My name is Gabriela Rosa. I have brown hair. I'll be wearing sunglasses, a pink shirt and white slacks. I'll be reading *Jornal do Brasil* and I'll have my white bag on the table. I will be alone. Are you coming alone?"

"Yes."

"Give me your name."

"No name. I'll find you."

"Fine, meet me at two sharp. I'll give you my cellphone number in case you must cancel. Do you want to give me a number?"

"No. I will be there at two."

"Can you give me some sense of what this story is?"

"I will tell you when we meet."

Afterward, as Rosa finished her feature, she took stock of the empty office. The bureau chief was out of town. The stringer and photographer were on assignments. The news assistant was off. Rosa was alone as she pondered her tip and WPA's rules for staff called out to meet unknown sources: "Tell people where you are going, who you are meeting and never go alone."

Rio was one of the world's most beautiful cities. It was also one of the most violent. Much of its major crime arose from drug dealing and gang wars afflicting the favelas, the crowded shanty towns that blanketed the hillsides overlooking the metropolis.

Rosa, like other news reporters in Rio, was mindful of the risks. Criminals had kidnapped and murdered journalists who threatened to expose their networks. She would not meet her source alone. She called a cell-phone number.

"*Alo,* Verde," a man answered.

"Marcelo, it's Gabriela. Are you getting back soon? I need you for a job."

"I'm leaving Santa Teresa now. Got some very nice pictures New York will love. I have to get lunch."

"No. Meet me on the street in front of Café Amaldo. I'll buy you lunch."

"That's a deal. What's the job?"

"I'm meeting a source and you're my backup. Be there at one-thirty. Don't be late. Call me if you are delayed."

Later, as Rosa prepared to leave the bureau, she called John Esper, her husband, who was also the bureau chief and who, by her estimation, would now be on a return flight from São Paulo, where he'd helped cover news of the upcoming visit by the U.S. vice president. Rosa left Esper a voice mail on his cell phone advising him she would be meeting an anonymous source at the Café Amaldo but would be with Marcelo.

Rosa walked to her meeting, absorbing the bustle of downtown Rio with its beautiful colonial buildings juxtaposed with highrises, shops and corporate towers. Some days, she could feel the city's excitement mounting in the lead up to the World Cup and the Summer Olympics. But today, as she neared the café, she thought only about the call she had received.

Sure, it could be something but these things never amounted to much. Usually, they had more to do with a personal matter of a malcontent who wanted a reporter to publicly embarrass their adversary. If that happened today, it wouldn't be a total waste. She would at least have lunch at Café Amaldo and a tale to tell Esper.

Marcelo met her near the restaurant. He was one of Brazil's best news photographers, an ex-beach bum from Copacabana who was also a bodybuilder.

"My source is meeting me here in thirty minutes. A woman," Rosa said. "You know the drill. Can you set up over there?" She nodded to the cantina across the busy street.

"Sure." He had his hand out. "But you promised me lunch."

Shaking her head, Rosa put a few bills in his palm.

"I want a receipt and the change, buddy."

Marcelo winked then left Rosa, who found an outdoor café table with a clear line of sight for Marcelo. She put her bag on the table, adjusted her sunglasses and read her newspaper.

Twenty minutes later, a taxi stopped near the café, cuing a chorus of horns. As the female passenger paid the driver, a motorcycle with two people aboard growled around it. After scanning the crowded café, the taxi's passenger approached Rosa's table and stood before her.

"May I help you?" Rosa asked.

"Gabriela?"

"Yes."

"I am the woman who called."

She had a tight grip on the strap of her bag, running her thumb over her knuckles as she took quick stock of the busy restaurant. Rosa set her newspaper aside.

"Sit down, please."

The two women filled Marcelo's lens. As he prepared to take his first shot from his table across and down the street, a large truck making a delivery blocked his view. Marcelo cursed under his breath, left money for his drink, grabbed his bag and trotted toward the Café Amaldo, passing by the mouth of a dark alley.

He did not notice that the same motorcycle, which earlier had sped by the cab, was now in the alley, sitting back from the street. Two men stood next to it, their attention fixed on the café. The driver talked in low tones on his cell phone. His passenger, dressed in a suit like a downtown banker, checked his hair in the side mirror. He slid on dark glasses, then he unfastened a tan leather briefcase that was strapped to the motorcycle's backrest.

At the café, Marcelo found a table inside, next to the large open-air window that looked out over the alfresco area. He liked the Amaldo and had used it many times like this with reporters. It had Wi-Fi wireless access. And with his camera's Eye-Fi card preconfigured, he was good to go.

Marcelo ordered a soda and sandwich then worked ever so casually, so that anyone watching would conclude he was merely cleaning his lens, when in fact he was shooting photos.

Rosa tapped her pen on her notebook while waiting for the woman to tell her story. The woman was in her twenties. She had a good figure and was pretty. She seemed educated and poised but her hand shook and she spilled some of the cream meant for her coffee.

"Forgive me, please. I'm nervous."

"What are you nervous about?"

"They could be watching me."

"Who?"

"Give me a moment. I want to do this. But I need to go to the lavatory."

Rosa was a veteran reporter, not easily frightened or fooled. She sensed something genuine about this woman and was relieved when a few minutes later she returned.

"You know," Gabriela said, "you should tell me what's going on."

"No one will believe it. It goes beyond Brazil. It's why I chose your news agency. You must tell the world." The woman extracted a brown envelope from her bag. "You have to investigate, it has to be exposed."

"What has to be exposed?"

"Some of it is in these documents."

At that moment, a man in a suit, wearing dark glasses, navigated his way among the tables of the crowded café. He reached inside his jacket for his wallet but dropped it.

As he bent over to retrieve it amid the din, no one saw him place his tan briefcase under a chair occupied only by shopping bags. The chair was being saved for someone who had not yet arrived at the crowded table.

Brushing off his wallet, the man walked into the restaurant and left unnoticed by a side door. He strode to a corner while pressing several numbers on his cell phone. A motorcycle stopped next to him and he put on a helmet then climbed on behind the driver.

At her table, Rosa began flipping through the documents as her source explained the story.

Two tables away, as a group of well-dressed women cleared the chair of shopping bags for their friend who had arrived, the tan briefcase under it fell over.

The woman nearest to it blinked in question.

One of them reached down toward it, but the briefcase disappeared in a blinding flash of hot light. Glass in buildings near and above the café exploded in the concussive wave. Blood, flesh and debris showered on the street, pelting people a block away.

A fireball rolled skyward.

3

New York City

The World Press Alliance headquarters is at midtown Manhattan's western edge.

Jack Gannon hurried back to it, walking by the Long Island Railroad maintenance yards, where Thirty-third Street slopes into a bleak wasteland near the Hudson River. From here, he could see the helicopters lifting off and landing at the West Thirtieth Street Heliport.

Beyond that: New Jersey.

His cell phone vibrated again. Another text message: Where are you?

Be there in ten, he responded.

Nearly trotting now, he passed the graffiti-covered wall of a shipping depot where shopping-cart pushers sorted their morning bounty of cans. One man in dreadlocks and a faded Obama T-shirt was dismantling a TV for recycling.

"Can you help your brother? I need food."

Gannon reached into his pocket where he still had the change from his hot-dog lunch and fished out a crumpled five.

"Bless you. Have a long, happy life."

Gannon was still new to the city, and his heart had not hardened toward the hard-luck cases he saw every day.

Since he'd left Buffalo for his new job at the WPA, he'd taken to walking New York's streets whenever he could. He was on desk duty today and had come to this isolated tract on his lunch break to be alone.

To think.

He was five months into his dream of working at one of the world's largest news organizations and he still had not landed a good story.

So far he'd reported on a homicide, and helped with the coverage of a school shooting in California and a charter bus crash near the Grand Canyon. He'd inserted national paragraphs into stories from WPA's foreign bureaus. He had also been assigned to night shifts helping edit copy on the national and world desks. Soon, he realized that not everyone at WPA wanted him there, something made clear the night he'd overheard two copy editors kibitzing by the features desk.

"What do you make of Jack Gannon?"

"I haven't seen any pizzazz. He's out of his league."

"Didn't the *Buffalo Sentinel* fire him, or something? I missed all that."

"He's one of Melody Lyon's projects. She hired him after he broke that story on the Buffalo detective and the missing women."

"That one wasn't bad."

"Gannon's got more luck than talent, if you ask me. What's he done since?"

"Not much."

"That's my point. And you're right, he was fired by the *Sentinel,* so was his managing editor. It was a stinking mess. I heard that O'Neill and Stone were against Gannon's hire but that Melody wanted it done. I hear he's disappointed people and there's talk they might let him go."

"Really?"

"It's a rumor. I think he should be punted back to Buffalo."

"Didn't his bio say that he'd been nominated for a Pulitzer way back for the story on the jetliner and the whacked-out Russian pilot?"

"A Russian-speaking guy in the *Sentinel*'s pressroom did all the talking to sources overseas, Gannon just took dictation."

That was a load of bull!

Gannon had bristled on the other side of the file cabinets, out of sight.

They were wrong about him.

Dead wrong, he repeated to himself now, as he jogged to a crosswalk to make the light. He'd earned his shot with the WPA, crawled through hell to get to New York. He belonged here and he'd prove it.

Gannon entered the twenty-story WPA building, swiped his ID badge at the security turnstile and stepped into the elevator.

He checked his phone. Nineteen minutes since Melody Lyon, the deputy executive—the WPA's number two editor after Beland Stone—had summoned him with her first text.

We need to see you now.

He got off the elevator on the sixteenth floor with a measure of honor as he strode by the reception wall displaying WPA news photos of history's most compelling moments from the past hundred years.

The World Press Alliance was one of the world's largest news wire services, operating a bureau in every major U.S. city, and two hundred bureaus in seventy-five countries, providing a nonstop flow of information to thousands of newspapers, radio, TV, corporate and online subscribers.

The WPA's demand for excellence had earned it twenty-two Pulitzer prizes and the respect of its rivals, chiefly the Associated Press, Reuters, Agence France-Presse, Deutsche Presse-Agentur, Bloomberg, China's Xinhua News Agency and Russia's fast-rising Interfax News Agency.

Gannon entered the newsroom with a sense of foreboding.

Something was breaking on the flat-screen monitors that streamed video and data from around the world. Whatever it was, it had hit the WPA. Some reporters looked shaken. A few were standing, hugging each other.

"Did you know Gabriela? Poor John."

A few editors quietly cursed at their keyboards.

Gannon was headed toward Melody Lyon's office when a news assistant caught up to him.

"Jack, they're all in the conference room. Go there now."

A teleconference was in progress, and solemn-faced senior editors sat around the polished table. Concentrating over her bifocals on the call, Melody Lyon, who was running the meeting, pointed at an empty chair beside her. As Gannon took it, an assistant passed him a folder.

"Sign this." Her pen tapped a signature line on the documents. Gannon glimpsed the words *Consulado-Geral do Brasil em Nova York—Visa Application form* and a note affixed: "Request for Urgency."

George Wilson, the third most powerful editor after Lyon, was in charge of WPA's foreign bureaus. He eyed Gannon, checked his BlackBerry then said to the caller, keeping his voice loud: "Everyone, Reuters just moved an item claiming two journalists are among the victims. No other details. Frank, let's run through that again."

Frank Archer, WPA's São Paulo bureau chief, who was on the speaker phone, kept his emotions under control. He had landed in Rio de Janeiro and was at the scene. Sirens could be heard in the background.

"John Esper was returning to Rio from São Paulo where he was helping with coverage of the U.S. vice president's upcoming visit," Archer said. "John landed in Rio about four hours ago and learned the news about the Café Amaldo bombing. At that time he picked up Gabriela's message saying she was headed to the café with Marcelo Verde—"

Gannon read the note Lyon had passed to him:

"John Esper is WPA's Rio de Janeiro bureau chief. Bureau reporter Gabriela Rosa is his wife. Marcelo Verde is WPA's Rio photog."

Archer continued, "John first thought Gabriela and Marcelo were en route to *cover* the bombing but when he couldn't reach them, he rechecked her message about meeting a source at the café. That's when it hit him—they were there when the bomb exploded at the café. It was the last thing John said to me before I rushed to the airport. I can't reach him now."

"Frank, it's George," Wilson spoke up. "John texted us saying that he'd gone to the hospital where they took most of the victims."

"Wait!" Archer said. "A friend at Globo just told me that police have found Marcelo Verde's wallet and Gabriela Rosa's bag among the dead and debris."

"Oh, my lord." Melody Lyon cupped her hands to her face. "It's true."

Gannon's stomach tightened.

"The toll," Archer struggled, "is now seven dead and several critically injured, so it will rise. George, we need help down here." Archer was fighting emotion. "Our Rio bureau's been—George, we need help."

"We're on it, Frank. I've sent in our people from Buenos Aires and Caracas. We're also sending help from New York."

Wilson looked at Gannon.

"Melody here, Frank. Any claims of responsibility? Any thoughts on who's behind the attack?"

"*O Dia* says it's narco gangs from the favelas, but who knows. I have to go."

"Keep us posted, Frank."

George Wilson removed his glasses, rubbed his eyes and took stock of the other editors, stopping at Melody Lyon, who outranked them all.

"Jesus, Mel, I think we just lost two of our people. Did you alert Beland?"

"He's in Washington. We told him when the unconfirmed reports first broke. I've been updating him."

A soft rap sounded at the door. "Excuse me, Melody?" The news assistant had returned.

"Yes, Rachel."

"Melissa's left in a cab to the Brazilian Consulate to get Jack's visa application processed. Our consular contacts expressed concern and agreed to expedite Jack's application."

"Thank you, Rachel."

"Jack." Lyon turned to Gannon. "There's a TAM flight that leaves JFK in five hours. It's direct to Rio de Janeiro, arrives 8:30 a.m. tomorrow."

"You're sending me to Brazil?"

"We need you to help our team there."

Gannon's heart beat a little faster.

"Certainly," he said, "but you should know, I've never been there and I don't speak Portuguese, or Spanish."

"Local support staff will help you," Lyon said. "Go home and pack."

A vein in George Wilson's temple pulsed as his steel gray eyes locked on Gannon.

"I want you to know," Wilson said, "that I don't think you're the right person to send down there at this time."

"George, please," Lyon said, "we've been over this."

"Melody's the boss, Gannon, and she believes your fresh eyes, as she calls them, could be an asset."

"I will do my best," Gannon said.

"You'll do as you're told," Wilson said. "You'll take direction from New York and from my correspondents down there who have far more foreign-reporting experience than you ever saw at the *Buffalo Sentinel,* and you will stay out of the goddamned way."

That's not what I do.

Gannon looked to Lyon for support but she was pondering the Empire State Building, Manhattan's skyline and her anguish. Everyone's hurting now, he thought. Out of respect, he bit back on his words and absorbed Wilson's misdirected insult.

"I will do my best, George," he repeated.

4

Rio de Janeiro, Brazil

Gannon's jet landed at Galeão airport.

As he walked through the terminal, the satellite phone the New York office had given him blinked with a message from George Wilson.

When you arrive go to the WPA Bureau, Rua de Riachuelo 250 in Centro. See Frank Archer.

Gannon collected his bag, got his passport stamped at customs and stepped into the equatorial humidity to find a taxi. The driver nodded after seeing the address Gannon showed him. As they drove down a southbound expressway, his satellite phone rang.

"Gannon."

"It's Melody in New York. Where are you?"

"In a taxi headed downtown."

"Jack, last night—" she paused to clear her throat "—we got official confirmation. Gabriela and Marcelo were among those killed."

"I'm sorry."

"We're all reeling. Wilson's taking this very hard."

"I understand."

"We've suffered a huge loss. Bear that in mind when you're dealing with everyone down there."

"I will."

"You didn't know Gabriela and Marcelo. Your thinking won't be clouded with grief and anger. I need you to help us find out who is behind this attack on the café and why. We must own this story, Jack, no matter where it leads. This is how we will honor the dead."

Adrenaline surged through Gannon as his taxi fought traffic and Rio de Janeiro rose before him. He exhaled slowly, marveling at the sprawl. Rio's skyline stood in contrast to its favelas, which ascended in wave upon wave of ramshackle houses shoehorned into crowded slums, notorious for drug wars and gun battles. The shanty towns clung to the hills that ringed the city and overlooked the South Atlantic.

Was Wilson right? Could he handle this story?

The taxi's open windows invited warm salty air. He saw azure patches of Guanabara Bay and the map he'd studied on the plane came to life as he recognized landmarks during the drive to Centro.

The bureau was in a tall glass building that reflected the clouds.

The guard in the lobby studied Gannon's passport and business card, made a call and minutes later a man barely out of his teens emerged from the elevator to buzz him through and greet him.

"Welcome to Rio, Mr. Gannon, I am Luiz Piquet. Come with me, please." He took Gannon's bag and in the elevator he asked, "You had a good flight, sir?"

"Call me Jack. Yes, Luiz, it was fine."

The elevator was slow. Gannon turned to Luiz.

"Are you a staff member with WPA?"

"I am the bureau news assistant. I recently received my degree in journalism from the Federal University. I will be helping you."

The elevator stopped on the tenth floor. The brass plate across the hall said *Aliança da Imprensa do Mundo*—World

Press Alliance. Luiz opened the glass door to a large room that was lit only by daylight from the floor to ceiling windows at one end.

It was typical newsroom decor, an open office with half a dozen desks, each with a monitor and a keyboard; each cluttered with phones, newspapers, file folders, documents, coffee cups.

Gannon noticed the far wall: two large TV screens were suspended from the ceiling and tuned to news networks. The sound was turned low. The wall had large news photos of children in slums, a SWAT team and shooting victims on bloodied streets, the pope waving to crowds at a stadium, girls in bikinis on the beach.

The only other person in the office was a man finishing a phone call.

"Frank Archer em WPA. Você tem o número!" he said before slamming down the phone and cursing in English.

With his back to Luiz and Gannon, he doubled over in his chair, set his elbows on his knees and put his bald head in his hands.

Not certain he was aware of their presence, Gannon said: "Frank Archer?"

The man swiveled in his chair.

Like Gannon, Archer was in his early thirties. He was wearing jeans and a white shirt. His face was sullen.

"Jack Gannon. I just got in from New York."

After an awkward silence the man stood; he was about six feet tall with a medium build, like Gannon.

"Frank Archer." The two men shook hands. "Gannon, I'm going to be blunt. I don't know why you're here."

"On the call yesterday, you said you needed help."

"And we've got it. Our people from our bureaus in Caracas and Buenos Aires have flown in and are out on the story. We've got stringers on it, too. Everyone is fluent in Portuguese and Spanish, all experienced. Wilson said you're from where? Rochester or something like that?"

"Buffalo."

"Right."

"Frank, I was sent down to help. Let me help."

Archer flipped through some papers then rubbed his face.

"Gabriela and Marcelo were my friends."

"I understand that."

"I was with John at the hospital last night when they told him Gabriela had died. Marcelo died in the ambulance. I've been through a lot of shit but that was one of the worst moments of my life."

Gannon nodded, letting Archer go on.

"John met Gabriela in Miami when she was a correspondent there for Reuters. I went to their wedding. Now he's at the consulate with Gabriela's father, who flew down from Miami. They're trying to make arrangements to fly her back to Florida in a few days to bury her there. Marcelo's family is preparing a funeral for him."

"I understand."

"I've lost friends in Afghanistan, in Africa, but this one hits home hard."

"Frank, do the police have any leads on who's behind the attack?"

"The strongest theory is that it's narco terrorism. Globo, the TV network, is reporting that a Colombian drug lord's daughter is one of the victims. There's speculation she was the target in a vendetta with a Rio drug network."

"What's the thinking on Gabriela's being at the café?"

"That's a mystery, for now."

"I understand she left a message for John that she was meeting a source."

"She did." Archer turned to his phone and pressed numbers. "John gave me his access code. It's not much, listen. It's in English."

After a few tones, Gabriela Rosa's last words to her husband played through the speaker, her voice filling the darkened bureau.

"Hey, it's me. Finished that story about pickpockets on the metro, you've got it. Meanwhile, I got a call from an anonymous woman who claims to have a big story and documents for us. I set up a meeting at the Café Amaldo for this afternoon, with Marcelo to back me up. Hope São Paulo was fun. Did you say hi to Archer for me? Tell him I found a girl for him. Have a safe flight home, catch you later. I love you."

Gannon fished his small digital recorder from his laptop bag and Archer replayed the message so he could record it.

"Do you think Gabriela's source could have wanted to tip her to the narco attack and something went wrong with the timing?" Gannon asked.

"I don't know. It seems unlikely since Gabriela picked the location."

"Has the bureau here written anything recently that threatened any of the criminal networks?"

"Not really—the crime gangs usually target the local press." Archer glanced at his watch. "You flew overnight, you must want to drop off your bags at your hotel, wash up. Get something to eat, right?"

"I could use a coffee and a hot shower."

"We got you a room at the Nine Palms Hotel. It's a good place and nearby." Archer handed Gannon a large envelope. "The address is in here. Tell the taxi driver *'hotel de nove palmas.'* You got some cash? You want Luiz to go with you?"

"I have cash and the company card." Gannon peered in the envelope. "I should go myself."

Archer's phone rang. He answered, saying something quickly in Portuguese before cupping his hand over the mouthpiece.

"Jack, I have to interview a source with Public Safety, then the café owner. Meet me back here in ninety minutes. I'll have something for you."

The Nine Palms was three kilometers away, off a busy

thoroughfare, hidden atop a narrow cobbled street. The greenery was so lush Gannon almost missed seeing the hotel behind a set of wrought-iron gates.

It was a modernized massive nineteenth-century colonial mansion with shuttered windows, ceiling fans and dark mahogany floors. In his room, he ordered food then took a hot shower before it came—a plate of fruit, fresh baked bread, juice and coffee.

It recharged him.

As he ate, Gannon struggled to comprehend coverage of the Café Amaldo bombing in Rio's newspapers but didn't get far before someone knocked on his door. Through the peephole, he saw Luiz Piquet.

"Sorry to disturb you, Jack, but Mr. Archer sent me. He's had to change his plan because he's going to be tied up on calls while putting the latest story together with the other WPA correspondents. He said to tell you that senior editors Beland Stone and Melody Lyon are flying to Miami to attend Gabriela's funeral. George Wilson is flying to São Bento do Norte, to assist Marcelo's family with his service there."

"So what does Frank want me to do?"

"He wants me to take you to the Café Amaldo, now."

"The crime scene?"

"Yes, his instructions are for me to help you to talk to the lead investigators, to push them for more information. Then go directly to the bureau, to help update the story."

"Let's go."

5

An eerie quiet enveloped the air around the café.

Rio's Centro traffic had been diverted around the blast area or, what one newspaper called *"A Zona da Matança."*

"It means the Zone of the Slaughter," Luiz translated for Gannon as they left their taxi and walked to the inner perimeter.

Knots of police vehicles, their emergency lights flashing, secured the street. Farther along, where the satellite trucks and news crews had parked, it was cordoned by barricades and tape, and several dozen people were rubbernecking the investigation.

Beyond the police lines, Gannon saw the office buildings and shops smashed by the blast. The awning of a boutique drooped above its shattered windows. Mangled chairs, tables and debris littered the street. The sign above the café had split, both pieces swaying now in the breeze, signifying the wound in the aftermath of the attack.

Stick to the basics, keep your notebook out of sight and observe. Gannon knew how to work a scene.

As they drew near, he indicated to Luiz that they should go to the far end of the barricade away from the other news people.

From there, they saw the technicians in their white coveralls, yellow shoe covers and latex gloves picking through wreckage on the patio and sidewalk, collecting evidence. Others photographed the devastation, took measurements and made notes. A police dog, its snout to the ground, sniffed for trace material, while a soft wind carried flakes of ash and papers down the avenue and alleys.

"Não aqui! Você deve mover-se!" An unsmiling uniformed officer appeared before them.

"He wants us to move, to join the other reporters," Luiz said.

"Tell him I'm a reporter with the World Press Alliance from New York and that two of my colleagues were killed here. Gabriela Rosa and Marcelo Verde. Tell him I need to speak to the lead investigator, possibly, to share information. Stress *possibly*."

As Luiz translated, Gannon held up his WPA identification. After listening and looking at it, the cop spoke into his radio.

A moment passed and a response crackled back.

Gannon saw another uniformed officer amid the scene talk into his radio, then to the two men in polo shirts and jeans beside him. One of them looked from his notebook to Gannon, then waved him through. Gannon had figured the plain-clothed men for detectives. The first one held out his latex-gloved hand before him and spoke in English.

"Give me your passport, please."

The man reviewed it and wrote down Gannon's passport number while his partner took Gannon's picture with a small camera.

"Am I to understand that you have information on this crime, Mr. Jack Gannon?"

Gannon glimpsed the cop's ID on the chain around his neck and the words *Polícia* and *Roberto something Investigador*. His face was somber as if the weight of the world were pressing on him. A tiny scar meandered down his left cheek as his hooded brown eyes measured Gannon.

"I would like to discuss things first," Gannon said.

"No discussion, if you have information relating to this crime, you must tell me." The detective angled Gannon's passport so his heavyset, pock-faced partner could read Gannon's passport number. Then he spoke in rapid Portuguese and his partner nodded and made a phone call. "If you interfere with our investigation we can revoke your visa and send you back to New York."

"What?"

"Or we can arrest you."

"Hold on a second."

"Do you have information relating to this crime?"

Gannon heard the partner say "Jack Gannon" into his phone and grew uneasy. This was not like a crime scene in Buffalo. What had he stepped into? Sweat rolled down his back. His mind blurred with the reports he'd read on the plane of how elements of the Brazilian police were feared for alleged corruption, brutality and, according to human-rights groups, executing criminal suspects.

A New York detective might have offered a few words of condolence for the loss of Gannon's colleagues. Not this Roberto guy, who was tapping Gannon's passport in his palm.

"Your response?"

Gannon studied the man's ID. "You're Roberto Estralla?"

"Yes."

"The lead detective?"

Estralla nodded.

"May I have my passport back?"

"You have failed to answer my question."

After quick consideration, Gannon said, "Would you exchange information confidentially?"

Estralla stopped tapping Gannon's passport. "Are you attempting to bribe me? Because that is a crime."

"No."

"Tell me what information you have, before I exercise my authority."

"I believe Gabriela and Marcelo were supposed to meet a source here."

"And what is the name of this source?"

"I don't know."

"What sort of business did they have with this source?"

"I don't know."

Estralla spoke to his partner in Portuguese then continued, "Where did you learn of this information about the meeting?"

"We heard it at WPA headquarters in New York before I was dispatched to Rio de Janeiro."

Estralla studied Gannon's face for an icy moment.

"In which hotel are you staying?"

"Nine Palms."

Estralla nodded to Gannon's cell phone.

"Your telephone number?"

Gannon recited it and the moment Estralla finished noting it, Estralla's cell phone rang. He returned Gannon's passport. "You may go," he said, hailing a uniformed officer before taking his call.

"Wait," Gannon said, "I have some questions." Estralla waved Gannon away to take his call but Gannon persisted. "Do you have any suspects or leads? What about a motive, or the type of bomb?"

Estralla and his partner walked away. A uniformed officer took Gannon's arm and escorted him to the police line where he was suddenly awash in bright lights from the news cameras.

"Jack Gannon," an attractive woman wearing flawless makeup, a tailored suit and a sense of urgency beckoned him. She gripped a microphone. A man with a TV camera on his shoulder stood behind her. "You are with the WPA?" the woman asked.

The police officer nodded and nearly two dozen journalists and photographers crowded around Gannon.

"I am Yasmin Carval from Globo." The rings on her fingers glinted as she extended her mike to Gannon. "Did the police tell you who is responsible?"

"No, I'm sure you know more than me."

"Two of your WPA press friends were killed. Can you say something to us about that?"

The lights from the five or six TV cameras around him were intense. Gannon glimpsed Luiz at the fringe of the pack and caught a hint of Yasmin Carval's strong perfume as she stepped closer.

"Mr. Gannon, what has been the impact?" Yasmin Carval asked.

"The loss has taken a toll on our entire agency."

"Do you think Gabriela and Marcelo were targets?"

"Targets?"

"Was Gabriela working on a story about drug gangs?"

"I don't know."

"There is speculation that narco gangs are behind the bombing."

"I don't know anything. I can't say more, I have to go."

Gannon shouldered his way through the pack and when he reached Luiz, they started walking toward the bureau. It was a few blocks away.

"What the hell was that?" Gannon said. "How did they know my name and everything else?"

"When they spotted you inside the line, they thought you were getting preferential treatment and complained to the other officers, who told them you were with WPA."

"Preferential treatment?" Gannon shook his head, glanced over his shoulder, relieved no one was following them. "I didn't get any stinking preferential treatment from that detective."

"Roberto Estralla."

"That's right."

"He's one of Rio's most respected investigators but he detests reporters. Those at the barricade were impressed he allowed you to cross the police line and talk to him."

Different town, different rules, Gannon thought, taking a parting glance back at the scene. There was something there.

Something he was overlooking.

6

When they returned, Gannon saw himself on one the bureau's TV screens.

The sound was muted.

Frank Archer was in the office with two other people. A man sat at a desk talking softly in Spanish on his cell phone, while Archer worked with a woman typing on a keyboard.

"You're amazing, Jack," Archer said. "Within hours of landing, you've become the official spokesperson for the World Press Alliance while also helping the Rio press with their stories."

"Excuse me?"

"Globo and SBT both carried you live from the scene. They'll run your performance all day. Good job, Gannon."

"Those networks reach about one hundred million people," the woman said without looking at Gannon.

"I'm sorry, have we met?" he asked her.

The tanned woman was in her early thirties, wearing a print shirt and white slacks. She had short blond hair and a cool hand when Gannon shook it.

"Sally Turner, Caracas Bureau. The grump on the phone is Hugh Porter from our Buenos Aires Bureau."

Porter extended his hand while remaining on his call. Gannon shook it then saw the second TV cut back to news.

"Jack," Archer said, "are you aware of the WPA policy about reporters granting interviews to other reporters?"

Gannon shook his head, keeping his attention on the TV screens.

"We don't comment on the news," Archer said.

"Well, now we *are* the news, Frank. I didn't say anything wrong. Besides, my instructions from you were to go to the scene and press the lead investigators for information and that's what I did."

"What did you get from Estralla?" Porter asked after finishing his call.

"Attitude."

"Anything to contribute to our story?" Archer asked.

Gannon didn't answer. He was watching the news reports on the TV screens, footage of him talking with the detectives. Archer turned on the sound and Gannon heard his English dubbed into Portuguese. Then he saw his name in the graphic at the bottom, *Journalista de Jack Gannon, Aliança da Imprensa do Mundo.*

Gannon scrutinized the TV images. He was missing something.

"Jack," Archer said, "anything for the story? We have to file to New York."

"No."

"I didn't expect anything." Archer turned to the others. "Porter?"

"My source in Bogotá says one of the victims is Angella Roho-Ruiz, daughter of Paulo Roho-Ruiz, a high-ranking member of a powerful Colombian cartel."

"That fits with what I'm picking up," Turner said. "This is a retaliatory hit arising from a debt or vendetta with a gang from one of the favelas."

"Angella Roho-Ruiz had to be Gabriela's source," Porter said.

"You know that for a fact?" Gannon asked.

"Not yet."

"Do you know for certain that Gabriela even met this Angella?"

"What is this, Gannon?"

"You've ruled out other possibilities, like this source Gabriela was supposed to meet, or didn't meet."

"What do you know about anything?" Porter said. "You've been here all of what, a few hours?"

"Hold off, Hugh." Archer turned to Gannon. "Jack, we talked about this. Gabriela was not lured to the café. She chose it, which is our practice when meeting sources. It's possible that Angella Roho-Ruiz was followed and targeted at her meeting with Gabriela."

"You're making assumptions. You haven't confirmed if Gabriela met her source or who her source is, or was. You're assuming that since Angella Roho-Ruiz is among the dead, then she must have been the source and this was a narco hit."

"Listen, Jack, right now, everything points to narco terrorists," Archer said. "Angella Roho-Ruiz comes from a mighty cartel. At this level, this kind of bombing is their signature."

"Is it?" Gannon asked.

"It is," Porter said. "But you wouldn't know that, coming from Buffalo."

"Fuck you."

"Hey!" Archer said. "Everybody, dial it down. We're all pissed off and on edge over Gabriela and Marcelo, so let's just dial it down and work."

Archer gave Gannon names and phone numbers of employees at businesses near the bombing. Most were still operating. Then Archer and the others went back to concentrate on the story.

With Luiz's help, Gannon spent the rest of the day mining the list for a break. Other than hearing the explosion and seeing the chaotic response, no one had witnessed anything unusual, leaving Gannon to figure Archer just wanted him out of the way.

After they'd filed, Archer, Porter and Turner left to interview security officials and other sources for new information. They returned at the end of the day and filed another update. Then they invited Gannon to an early dinner in

Santa Teresa. The restaurant was in a colonial building on a narrow, curving palm-lined street. They monitored their cell phones and BlackBerries while they ate. After the meal, they all drank, except for Gannon.

He wasn't a drinker.

"Are you curious," Porter turned to Gannon after his fourth beer "as to why everyone's giving you a hard time?"

Gannon shrugged.

"Down here, we bleed for our stories. We've all stared down the barrel of a gun. We've all faced jail, abduction, threats, intimidation and beatings."

"The thing is," Turner said, "we know about your hiring and the bit of stink around your situation at your former rag, the *Buffalo Sentinel*."

"Is that right?"

Turner bobbed her head in a big alcohol-laden nod.

"You should be glad you're not working there anymore," Porter said. "The print newspaper industry is melting. But the WPA will survive as one of the world's biggest online content providers…. I digress."

"You digress," Archer agreed.

"Jack," Porter put his arm around Gannon. "We heard about your little adventure story about that cop out of Buffalo that impressed Melody so much that, despite everyone's advice to the contrary, she hired you. And from what we understand, the story was more luck than journalism."

Gannon shook his head, smiling at their inebriated arrogance.

"You guys are good."

"Well," Porter chuckled, "we are." He pointed to Archer, Turner and himself. "All Pulitzer winners, pal."

"It's amazing that you know what I went through for my 'little adventure story' sitting all the way down here in South America, because I didn't bump into any Pulitzer winners while I was living it. In fact, it was the WPA who begged me to help its reporters."

"Loosen up." Porter slapped Gannon's back. "Giving the rookie a hard time is a right of passage. Ain't that right, Sally?"

The three drinkers raised their glasses, laughed, then bought another round to honor their dead friends as the afternoon morphed into a wake of teary tributes to Gabriela and Marcelo, leaving Gannon alone with his thoughts.

He withdrew into his memories of growing up a blue-collar kid in Buffalo where his mother was a waitress and his father worked in a factory that made rope. He remembered how his big sister, Cora, got their parents to buy him a used computer and encouraged him to write and pursue his dream of being a journalist.

You're going to be a great writer some day.... I see it in your eyes. You don't let go. You don't give up....

Gannon worshipped Cora, but they grew apart. She got into trouble with drugs before she ran away from home. Over the years, while he graduated from college and got a job as a staff reporter at the *Sentinel,* his parents tried to find her.

At times Gannon would push aside his anger and search for Cora himself.

Always in vain.

While he gave up, his parents never stopped trying, right up until they were killed when a drunk driver slammed into their car just over a year ago.

Gannon had no other family.

No wife, no girlfriend. He was alone in the world.

But that was fine with him, he thought, glimpsing himself on the Globo TV news report on the set over the bar. As it played, he studied the few seconds of footage of the scene and the breeze kicking up ash.

That's when it hit him. The piece he'd been missing.

"Excuse me," he said to the others. "It's been a long day, I'd like to head back to my hotel." He pulled several bills from his pocket and left them on the table.

Turner plucked out a couple and put them back in his hand.

"Tomorrow—" Porter started a new beer "—they may have the complete victim list. We'll work on that."

"You get to your hotel while it's still light out, Jack," Archer said. "This town isn't safe after dark. You remember what to tell your taxi driver?"

"Hotel de nove palmas."

"Good."

But five minutes later, when Gannon got into a cab, he told the driver to take him to the Café Amaldo, the *A Zona da Matança*. Returning to the blast area, he saw police officers still protecting the scene while a few forensic people continued to work. Most of the news crews had left.

He walked along the fringes, wondering why the experts ignored a basic rule by not protecting transient physical evidence. All day long, the wind had been lifting ash and papers from the blast site.

The stuff had been carried along on a virtual flight path.

Sloppy police work, he thought. It helped explain why Rio's homicide clearance rate was around 3 percent, while the average back home was about 65. Using what he'd seen at the site, and on the TV footage, to guide him, Gannon figured that most of the material had ended up in the alley across the street from the café.

Although police were present, the alley was not sealed. The narrow passage between the tall buildings was vacant and dark, but there was enough natural light remaining. Gannon's pulse quickened.

A number of papers were on the pavement among other debris, or pressed to the walls. He began collecting them. Were they from the blast? Who knew? He'd study every one he could find.

"Hey! Que você está fazendo lá?" a voice boomed down the alley. He was in trouble.

"Que você está fazendo lá?"

The voice was now closer; two figures were approaching from a distance. Gannon turned and walked in the opposite direction.

"Batente!"

The figures were moving faster, Gannon's breathing quickened and he started a fast trot.

"Polícia! Batente agora!"

His heart pounding, Gannon ran from the alley.

Don't let the police get near you.

He cut across a busy street to a large hotel, entered the lobby and rushed through it, finding a rear exit that opened to an ornate gurgling fountain, which led to a plaza.

Sirens echoed through the city.

Were they for him?

Fueled by adrenaline, he kept moving.

Without looking back he hurried around the plaza's statues. Two or three blocks away, the lights of a theater, nightclubs and restaurants glittered in the dusk. He slipped into the crowds on the sidewalk and made his way toward the restaurants until he saw a taxi.

The driver was in his fifties, wearing a white cap. Gannon neared the cab, pointing at it then himself. The driver nodded, making the small silver cross on the chain around his neck sway a little.

"Hotel de nove palmas," Gannon said after getting in the back.

The taxi pulled away. No police were in sight.

As Gannon's breathing settled, he analyzed the situation. All he'd done was gather trash from a public street in an unsealed area near a crime scene.

Still, if Estralla learned of it, it would be disastrous.

Gannon dragged the back of his hand over his moist brow and glimpsed the driver's eyes studying him in the rearview mirror. Gannon felt a small ache in his right hand. He was still gripping the papers, a sheaf nearly half an inch thick.

As the cab worked its way through Centro, Gannon inserted his earpiece into his digital recorder and played Gabriela's last message, cuing up the key aspect.

"...I got a call from an anonymous woman who claims to have a big story and documents for us. I set up a meeting at the Café Amaldo..."

Gannon replayed "and documents for us," several times.

If Gabriela met her source, and if that source brought records, then it's possible the blast scattered some of them to the street.

Those documents could be in his hands now.

A few of the papers were charred. Some had burned edges.

They had to have come from the blast.

Gannon caught his breath when he stopped at one page.

It looked like it was smeared with blood.

As soon as he got to his hotel room he started working.

This wouldn't be easy. The papers were in Portuguese. He set them out on the desk and switched on his laptop. Some papers had letterheads, some looked like spread sheets, sales records, membership lists, business correspondence.

He typed phrases into free online language services and translated what he could into English. It gave him a sense of what each record was. When he found pages that obviously belonged together, he grouped them. The documents were from computer companies, law firms, banks, churches. It was meticulous work but he kept at it until exhaustion overtook him and he went to bed.

7

Big Cloud, Wyoming

A continent away, Emma Lane was plunging through darkness with her eyes closed, her thinking unclear.

They're gone, Emma.

Nooooo…

Joe and Tyler are with the angels now.

She was trapped in a nightmare.

There was a flash, a scream on a rushing wind, then her world vanished and she floated out of herself but came back to now.

Emma smelled the antiseptic smell of a hospital. A faint message echoed on the PA and she sensed laundered linen, a pillow under her head. She was thirsty, and her head ached as her mind streaked with images: of a perfect day, of driving to the river for a picnic, of Joe and Tyler laughing.

Let me stay here with them.

She struggled to hold the images but couldn't.

Joe's smile disappears…their SUV swerves to miss the car coming at them head-on…their SUV rolls…Emma is thrown…. Tyler's strapped inside…Joe's hurt…Emma reaches for him, touches him, feels Joe die…then in the chaos someone's pulling Tyler clear before the inferno…

No!

They're gone, Emma.

The nurses.

Joe and Tyler are with the angels.

That's what the nurses had been whispering so that when Emma regained consciousness, she would have absorbed the horror: that her husband and baby boy died in the crash.

"No! No! No!"

Emma's eyelids fluttered open. She bolted upright, eyes bulging, her face a mask of cuts, bruises, fear, her arms reaching out.

"Tyler!"

A nurse and doctor moved to calm her. The room tensed with concern before it vibrated with a deafening keening.

"Oh, God!"

"Easy, dear, easy," the nurse said.

"Where is my baby? Give me my baby!"

"Emma, take it easy. Lay back, sweetie," the nurse soothed her as she and the doctor gently forced her back down on the bed and prepared a hypodermic needle. Emma saw the tubes taped to her arm, the monitor on her finger tip, felt the tube under her nose, saw the IV line. She had no physical pain, just medicated muzziness.

It did not happen.

Yes, it did.

The monstrous truth stared back from the eyes of the people in her room: the nurse, the doctor, another medical person, Emma's aunt Marsha and uncle Ned from Des Moines?

"Oh, Emma. When the police called, we got on the first plane." Her aunt bent down and hugged her. "We're so sorry."

"We're going to get through this." Uncle Ned, the retired Marine, who had *Semper Fi* tattooed on his forearm and smelled of Old Spice, patted her hand. "We'll get you through."

The doctor shone a flashlight in Emma's eyes, uncollared his stethoscope and pressed it to her chest. "You were in a terrible car accident but, fortunately, your physical injuries are relatively minor. You've got a concussion, bruised ribs and abrasions." He injected something into Emma's IV. "You're undergoing trauma. Your husband and son did not survive the accident. I'm so sorry. We've got someone here to help you."

"No. I saw someone rescue Tyler."

Silence fell over the room.

"Where are you keeping Tyler? Bring him to me."

The doctor, the nurse, her aunt Marsha and uncle Ned exchanged glances, then looked to the other medical staff member in the white coat.

"Emma, I'm Dr. Kendrix, I'm a psychiatrist. I'm here to help you with the deaths of your husband and son. You've suffered a cataclysmic loss, Emma, and we're going to help you."

"Stop!"

Emma held up her palms, and the tubes tethered to her arms trembled. Everyone was taken aback by the unyielding ferocity burning in her eyes.

"I know Joe is dead. I know that. I held his hand. I felt him die. I know he didn't suffer. Oh, God!" Her voice quavered, but she cupped her hands to her face then removed them and continued. "But my son is not dead!"

"Emma—" Aunt Marsha stepped closer.

"No! Someone rescued him just before the fire. I saw it happen."

"Emma," Uncle Ned said. "That's not how it happened, you have to accept that."

"No!"

"Emma—" Dr. Kendrix sat on the corner of her bed "—according to the troopers, Tyler remained buckled in his car seat. Now sometimes—"

"You're wrong!"

"Okay. It's okay. Your anger is justified," Kendrix said, "but sometimes, Emma, the mind in shock, facing overwhelming trauma, denies the unthinkable when it happens."

Emma buried her face in her hands as her aunt took her shoulders and held her.

"I want proof," Emma said.

"Proof?"

"I want proof that Tyler died in the crash."

Kendrix searched Emma's face as he weighed her demand. It was not unreasonable. In fact, it was not uncommon.

"All right."

"But, Doctor—" Emma's aunt was apprehensive "—don't you think it's too soon. I mean..." She hesitated. "It's just too soon."

"I understand your concern," Kendrix said to her. "These things are never easy, but in this case, given the circumstances, I think it's warranted."

He turned to Emma.

"All right, you've had a lot to deal with. We'll take care of it after you've rested."

8

Fairfax County, Virginia

While Emma Lane rested in Wyoming and Gannon slept in Brazil, Robert Lancer was hard at work in metropolitan Washington, D.C.

He undid his collar button and studied a file while walking down a third-floor corridor of the National Anti-Threat Center. The complex sat amid the wooded suburbs northwest of the capital.

In this building, behind the bullet and blast-proof windows, hundreds of security experts from a spectrum of government branches worked 24/7 analyzing threats to national security.

Lancer re-read his file on his way to the center's East Africa section, hoping that this latest "urgent" interruption warranted pulling him away from his other duties.

He reached the section's locked door, swiped his card, then punched the alphanumeric code into the keypad.

Access approval beeped, and he entered.

The room glowed in the light from the screens and computerized GPS maps suspended above a bank of modular desks where several analysts were entering data into computer keyboards.

Martin Weller, the section chief, was updating his staff and paused when he saw Lancer arrive.

"Bob, thanks for coming. I know you've got plenty on your plate."

"What've you got, Marty?"

"Not sure. Pull it up, Craig."

An analyst entered some commands on his keyboard and photos of a man in his late twenties filled one of the large monitors.

An arrest photo.

"This is Said Salelee, a painter who lives near Msasani Bay, one of the poorer sections of Dar es Salaam."

"Our people in Tanzania called this in?"

"One of the local nationals employed at our embassy reported him acting strangely outside the gate."

"The sheet says he was taking pictures and making notes?"

"He was doing it for several days. The staffer told her boss, who alerted the Ministry of Home Affairs and the national police picked him up. Turns out he's linked to the Avenging Lions of Africa."

"How did they discover that?"

"They threatened to feed him his testicles."

Staring at Salelee's face, Lancer, one of the center's leading senior operational agents, weighed matters. The mission of the Avenging Lions of Africa was to make developed nations suffer for enslaving Africa in poverty. Regionally, the Lions had been linked to bombings, shootings and hostage takings in Kagera, Pemba North, Kigoma and Zanzibar. Lancer had considered them minor league until last year when they attacked the British Embassy in Cairo.

Cairo.

That was a psychological trigger for Lancer.

Ten years earlier, everything in his world went black in Cairo. His wife, his daughter, his life, all changed in Cairo. Since then not a day passed without a word, fragrance or other mundane matter ripping open his wound.

It would never go away.

But Lancer always rode it out, always focused on his work. His determination deepened because he had a personal stake in the job.

Now, everything he did, he did for them.

He flipped through the pages of classified situational reports on Salelee. The CIA and State Department tied the Lions to funding operations through drug networks, human trafficking and Internet fraud.

As he studied Salelee, Lancer thought back to 1998 when terrorists bombed the U.S. embassies in Nairobi, Kenya and Dar es Salaam, foreshadowing September 11, 2001.

Never underestimate any piece of intelligence.

"All right, Marty," Lancer said, "where are we at with Salelee?"

"The Tanzanians have been going at him for two days— nothing to eat but bread and water, no sleep, not to mention a few other methods that are not pretty."

"They're compensating for moving too quickly in picking him up," Lancer said. "They should have put surveillance on him."

"They were eager to help. Today, our people in Dar es Salaam set up a satellite link in the interview room. Since the original complaint involves U.S. property, Tanzanian officials have invited us to ask Salelee questions. They think he could be ready to talk. Craig, are they set?"

An analyst talking on a landline nodded.

"Bob, as you know, Craig is fluent in Kiswahili. Ask your questions, and he'll repeat them to the police in Dar es Salaam."

"Fine," Lancer said, "but I don't expect much. Besides, when you're aggressive, a prisoner will most likely give you bullshit intelligence."

Within minutes a clear satellite link was activated. In a stark room, a number of men stood around a seated figure whose hands and ankles were bound to the chair. Salelee's face was a stew of swollen cuts that forced his eyes shut. His body sagged with exhaustion.

For nearly forty minutes, the local police questioned Salelee.

There was the drone of Kiswahili with Craig translating quickly and softly. Watching and listening, Lancer noticed two landline phones on the table in the room in Dar es Salaam; one in use that was connected to Craig's line, and a second one not in use.

Lancer thought of strategy, mulling it over as the questioning went on.

"What is your interest in the embassy, Salelee?"

"I told you it is painting. I am a poor painter working hard to support my wife and children. I had learned the Americans want to paint the building. I was sizing up the job to offer—"

"Tell us the truth."

"I am."

"We know you are with the Lions."

"No, I attended a meeting, that is it."

"Do not lie to us, Salelee, you're a leader."

"No, I am a poor painter from Msasani. I have a family—"

Lancer waved Weller over, pointed at the screen and asked about the second phone in the room.

"Can we call into the room and make that phone ring?"

Weller whispered to Craig, who checked his computer, then nodded.

"Call in," Lancer said. "When it's answered, explain who we are, then tell the man to say aloud for Salelee's benefit, 'hold everything, something has happened.'"

Craig dialed and within ten seconds the line rang.

On the screen one of the interrogators moved to answer in Kiswahili, and Craig spoke Lancer's words. The man in the room repeated them aloud in Kiswahili.

"Now tell him to say to Salelee that police have arrested the others and they're revealing everything about the plan. You, Salelee, are implicated. They fear you have exposed them already."

The man came back to the phone.

"Tell him to say 'This is bad for you, Salelee, very bad.

Your friends have moved quickly to implicate you. You'll suffer the most.'"

Salelee's head bowed.

"Tell the man on the line to keep the line open. Tell Salelee now is the time to save himself. We will send people to his house to get his wife and children, for their safety, because the others think Salelee's betrayed them."

A moment passed before Salelee began nodding.

"He says, 'I will give you some information on a different plan, but you must protect my family,'" Craig translated.

Lancer crossed his arms and stepped closer to the screen.

"Tell Salelee to tell them now, for the safety of his family."

The Tanzanian cop repeated the words.

"He says, 'First, let me talk to my wife on the telephone.'"

The Tanzanian cops, on the earlier advice of the Americans, had already placed Salelee's wife in custody in another office within the building where she sat now with two police officers. The cops with Salelee telephoned her, allowing Salelee to hear her plea for him to cooperate for the sake of their children.

Salelee was prepared to cooperate.

"What was he really doing at the embassy?" Lancer wanted to know. The Tanzanian police asked him.

"The Lions wanted information to target it for a bombing operation on the Independence Day as declared by the Lions."

"That is not the full plan, what is the operation?"

"It is a separate operation."

"What is it?" Lancer asked Craig, who conveyed the question.

"An attack," Salelee said.

"How do the Lions know of this attack?"

"We have a small role."

"What is that role?"

"We passed coded e-mails, spam, lottery announcements and appeals for large cash transfers. Information relating to the operation is hidden in a few of the millions of spam we send out around the world."

"What is the nature of the operation?"

"An attack."

"An attack against the United States?"

"Yes."

"Any other countries?"

"Yes."

"Who?"

"Many, most countries."

"And the weapon is through computers—cyber?"

"No, some of the communication from one group to another is through the spam. We know nothing of the weapon."

"Who is behind it?"

"We don't know. We were paid great sums through go-betweens."

"Who are they?"

"We don't know."

"What is the weapon—is it planes?"

"No."

"Bombs? Suicide bombings?"

"No."

"Hostage takings?"

"No."

"Nuclear or chemical, what is the weapon?"

"I don't know."

"Who is behind it?"

"I don't know."

"When will the attack take place?"

"Soon."

"When? Days? Weeks? Months?"

"They told us that it is too far along for anyone to stop them."

9

Rio de Janeiro, Brazil

A phone rang and Jack Gannon awakened in a strange room. He looked at the walls, the sunlight streaming through the shutters.

He lifted the phone.

"Good morning, Mr. Gannon. This is your wake-up call."

"Thank you."

Piece by piece, it all came back to him as he rubbed his face. He took two aspirin, shaved, showered, dressed, grabbed some breakfast, got his bag and headed to the bureau. When he arrived, Luiz, the news assistant, was the only person there.

"What's going on, Luiz? Where is everybody?"

"Much has happened. Mr. Archer is interviewing an official with the *Departmento de Polícia Federal.*"

"They're like our FBI and Estralla is with the Civil Police?"

"Yes. And Mr. Porter and Ms. Turner are interviewing people about the Colombian narco connection to the bombing."

"Porter said the victim list might be released today?"

"Yes, but not yet. Not officially. Mr. Archer wants me to help you follow today's major story. JB has obtained the list."

"JB—what's that and what did they get?" Gannon switched on his laptop.

"JB has broken the story identifying all the bombing victims," Luiz held up a newspaper, *Jornal do Brasil,* with the main headline: *Caras dos Mortos,* over a gallery of ten head shots superimposed on a photo of the ruins of the Café Amaldo.

Gannon did not have to understand Portuguese to see that the newspaper had beaten its competition by obtaining the victim list in advance.

Gabriela Rosa and Marcelo Verde were on the newspaper's front page, staring back from WPA file photos.

Luiz blinked back tears, staring at the newspaper.

"Seeing it now in the paper like this is hard," Luiz said. "Gabriela was kind to me, she helped me write travel features for WPA. She took me out for lunch on my birthday."

Luiz gazed at Gabriela's empty desk, orderly and uncluttered compared with Marcelo's desk. His was heaped with magazines, manuals and empty food wrappers. Marcelo's monitor was feathered with two dozen small yellow notes.

"Marcelo was a consummate photographer, an artist who loved his work. He was fun, always joking but so forgetful with many things. He needed all these notes."

Gannon studied the *Jornal do Brasil* and the faces of the ten victims, five men and five women. There were small bios about each of them. It was good work. He tapped the picture of Angella Roho-Ruiz, a beautiful woman in her twenties, smiling under the headline: *Era uma Execução do Narco?*

Luiz nodded.

"That is Paulo's daughter on a shopping vacation in Bogotá, Colombia. The headline *Era uma Execução do Narco?* is asking, Was this a narco execution?"

Gannon took a moment to process the growing speculation that the bombing was the result of a drug war.

Was everyone else right about who was behind it?

Was he an idiot to question reporters who worked, lived and breathed in Brazil everyday? Was he out of his league?

Gannon looked at the other victims. Was Gabriela's source among them? Maybe they'd met and the source left? Or maybe the source never showed up at all?

The sheaf of charred and bloodied papers from the alley sat next to his laptop. If he could connect the victims to any of these documents, it would be a key puzzle piece.

First, he had to take precautions. His little adventure from last night underscored the need to protect his documents, for now.

"Luiz, will you do a confidential favor for me?"

"Of course."

"Copy these pages, keep a set in a safe place, but tell no one. Do you swear to me you will do this?"

"I like working with you, Mr. Gannon. You're different from the others. I give you my word I will do as you ask."

"Good, these pages could be very important, we need to be careful. But I don't want you to tell anyone. Do you understand?"

"Yes."

Luiz flipped through the papers. "It won't take long." He disappeared into the small supply closet. As the photocopier hummed, Gannon reviewed the faces in the newspaper and tried to think of a strategy to determine the café's seating situation at the time of the explosion. Maybe talking to the families of the victims would be a good start.

Luiz returned the original documents and Gannon put them in his bag.

"I've hidden my copies in our supply room," Luiz said. "I will not speak of them to anyone."

The bureau's door opened and two uniformed police officers entered. They were grim faced, and spoke in gruff, rapid Portuguese to Luiz before they approached Gannon.

"Jack Gannon, American citizen of New York City, U.S.A.?" One of the cops stood before Gannon, unfolded a single sheet of paper, glanced at it, then at Gannon.

"Yes."

"Your identification, please?"

Gannon retrieved his passport from his computer bag. The officer looked at it, then tucked it in his breast pocket and snapped the flap closed.

"You will come with us to police headquarters."

"Why, what's this about?"

"For questioning."

"Questioning? About what? Do you have a warrant?"

"No warrant, come with us."

"Not without a warrant, or lawyer."

"You will come with us now."

"Am I being charged? Am I under arrest?"

"You will cooperate and come with us now, or you will face immediate expulsion from Brazil."

The second officer stepped around Gannon. Their body language was loud and clear. Gannon looked at Luiz, then back at the cop and got his bag.

"I will cooperate. Luiz, call Frank, tell him to alert New York and the U.S. consulate that I have been arrested without a warrant."

10

The officers took Gannon to a patrol car in front of the building.

They took his cell phone, his bag, searched it for weapons, locked it in the trunk, then held the rear door open for him. The back reeked of lemon-scented cleaner, perspiration and vomit.

The officers laughed at a private joke as they drove.

The radio issued coded transmissions. As the cop in the passenger seat worked on the keyboard of the car's small computer terminal, Gannon studied himself in the rearview mirror. Day two in Brazil and here he was in the backseat of a Rio police car. The officers didn't speak to him as they sailed through Centro's traffic. He had spent enough time on the crime beat in Buffalo to know that he was nothing more than a package to be delivered. They hadn't put him in cuffs. They hadn't been rough. This had to be about last night, or something about Gabriela and Marcelo.

He'd find out soon enough.

They went several blocks before turning onto Rua da Relação and stopping in front of a fourteen-story building—Gannon counted the levels—that looked like an attempt at 1970s Soviet disco-era architecture.

The sign in front said, *Polícia Civil*.

The officers got his bag and escorted him into a packed elevator. He'd lost track of the floors by the time they reached their destination.

They went down a hall to the squad room. Plainclothes detectives were talking on the phone, reading reports or interviewing people. Gannon's escorts stopped at an empty desk and put him in a folding hard-back chair beside it.

"Don't move."

"What about my passport and bag?"

They ignored him and walked away.

Gannon looked at the desk pushed against the wall to the left that displayed a framed degree from the John Jay College of Criminal Justice in Manhattan. He couldn't read the name on it.

Under the degree was a corkboard with a calendar, along with memos and an enlarged photograph of a man and boy holding up fish by a mountain lake. The man held up a tiny fish while the boy struggled with a catch that was over two feet long.

Gannon recognized the man as Roberto Estralla. The boy looked to be about ten and had Estralla's smile. Gannon glanced at the desk, a copy of today's *Jornal do Brasil* with the ten victims, file folders, a notebook, and something titled Café Amaldo, which looked like a floor plan.

Gannon was about to lean in for a better view when a hand reached across him from behind and snapped a business card on the table for *Hotel de nove palmas.*

His hotel.

Estralla then dropped Gannon's bag and cell phone on his desk before he deposited himself into his chair. He was wearing jeans, a T-shirt, his ID and a shoulder holster holding a pistol.

He set Gannon's passport on the desk, then tossed a piece of gum into his mouth, chewing hard as he assessed Gannon.

"Are you comfortable, Mr. Gannon?"

"I'd like to know what's happening. My bureau in New York will be notifying the U.S. consulate."

"Last night," Estralla said, "officers at the bomb scene

chased a man acting suspiciously in an alley. This hotel card fell from his pocket as he fled. They saw him get into a taxi then contacted the company. After further investigation at your hotel this morning, and by the description and time, we've concluded it was you, Jack Gannon."

Estralla leaned forward.

"What were you doing at the crime scene?"

Gannon's pulse quickened as the circumstances rose around him. No matter what explanation he offered, he would lose. The threat of expulsion was real. He glanced at Estralla's fishing photo, reasoning Estralla had a human side. All he could do was play to it.

"When I met you at the scene," Gannon said, "and later watching the TV news reports, I noticed the wind was scattering papers from the explosion. So I went to the alleys nearby and collected all the papers I could find."

"These are the papers?"

Estralla removed the originals from Gannon's bag and began flipping through them carefully.

"I am seizing these."

"But they're mine."

Estralla shrugged.

"I don't understand why your crime scene people did not protect this kind of potential evidence," Gannon said.

"They did."

"Did they? Their work was sloppy. It's probably why you have trouble clearing crimes down here. That and the reputation Brazilian police have with human rights groups."

Estralla's eyes narrowed at Gannon.

"Are the LAPD and the NYPD without sin? And didn't London police shoot dead an innocent man? A Brazilian student, they wrongly suspected of being a terrorist? All police should not be judged by the actions of a few."

Gannon chided himself for saying something so asinine to the cop holding his passport.

"I apologize—I was out of line," Gannon said. "Maybe

it's the stress of two murdered colleagues and of flying down here on short notice where I don't know the language or the culture, or much else."

Estralla resumed chewing his gum and reappraised Gannon.

"We had nets on the scene, but removed them to take photographs and give the dog unit access. We were slow to return them."

"Look," said Gannon. "Now that I've explained everything, may I leave with my belongings?"

"No."

"Why not?"

"I have the impression you know more about why Gabriela Rosa and Marcelo Verde were at the café, more than you're telling me."

"If I help you, will you help me? Not as cop to reporter, but as two men trying to learn the truth about the murders?"

"We make no deals with journalists."

"I think you do." Gannon tapped the *Jornal do Brasil*.

Estralla's chewing slowed as he thought.

Gannon took his shot at the cop's human side.

"So, how did you come to attend John Jay in Manhattan?"

"My father was a diplomat at the UN. We lived in New York for ten years."

"Then you know the city better than I do. I moved there from Buffalo a few months ago."

"Home of the Bills."

"You a Bills fan? You like American football?"

Estralla shifted his weight in his chair and changed the subject.

"At this moment, my partner is preparing the documentation for your expulsion. You should tell me what you know now."

Gannon let a few moments pass. This was it.

"There's a small recorder in my bag, may I play it for you?"

Estralla nodded and Gannon played Gabriela's last message.

"We were aware of the message," Estralla said. "Gabriela's husband transcribed it for us but said that in his grief he accidentally erased it."

"That may be, but he forwarded it to a WPA colleague. I recorded it."

Gannon played it again for Estralla who listened intently.

"The part about documents is important," Gannon said. "I think these documents can lead us to the source. Her source could have been among the dead or injured. Did you create a seating map, showing where everyone was sitting at the time of the blast?"

Estralla thought, then placed a call, speaking quickly in Portuguese before coming back to Gannon.

"Nothing we discuss must be published. We can charge you with tampering with a crime scene. Do you understand?"

"I do."

"There are many theories we and the DFP are following. Because Angella Roho-Ruiz is among the victims, the narco-terrorist link is one. But criminal intelligence from the favelas to Bogotá has yielded nothing to back it up."

"What are the other theories?"

"An employee who was fired last month for stealing cash threatened to come back to the café and kill everyone. We have yet to find this ex-worker and confirm his whereabouts."

"That's it?"

"The restaurant was badly managed and carrying massive debts. But it was heavily insured. We received a tip that one of the owners had made inquires to criminals about arson bombs."

"Does the physical evidence point to anything, the type of bomb? The materials used? Is there a signature?"

"We've found nothing conclusive so far. It was very professional."

"And the seating map?"

Estralla opened a folder and showed him the detailed diagram.

"This was composed based upon where we found the bodies, food orders and our subsequent interviews with the survivors."

Gannon saw circles representing the tables, and the names, as Estralla explained the symbols for the dead and the injured.

"Marcelo Verde was here, alone." Estralla touched the table by the window overlooking the patio. "We found his camera. It was destroyed by flying debris and the fire. And Gabriela was here."

Estralla pointed at the square representing her table. No other names were assigned to it.

"She was alone?" he asked.

"No one can place anyone there at the time of the blast. Some recalled seeing a woman with Gabriela, others contradicted them. It means we still have a lot of work to do."

Estralla passed Gannon his bag and stood.

"The officers will return you to your bureau."

"May I have my passport?"

"No. Your visit remains under police scrutiny."

"How about a copy of that floor plan?"

Estralla looked at it, chewing his gum thoughtfully.

"From one Bills fan to another?" Gannon asked.

11

Big Cloud, Wyoming

Emma didn't know how long the sedative had made her sleep.

She woke up alone to battle her grief.

It's a dream. Wake up.

If she could stop thinking she could stop it from being real.

Emma stared at the ceiling, at the corners where the drab paint had dried and fractured. Suddenly those tiny lines of cracked paint moved, growing until they raced down the walls like fingers of lightning and pierced her heart, forcing her to tense with pain.

My husband. My son.

It can't be.

She could still feel Joe's hand; his shirt, his favorite faded denim shirt, softened by a thousand washings. She could feel his skin, smell his cologne. She still tasted his cheek on her lips.

And Tyler.

Her angel laughing in the brilliant sun before everything exploded. Emma smelled gas, heard Tyler screaming, and in the chaos, she saw someone take him to safety.

She saw it!

Then the ground shook, the air ignited and everything burned.

It can't be happening again.

Fire had first devastated Emma's world all those years ago, when she finished college in Chicago. Her mother and father had driven from Iowa for her graduation.

"We're so proud of you, kiddo." Her mother's hug was crushing.

The day after graduating, Emma flew to Boston to start her new job with a travel agency while her parents took a vacation drive home. They'd stopped in Wisconsin at an older motel. Her dad loved them. "They've got character, not like the chains. All clones."

But at this one the owner had scrimped on repairs. The new air conditioners strained the outdated wiring, which resulted in a fire that killed Emma's mother, father, and a family with three children from North Dakota.

After the tragedy, Emma went through the motions of living, thinking she would not survive. Friends encouraged her to keep going and she used the insurance money to travel and write articles.

If she kept moving, she could stay ahead of her pain.

She did that for nearly ten years before she met Joe Lane, a carpenter in Big Cloud, Wyoming, where she'd come to write a travel story for the *Boston Globe*. They'd met at a diner, had a beer at a bar and a month later she found a reason to return. Emma was taken by Joe's strong gentle way, and the bittersweet sadness in his eyes. His mother had died when he was nine. His father, an electrician with the state, had died of a heart attack just the previous winter.

Joe was a loner.

But being with him made her feel like she was in the place she needed to be. They got married and Emma, who'd minored in education at college, got a job as a teacher.

She loved her new life in Big Cloud.

It was as if she'd been reborn.

Joe was her rock and Tyler was their gift.

But now Joe is dead and Tyler is gone.

"No!"

Emma pulled her fingers into a fist and pounded the stand at her bedside, toppling the tray. The water jug splashed to the floor. She brought her fist down again, and the stand crashed against the wall and equipment cart.

Nooooo.

Emma's heart rate soared, the monitor beeped. Alarmed nurses rushed into her room.

"I'm sorry," she sobbed, "it's my fault!" Her hands flew up to her mouth. "I'm the one who said we should drive to the river for a picnic. It's my fault!"

"No, it's okay, Emma." The nurses lowered her head back. "It's okay."

The next sedative put her down for hours.

Emma woke in dim light to several silhouettes.

Her aunt Marsha, her uncle Ned, Dr. Kendrix, a nurse and several other people were gathered in her room.

She heard the soft chink of keys, the leathery squeak of a utility belt then the whiz of a nylon club jacket and nervous throat clearing.

"Emma," Kendrix said, "you know Lyle and Darnell."

As her eyes adjusted, she recognized Lyle Spencer with the Big Cloud County Fire & Emergency Services and Darnell Horn, a deputy with the county sheriff's office. Both had made safety presentations at her school many times. She knew their wives, their children.

"Yes."

"They were both at the scene, do you remember?"

"No."

"We're so damned sorry," Lyle said. "Most of the guys at the department knew Joe. They're taking up a collection."

"Ruthie sends her love," Darnell said. "If there's anything we can do."

"What have you done with my son?"

Keys chimed. Darnell shifted his weight as he braced to explain.

"Emma, I'm so sorry but he didn't make it. Tyler and Joe didn't make it."

"You're a liar!"

"We were called to the scene." Darnell cleared his throat. "We helped the highway patrol. Joe lost control. The guys at Joe's site said he'd been putting in long hours, we figured he drifted off."

"No! Someone swerved into our lane!"

"There were no other witnesses, no skid marks. The people that stopped afterward to help you did not report seeing anyone."

"I'm your witness! A car was coming at us and Joe swerved."

"Do you remember the color? The make?"

"No, dammit, it was all too fast!"

"Emma, some of the guys at Joe's job site said that in the past few days he would sleep at lunch or fall asleep in his truck before heading home."

"No."

"He was working god-awful long hours."

"Don't you dare blame him! You can't blame him, I was there!"

"Emma," Lyle said. "The doctors said you had a concussion."

"Why are you doing this?"

"We're trying to help you."

"You're all lying! Is it because of Tyler? Where is he?"

"Emma, sweetheart," her aunt said. "Everyone understands this is a horrible time. They're only trying to help."

"What did they do with my son? I saw someone rescue my son!"

Kendrix sat in the chair beside her and positioned it nearer.

"Sometimes," he started, "Emma, sometimes the mind

will create—fabricate—scenarios, such as rescue scenarios. It's a psychological defense mechanism, a means of coping with the unbearable. Perhaps your rescue scenario is representative of angels pulling Tyler free from being consumed by the fire, to give you solace."

"No, no."

Kendrix nodded at Darnell.

"Emma," Darnell said, "you were thrown from your vehicle. Joe was partially ejected, then thrown clear by the explosion and fire. But Tyler—" Darnell glanced at the others, and Kendrix urged him on "—Tyler remained inside."

She started shaking her head.

"Why are you doing this, Darnell? Why, Lyle? You knew Joe. You're both fathers. I know your children. I know Joe died. *I felt him die.* But why are you lying to me about Tyler?"

"No one is lying," Lyle said. "This is the hardest thing I'm going to have to tell you. The fire was intense." Lyle paused. "It consumed Tyler. The heat was so ferocious he was incinerated. I'm so sorry, there was nothing left."

"Nothing left?"

Lyle brought out a small brown paper bag from his pocket and placed it in her lap.

"This is all we recovered."

Emma stared at it.

It weighed nothing. It was a new lunch bag. She wondered if Lyle brought it from his home. When she opened it, it crackled, exhaling a whiff of smoky air as she peered inside at two small shoes.

Tyler's little sneakers.

Charred.

"It's proof, Emma," Kendrix said.

She touched them to her face, and her tears streaked over the toes, making tracks along the scorched canvas.

12

Rio de Janeiro, Brazil

Frank Archer was pacing with his cell phone against his ear when the Rio police returned Gannon to the bureau.

"He just walked in. We'll set it up in two minutes." Archer turned to Luiz. "Go ahead, set up the call."

Archer tossed his cell phone on his desk and put his hands on his hips.

"Dammit, Gannon. What the hell's going on?"

"It was a misunderstanding with police."

"They arrested you."

"They wanted to talk to me—it's been cleared up."

"Good. Do you have your passport? Luiz is booking you a flight back to New York. George agrees, having you down here is a liability."

"Wait, Frank—I think I've got some leads."

"What leads?"

"It might not be a narco hit. There's a disgruntled employee who made threats, and there's also a chance the bombing is linked to financial troubles the café was having. And there's the mystery woman Gabriela was supposed to meet."

"We've been through those theories. Our contacts say this was an act of narco terrorism."

"Have you confirmed Gabriela's source?"

"Gabriela's anonymous source never showed. According

to what Porter and Sally got from their police contacts, Gabriela was alone at her table."

"The sense I get is that the lead investigators have not exactly confirmed that Gabriela was alone. They've got conflicting reports that a woman may have been with her."

"Are you kidding me, Jack? Collectively, Hugh, Sally and I have worked in South America covering coups, earthquakes, drug wars, for nearly twenty years. You've been here about twenty minutes and you're going to tell me you have better inside police information?"

"Call's ready," Luiz said from the meeting table nearby where he'd entered the required codes on the telephone console for an urgent WPA teleconference call. The phone's speaker hissed with static.

George Wilson was on his cell phone at São Paulo's airport about to make his connection for Marcelo's service. Melody Lyon was in Miami for Gabriela's funeral and was calling from her hotel room.

"It's Luiz in Rio. Everybody's ready?"

"Is Gannon there with you, Frank?" Wilson asked.

"I'm here," Gannon said.

"Not for long," Wilson shot back. "Frank, give Melody an update."

"We no longer need Jack's help. Sally, Hugh, the stringers and I have got this covered. We appreciate that Jack rushed down here, but we're good."

"Don't sugarcoat this, Frank," Wilson said. "Mel, I don't want to say I told you so, but Gannon's screwed up royally."

"Jack," Lyon said, "I heard you got into trouble. What happened?"

"There was a misunderstanding with police and it's been cleared. Now, I have a few leads on tracking down who might be behind this."

"Oh, for Christ's sake," Wilson said. "Gannon, admit you messed up. You get yourself on Brazilian TV, get your picture in the papers, then you get arrested for tampering with evidence at the crime scene."

"I did not tamper with evidence. I was outside the scene. I just got back after talking to one of the detectives on the case. He's fine, he let me go."

"You're embarrassing the WPA at a difficult time," Wilson said. "Mel, I want him out of there."

"Wait, George," Lyon said. "Jack, how solid are your leads?"

Gannon thought of the document in his back pocket, the diagram of where the café victims were seated at the time of the blast. Estralla agreed to share it with him in confidence.

"They're good leads."

"Mel, send him back to New York. He needs more experience on the national desk," Wilson said. "This was a narco hit and our people were caught in the crossfire."

"Give me a few more days," Gannon said.

"Frank—" Melody came on the line "—are you, Sally and Porter attending any of the services? We hear the Rio Press Club has arranged something there?"

"Yes, we're going to a memorial today. Then I'm flying to Miami tonight. John asked me to go with him. Sally and Porter are going to meet George for Marcelo's service. The stringers are standing by and will file any breaking news to New York."

"Okay," Lyon said. "Jack you're staying in Brazil."

"Thank you," Gannon said.

"For now," Lyon stressed. "You and Luiz will mind the bureau while we're down for the next few days. And you will stay out of trouble and keep me up to speed, is that clear?"

"Yes."

"After that, we'll see where the story is and decide your assignment," Lyon said. "Are you good with that, George?"

"It's your call, Mel. I have to go."

"Thank you, everyone," Lyon said.

As he tightened his tie and slid on his jacket, Archer stared at Gannon.

"I have to meet Sally and Hugh at the church in Copacabana for the memorial service. Luiz will give you the spare keys. Lock up if you go out."

"Thanks."

Archer shook his head.

"You're a piece of work, Gannon."

Archer left, the tension in the office eased and Luiz went out for pastries, leaving Gannon alone. He exhaled slowly as he studied the seating diagram Estralla had given him.

There had to be something more to this.

Who was Gabriela's source? According to Estralla, a woman appeared to have met Gabriela at the café but then disappeared. Maybe she went to the restroom?

He grabbed the *Jornal do Brasil* and reviewed the faces and bios of the victims. The diagram allowed him to consider who they were and where they were situated at the time of the blast. He pondered it and the pictures until Luiz returned.

Gannon had given little thought to the fact he was sitting at Marcelo's desk until he absentmindedly gazed at all of the notes framing his computer's monitor, then at some of the photo equipment.

That was when it hit him.

"Luiz, help me out here. Marcelo accompanied Gabriela to the café to meet the source, we know that much."

"Of course."

"But as I understand it, he went for more than a matter of bureau practice and safety. He probably wanted to take a few photos of the source without her knowing. I mean, we did the same thing in Buffalo, in case a source was going to feed you a bad story. If they burned you, you had their picture."

"I understand, yes."

"What if Marcelo managed to take a few pictures before the café exploded?"

"But Marcelo's camera was destroyed."

"I know."

But in his years of working with the news photographers, Gannon had learned a bit of the technical side of things and an idea was taking shape.

One that could pay off.

"I have a hunch about something, Luiz, and I'm going to need your help."

13

Gannon swayed in the chair of his murdered colleague, nurturing his new hunch.

Taking stock of Marcelo's desk, Gannon considered an empty package for an Eye-Fi card, thinking about what the photographer could have done at the café.

"Marcelo was obviously familiar with wireless transmission of photos."

"Most photographers are," Luiz said.

"And the Café Amaldo had Wi-Fi wireless access."

"Yes, the journalists went to the Amaldo often with their laptops."

"With this—" Gannon held up the Eye-Fi package "—Marcelo had the ability to ensure that any picture he took at the café was immediately transmitted and stored securely online."

Gannon studied Marcelo's keyboard as if it held the answer.

"We've got to get into his computer." Gannon switched it on.

After several moments of whirring and beeping, the system came to life and the password window popped up, stopping him cold.

"Do you have Marcelo's password?"

"No, each member of the bureau has a secret password."

Gannon tapped a finger next to the keyboard and searched the notes affixed to the edges of the computer monitor.

"You said he was forgetful?"

"It is why he attached all those notes to his screen."

"Let's go through them. Maybe he posted his password here?"

Luiz and Gannon scrutinized the notes one by one with Luiz reciting names, dates, numbers, addresses and phone numbers as possible passwords. Gannon submitted candidates, and each time they were denied access. He knew it was likely futile, given the upper- and lower-case combinations. But they tried for nearly an hour, including restarting the computer when they exceeded the number of failed attempts to log in.

No luck.

"I could call technical support," Luiz suggested.

"No. I want to keep this between us for now," Gannon said. "Think, Luiz. Did you ever see him submit his code or get a glimpse of any of the key strokes?"

"No, but I heard it all the time. It went like this—" Luiz tapped four quick strokes on the desk, paused then tapped a fifth. "One, two, three, four. Always like that."

"So it's a four-character code, because the fifth would be the enter key. Four characters. That's pretty short for a password. Okay, let's check the notes for a four-character word, or name."

They had studied them for fifteen minutes when Luiz froze.

"I think I know Marcelo's password. His girlfriend's name is Anna, spelled A-N-N-A, that's four characters."

Gannon entered the name with the first letter in upper case.

It failed.

"Try with no capital letters," Luiz said.

Gannon typed *anna* and pressed Enter.

The screen flashed to Marcelo's desktop and screen saver of Rio de Janeiro's skyline at night, a shot he'd taken himself.

"That's it!" Luiz said.

"We're in! It would be an Internet link. Go to his favorites." Gannon got out of the chair. "Luiz, you do it. You'll recognize names faster."

Luiz translated after he'd pulled down a list of links for sports teams, a bank, camera stores, weather, magazines, an auto shop and restaurants.

"This could be it," Luiz translated, "Onlinephotocapture."

"Hit it."

An array of news and feature photos came up. Luiz translated the text.

"Onlinephotocapture…welcome to Onlinephotocapture…the secure members-only Web site for storing visual data…."

"This might be it," Gannon said.

It was secure with a member's log-in tab, requiring a user ID and another password. Gannon cursed under his breath.

"It's no problem," Luiz said. "This one has a password recall feature. Marcelo's locked in his password, see?"

A couple of clicks and they had entered Marcelo's page. Luiz translated: "Marcelo V. Storage Inventory." Gannon felt a chill rush up his spine. Topping the item list: Café Amaldo and the date of the explosion.

"Open it."

Half a dozen thumbnail photos appeared on the screen.

"Open the first one," Gannon said.

It presented a well-framed photo of a beautiful woman alone at a table of the busy café. A long silence passed as Luiz and Gannon realized the significance of the image.

"That's Gabriela." Luiz swallowed. "Before her death."

"Jesus," Gannon whispered.

Luiz clicked to the next picture.

A woman in her late twenties, dressed in a blazer and skirt, was gripping the strap of a shoulder bag and standing before Gabriela's table.

Luiz clicked.

Next, a close-up of the woman, worry creasing her face
and making her appear older than her wardrobe and pos-
ture suggested.

Next, the woman sitting at Gabriela's table, removing a
legal-sized envelope from her bag. Next, Gabriela reading
documents from the woman's envelope, which was open on
the table before them.

When the last picture came up, Luiz gasped.

Tentacles of smoke spattered with debris shot out in all
directions radiating from a red-yellow fireball. Marcelo had
photographed the instant of the explosion within the mil-
lionths of a second he and the others were killed by it.

And like the others, this image was transmitted immediately to his page at Onlinephotocapture.

"My god!" Luiz said.

"Unbelievable," Gannon agreed. "Marcelo photographed
the moment of his death." He shook his head. "No one has
seen these pictures, right, Luiz?"

"No, no one knows they exist. None of the others here
have thought to look for them as you did, Mr. Gannon."

"Don't tell anyone. I need time to follow this up my way."

"But they're so amazing. WPA's news subscribers around
the world would want these pictures."

"I know."

"And what about the police? Isn't this evidence we
should give to them?"

"We'll sort that out later. I need time to chase this lead.
Swear to me you won't tell anyone just yet, okay?"

Luiz nodded.

"Pass me that copy of the *Jornal do Brasil,* please."

Gannon spread the newspaper over the desk's clutter so
he and Luiz could study the ten victims of the bombing.

"This one—" Luiz pressed his finger on one of the pictures "—her name is Maria Santo. She is the woman in
Marcelo's pictures, Gabriella's source."

Gannon unfolded the floor plan Estralla had given him.

It put Maria Santo at the table of architects and secretaries next to Gabriela, but her chair was flagged with a question mark, meaning the investigators were uncertain as to where exactly Santo was positioned.

Marcelo's photographs confirmed where she was seated.

Luiz translated the newspaper's small biography for her, telling him quickly that she was twenty-nine and had grown up in one of Rio's harshest favelas. Her mother worked as a domestic for the wealthy, her father in a sheet-metal factory. Maria Santo had worked in shopping malls as she struggled to pursue her education, before finding work at various office jobs downtown.

On the day she died Maria Santo was working as an office assistant at the international law firm, Worldwide Rio Advogados.

"'We're saddened by this tragedy,' said a spokesman for the firm, who would not elaborate or disclose his name," Luiz finished reading.

Worldwide Rio Advogados? It was familiar to Gannon from the papers he'd collected near the scene of the bombing.

"Where are the copies of the documents I asked you to store?"

Luiz got them from the supply room. Paging through the papers, Gannon found a few records on the letterhead of Worldwide Rio Advogados.

These were the bloodied pages.

Looking them over again it appeared that they held little information.

A list of a dozen or so file numbers and a short note in Portuguese. As Luiz translated, the significance of the information dawned on Gannon.

"Please ensure all versions of these noted files, hardcopy and electronic, are destroyed and that no record exists in the firm that makes mention of their existence, including this one which should be destroyed after these instructions are carried out."

Luiz looked at Gannon.

"This woman was on to something," Gannon said.

Maria Santo's eyes met Gannon's from the front page of the *Jornal do Brasil*. As he stared into them, he wondered why she had needed to meet with a reporter from a global news agency.

Why did the firm where she worked need their files to disappear?

Were these the secrets Maria was planning to reveal in the moments before her death?

"Luiz, I'm going to the law firm to see what I can find out."

14

The offices of Worldwide Rio Advogados were in a skyscraper in Centro's east side, near Guanabara Bay.

As the elevator rose to the twenty-eighth floor, Gannon weighed the pros and cons of a cold visit.

Sure, he risked being turned away. But the fact that the *Jornal do Brasil* had already reported the firm's connection to the bombing might help—press interest would be expected.

According to its Web site, Worldwide Rio Advogados was a global operation that practiced in international trade, labor, family law, international adoptions, banking, patents, corporate law and the list went on. The firm functioned in several languages, including English. Gannon had decided to go alone, realizing that his chances of obtaining new information were slim.

Still, he had an edge.

His agency and the law firm shared a common bond in the tragedy—they had both lost staff to the bombing.

But it was the firm that had secrets linked to it.

Gannon had to learn those secrets and he had to do it now because time was working against him. At any moment, someone could beat him to it. Or Estralla could force him back to New York.

Gannon considered the bloodied pages he'd gathered from the street.

Copies were now folded in his jacket pocket as he stepped

from the elevator to a polished stone hallway and passed
through the brass-plated doors of Worldwide Rio Advogados to the reception desk. The woman seated there finished
a call.

"May I help you," she asked in English, then Portuguese.

"Jack Gannon, from the World Press Alliance." He
placed his card on the counter. "I don't have an appointment
but I'd like to speak to Maria Santo's supervisor. It will only
take a moment."

"World Press Alliance?" She read his card, looked around
her desk sadly as if searching for a response, then said,
"Yes, please sit down. I will call someone."

She spoke softly into the phone as he went to the waiting area and sat in a thick-cushioned leather chair. To one
side, a large window offered views of the bay and planes
landing at Santos Dumont Airport. Down the hall, he saw a
room with files.

"This way, Mr. Gannon, please." The receptionist led
him to a door bearing the nameplate, Drake Stinson, then
opened it for him.

"Jack Gannon?" A tall, silver-haired, well-built man in
his late fifties stood. He wore a tailored suit and a smile as
he crushed Gannon's hand in his. "Drake Stinson, I'm here
by way of Washington, D.C. Always nice to see a fellow
countryman—too bad about the circumstances. Have a seat.
Are you hearing anything new on the investigation?"

"Only that the victims' names have been released. You
know we lost two of our bureau people."

"Yes, terrible." Stinson handed Gannon his card, and
Gannon glimpsed Stinson's title: special international counsel. "What were they doing there? Anything to do with the
press reports that this was an execution in a drug war with
the Colombians? Did your agency have an inside scoop?"

Gannon cautioned himself.

He was not there to reveal information, but to obtain it.

"No, we think Gabriela Rosa and Marcelo Verde just

happened to be at the Café Amaldo for lunch. It's a short walk from our bureau."

"I see," Stinson said, "and I think that is how we lost Maria. She was at the wrong place at the wrong time."

"Which is why I'm here." Gannon opened his notebook and pen.

A hint of unease flickered across Stinson's eyes.

"We're profiling the victims," Gannon said, "and I was hoping you could tell me about Maria Santo."

"The firm won't comment other than to say we are saddened by this horrible event and our thoughts go to the families of the victims."

"Can't you elaborate? Both of our organizations lost people here. Can you tell me the kind of person she was?"

Stinson shook his head.

"Why not? You lost an employee—why not offer a few compassionate words to let people know just what kind of innocent person was murdered here?"

"I can't." Stinson paused. "Would you consider going off the record?"

"What's the information?"

"I have your word you will not attribute what I'm going to tell you to this firm in any way?"

"Go ahead."

"This is terrible to say but Maria was going to be let go."

"Why?"

"We think she was stealing files. One of the other girls saw her leave with case files in her bag and that's a firing offence."

"Which files? Which case?"

"I'm not certain."

"Any idea why she was stealing files?"

"Who knows? Maybe she had thoughts of selling them to narco terrorists, corporate competitors of our clients, other law firms that were opposing us on cases?"

"Would she want to go to the press about anything?"

Stinson took a moment to assess the question.

"You're talking about the coincidence of Maria and your people being there at the same time?"

"Just trying to get a sense of the files."

Stinson shook his head.

"No, our files are legal mumbo jumbo, nothing newsworthy."

"I thought you didn't know which case she was taking files from?"

"I don't, but I know the type of cases we handle and it's really all contractual stuff."

"Contractual stuff—that is of interest to narco terrorists? You said she could've wanted to sell the files to narco terrorists."

"Look, the files contain personal information on some wealthy clients. Hostage-taking for ransom is a business down here. Bottom line—we really don't know why she would be taking files," Stinson said. "She had a rough upbringing in one of the gang-controlled favelas. She'd been with us less than a year. Came to us through a temporary placement service, the Rio Sol Employment Agency. I hope this helps you understand our position." Stinson stood. "And on behalf of the firm, our condolences for the loss your news organization suffered."

Gannon finished making notes and stood.

"Thank you. Yes, this helps."

"We're clear on quoting me then?" Stinson went to the door.

"Right." Gannon tucked his notebook in his jacket. "I'm curious, how did you come from Washington to be—" Gannon glanced at Stinson's card "—special international counsel for this firm?"

"Me?" Stinson smiled. "I'm from Connecticut—Hartford. I went to Yale, practiced in D.C. a lifetime ago. Dry government stuff, then I retired. Then my wife passed away. I couldn't stand living alone. Submitted my CV to a global headhunting firm, got back into the game with a job here where the weather suits me. Coming from Buffalo, you'd know about winter weather."

Gannon stopped.

Stinson smiled.

"I checked you out online when we saw you on the Rio news channels. You used to write for the *Buffalo Sentinel* before you joined WPA. You were nominated for a Pulitzer. Interesting what you can find out about people on the Internet, don't you think?"

"Yes."

Afterward, as he descended in the elevator, Gannon tapped his notebook to his leg trying to decide how much of what Stinson had told him was a twisted version of the truth and how much was a flat-out lie.

In his taxi back to the bureau, he unfolded the blood-stained pages from the files Maria Santo had shown to Gabriela.

There's a story here, he told himself, looking off to the favelas blanketing the hillsides around Rio de Janeiro.

15

It was not the same house.

How could it be?

Three days after Emma had left with Joe and Tyler for a picnic by the Grizzly Tooth River, she'd returned home without them. Their ranch-style bungalow stood empty in the Bluffs, a suburb at Big Cloud's edge.

Emma stared at it from the car.

Aunt Marsha squeezed her hand and hugged her tight as Uncle Ned eased the airport rental into the driveway. They sat without speaking for a long time.

"It's going to be hard, dear." Her aunt smiled.

Emma nodded.

Uncle Ned fumbled with the house keys, the new ones he'd had cut at Gorten's Hardware. Her aunt and uncle didn't want her using the blood-speckled, scorched keys recovered from the SUV.

The door opened and Emma caught her breath.

A breeze tortured her with familiar smells: Joe's cologne and Tyler's sweetness. *But they're not here.* She inched into the kitchen expecting the floor to collapse and drop her into a pit. She steadied herself.

Their last moments together had been frozen in time.

Here was Joe's favorite coffee mug in the sink, the chipped one from Treeline Timber. He'd gulped one last cup before they'd left for the picnic. Emma traced its rim with her fingertips. And here was Tyler's ring-toss game, the bright colored plastic donuts he'd played with before she'd bundled him up for the trip. Emma had piled the rings on the counter, on top of the flyer she'd pulled from their mailbox.

She'd noted the sale on something they needed. She couldn't remember what.

How was she to know these would be the last moments of her happiness?

Her hands were shaking.

"Easy, honey." Uncle Ned helped her to the sofa. Aunt Marsha got her a glass of water and pills rattling in a plastic bottle.

"The doctor said these would help, Emma."

"No pills now."

Emma finished the water and sat motionless for a long time, listening to the clock ticking above the mantel, before she found herself walking through her home, room by room, expecting Joe and Tyler to be there.

Wanting them to be there.

Aching for them to be there as she touched Joe's work shirts and thrust her face into Tyler's blanket, muffling her screams. *Bring them back. Please bring them back.* She lay down on Joe's side of the bed and questioned the distant snow-capped mountains.

Why was God punishing her again? What had she done?

The afternoon blurred into a flow of friends bearing salads, sandwiches and condolences, mourners in their Sunday best, smelling of perfume, mouthwash and alcohol. They touched her shoulder, kissed her cheek and embraced her, whispering words of sympathy and scripture.

The men huddled in corners, spoke in low tones about Joe, Tyler and the "damned shame" of it all, while the women collected around Emma. These were people descended from pioneer stock, people who endured.

Emma loved them for what they had done for her.

But by early evening, after the majority of her visitors had left, she couldn't remember a single word or face. A few of the women stayed behind and cleaned up. By nightfall the only people who remained were her aunt, uncle and her friend, Judy Mitchell, who taught at Emma's school.

"Sweetheart," her aunt said, "Judy's already helped us start with some of the arrangements."

"Arrangements?"

"For the funerals, Em," Judy said. "Tomorrow we'll go with you to help finalize things."

Emma was numb.

That night while Uncle Ned and Aunt Marsha slept in the spare bedroom, Emma lay alone in her bed for hours.

She didn't move.

She didn't breathe, as agony and darkness swallowed her.

Do something.

She went to Joe's side of the closet and pulled out his heavy flannel shirt. The blue-and-black plaid one he wore to work each day. She slipped it on. Then she took Joe's pillow, their bedspread and went to Tyler's room. She stood before his empty crib. It glowed in the pure moonlight and she reached in for his stuffed bear.

She lay on the floor, pulling Joe's big shirt tight, feeling his warmth, his arms around her. Crushing Tyler's bear to her face, she swore she could feel his tender cheek against hers. And in the furthest corner of her heart, Emma found a pinpoint of light.

Hang on, she told herself. Hang on.

The next day Emma, her aunt, her uncle and Judy Mitchell arrived at the Fenlon-Wilter Funeral Home, a grand Victorian mansion built in the late 1800s by a mining millionaire before it was sold during the Depression.

Emma carried a small travel bag with the clothes she'd picked for Joe: faded jeans and a T-shirt, the clothes he loved. "Whatever you do, Em, don't bury me in a damned suit. I hate them," he'd joked to her one night.

But she knew he'd meant it.

Emma also brought Tyler's shoes, which had been deemed his only remains and were to be placed in Tyler's casket. She hadn't slept and didn't hear what the funeral director was saying.

This is not real. I am not here. This isn't happening.

Emma's aunt, uncle and Judy guided her with decisions, showed her where to sign.

The funeral home had deep-pile carpet that absorbed sound as they moved to the viewing room where Emma agreed to a dark oak casket for Joe. She then heard the gentle strains of a harp wafting through hidden speakers as the director led them upstairs to the children's viewing room.

It was small, occupied with five small caskets, models for preteens, children and the pearl-white box for babies. The walls had sky-blue murals of cherubs frolicking amid clouds pierced by sunbeams.

Emma stood there among the children's coffins, holding Tyler's stuffed bear, unable to think or breathe until finally she pressed her hand firmly on the Angel's Wings model.

That was the one.

The funerals were at the Sun View Park Cemetery west of town.

Two hearses and a long line of vehicles moved over the rolling range land that stretched to the mountains under an eternal blue sky. The procession, led by two deputy patrol cars from the county, came to a stop at two open graves next to mounds of dark, fresh earth. Abner Fenlon, the owner of the funeral home, and his assistants, helped the pallbearers, men who knew Joe—carpenters, electricians—and Emma's uncle, position the caskets.

About fifty mourners were gathered, as Reverend John Fitzgerald, who'd officiated at Emma and Joe's wedding, produced a worn bible.

In keeping with what Joe would have wanted, Reverend Fitzgerald spoke briefly of death and God's love before moving on to the readings.

Emma's ears began ringing during the service. She did not hear Reverend Fitzgerald's recitation of passages from Isaiah as she stared at the two caskets.

Her breathing quickened.

Earlier, at the funeral home, she was left alone to say goodbye to Joe before his casket was closed. His handsome face bore some scarring from the crash. A heavy coating of makeup muted his cuts and bruises. Her tears fell on him as she bent down to give him a final kiss. Emma knew and accepted that he was dead.

She nodded for the lid to be secured.

Now at the cemetery, as Reverend Fitzgerald finished reading, Abner Fenlon gestured to Emma and she kissed Joe's casket and placed a white rose upon it. As it was lowered into the ground, Emma, standing in shock, glanced at Tyler's tiny casket. Abner Fenlon invited her to say goodbye to Tyler before his casket was lowered. Emma did not respond.

"Mrs. Lane," Fenlon whispered again, "you may come forward."

Emma did not move.

Abner Fenlon had five decades of experience in the funeral business and reasoned that Emma, paralyzed with grief, was likely not going to do anything without help. He wanted her to have the opportunity to say goodbye to her dead baby, so he offered it a second time, shooting glances at Emma's aunt and uncle, who whispered in her ear.

"Say goodbye to Tyler, Emma."

Emma did not respond.

Fenlon stepped up to Emma.

"Mrs. Lane, do you wish to say goodbye to your son?"

Emma was numb.

"I understand, Mrs. Lane." Fenlon nodded to his staff.

At the funeral home, Emma had been invited to place Tyler's stuffed bear inside his casket, alongside his little charred shoes. She had refused to part with the toy bear.

There's nothing in there. I saw someone rescue my baby.

Now, as she watched the casket disappear into the earth, she pressed the stuffed toy to her face.

I know you're not dead. Mommy's going to find you.

16

"Got it! Rio Sol Employment Agency, in the financial district."

Luiz had looked it up online for Gannon as soon as he had returned to the WPA bureau from the law firm. Luiz called and pleaded in Portuguese for a meeting on Gannon's behalf before hanging up.

"They will help us."

Minutes later they were in a taxi weaving through traffic in Rio de Janeiro's financial district. Gannon didn't have much time to pursue this angle before the others would return from the funerals. He had to find out what role the documents from the law firm played in Maria Santo's meeting with Gabriela. He needed to get to someone who knew Maria Santo.

Someone she trusted.

A few blocks after they'd passed by the Petrobras building with its sugar-cube architecture, the taxi stopped at the complex where the Rio Sol Employment Agency was located.

They were directed to the north wing, phase two, and the office of Francisco Viana, a small, officious man with a neatly trimmed beard. "Francisco's English is not so good," they were told. But Gannon was encouraged when he saw Maria Santo's file on Viana's desk.

After introductions, Viana offered his guests seats.

"The tragedy of the Café Amaldo was such a terrible act, my sympathies, Mr. Gannon."

"Thank you, and our condolences, as well."

"On the call, Luiz said that you wanted to pay tribute to Maria Santo."

Viana's English was stronger than Gannon had expected.

"Yes." Gannon withdrew his notebook. "We're profiling all the victims."

"I see," Viana said. "You cannot use my name, or the company's name in any news report. We have client confidentiality agreements."

"How about I take notes for background? And if the agency decides to make a formal statement of condolence, I will use that for my report?"

"Very well, on background as you say, not for publication."

"Did you know Maria well?"

"She had been my client for three years. She was a very determined young woman."

"How so?"

"She came from a very tough favela. Like the papers say, her father was a factory worker, her mother was a maid for wealthy people around Gávea and Leblon. Maria's parents wanted a better life for her and sent her to school outside the slum."

"What kind of a student was she?"

"Excellent." Viana tapped her file. "She became very committed to human rights, social justice. She was a community activist and a conscientious worker. She was taking courses to be an administrator."

"How would you rate her honesty, her integrity?"

"She was beyond reproach. She was one of our best workers."

"Were there any problems with her work at Worldwide Rio Advogados?"

"None. Wherever she went, she was praised. At Worldwide Rio Advogados Maria was filling in for a worker on maternity leave. It was one of her longer assignments." Viana stroked his beard as if coaxing a memory. "There is one odd thing about the firm and Maria."

"What's that?"

"She was always interested in postings at that specific firm."

"Why?"

"Again, I must emphasize that this is not for publication?"

"Certainly."

"There were rumors that Worldwide Rio Advogados represented the interests of big narco networks," Viana said. "Some said they set up shell companies for the CIA, or numbered companies operating child labor sweat shops in contravention of UN treaties. All of it rumor, nothing ever surfaced. If it had, we would never send our people there."

"Yes, but would Maria be the kind of person who would want to expose such activities if she'd found evidence, say documented evidence?"

"Perhaps. She was passionate about human rights, but really—" Viana shook his head as if to downplay the subject "—I don't know. Those are only rumors and my speculation is not for publication, please."

"Where did Maria live?"

"In the favela with her parents, Pedro and Fatima Santo."

"She never moved out?"

"No, she wanted to make life better in her neighborhood."

"Which favela?"

"Céu sobre Rio. Loosely translated, it means, heaven over Rio," Viana said.

"Do you have a specific address? I'd like to go there and talk to her family and friends."

"That's not advisable," Viana said.

"As a journalist, I must go. Luiz here can be my guide."

"No, I could not," Luiz said. "It would not be safe for either of us. Céu sobre Rio is one of the most dangerous favelas in all of Rio de Janeiro."

"The drug gangs live there and control it," Viana said. "As you may know, they control many favelas. In exchange for loyalty, they protect the residents and provide them with the things governments don't," Viana said. "If you enter as a stranger without permission, you could be robbed or beaten, taken hostage for ransom, or worse."

"I understand it can be dangerous."

"Especially for people like you, Mr. Gannon," Viana said. "A year ago, a Brazilian TV crew doing interviews in the favelas was taken hostage after the narco chiefs accused them of being police sympathizers. They were tortured for days, their agony recorded with their own TV cameras."

"I recall reading about that case. They were killed?"

"Executed," Viana said. "No one was arrested. Then just last month, a reporter and photographer from Spain went into Céu sobre Rio. No one heard from them for five days— that is when their bodies were found in a Dumpster behind a Zona Sul police station. The drug bosses had suspected them to be undercover international police posing as foreign journalists. They were tortured, their torment recorded on a disk left on their bodies. It shows their killers, their faces hidden under bandannas, warning other 'foreign police rats' to stay away. It was on the TV news."

"I understand," Gannon said, taking a few moments to ponder Viana's advice. Then he asked a few minor questions before closing his notebook and thanking him.

The taxi trip back to Centro was a long, silent one until the cab neared the bureau and Luiz turned to Gannon.

"You did some good digging, Jack, finding out Maria Santo was Gabriela's source and everything else we learned today."

"We got lucky there."

"I guess we've reached a dead end at the favelas."

"I'm not sure where we go on this story next," Gannon said.

"The others are due back the day after tomorrow. It doesn't leave you much time."

The taxi had stopped in front of their building.

"It's been a long day, Luiz, thanks for your help. Send a news status update to New York, say that follow-up stories to the bombing are in development, then go home. I'll see you tomorrow."

"Okay, thank you."

After Luiz entered the building's lobby Gannon said to his driver, "Do you speak English?"

"A little."

"Take me to a restaurant that is as close as possible to the entrance for Céu sobre Rio."

"Céu sobre Rio?" The driver raised his eyebrows, shifted his transmission and eased into traffic. "Okay."

After negotiating heavy late-day traffic, the driver came to a collection of boutiques and shops bordered by rising hills. The taxi stopped at a small restaurant called the Real American Diner, where Gannon got a table outside on the patio and ordered a burger made with beef from Argentina. In making awkward small talk with his waiter, Gannon confirmed that ascending beside him was the favela, Céu sobre Rio, an explosion of clustered shacks, jutting at all angles, piled on top of each other as they clung in defiance to the steep hill. While the sun sank behind the hill, Gannon asked his waiter if any of the staff lived there, or if he knew anyone who lived there.

After several minutes, Gannon was invited into the darkened restaurant, to the end of the bar where some of the staff had gathered. A man in his thirties, who bore a friendly face and spoke English, nodded to the youngest in the group, a teenager wearing an apron over jeans and a white T-shirt.

"Alfonso, our dishwasher, lives in the favela."

"I am a journalist from New York City." Gannon showed them his laminated WPA ID, then the clipping about the bombing victims. "I need to find the family of this woman." He tapped Maria Santo's picture. "Pedro and Fatima Santo. I need to visit them in the favela and talk about Maria."

The older man translated and Alfonso began nodding.

"He knows Maria's family."

"Will he take me to them? Will he be my guide? I will tip him."

The older man asked the boy, who spoke for a moment.

"Yes, he says. Meet him out front of this restaurant tomorrow at noon."

"Can't we go now?"

The man asked the boy.

"No, it is almost night, tomorrow is Sunday, it will be safer to take you then."

"Good."

Energized by the break and the meal, Gannon tipped the staff, who called a cab for him. As he waited, twilight fell and he gazed up at the Céu sobre Rio. The echo of traffic, shouting and throbbing hip-hop music rolled down in the evening air.

Every now and then, Gannon heard the sporadic pop of gunfire.

17

After the funeral, time floated by Emma like fog.

She'd lost track of it as she grappled with the emptiness.

She'd sit alone in Tyler's room for hours, rocking in the chair where she had nursed him. Joe had made the chair for her from Canadian maple. Its rhythmic squeak comforted her as she held Tyler's teddy bear while images of the crash whirled around her.

Each time Emma replayed the tragedy, she saw Tyler being saved.

Was she crazy?

Oh, Joe, tell me what to do. Please, tell me!

Emma could feel Joe pulling her back to that day.

"You're one of the most fearless people I know. Woe to anyone or anything that comes between you and Tyler."

That was her answer.

Emma could not allow a lie to come between her and their baby. Emma needed proof, evidence that what she saw, *that what she felt with all her heart,* was wrong. And until she had it, she would never ever let go of her belief that Tyler was alive.

Never.

She found the binder holding papers from the funeral director and snapped through it, coming to the documents she needed.

"What is it, dear?" Aunt Marsha asked.

"I need to go out, to see to matters."

Emma showered, dressed, made phone calls from the bedroom, then collected her purse and files.

"Are you sure you're up to going out alone?" her uncle asked. "What matters are you talking about? Maybe we can see to them for you?"

"Thank you, Uncle Ned, but this is something I have to do myself."

Emma got into her Chevrolet Cobalt and caught her breath.

Tyler's car seat and some of his toys were in the back. Joe had insisted on getting a car seat for each vehicle so they weren't constantly moving one from the Cobalt to the SUV.

Emma touched it, then turned the ignition and headed to Deer Creek Road and the office of the chief deputy coroner.

"Emma Lane. I called," she told the woman at the desk.

The receptionist's eyes went briefly to the scrapes on her face, a subtle verification that this was the woman who'd lost her husband and baby in the crash. "Hold on, I think Henry's free."

Henry Sanders, M.D., was in his forties. He was wearing a white smock with a pen in his breast pocket. His thick, dark-framed glasses had slid to the end of his nose when he came out from behind his desk to greet her.

"I'm deeply sorry for your loss, Mrs. Lane. I'll try to answer your questions." Sanders shook her hand. "May I get you a glass of water, coffee, maybe some tea?"

"No thank you. Dr. Sanders, what proof do you have that my baby died in the crash?"

Sanders's face dimmed and he nudged his glasses.

"It was a terrible accident," he said.

"Dr. Sanders, I was there. Now, according to my documents from the funeral director, you signed the death certificates for Joe and Tyler."

"That's correct."

"And I understand that you filed them with the state."

"Yes, with the local registrar."

"I would like copies, please."

"You can order them through vital statistics, but we'll get you copies."

"What did you list as the cause of Tyler's death?"

"In Joe's case, cause was attributed to a broken neck. In Tyler's case, given the circumstances, I concluded fire was the cause of death."

"But how can you say that without evidence? You didn't find any of his remains." Emma stifled an anguished groan. Keep going, she told herself. Keep moving. "No teeth, no bones. Just his shoes, which I had removed during the trip and put in the front seat with me."

"Mrs. Lane, I know this is a traumatic time when people cannot conceive of the reality of what has happened."

Emma noticed the framed degrees and certificates displayed on the wall behind Sanders.

"Did you find any remains belonging to my son? Any bones or teeth because—" Emma's chin crumpled "—I understand teeth can survive fire?"

"No, Mrs. Lane, no remains belonging to your son were found."

"Well then, how can you say—"

Sanders removed his glasses.

"The impact of the crash situated the baby's seat upon the fuel tank, so that at the point of ignition it was akin to being at the hypocenter of a powerful explosion where the heat and gasses are the most intense. I am so sorry, but Tyler was incinerated. And under the regulations of this state, I am authorized to reasonably conclude that death occurred as a result of this event. Again, my condolences, Mrs. Lane."

"But I saw someone rescue him."

Sanders blinked sadly.

"Mrs. Lane, I understand the monumental loss you're

facing. Acceptance is difficult, denying the tragedy is understandable. Perhaps—"

"I'm not denying it. I know my husband is dead, I just—"

"Perhaps," Sanders continued, "if you haven't done so already, you should consider seeking counseling. There's someone in Cheyenne I could recommend, if you like."

Emma cupped her hands to her face and shook her head slowly.

"No, thank you."

After leaving the coroner's office, Emma drove across town to Blue Willow Park, where she used to bring Tyler. She stared at her copies of the death certificates until deciding to drive to the Big Cloud County Sheriff's Office on Center Street, to see Darnell Horn, the deputy who'd brought Tyler's burnt shoes to her in the hospital.

Horn had been the first officer on the scene.

"Is there something I can help you with, Emma?" Reed Cobb, Darnell's supervisor, asked at the front counter, concern rising in his eyes. "Darnell's out. But I expect him back any minute."

"I want to see the reports, pictures, everything on the crash."

"Emma, geez, I don't know. It's a terrible shame what happened, but it was a bad crash. One of the worst we've— I don't think you want to look."

"I want to see them."

Glancing at her bruises, Cobb reasoned she had a right to see the file.

"Come around this way."

He led her to a small room, left, then returned with a folder.

"Everything we have is in there, and we shared it with the Wyoming Highway Patrol."

Emma took a breath, opening the folder to a collection of reports and photographs. There were color prints of charred metal, the contorted remnants of their family SUV on its roof. This was the car Emma used to load with their groceries, the car she'd dreamed in, the car she'd taken on class trips; the car Joe had driven when they went to the County Hospital where Tyler was born.

Now it was twisted metal and melted plastic, a grotesque headstone to her life. Emma's vision blurred as she searched for proof that her son had survived.

She found none.

The reports were clinical. Phrases leaped out at her.

Single Vehicle Fatal Accident
Fatalities: Lane, Joseph, Age 34. Lane, Tyler, Age 1.
Injured: Lane, Emma, Age 31.
"...survivor Emma Lane, front-seat passenger, reported that her husband swerved to miss an oncoming car. However, investigation of the scene determined no evidence of a second vehicle...no indication of mechanical failure...

NOTE: Joseph Lane, driver, prone to sleeping in vehicle on job site possibly due to long hours of work as carpenter as reported by coworkers...

ON SCENE: Vehicle was traveling northbound on Junction Road 90. Discovered 40 feet east of highway on shoulder on its roof by...Herb Quiggly, Age 53, Mave Quiggly, Age, 52, and Rolly Quiggly, Age 17, of Ram River Ridge, traveling northbound. First Aid administered to Emma Lane by Mave Quiggly, part-time nurse...Emma Lane discovered traumatized, hysterical...Quiggly family was also northbound on Junction Road 90 prior to coming upon accident scene...could not corroborate Emma Lane's reports of second vehicle...as no vehicles southbound on Junction Road 90 were seen by Quiggly family.

CONCLUDING OBSERVATIONS: Cause unknown, contributing factors, driver error due to fatigue…"

Tears fell on the pages as Emma shook her head.

"You okay?"

Emma looked up to see Reed Cobb and Darnell Horn watching her. She had been so absorbed in the documents that she hadn't noticed Horn arrive.

"This is wrong."

"Wrong, how?" Cobb asked.

"There's nothing here about the car. I saw a car."

"Emma, you were hurt," Cobb said.

"And there was that strange car down our street a little while ago."

"Emma."

"Like a stranger was watching us. Maybe it's all connected?"

"Emma, you're not making sense," Cobb said.

"And some hang-up calls. I told Joe but he said not to worry."

"Emma, you should take it easy," Horn said.

"There was a car, dammit!"

"Emma, now, please—" Cobb murmured.

She thought for a moment before returning to the witness statements and copying the address and telephone number of the Quiggly family in Ram River Ridge on the back of her file from the funeral director.

"Why are you taking notes on the Quigglys, Emma?" Horn asked.

"So I can thank them for what they did. Can I do that?"

"I don't see a problem," Cobb said. "Are you finished with the file?"

"Yes, thank you."

"It's a damn shame what happened, Emma." Cobb gathered the folder. "Sanders gave us a call, said you'd visited him, too, and that you're having a hard time with this. We understand."

"Thanks."

"You'd best go home now," Cobb said. "Let this thing run its course. I'll have Darnell drive you and get someone to bring your car home later."

"No. I got myself here, I'll drive myself home."

Emma knew what she had to do now, and as hard and painful as it would be, she had to do it alone.

18

It was late.

Robert Lancer downed the last of his tepid coffee then dragged his hands over his face.

The unconfirmed intel out of Dar es Salaam concerning an imminent attack weighed on him. He'd been searching for anything to connect this dot to the next one. Before this had surfaced he had been working on a letter from a troubled ex-CIA scientist living in Canada.

His line rang.

"Lancer."

"Bob, it's Atkins at Homeland. We've got zip so far on Salelee."

"Nothing to substantiate?"

"Zilch. The Tanzanians are keeping him for a while. He could've been blowing smoke. You know how these guys make claims to leverage deals, or deflect attention."

"Keep looking and keep me posted."

Lancer reached for his mug, remembering it was empty.

Like my apartment. Like my life, he thought, glancing at the framed photographs of his wife and daughter next to his phone.

Take nothing for granted.

He sat up and went back to Salelee's file.

He realized that this latest threat was at risk of being

rolled into so many others that had arisen over the years. As of last fall, U.S. security agencies were tracking about five thousand people, two hundred suspicious networks and investigating at least seventy-five active plots.

Lancer reviewed a few in the database. There was a threat to destroy a U.S. airliner over the Pacific. Nothing came of it. Then there was the group in New York arrested in a plot to use fertilizer-based explosives in attacks on packed nightclubs. On the international side, in the Chechen Republic, a man tied to extremist groups, who possessed large amounts of the lethal poison ricin in a barn outside of Grozny, had tickets for a charter tour of Washington, D.C., which included a visit to the White House. And in Turkey, a plot to bomb the U.S. embassy in Ankara was foiled.

Lancer exhaled. That was just a sampling.

He'd been deployed to the Anti-Threat Center from the FBI because he'd requested it. Besides, the people at the center wanted to take advantage of his counterterrorism experience. But Lancer knew he was afforded special consideration because of his "personal investment in U.S. national security," according to the handwritten letter he'd received from the director.

He looked at the faces of his wife and daughter.

My personal investment in U.S. national security.

Lancer was given a special assignment, allowed to operate as a one-man flying squad, investigating where his skill and instinct took him. He was cleared to cut across jurisdictional and agency boundaries to help on hot files and cold cases. His primary concern was soft targets that could yield the highest number of civilian casualties on U.S. soil.

Salelee's claim could involve a soft target, Lancer thought and reviewed possibilities, the bigger ones.

There was an upcoming spiritual gathering at the L.A. Memorial Coliseum that would draw one hundred thousand attendees. The Texas State Fair in Dallas would see over two million people pass through its gates. In Columbus, a music festival was expected to bring one hundred thousand people to Ohio Stadium.

Then Lancer looked at another big one: the Human World Conference coming up in New York City. It would be a family-friendly gathering of music and love, aimed at spreading harmony around the planet. There would be addresses by Nobel laureates, actors, authors, artists. Music groups would perform free concerts. It was set for Central Park and was expected to draw about one million people.

This one was on the radar of every local, state and federal security agency. There was a long list of potential attack methods to consider: suicide bombers, a truck or bus filled with explosives or a chemical, biological or radiological device—a dirty bomb.

Lancer considered recent history.

Some terrorist groups claimed to have chemical, biological or radiological weapons. While there had been few attacks on civilians employing such methods, those carried out were lethal.

In 1995, a cult known as the Supreme Truth released sarin, a deadly nerve agent into the Tokyo subway system killing a dozen people and injuring at least five hundred others.

In 2001, a series of anthrax attacks was launched in the U.S., using letters containing anthrax spores. At least five people were killed. In 1979, nearly nine hundred miles east of Moscow, several vials from top-secret biological and chemical military experiments vanished.

Take nothing for granted, Lancer thought and went back to the letter he'd been reviewing. It involved an older case and was written by a dying CIA scientist who'd overseen deadly classified U.S. military experiments that were long abandoned. The letter went first to the CIA, but upon assessing it, the agency referred it to the National Anti-Threat Center.

The scientist was concerned about rumors among fringe

elements of the underground research community that an unknown international group was somehow now attempting to replicate parts of those "terrible experiments."

Lancer questioned himself: *Doesn't that constitute a threat? Doesn't it require investigation?* He looked at the letter. The scientist was living out his final days in a remote cabin in Canada.

If Lancer chose to follow intelligence of this sort, policy required he make a face-to-face interview.

He read the letter one more time.

Take nothing for granted.

Lancer picked up the phone to make travel arrangements to Canada.

19

The Quiggly place was thirty miles outside of Big Cloud in the foothills of the Laramie Mountains.

In the late 1800s, Lance Quiggly drove his herd from Texas to establish his Five-Spur brand here after purchasing five hundred acres of grassy rangeland in the river valley. But each time the operation was passed to a succeeding generation, it was parceled and subdivided.

All that remained were forty acres where Emma Lane had come to search for answers. She turned down the dusty road to the ranch, praying the Quigglys would come to her aid again.

"Of course we'll talk to you," Mave Quiggly told her earlier when she'd called. "Anything we can do to help."

Driving out, Emma sensed the purity of this place and the goodness of its people. When she reached the house, Mave stepped from the porch and greeted her with a hug.

"Come on in, I'll put the kettle on."

She took Emma to the sofa in the living room, which opened to the large kitchen, where Mave gazed out the window.

"The fellas saw you drive in, they're coming up from the river now."

As the older woman busied herself, she punctuated her tasks by checking on Emma's well-being, patting her hand and shoulder.

"We went to the funeral service," Mave said. "We sat at the back of the church."

The kettle boiled and Emma struggled to hold herself together as Herb Quiggly and his teenaged son, Rolly, entered the kitchen from the rear door, telegraphing concern as they approached her.

"Herb Quiggly." The elder man shook Emma's hand. "This is our son, Rolly."

Rolly's acne-ravaged face was as still as a mountain lake as he nodded to Emma, his eyes lingering on her cuts and scrapes.

"You drove out here all by yourself, in your condition?" Herb asked.

"Hush now." Mave set a tea set down. "Emma's a strong young woman. She wants to talk to us and after all she's been through, we're going to listen."

Emma slid both hands around her teacup to steady herself.

"I need to know what happened that day, what you saw. Did you see the second car?"

"No, we saw nothing at all. We told the deputy we'd been out to Three-Elk Point. Rolly and I wanted to look at a bull J. C. Fargo was selling.

"We were northbound on that stretch, not another vehicle in sight until we saw your SUV on its roof. Rolly said he thought they were making a movie, or something. Kevin Costner shot part of one of his films out here years back."

Rolly nodded.

"But he didn't think that for long," Mave said. "We saw you there—saw your husband halfways out, saw the baby's seat caught up in the twisted metal like it was in a steel web."

"Did you see Tyler? Could you see him inside?"

"No," Rolly said. "Just saw that baby seat in the mess, heard you and smelled the gas."

"Could you hear Tyler crying?"

"I don't recall—you were screaming pretty loud," Rolly said.

"We had to get everyone out of there on account of the gas," Herb said.

"But you didn't actually see Tyler in his seat?"

Herb and Rolly shook their heads.

"It was twisted up in there," Rolly said.

"And you saw no other cars in the area?"

"Nothing," Herb said.

The Quigglys were patient with Emma as she continued pressing them. But as they recalled details for her, their voices faded until she heard only fragments.

"It happened fast…like a blast furnace…nobody could've survived…"

Their recounting of the aftermath had catapulted her back to those terrible moments on the highway.

Emma struggled with what the Quiggly family was telling her: There was no other car.

It can't be true because if it is it means my baby burned to death. But I saw someone. I saw someone save him.

Didn't I?

Emma's hands shook.

"Careful, Emma, careful." Mave rushed to her.

Hot tea had splashed over the cup's rim, onto Emma's hands and to the floor.

"I'm sorry."

Mave hurried her to the kitchen sink and ran cold water gently over her wrists and hands. It was an act of kindness and as the water soothed her skin Emma felt something deep inside break apart. Mave Quiggly comforted her until she was calm again.

"Thank you," Emma said. "I should be going."

"Maybe we should take you home and have Rolly drive your car back?"

Emma shook her head then collected her purse.

"You sure, you're okay?" Herb asked as they saw her to the door.

"I am convinced there was another car."

Rolly was scratching the back of his head, a habit familiar to his parents when something was gnawing at him.

"What is it?" Herb asked.

"Well, I was just thinking."

"Is it something Emma needs to hear?"

"Well—" Rolly continued rubbing the back of his head "—there *was* a car."

Emma stared at him.

"I didn't see any car," Herb said.

"Rolly, don't be talking this way if you're not sure," Mave said.

"There was a car in the area," Rolly said.

"But, Rolly," Emma said, "in the statement you gave to police, in all of your statements, no one saw a second car at the scene, or on the highway."

"That's just it," Rolly said. "The deputy asked me if I saw any cars *at the scene or on the highway,* and I didn't. But I saw this car just before we came to yours."

"Where was this?" Mave asked him.

"At the junction. Mom, you had leaned over to look at the gas gauge and tell Dad how he shoulda stopped in Big Cloud. I just looked east and it was way out there. I couldn't tell you the make. It could've been white. This car was way off by the T-stop near Fox Junction, way off kicking up dust on that dirt road. It was moving real fast."

Less than an hour later at the Big Cloud County Sheriff's Office, Reed Cobb's head snapped up from the glossy pages of a hunting magazine. Some fool was spanking the hell out of that bell at the front counter. Cobb's utility belt squeaked as he got up and went to straighten them out.

"Emma? What the—?"

"There was a second car," she said.

"What?"

"There was a second car fleeing the crash! Rolly Quiggly saw it. I just came from the Quiggly ranch."

"Hold on—"

"This means someone saved Tyler! My baby's alive!"

Emma's commotion drew other deputies and clerks to the counter.

"Emma, you should be home resting." Cobb gave a little nod to the others.

"No! You should get your people out there looking for that damn car!"

"Emma, you're upsetting yourself." Cobb exchanged glances with the other staff members. "We're going to get you home. John and Heather are going to make sure you get home safely."

"No!"

"We can take of care your car later."

The deputies, John Holcomb and Heather MacPhee, approached Emma. She knew them a little from school fundraisers down at the Big Cloud fair grounds. Holcomb was a part-time rodeo clown who operated a dunk tank and MacPhee sold home-baked pies and tarts. Her apple pie was very good. The deputies each took one of Emma's upper arms.

"No," Emma said. "Stop! What are you doing?"

"Take it easy now, Emma." Holcomb's grip was firm.

"My baby's alive! Help me find him!"

"Emma, you have to stop this kind of talk," Cobb said. "It's not doing you any good."

"No!" Emma struggled. "Why are you doing this? Help me find my son!"

20

After landing in Ottawa, Robert Lancer drove southwest for nearly two hours before turning his rental car onto Burnt Hills Road.

The side road led to secluded parts of cottage country, where Foster Winfield, the CIA's former chief scientist, was living out his last days. Upon crossing a wooden bridge over a waterway, the pavement became a dirt road winding through sweet-smelling forests. Gravel popped against the undercarriage and dust clouds rose in his rearview mirror, pulling Lancer back to Said Salelee's claim of a looming attack.

Marty Weller's team was following Salelee's information. Tanzanian police and U.S. agents were searching for other Avenging Lions for questioning, to determine who was behind the operation.

Was Salelee's information valid or, like most raw data, unverifiable?

They had to be vigilant.

As I should've been with Jen and Becky.

As Lancer drove, he remembered the events of a decade ago.

Seeing his wife and daughter off at the airport for their trip to Egypt.

Becky, who was attending school in New York, had received a scholarship to study Egyptian art in Cairo for a year. Jen, who had worked in Cairo when she was a cultural attaché with the State Department, was going to help her set up. Back then, he was with FBI Counterterrorism.

Watching their plane lift off that night in the rain, Lancer had felt a drop of concern ripple through him because of threats against the West by 37MNF, a new militant faction in Egypt. U.S. analysis said the group was poorly organized and poorly funded with little means to carry out an action.

That analysis was dead wrong and the life Lancer knew ended the moment his section chief called him into his office and told him to sit down.

Jen and Becky were on a tour bus near the pyramids on Cairo's outskirts when 37MNF extremists hijacked it to the desert where they murdered all forty-two tourists, the driver and tour guide.

Egyptian police later tracked down the militants and shot them.

Lancer blamed himself.

While the analysis was not his, it reflected the work he did, and it had concluded that 37MNF did not constitute a valid threat.

Not a threat?

Then why did my wife and daughter come home in boxes?

Their deaths haunted him and led him to doubt what he did for a living and to doubt everything he had ever believed in.

After Lancer took bereavement leave, September 11 happened, and in the aftermath he used his rage to forge a new purpose. He was deployed to the National Anti-Threat Center where, in the years that followed, he buried himself in his work.

Now, as he drove, Lancer glimpsed his folder with Winfield's file on the passenger seat.

Foster Winfield was born in Brooklyn, New York, where his father was a chemist and his mother was a math professor. Winfield was a gifted scientist. He'd been a professor at MIT before working with DARPA, the Defense Advanced Research Projects Agency. He then left DARPA for the CIA to head some of its top-secret research.

Lancer left the dirt road for a grass-and-rock stretch that twisted down to the lakeshore and an A-frame cottage.

Winfield cut a solitary figure standing on the deck watching Lancer approach. The old man was wearing a rumpled bucket hat, khaki pants and a faded denim shirt with a pocket protector from which pens peeked out. He stood a few inches above Lancer's six feet and had a firm handshake.

"Thanks for coming, Bob. Coffee?"

While they waited for the coffee to brew, Lancer noticed a golden retriever on the floor.

"That's Tug, the neighbor's dog. He comes by every day."

Lancer's gaze went to Winfield's desk: a laptop hooked up to the satellite dish outside, a phone, files, a framed photo of Winfield's wife, who'd died years earlier. They had no children.

It underscored a void familiar to Lancer.

The two men took their coffee out to the deck, where they sat in Adirondack chairs and Winfield talked about his terminal condition while he stroked the dog.

"I take medication—there's no discomfort. They gave me six months, five months ago," Winfield said. "It's come full circle for me. My parents had a cottage here. Some of the happiest days of my life were the summers I spent here as a boy."

Winfield gazed out at the tranquil lake.

"Forgive me, you're not here to listen to an old man reminisce."

"It's all right, Foster."

"As you know, DARPA was created in the late 1950s, after the Russians launched Sputnik. I came aboard many years later, after they'd headhunted me at MIT."

After several years with DARPA, Winfield had been approached by the CIA.

"The Cold War was in its death throes and the CIA wanted me to put together a secret research team to ensure the nation did not let its guard down—exciting stuff but lots of pressure. I got the best people I could, Andrew Tolkman, very brilliant, from Chicago, Gretchen Sutsoff from San Francisco—she was our youngest team member and known for her strong will and strong views. We had Lester Weeks from Chicago, very even-handed, Phillip Kenyon, the über-intellectual from Harvard, and several others from MIT, Cornell and Pittsburgh. Our objective was to ensure that the U.S. not be surprised by an adversary's technological advances in weaponry.

"First, we were to defend against, match, then surpass any work by the Soviets or Eastern Bloc scientists, or the Chinese, or North Koreans, or some Middle East and Gulf states whose research was emerging rapidly.

"The CIA provided us with historical intelligence on research by Nazi, Chinese and Japanese scientists, up to our time and on dangerous advances made by enemy states."

"What kinds of stuff are we talking about, Foster?" Lancer asked.

"It was a spectrum of research over the years, ways to destroy your enemy's crops with infestations, ways to contaminate the water supply, the air. We analyzed their work on mind-control experiments, the effects of chemical compounds on humans, parapsychology, engineered pathogens, advances in chemical and biological warfare, human endurance studies, medical breakthroughs and human engineering."

"Sounds like a Pandora's box."

"Not all that long ago we learned that some African rogue states had initiated work on genetic attacks. They'd planned to secretly introduce malevolent microorganisms to attack the DNA profile of certain races by secretly contaminating a national health initiative, like flu shots. The microorganisms were designed to cause an extremely high rate of miscarriages in that race, with the aim of wiping it out. That work was covertly thwarted.

"Another disturbing file concerned biological warfare. One of the Soviet satellite countries was developing a new lethal airborne virus that could be used to infect enemy troops. The scientists who engineered the virus also created the antidote, so that the weapon could not be used on their forces and population. That threat was also contained. And, more recently, we learned of something called File 91."

"File 91?"

"North Korean scientists had made advances on hyper tissue regeneration, to accelerate and increase survival rates of battlefield wounds. The research used nanotechnology, essentially, microscopic robots introduced into the body that are programmed and controlled by computer via low-frequency radio signals to read DNA and engage in rapid rebuilding—molecular manufacturing of cells, tissue and bones."

"It sounds miraculous."

"Yes. But there's a flip side. The CIA had learned that other rogue states and terrorist groups wanted to exploit the technology to reverse the process, to manipulate it to attack and destroy, rather than rebuild."

"I'm not sure I follow you."

"We feared File 91 technology could, in theory, be used to deliver a synthetic biological agent or microorganism that was unlike any known pathogen."

"Would it work?"

"With File 91, it is theoretically possible to create a new deadly microbe you could introduce into a host, but it would not harm the host. The host could be your mode of delivery. You could manipulate and control release of the new agent, control infection or even target infection of a certain population using DNA profiles, using cutting-edge nanotechnology and state-of-the-art genetic manipulation."

"That's a nightmare. How would you stop it?"

"That was the crux of our job through a classified program called Project Crucible. Research by our enemies, rogue states and terrorist groups was aimed at killing large numbers of people. Without our scientific understanding of it, the United States would be helpless to defend itself and its allies. Through Project Crucible we worked to defend against, and to dismantle, that work. But in order for us to gain effective knowledge we had to replicate it and, most important, test it.

"Some CIA agents gave their lives providing us with intelligence on the research. It was a key component but it was not all we needed. We had to embark on the most critical aspect—secret human trials. It was the only way we could get accurate results."

Lancer shook his head slowly.

"Traditionally," Winfield said, "we used inmate volunteers, usually those serving life sentences. They were told about military research and signed their consent to be test subjects. All work was done with their knowledge, consent and cooperation. Still, some of our team were hinting at modifying trials on Project Crucible to be conducted on civilian populations."

"What?"

"Not using anything lethal," Winfield said, "but substituting the agent with something as harmless as a common cold, to study the effectiveness of delivery and other aspects even more accurately because you're using the real environment, or theater of application."

"But with the public's knowledge?"

"That's a sensitive area. As you know, throughout history there've been cases of secret experiments on humans without their consent or without them understanding the risks involved. I'm talking about notorious experiments conducted on soldiers, on unsuspecting groups like the poor, POWs or concentration camp victims. Such work is crimi-

nal and morally repugnant to doctors and scientists. It gave
rise to the Nuremberg Code."

"Which deals with consent."

"The code holds that the voluntary consent of a human
subject is essential for research. Now, Gretchen Sutsoff was
a leading expert on genetic manipulation and diseases. She
was a passionate firebrand and in the case of File 91 she was
convinced it was flawed. To prove it, she advocated that
Project Crucible's trials be conducted on a civilian population without consent."

"Without consent?"

"Tolkman and Weeks said her strategy was a clear violation of the Nuremberg Code."

"How did she react?"

"Not well. We argued. I told her we would never allow
public trials to happen without consent, but I needed
Gretchen on the team. I admit she was arrogant, impatient,
isolated and lacking in social skills. She had a troubled life.
But she was also one of the world's most accomplished scientists. She was astounding. I admired her, respected her and
valued her insights and contributions. I felt she was getting
burned out, suggested she take a leave, travel, clear her
head."

"Did she?"

"Yes, but ultimately she resigned. She debriefed with
the CIA, severed all ties, then disappeared. A legend grew
around her departure. She was ostracized by much of the
scientific community. Rumor had it that she found lucrative
research in some poor country after she left the U.S.
Might've even taken up citizenship in another country, Sen-
egal or Aruba, or someplace. No one in our old circles has
been able to find her. It's not surprising—she was embittered
when she left."

"What happened with File 91 and Project Crucible?"

"Our agents worked covertly to destroy File 91." Winfield peered at the bottom of his coffee cup. "I know we pro-

duced some good work, work that saved lives, but ultimately all research we'd completed to that stage of Project Crucible was shelved. All our Crucible work was destroyed or locked up. A new generation of scientists has carried on with new research that seems to focus on cyber threats."

"Foster, you'd said that you feared Project Crucible's experiments are now being replicated?"

"Elements have surfaced in some obscure online discussion groups. I've alerted the CIA to my concerns and they've concluded that they are without substance. They've suggested I've misread things. I know they've written them off as the age-impaired ramblings of a dying old man."

"What do you think?"

"Few people alive know the contents of Project Crucible as well as I do, and I am convinced that from the snippets I've picked up online that someone is out there now attempting research arising from Crucible's files. And in the time I have left, I will continue sounding the alarm."

"Who do you think is behind it? Gretchen, or maybe someone from your old team?"

"We don't know. I've been in touch with a few of the remaining Crucible scientists. Not everyone agrees with me and we've debated my concerns. Maybe someone sold research, that's one possibility. But we don't know. However, something's come up that may help."

"What's that?"

"This morning, before you arrived, Phil Kenyon e-mailed me saying he's got a lead on something recent he thinks is tied to Gretchen Sutsoff."

"Will he talk to me?"

"I'll arrange it. He's in Chicago."

21

Rio de Janeiro, Brazil

A fine rain was falling the next day when Gannon returned to the diner to meet Alfonso, his guide into the slum.

He was waiting in the street, straddling a motorcycle and wearing a helmet and a baggy flowered shirt. He waved, and Gannon approached him.

Alfonso pointed to the gas tank and the hills and held up four fingers. Gannon gave him about forty reais, roughly twenty bucks U.S. Alfonso stuffed the bills in his jeans and nodded for Gannon to strap on the spare helmet and climb on behind him.

"You will take me to the parents of Maria Santo, Pedro and Fatima Santo?"

Alfonso gave him a thumbs-up, the motorcycle roared and they raced off along the crowded streets. Small shops, kiosks and parked cars blazed by as the commercial fringe of Zona Sul morphed into a narrow road, twisting into a lush jungle gateway to the favela.

The road continued slimming, coiling up and up. The engine growled as Alfonso shifted gears, threading through traffic. His body slid back and Gannon saw something sticking out from Alfonso's waistband. When a breeze lifted Alfonso's shirt, he saw the butt of a pistol.

They climbed for an eternity, the hills growing steeper, the road shrinking until finally they stopped at a side street.

The engine sputtered into the quiet of Céu sobre Rio on a Sunday.

Gannon turned to the God's-eye view of downtown Rio de Janeiro, the beaches, the bay, the statue of Christ on Corcovado Mountain. The upward sweep over the endless jumble of rooftops was amazing. Shacks and multi-story houses covered every speck of land, every outcropping; they were crushed together, battling for sun, angling to stand free as somewhere church bells tolled.

Alfonso led Gannon to a stairwell slicing between buildings and taking them higher. As they climbed, Gannon extended his arms, touching the lichen-laced walls on either side of the canyon they passed through. From time to time he saw large nests of wires and cables, common in favelas where residents spliced illegally into city utilities.

Drenched with sweat and breathing hard, Gannon guessed the temperature at more than a hundred degrees Fahrenheit, when they veered down a tight passageway that led to a side street.

Here, the low-standing concrete walls in front of the houses were coated with graffiti and bullet-pocked from gang shootouts with police.

They pushed on, passing more walls and shacks, then a pack of dogs yipping at children who were using sticks to probe garbage in the middle of the street. Watching them were several teenaged boys, smoking pot and sitting on a seat ripped from the rear of a car. Each of them had a gun and regarded Gannon as if he were new merchandise.

Alfonso gave a little whistle and led him down an alley that was slivered into yet another ascending canyon of stairs. This one opened to an oasis of well-kept houses, painted neatly in coral pinks, blues and lavenders. They were small houses with clean stone walls and ornate metal gates. Most had flower boxes in the windows.

Pretty, Gannon thought, as Alfonso stopped at one and unlatched the gate. They stepped into the cramped stone landing that welcomed them to a sky-blue house with a bone-white door.

"Santo." Alfonso nodded to the door, holding out his hand for payment.

Gannon gave him another forty reais then knocked.

The door opened to a man in his fifties. His haunted, tired eyes went to Alfonso then traveled sadly over Gannon. His white mustache was like snow against his leathery skin.

"Pedro Santo?" Gannon asked.

The man nodded.

Alfonso spoke to him in Portuguese and the older man looked at Gannon.

"Do you speak English?" Gannon asked

Pedro Santo shook his head.

Gannon turned to Alfonso who shouted in Portuguese to some girls down the street who were skipping with a rope. One, who appeared fourteen or fifteen, approached them. Alfonso spoke a stream of Portuguese to her. She looked to Gannon and said in English, "Hello, sir. My name is Bruna. I will try to help you. I am learning English from the British ladies at the human-rights center where Maria Santo has many friends."

Bruna listened intently as Gannon told her that he was a journalist from New York with the World Press Alliance and needed to talk to Pedro Santo and his wife about Maria. After Bruna translated, Pedro opened his door wider, inviting them inside.

The house was immaculate but small with a living room and adjoining kitchen. Pedro Santo introduced his wife, Fatima, who was washing dishes at the sink. Pedro spoke to her in Portuguese and she gave Gannon a slight bow then began fixing him a fruit drink, indicating he sit in a chair at their kitchen table.

A moment of silence passed.

Over his years as a crime reporter, Gannon had come to learn a universal truth—that it didn't matter if it was Buffalo or Rio de Janeiro, a home visited by death was the same the world over, empty of light. Like a black hole left by a dying star, its devastation was absolute.

When Fatima Santo set a glass before him, Gannon noticed her hands were scarred and wrinkled from years of cleaning the houses of the rich. Her eyes were dimmed with tears, her body weighted with sorrow. A gold-framed photograph of her murdered daughter was perched on the shelf above the TV, draped with a rosary.

"Please tell them—" Gannon turned to Bruna "—that I give them my sympathy for the loss of their daughter."

Bruna nodded then translated, softening her voice as she grasped Gannon's intentions. That small act, the inflection of Bruna's voice, won his immediate respect, for he realized that in Bruna, he had the help of an intelligent young girl.

Gannon began by asking Pedro and Fatima to tell him about the kind of person Maria was. Bruna put the question to Fatima, who buried her face in her hands and spoke in a voice filled with pain.

Bruna translated, "She says that Maria was a good girl who went to mass and worked hard at important jobs in big offices. They wanted her to leave the favela for a better life but she insisted on remaining in Céu sobre Rio. Maria wanted to make life better for everyone, the children of the favela, the whole world."

Pedro spoke in a deep, soft voice to Bruna, who nodded.

"He says that is why Maria worked with the human-rights groups, the earth groups, the unions. She was committed to social justice."

A motorcycle thundered by, rattling the door, distracting Gannon momentarily as he resumed taking notes.

"I am interested in the kind of work Maria did for these causes." Gannon gestured. "Did she keep files, records or notes here?"

Bruna translated and Pedro led them to a small bedroom, neat and evocative of a monk's cell. It smelled of soap and contained a single bed, a dresser with a mirror, a desk, posters from Amnesty and other global and environmental groups. In one corner stood a four-drawer steel file cabinet.

As Pedro spoke to Bruna, there was a burst of shouting outside and the sound of people running near the house. It lasted a few seconds then Bruna turned to Gannon.

"He says you can look at anything, but be respectful."

Gannon and Bruna immersed themselves in Maria's files, which were all in Portuguese, spreading them out on the desk, floor and bed. Items on the dresser began ticking from the vibrations of loud hip-hop music pounding from someone's sound system nearby.

Bruna raised her voice a bit as she translated excerpts of reports, studies and news clippings on human rights, child labor, human smuggling, environmental issues, police corruption, religious and political persecution.

Gannon noticed something: A low side drawer on the desk had a very slender sleeve inside holding a leather-bound notebook. He opened it to pages filled with dates and notes written in longhand in Portuguese.

A diary.

Outside, the music's volume increased, and Gannon never heard the front door latch click over its menacing throb, never heard the living room floor creak as the house filled with people.

Gannon had passed Maria's journal to Bruna and she was reading over the entries for the last three days of Maria's life.

"I have located the documents the law firm thought it had destroyed. It proves what we have suspected. I have copied the thirteen pages and shared them with SK at the center." Bruna paused.

Gannon held up his hand before he reached into his back pocket and unfolded the documents he'd found near the bomb scene. He had pages two, five and nine. There were thirteen in all. He needed to see all of them.

Who was SK at the center? What center?

As Gannon nodded for Bruna to resume, "We agree we must go to the press with these records—" he noticed a flash in the mirror, a diffusion of light "—I will contact the WPA and give the documents to a journalist—"

Music hammered the air, and in a heartbeat Gannon turned to glimpse Pedro and Fatima held at gunpoint by people—a dozen, maybe more—brandishing automatic guns, their faces covered with bandannas.

Without warning Gannon's head was swallowed by a large black hood.

His head exploded into a starburst of sudden pain.

22

Gannon was drowning.

Oh, Christ!

He couldn't breathe. He couldn't see. His head was wrapped in cloth and held underwater. His lungs were splitting, he struggled but his hands were bound behind his back.

God, please!

Mercifully, his head was pulled up. As he choked on air, he was tossed onto a mattress in a darkened room.

Who was doing this? Why? Where was he?

Someone jerked him upright, yanked the cloth hood from his head. Blinding light burned his face and a voice he didn't recognize mocked him in accented English from the darkness.

"Jack Gannon, reporter, World Press Alliance, New York."

Gannon coughed.

"Your card identifies you as an American reporter. Is this true?"

Gannon said nothing, then a fist smashed the side of his head. He tasted blood, gritted his teeth and was pulled to his feet.

"Answer! You are an American reporter?"

"Yes."

"You lie. You work for police. You're here to frame us for the bombing!"

"No, I don't know who you are. I've come to learn about Maria Santo."

A knee flattened Gannon's groin. Lightning flashed in his eyes, and he doubled over, groaning in agony.

Gannon wheezed, "You're making a mistake."

"There is no mistake."

The man barked in Portuguese. A small video player was shoved into Gannon's face. He blinked, his eyes adjusting to the light.

It was a TV news report of him talking to Detective Roberto Estralla beyond the yellow tape at the crime scene of the attack on the Café Amaldo. The report cut to Gannon close up. The video player vanished, then newspapers were thrust before him, a flashlight haloed on the photograph of him taken with Estralla at the scene.

"Did you think you could walk into our turf and plant evidence in the home of Maria Santo?"

"No. No, you don't understand," Gannon said.

"We are going to send a message to your police friends that we had nothing to do with the bombing."

A chrome-plated revolver materialized. Gannon's captor spun its cylinder, showing the empty chambers, then he held up a bullet before sliding it into one of the chambers. He spun the cylinder then clicked it into the frame.

"Don't. Please."

The barrel was drilled into Gannon's mouth, he tasted metal.

"Our message will be written on your corpse."

Gannon's stomach heaved, a finger squeezed the trigger. As it went back, he shut his eyes.

God help me.

Click.

Empty chamber.

Laughter filled the room.

The gun was removed, Gannon's heart nearly burst.

"So you live a little longer. Spend the last moments of your life dreaming of your execution."

A sudden blow to his head sent Gannon falling to the mattress and falling back through his life….

He is ten years old in the Buffalo Public Library where his big sister Cora is telling him he must read books because he's going to be a writer…I see it in your eyes, you don't give up…his mother, the waitress, in her white apron…his father in the rope factory, his blistered hands…his mother sobbing…they've lost Cora to drugs…she's run off…they can't find her for years…he resents Cora for the pain she's caused…he loves Cora for his life follows the course she envisioned…he's a news reporter with the Buffalo Sentinel*…he meets Lisa Newsome on assignment from the* Cleveland Plain Dealer*…Lisa wants to get married and have kids…he could be cutting his lawn in suburbia, taking the kids to the mall…not him…he breaks Lisa's heart…ghosts will haunt you…his parents keep looking for Cora…she may have children…she may have a new life…what became of Cora?… A New York State Trooper, standing at his apartment, hat in hand…a pickup driven by a drunk driver has smashed into his parents' Ford Taurus, killing them both…he aches to get out of Buffalo but is afraid to leave….ghosts…nominated for a Pulitzer…for convincing the brother of the suicidal Russian airline pilot who plunged his jet into Lake Erie to talk…think of the dead, their ghosts will haunt you…he got what he wanted…Buffalo behind him…working for the World Press Alliance…wasn't that what he wanted?… No one to mourn him…he was alone… Wasn't that what he wanted?… To die in the slums of Rio de Janeiro…ghosts will haunt you… don't ever give up, Jack…*

Jack…

"Jack Gannon."

His eyes opened then squinted.

He was on a bed in a bright room with an open window, fresh air. He had been moved. A woman was sitting near, tending to his face. She had a British accent.

"Can you hear me, Jack? I only have a few minutes."

He turned to her, a woman in her early thirties with brown hair and dark eyes filled with worry.

"My name is Sarah Kirby. I'm Maria's friend from the Human Rights Center, at the bottom of the favela."

"Help me get out of here."

"I'm trying. You must listen. You were taken by the Blue Brigade, the drug gang that controls the Céu sobre Rio. They have places to hide people here, but everyone knows them. Bruna came for me."

"Did they hurt her? Did they hurt Pedro or Fatima?"

"No, the narcos protect the people of the favela."

"But how did you get in? We have to leave! Untie my hands!"

Someone outside shouted to Sarah in Portuguese and she responded, then turned back to Gannon.

"No, we have no time, listen—"

"*No!* They're going to kill me! They think I'm a police informant!"

"I know. It's Dragon, the leader of the Blues, he's psychotic. He fears the Colombians are coming for him because of Café Amaldo. Dragon fears police are trying to fuel a drug gang war so that the narcos exterminate each other. He swears the Blue Brigade had no role in the bombing."

"Great, let's get out of here!"

"Jack, we can't leave, you must listen, they trust me, they trusted Maria because of the work we do in the favela."

"Well, it was Maria who came to the WPA with documents from her firm for a story."

"I know."

"Then for God's sake, untie me and let's get out of here!"

"No, listen! They're waiting outside this door. I have negotiated for you, now listen, please!"

Gannon listened.

"Maria discovered evidence that the law firm was linked to criminal activity," Sarah said.

"I found a few of her pages at the bomb scene. Is it about drugs?"

"We think it's about human trafficking or the illegal adoptions of children, stolen children."

"What?"

"Maria was working with our human-rights networks. We kept it secret. Only a few knew—we had to get the story out. Maria agreed to contact the WPA. She was so afraid and so brave."

Someone thudded on the door, Sarah hurried.

"After the explosion those of us at the center were terrified. We didn't know what to think. Was it a gang hit, or was Maria the target? Were corrupt police involved? How big was this illegal operation?"

"Jesus," Gannon said. "Estralla, the cop, has my documents!"

"Listen, I have told Dragon a little about Maria's work, her connection to WPA, the café. I told him that killing you was stupid. He must keep you alive so you can get the truth out through your worldwide news agency."

"Did he buy it?"

"He's allowed me a few minutes to get your vow that you will write the truth about the bombing, if he lets you live."

"Dammit, that's why I'm here. Tell him yes."

The door strained with banging.

"Time is up," Sarah said. "If we get out together I'll give you copies of all of Maria's documents and our contacts in Europe. We think this is bigger than you could imagine."

Sarah rapped on the door, it opened and Sarah left.

Gannon was alone, unsure how much time had passed before the door opened again and several armed men entered. Blue bandannas covered their faces as they leveled their pistols and M-16s at him.

A scrappy man in his mid-twenties followed them into the room, the grip of a chrome pistol sticking out of his waistband. His eyes were sharp and icy as he inventoried Gannon.

"The woman assures me you are not with police, that you will write the truth about the café bombing, which is that the Blue Brigade did not do it."

"I give my word."

"If you fail, we will not harm you."

Gannon was relieved but confused as Dragon nodded to a gang member who again displayed a digital recorder. The images jerked but showed Luiz walking the streets of Centro, then cut to Sally Turner, Hugh Porter and Frank Archer getting out of taxis at the bureau.

"We will kill your friends. You have two days."

"I need more time."

"Two days."

Dragon nodded and a gang member pulled out a knife and sliced away Gannon's bindings. The others surrounded him and escorted him through the house. Sarah Kirby was waiting in the living room where Gannon's wallet and cell phone were handed back to him before the group left the building. As Gannon and Sarah began walking down the street amid Dragon's armed posse, Gannon noticed something odd.

Life was absent from this area.

Silent and still. Too still. As if the neighborhood was holding its breath.

Not even birdsong, the echo of children playing or a dog barking. It was the kind of deathly silence Gannon knew. It was familiar to him. Realization landed on him, he felt an arm lock around his chest and a gang member had suddenly made Gannon his shield.

Gannon saw Sarah pulled close to another gang member, then he glimpsed a police sniper behind a stone wall, eye clenched behind a scope, fire flaring from his rifle muzzle.

A bullet tore through the cheek of the gangster holding Gannon as the street exploded in gunfire. Bullets whizzed in the air and ricocheted off of the stone walls, the street, sparks, dust, blood and debris flying.

Gannon turned but failed to find Sarah in the chaos. Bullets ripped through the air near his head, and he dove to the ground.

Men shouted. Police vehicles, their radios squawking, appeared from nowhere and the sky thundered with a helicopter. Gannon crawled to the shelter of a doorway, pressing his body to a low wall.

He kept his head down until the gun battle subsided.

In the dust-filled air of the aftermath Gannon saw several police officers toeing the bodies of dead gang members in the street. As radios crackled, Gannon was certain he recognized Roberto Estralla in the distance, wearing dark glasses, watching from the open door of an unmarked car.

Then Gannon heard sirens and his attention went back to the dead and wounded on the bloody street.

That's when he found Sarah Kirby, in a puddle of blood.

23

Several days after her breakdown at the county sheriff's office, Emma sat in Wally Bishop's office at Silver Range Insurance downtown.

"Thanks to your uncle's help, we've expedited the claims. Never saw anything move so fast." Bishop made little Xs on the documents he'd slid toward Emma, then passed her a monogrammed fountain pen. "I need you to sign here and here."

But Emma was looking at the great gray owl mounted on Bishop's wall and thinking back to last year when she sat here with Joe, updating their policies. All the way home, he'd gone on about how much he liked that owl because neither one of them wanted to hear another word about death benefits.

We've got a lot of living ahead of us, Em. But if I go first you can stuff me like that owl.

"Emma?"

Uncle Ned pulled her attention back to the business before her: paperwork for a check for $225,000 for Joe's life insurance, and one for $25,000 for Tyler.

Emma gripped the pen, took a deep breath, held it and signed for the larger check. When she poised it over the signature line for Tyler's, she froze.

"Is there a problem?" Bishop asked.

"I can't sign for Tyler."

Because I don't believe he's dead.

Bishop's focus shifted to her aunt and uncle, then back to Emma.

"Emma," Aunt Marsha said. "We know it's hard but you have to sign."

"The second one can wait," Uncle Ned said. "We'll deposit the bigger check today and deal with the second claim later, okay, Wally?"

"Of course, I understand," Bishop nodded. "This is never easy."

On the drive to the bank, Emma said nothing.

She had spent the past few days battling the grief, fear and rage that swirled around her. She was nearing an abyss, slipping closer toward its yawning black jaws.

Was she losing her mind?

"Emma? Are you expecting a delivery?"

Delivery?

Aunt Marsha's question had startled her.

They had left the bank but every aspect of their time there—sitting in the manager's office, accepting condolences, dealing with the large check—had not registered with Emma. She had been submerged in her thoughts of Tyler. Now, she recognized that they had returned to her house, and her aunt and uncle were curious about a van that had arrived at the same time.

"Looks like a courier," Uncle Ned said.

After parking, he went to the driver's door and signed for receipt of an envelope then passed it to Emma. She opened it to find a large, plain, sealed brown envelope marked "Confidential to Emma Lane."

She opened it and withdrew a white business letter and immediately recognized the sender's letterhead.

"What is it, Emma?" Aunt Marsha asked.

"It's from my doctor."

"The one who treated you at the hospital?"

"No, I'll open it inside."

The letter was from Dr. Glen Durbin, her obstetrician and gynecologist.

Sitting on her living room sofa, she read,

Dear Emma:

Please accept my sincere condolences for the tragic deaths of your husband, Joe, and son, Tyler.

I can only imagine the shock and the unbearable pain and void caused by this unthinkable loss.

As you know, Joe was loved and respected in Big Cloud. He probably helped build half the new houses in this town. He was a skilled craftsman and a good man. Joe was also a supportive husband and loving father, something he proved every minute of every day during the difficult time you faced together, bringing Tyler into this world.

I deeply regret that this tragedy brings me to my required contractual obligation.

As you may recall, I am legally bound to advise you that I have formally alerted Golden Dawn Fertility Corp., of Los Angeles, CA, of the terrible circumstances concerning Tyler's death so that the company may update its files concerning Donor #181975. (Copy attached).

Emma, please accept my deepest sympathies and know that I also mourn Joe and Tyler's loss.

You are in my thoughts,

Glen Durbin, M.D.

Emma's hand flew to her mouth and her body sagged. "What is it, dear?"

Aunt Marsha put her arm around Emma who passed the letter to her. After reading it, Marsha passed it to Ned, who looked up from the page.

"Tyler's not your biological child?" he asked.

Several moments passed before Emma could answer.

"I'm his biological mother. Tyler was conceived by an anonymous sperm donor from the clinic in California that we used."

"I never knew this. Marsha, did you know?"

"No one knew that Joe was infertile," Emma said. "It was something he'd agonized over. After we considered our options he agreed to an anonymous donor, provided we kept it secret."

"It must've been difficult," Aunt Marsha said.

"It was extremely hard. Joe's a proud man—*was a proud man*—oh, God," Emma gasped. "He did this for me, he ached to have a family but this threw him. He put my happiness before his own. He was so good."

Emma spent the remainder of the day resting.

She had no appetite for dinner, retreating, as she'd done since the funerals, to Tyler's room, rocking and thinking.

Dr. Durbin's letter had pulled her back.

Back to the troubling time when they'd learned the reason she'd failed to get pregnant was because Joe had poor sperm motility. For Emma, the prospect of being childless was the worst thing she'd faced since her parents' deaths.

"Actually, the chances of Joe fathering a child are about two, maybe three in ten, but you have options," Durbin explained to them.

After months of anguished consideration, Emma opted to have a child by using an anonymous sperm donor through a private clinic.

To her, a normal pregnancy, over adoption, was the best way to go.

But Joe was reluctant to do anything.

"I wanted you to have my baby, not a baby from another man."

"This will be our baby, Joe. A man needs to do much more than contribute DNA and genetics to be a real father."

"I just feel that I somehow failed you."

"No, this is where we work together to beat this and have a baby, *our* baby. Please say you'll do it for me, for us, Joe."

As he searched her face, his eyes brightened and he smiled.

"All right, if it's what you want, I'll do it."

Dr. Durbin had given them a list of clinics and they picked Golden Dawn Fertility Corp. After some initial telephone consultations and paperwork, they flew to Los Angeles to start the process.

Golden Dawn was a first-class operation located in a gleaming downtown L.A. office building where they treated Emma and Joe with the utmost care.

They first learned how the clinic screened donors.

All candidates were between the ages of twenty-one and forty and came from top universities or top professions. Their health had to be excellent. Their medical and genetic histories were scrutinized. Their blood and sperm samples were subjected to exhaustive testing to ensure they were free of disease, or of any risk due to lifestyle.

They were genetically profiled, their DNA collected. Doctors and psychologists interviewed them for personality traits and their family's genetic history.

The clinic introduced them to the donor catalogue, which offered general information, such as race, eye and hair color, weight, height, blood type, education.

Joe and Emma were not allowed to see a photograph, or know the names of the donors. However, they provided pictures of Joe and worked with clinic staff to narrow their choices to a donor that not only met their spectrum of choices, but ultimately resembled Joe as much as possible.

"Judging from that catalogue, I think we'll have a kid who's going to be a heck of a lot smarter than me," Joe joked with Emma as they walked on the beach to watch the sun set on the Pacific before heading home.

The whole process cost them about four thousand dollars.

The clinic worked with Dr. Durbin back in Wyoming to time the insemination procedure. When it was right, the vials from donor #181975 were shipped overnight from California to Durbin's office, where the doctor inseminated Emma.

"Now, Emma, I want you to consider this medical suggestion," Durbin said privately to her afterward. "You and Joe should make love tonight as many times as you can. Enjoy yourselves because you never know, this could be that one-in-ten time that Joe's sperm has a successful mission. It just might increase your chances of pregnancy."

"You read my mind, Doctor." Emma laughed.

When she returned for her next scheduled appointment her heart swelled.

"Congratulations, you're pregnant," Durbin said.

That night, Joe took Emma out to dinner at the Diamond Restaurant. Nine months later Tyler was born and their world had changed.

When she held him, she wept.

When Joe held him, Emma filled with joy because Joe was enraptured.

"Hey, Dad," she said. "He looks like you."

"Maybe," Joe beamed. "But he's got his mama's eyes."

Emma never believed she could be so happy and so in love.

She was living her dream, right up until the instant Joe swerved to miss an oncoming car.

Why? Why did this happen?

Now, as she rocked, she hugged Tyler's stuffed bear.

Someone had rescued Tyler from the fire. It happened. Didn't it?

Or was she losing her mind?

The police insisted she was wrong, the insurance company with its check told her she was wrong. Now Dr. Durbin with his letter told her she was wrong to think her baby had survived.

Another nail of reality had pierced her heart.

Emma cried out and her aunt came to help her to her bed.

"It's very late, sweetheart, you need to get some sleep."

Emma cooperated as she ached for rest. She undressed and got into her bed, letting sleep take her because when she slept, she could dream.

And when she dreamed she was with Joe and Tyler again.

In her dreams they were driving together near the snow-tipped Rockies, heading for the picnic north of town. There was no crash. They made it safely to their destination alongside the Grizzly Tooth River, the water sparkling like a rush of diamonds.

*Joe is crawling after Tyler who is toddling toward her, running into Mommy's open arms in the beautiful sunlight and they are so happy, so happy the air rings...and rings...until the mountains vanish...then Joe vanishes...and Tyler disappears into the dark void of night that is ringing...*like the telephone at Emma's bedside.

"What..."

Emma sat up and answered the phone, her head spinning.

"Emma Lane?"

She didn't recognize the female voice.

"Yes."

"Emma Lane in Big Cloud, Wyoming?"

The voice was ragged, raw with an underlying current of stress.

"Yes, who is this?"

"Listen to me. Your baby is not dead."

"What? Who is this? What did you say?"

"Your baby is alive. That's all I can tell you. I'm sorry."

"Wait!"

The line went dead leaving Emma to scream into the handset.

24

Kunming, China

Long before the sun rose Li Chen woke in the shack where she lived with her husband and son.

She began her day by lighting the stove.

Under the dying moon she stepped from her house that was shimmed tight against others in the village. She walked down the worn path to the water pipe where she washed, then brought water home for tea.

Her husband, Sha Shang, stirred, grunted a greeting then left to wash. After Li made their lunches, she made tea and breakfast: congee, which Li prepared in the rice cooker. While Sha joined the other men for their morning smoke, Li looked upon her three-year-old son, Pan Qin, asleep on his cot. Under the lamplight she drank in his flawless face and skin. One little foot stuck out from his blanket. Li traced the tiny birthmark on his ankle, shaped like two hearts touching.

It symbolized her eternal bond to her son.

Pan was her reason for living and dreaming.

Li and Sha were young peasants from the country when they married and migrated to the city two years ago. A cousin with city smarts got them this shack, while Li and Sha hoped that one day they would qualify for a modern apartment downtown with a private toilet, running water, bedrooms and a separate kitchen.

This was their dream.

When breakfast was ready, she teased Pan's hair until he woke. He kissed his mother, then, droopy-eyed, went outside to pee. His father smiled and called him a good soldier.

Dawn was breaking when they finished breakfast.

Sha kissed Li and Pan, climbed onto his bicycle and rode off to his job at a brick factory across the city. After Li tidied up, she and Pan set out for her job in the market. They had a long walk out of the village, which was in Kunming's Xishan District.

The sun peeked over the horizon, illuminating the smoggy haze that blanketed the metropolis, as the crammed bus took Li and Pan to Kunming's bird and flower market.

They walked by streets of old two-story shops with tiled rooftops, then to the market with its exotic smells like roasted chestnuts, fried duck heads, kebabs and other barbequed meats.

There were stalls with water tanks where live eels threaded amongst each other. The eels fascinated Pan as did the vendors selling parrots, turtles and large insects.

There were artists selling paintings, carvings, crafts, clothing, fabrics and jewelry. Farmers were selling corn, potatoes, onions, tomatoes, bananas, lemons and pungent goat cheese.

Li operated a small stall, selling spices.

Pan usually stayed with her all day.

While the market was popular, it was also a center for criminals, drug dealers, gangsters and child stealers. Like other working-class parents in the market, Li knew that the child traffickers kidnapped boys to sell to wealthy childless people who wanted to carry on the family line at any cost.

Li always kept a close eye on her son. She never let her guard down with him in the market. If Li had to step away, she entrusted Pan to a friend in a neighboring stall.

Lately, she'd grown increasingly comfortable with the young man and woman who'd appeared a few months back to conduct research on children in the market. At first Li was uneasy as she was not yet a legal migrant. But the researchers didn't care about her status. Their concern was collecting data on her son for a special government hygiene study.

The man and woman visited Li's stall every week and gave Pan a medical examination, swabbing his mouth, pricking his finger for a blood sample, making notes, taking his picture. They'd asked Li about his diet, bloodline, allergies, and similar matters.

Li was happy that Pan was getting personal medical care and was growing friendly with her regular visitors, even coming to depend on them. There were times when she left Pan with them while she stepped away from her stall for a brief errand.

The market was busy all morning. She'd wanted to buy Sha a present. His birthday was coming and there was a carving of a tiger that would be perfect for him. Li knew the artist and he'd offered her a good price.

By afternoon, the market crowds had increased.

Li was relieved when the medical researchers arrived.

"Good afternoon, Li. May we please examine Pan today?"

Li invited them into her stall.

"Would you watch Pan and mind the stall for me, while I run a quick errand?" Li asked them.

"Certainly." The young woman smiled. "We'll be right here."

Li kissed Pan, who gave her a wide grin because he knew that whenever his mother left, she returned with sweets. She moved through the market crowds to the vendor with the tiger and was disappointed. The artist who'd promised her a special price on the tiger was not there. A grumpy old man who wanted triple the cost was tending to the stall. Li bartered with him before the old crook relented.

Happy, she started back, stopping to get sweets for Pan.

As she neared her stall, alarm pinged in her stomach.

It was empty.

She went inside and looked around, puzzled and afraid.

What was going on?

She asked her neighboring vendors, who shrugged.

"It's been so busy, Li. We've seen nothing."

No sign of her son. No sign of the researchers.

"Pan!"

Her mouth went dry, fear slid down her throat and devoured her hope that he would appear.

"Pan Qin!"

Li left her stall, scanning the area, searching the faces of small children, running through the crowds screaming for her son. Her mind swirled. She didn't even have the names of the researchers, no cards, no documentation.

Nothing.

"Pan!"

The minutes bled into a half hour, which became an hour. Time swept by without a trace of her boy. The other vendors passed on the word, some sent people to Li's stall to help search the market.

The whole time Li accused herself.

Why weren't you watching your child?

Why did you trust him to strangers?

How could you be so stupid?

Two police officers came by and Li pleaded to them, told them about the medical researchers, the government's hygiene study.

"We know nothing of any study," one officer said, while his partner relayed details on the radio.

"There is no such study in the market," he said.

Li screamed.

This was a nightmare. She had to wake up. Yes. Sha would be waking her any moment now and she would tell him of her bad dream and she would go to Pan's cot and hold him so tight and cry tears of joy.

As the sun sank and the market crowds thinned, Li remained in her stall praying for Pan's return. Word got back to the village and Sha was alerted. He raced to the stall, his face a mask of disbelief.

Li collapsed in his arms.

"Kill me! Kill me for what I've done. I've lost our son!"

Sha only held her and stared at the empty market as a misting rain descended on them.

All night long, Li and Sha walked the abandoned streets, their voices echoing as they called out Pan's name. They never stopped because they could not bear to go home, could not bear to face his empty cot and the devastating truth.

Their little boy had been stolen.

25

Robert Lancer's hotel was near the Chicago River.

As he waited alone in a quiet corner of the hotel's restaurant, staring through the window at the buildings soaring skyward, he questioned if pursuing the old CIA file as a potential threat was the way to go right now.

He didn't have a lot of time.

He considered the upcoming Human World Conference. *Maybe I should be concentrating on Said Salelee's claim of an imminent attack?* Lancer was grappling with his circumstances when two older men, both in their seventies, approached his table.

"Bob?" the one with the close-trimmed beard asked.

"Yes."

"Phil Kenyon."

Kenyon set a laptop on the table and Lancer shook his hand, and then shook hands with the second man, who was wearing gold-framed glasses.

"Les Weeks."

Through Foster Winfield's arrangement, Lancer had expected to meet only Kenyon, who was in town attending an international science trade fair. But when Kenyon informed him on the phone that Lester Weeks was attending the same event, he agreed to meet both retired CIA scientists at the same time. The men kept their voices low.

"Foster talked to us about his concerns a few weeks ago," Weeks said. "But not all of us share his interpretation of the online chatter on some of the subject matter."

"Is that what you told the agency when it followed up?" Lancer asked.

"Pretty much," Weeks said. "Our work was advanced at the time but there've been breakthroughs since. I understand how Foster would be concerned about the appearance of someone using our work as the basis for engineering some sort of genetic attack."

"But is it possible that someone from the original team could be using that work to be plotting something? Chemical, biological or genetic attacks are rare, but this stuff from Project Crucible—and I admit I don't understand it all—but this stuff could produce a devastatingly effective weapons system if the right expertise were behind it."

Weeks and Kenyon exchanged glances.

"It's possible," Weeks said.

"So Foster's concerns are valid?"

"Absolutely." Kenyon's hand rested on his small laptop.

"In theory," Weeks added.

"That's where you and I disagree, Les," Kenyon said.

"Well, what about Gretchen Sutsoff?"

"Gretchen was a rare bird but absolutely brilliant," Kenyon said. "Once Foster and I were wrestling with a physics problem on Crucible. We had an equation plastered across the board in our cafeteria. For days we'd worked in vain on that monster and Gretchen read it while her kettle boiled. She walked over and solved it in about a minute flat. It was astounding."

"But would she be capable of trying to replicate unsanctioned experiments arising from Crucible?" Lancer asked.

"I don't think so," Weeks said.

"I disagree." Kenyon switched on his laptop and inserted a memory card. "Let me show you something I just received the other day from a friend with an Australian university who monitors fringe groups." Kenyon positioned his laptop so the three of them could see and hear it. "The speaker uses a voice changer and her face is obscured. It runs nearly ten minutes. Here we go."

A video emerged on the screen showing a woman at a podium. No markings anywhere to identify the location, the speaker or the event. Kenyon kept the volume low.

"Thank you, Doctor and members of the faculty. I am deeply honored by your invitation to lecture today at the Condition of Mankind's Progress Symposium. I am surprised and pleased at the recognition you've afforded my research. Your generosity has been boundless. You have made me feel more than welcome."

The lights dimmed and a mammoth screen lowered behind her with images to accompany her remarks.

"On the theme of the condition of mankind's progress, I'll begin by saying we are without question driving headlong toward calamity.

"In the early 1800s the earth's human population stood at around one billion. Today, we're in the range of seven billion…."

Images of cities choked by traffic, overcrowding, polluted by factories filled the screen.

"In less than forty years, notwithstanding the world decline in fertility rates, the world's human population will reach about nine billion, which would be like adding another China and another India to the planet."

She paused before resuming.

"In a little over two hundred years, we will have seen the human population increase nearly tenfold."

More grim images of poverty.

"This should be cause for alarm, yet political leaders are moving with glacial speed. Most movements parrot the same tired emphasis that rapid industrialization, rapid urbanization, out-of-control consumption and resource depletion have given rise to global warming, which is exacting a toll. The mantra of 'we must go green, we must reduce our carbon footprint, we must save the earth,' is a substitute for effective action."

The screen displayed images of spewing smoke stacks and melting ice shelves.

"This line of thinking is but a digit in the full equation; it is useless as a foundation for a solution, akin to a bandage on a terminal patient. It deflects attention from the root cause of our destruction of the planet.

"Overpopulation.

"To put it simply, the earth cannot sustain the current trend of population growth. There are simply too many of us putting too much strain on the earth. We are wearing it out. Birth control, contraception, sterilization, natural disasters and pandemics, even wars are not enough to alleviate the stress we have put on this planet.

"Within fifteen years, every corner of the globe will face acute water and food shortages, unlike anything we've experienced. While wealthy nations shield themselves with technological and financial resources, poorer regions with unchecked populations will grow desperate. It will lead to civil unrest, instability and chaos."

The speaker paused to drink water.

"We must take critical action now. As hope for the planet flickers, governments must take brave new steps. There are several options, but one that I put forward today is for the United Nations to champion a year of zero population growth.

"As it stands, there are approximately 140 million births each year worldwide and 55 million deaths. In order to address this ratio, in the face of our current crises, governments should be encouraged to enact legislation that outlaws pregnancy for one year."

The speaker paused for the murmur of disbelief then continued.

"At the same time, all programs that prolong, or extend

the life of anyone over the age of eighty, could be terminated for the same period. I am not advocating euthanasia, just removal of practices that thwart natural mortality and delay the inevitable. The combination of these initiatives holds the potential to curtail world population by some 200 million humans. China and governments of other populous nations have taken similar approaches, but they have not gone far enough."

The speaker drank water, absorbing further ripples of reaction.

"Some may call me an apocalyptic prophet. They may align me with fringe elements, doomsday cults, extremists or brand me an outcast for challenging popular opiate thought.

"That does not trouble me, for in my life I have experienced how humanity reacts in times of distress. I have seen the worst unfold before my eyes after warnings were ignored, after rational thought evaporated.

"I am your witness to reality.

"I advocate extreme action because we face an extreme situation. Time is running out on human existence on this planet. We are entering the panic zone…."

The video faded to black.

"This is extreme," Lancer said. "Is it Sutsoff?"

"No way of telling. No one's heard of this 'Condition of Mankind's Progress Symposium.' My friend thinks the video was made in Turkey or Africa."

"Or it's a complete hoax produced by undergrads at Yale or MIT," Weeks said. "I just don't think Gretchen is behind this, or anything like it."

"Really, and why not?" Lancer asked.

"To let a professional disagreement fester over time into motivation for a vengeful act, using our work on Crucible, is just unfathomable, impossible."

"Les, you didn't work with Gretchen as closely as Foster and I did. The stuff in this manifesto is precisely what she was leaning to before she left."

"Let me get this straight," Lancer said. "Gretchen Sutsoff could be using Crucible's research to put her extremist views into action?"

"That's the scenario Foster and I fear," Kenyon said.

"I just don't buy it." Weeks shook his head.

"Well, consider this," Kenyon said. "About a month ago the CIA looked into Foster's concerns about rumors online. They talked to me, too. I know that at first they dismissed Foster, but I recently heard from a friend at Langley who said the agency had reconsidered."

"Why?"

"I don't know. At this stage one can only speculate that they must have discovered something."

"Your video?"

"Maybe, and maybe something more substantial," Kenyon said. "Look at the circumstances. It's the stuff of nightmares. Maybe they don't want to alarm anybody. Do you know Gretchen Sutsoff's story?"

"Foster said she'd had a troubled life."

"Listen, our lives were put under a microscope when we were security-cleared to work on Crucible. I worked closely with Gretchen. She was very private, very guarded. Now we scientists can be eccentric in our own way, but she was different. Way out there. She seemed to have a pathological dislike of other human beings."

"Why?"

"I don't know. She refused to ever talk to anyone if it wasn't necessary, let alone open up to anyone. In my time with her I learned that her father had a military background and that her family traveled, lived around the world. Then there was some sort of tragedy and Gretchen was hurt, she suffered some kind of neurological disorder."

"Do you know what it was?"

"No, but it obviously didn't hinder her intelligence. I think she took medication. Still, every now and then, she'd have episodes."

"What sort of episodes?"

"Like an outburst. She had one around the time she left, when she'd advocated live human trials with File 91 without consent."

"Foster told me he denied her request, it violated the Nuremberg Code."

"Did he tell you what she said?"

"No."

"It's what precipitated her departure—I was the only one present with him and I'll never forget it. She said something like, *'These trials are for the public's own damn good. Most people don't have a clue what is best for them. They're lemmings. Believe me I've seen them at their worst. Rational minds need to do the thinking for them.'*"

"That sounds arrogant."

"There's more. She was storming out, when she stopped, turned and said, *'You know, Nazi scientists were responsible for many of the modern world's advances, and they did it because they were not restricted by boundaries. They had complete freedom to perfect the human race, to explore a vision.'*"

"A vision of what?"

"Hell, likely. I believe at that time Gretchen was on the verge of a breakdown."

"Do you have any idea how I can find her?"

"None. If the FBI can't find Hoffa, and the CIA can't find bin Laden, then nobody's going to find Gretchen Sutsoff. I heard she took out new citizenship with a small country, changed her name, maybe her appearance."

"What do you think is at work here?" Lancer asked.

"There are several possibilities—the North Koreans may have restarted File 91. Or some of the work may be on the black market or in the hands of an extremist faction. Or the possibility I fear most…"

"Which is?"

"Gretchen Sutsoff has lost her mind."

26

A seaplane flew low over Nassau's harbor.

It descended near the mammoth cruise ships and luxury hotels before it touched down, peeling curtains of spray from the clear Bahamian water. It glided to the terminal at the foot of the Grand Blue Tortoise Resort.

A lone passenger stepped onto the dock; a woman in her late fifties. She wore a sleeveless white shirt, white linen pants, a white straw braided sun hat and dark glasses. A tote bag was slung over her shoulder. She carried a small black case in her left hand and she carried herself with the poise of an executive arriving for a business meeting as she walked to the golf cart and the young Bahamian man sent to pick her up.

"Good morning, Doctor."

"Hello."

Dr. Gretchen Sutsoff did not smile or offer conversation.

Whenever possible, she preferred not to deal with people but it was unavoidable today. She'd left the solitude of her private island to come to the resort to tend to her business. Today she would conduct more secret trials. Her work was proceeding well, but if she was going to make her product more powerful she needed that overdue report from her research team in Africa, and she needed it now.

There was little time left.

The golf cart's electric motor hummed softly as Gretchen and her driver rolled toward the main structure. With two thousand rooms distributed through the complex, the Grand Blue Tortoise was one of the most luxurious hotels in the world. It offered restaurants, pools, casinos, shops and an amusement park on a thirty-hectare expanse of tropical property, ringed with pristine beaches.

The road from the dock was lined with tall palms nodding in the breeze. As the golf cart neared the central structure, the road started to congest with a stream of jitneys, cars and cruise ship shuttles. Having to contend with crowds triggered the onset of one of Dr. Sutsoff's throbbing headaches. She got out a capsule from a pill case in her bag as her driver maneuvered their cart to the entrance.

The lobby backed on to a restaurant bar. A giant flatscreen TV glowed from a dark paneled wall with a news report on the upcoming Human World Conference. She glanced at it as she passed by, reminding herself that she had much to do in very little time. Soon she would be leaving for her business meeting overseas. She checked her cell phone—still nothing from her primary research team in Africa. Everything was almost ready. But it was critical that she personally take charge of the final preparations.

Too much was at stake.

First things first, she told herself as she came to the breezeway that opened to a swimming pool and courtyard where suntanned guests lounged, reaching for drinks served on wicker trays.

Crossing the courtyard, she entered the south wing and a ground level area of the hotel. In the lush garden front, a wooden sign in dark mahogany identified the section as the Blue Tortoise Kids' Hideaway.

This was the resort's child-care service center. Its exterior walls were constructed with hurricane-proof glass. She saw toddlers and older children playing inside. Guests were required to use their room keys, and staff needed their swipe cards for access beyond this point. She fished in her bag for her security card and passed it through the reader. It beeped and she entered.

She was met with joyful chaos. The smells of baby powder, suntan lotion and fruit mingled in the air. It was a large operation handling scores of children from infants to preteens. It ran twenty-four hours a day, seven days a week and was staffed with trained caregivers and several nurses. It also had more than fifty top-flight babysitters on call for additional care on-site or in a guest's room.

The Hideaway offered computer games, movies, parties, sleepovers and crafts, as well as supervised excursions throughout the resort or to the amusement park. It was meant for parents who needed a break for a few hours.

And, in some special cases, longer.

It was expensive but families from all over the world praised the quality of the care. Staff members were thoughtful, compassionate. No one was neglected and someone was always available to speak to any visiting child in Spanish, German, French, Japanese, Chinese, Portuguese, Farsi or Russian—nearly every major language.

The child care was not provided by the resort.

The Grand Blue Tortoise had contracted an agency specializing in the service. The Blue Tortoise Kids' Hideaway was a numbered company that vanished in the labyrinth of the local tax system, the maze of Bahamian corporate law and the cloak of complex international banking operations.

The same shadowy entity also provided similar services at resorts in the United Arab Emirates, Greece, Australia, Maldives, Africa, the Mediterranean, Hong Kong, the U.K., China, Canada and the U.S.

Dr. Gretchen Sutsoff and her silent investors owned it all.

But no one knew that she was the invisible force controlling the company. Very few people knew her true identity. No one knew that, for years, she had been living under the alias of Elinor Auden, medical doctor, businesswoman and researcher. It enabled her to work with her international associates as they secretly strived to correct the mistakes of civilization.

"Good morning, Dr. Auden." Lucy Walsh, the chief executive assistant, acknowledged a young family. "As you know we were expecting Elena and Valmir Leeka, and their son, Alek. They're from Albania and have been vacationing in the United States."

"Yes, of course." Dr. Sutsoff smiled at the boy, squirming in his stroller. "Goodness, someone's not happy. If you'll indulge me for a minute, I'll be with you shortly."

The doctor entered her office alone, shutting the door behind her.

The quiet was calming.

She turned on her computers and glanced up at the bank of flat screens wired to the cameras monitoring the rooms, the outdoor jungle playground, and the pool where more children played.

Three muted TV panels monitored cable news channels.

No one knew the true nature of her research. No one knew the scope and reach of her operation and what it involved. She did a quick check, scrolling through files.

LA #212005 to New York67
LA #907864 to Texas908
LA #376274 to Minnesota9087

LN #77-487 to Bristol26
LN #F8-787 to Manchester98
LN #FF-879 to Dublin948
LN #00-977 to GlasgowS93

BN #JI-47-90 to Franfurt635
BN #K-489-86 to Munich875
BN #A-34-90 to Hamburg887

And the new ones: PRC #PQ-487-98 to Kunming967 and LA #181975 to Wyoming847.

The Chinese case would arrive soon. Now, she needed to focus on the extensive computer files she already had on the Albanians who'd arrived today with the Wyoming case. She had concerns with the Leekas but would get to them later.

Sutsoff's dedication to her work bordered on being pathological. Her staff worshipped her genius with zeal and fear. Her enigmatic mystique commanded unquestioned obedience, loyalty and absolute secrecy.

For the "special cases."

While most of the children at the center belonged to vacationing parents, there were those who were entangled in "complications," such as international custody disputes or "other matters."

"Their parents seek our service as a sanctuary," Sutsoff had told her staff. "For security reasons, these situations must never be discussed."

Consequently, the staff never questioned her about the strange cases or the cases of children who stayed for weeks, even months on end, as if they'd been abandoned.

Or hidden.

Dr. Sutsoff concentrated on these children, the ones her staff privately called, "the Children of the Hideaway."

The latest to surface was the Albanian case of little one-year-old Alek Leeka. His medical records had already been scanned into the secure computer system. Dr. Sutsoff had studied them on her island before flying in today. Now, after rereading them and double-checking her secure files, she thought the preliminary work done was flawless. The child's DNA signature was perfect, the best of them all to date.

But recent mistakes had been made in this case and it was time to deal with them. Sutsoff asked Lucy to usher the family into her private office. Lucy joined them, making notes of the meeting. The baby was on the verge of crying.

"Why so grouchy?" Sutsoff cooed. Then she said, "Hello, Elena and Valmir. You must be very pleased things have gone so well, so quickly?"

They smiled and nodded nervously. Elena was chewing gum.

"We are happy to have a son, finally," Valmir said.

"The files note that you are both dual citizens of Albania and the United States and that you're in the process of adopting your new child whom you've named Alek." Dr. Sutsoff nodded to Lucy. "Unfortunately, the boy was orphaned when his parents recently died in a tragic car crash in the United States. Ah, but for every ending there is a beginning. The adoption process has been expedited through an international law firm based in Brazil. Isn't that correct, Elena?"

Elena, who was working hard on her gum, stopped and nodded.

"That is correct, yes."

"It's been a little stressful," Sutsoff said to Lucy. "Elena and Valmir are going to extend their vacation. Now, if I may, I'll just have a look at Alek. I see he's a little crotchety. I think I can fix that."

Sutsoff looked at the baby in his stroller, taking stock as if he were a prized jewel, smiling to herself before turning and scrutinizing her computer files once more. Then she hefted him to the small table in her office, slid on her stethoscope and while Lucy steadied him, proceeded to examine the toddler for some twenty minutes, making detailed notes the whole time. Afterward, Sutsoff went into her small fridge and poured a little fruit punch into a plastic cup with dolphins on it. Then Sutsoff opened her small black medical bag, found a tiny brown bottle, unscrewed the lid and tapped a few drops into the juice.

"This medicine should help." She held the cup while little Alek gulped it down.

"That's a good boy." She patted his head. "Lucy, would

you mind getting one of the staff to take care of Alek. He's going to stay with us for this afternoon while his parents have some alone time."

Lucy took the toddler in her arms.

"Come on, sweetie," she murmured. "You can meet the other angels."

After Lucy closed the door, Valmir's head snapped to Dr. Sutsoff.

"Where is our fucking money?"

Sutsoff ignored him and checked a file on her computer.

"We want to be paid now," Valmir said.

"Valmir, you were part of the recovery team in the case of this Wyoming boy?"

Subtly, Valmir pushed his chest forward. "Yes."

"Your instructions were to obtain the baby. That accident could have killed him. You took a stupid risk."

Valmir shrugged as Sutsoff's computer printer came to life.

"There was miscommunication," Valmir said. "Our team was advised that you only needed his tissue. Whether he was dead or alive was no concern. But we grabbed him. He lived and we brought him to you as instructed. The mother and father died, so there is no problem."

Sutsoff handed him a news article.

"The father died, but the mother lived, Valmir. You made a dangerous error, risking everything. Fortunately, everyone assumes the baby died."

Valmir sucked air through his teeth. "So? It's a win-win. Pay us our fucking money if you want us to continue."

Sutsoff could barely contain her loathing of these two. She'd come to employ them through her international networks: Valmir, the onetime security agent turned human trafficker from Albania and Elena, the prostitute. Dr. Sutsoff hated them but needed them, as she needed the others like them. They were essential to the overall operation. But there was little reason for them to live beyond that. She would happily erase them later. For now, she pulled a thick envelope from her desk and tapped it in her hands.

"You are supposed to be convincing as proud parents. Valmir, you reek of cigarettes. Drink some mouthwash, shave, bathe and lose your tasteless jewelry. Elena, lose the gum, wear clothing that covers your tattoos and suggests you have a brain and are a good mother, not a moronic whore."

Sutsoff tossed the envelope to Valmir, who fanned the American bills, seventy-five thousand dollars in all.

"We're going to the casino now."

"Listen to me," Sutsoff said. "Stay sober. We have new passports for you and your son. Pick up the boy in five hours. We've arranged for you to join a cruise ship tonight. You are to conduct yourselves as a family on a Caribbean cruise. When your cruise ends, you will fly back to Nassau and stay in this resort. All your tickets and expenses are taken care of."

"That's it?" Valmir asked.

"You have one assignment on the ship."

"What is it?"

"A man and woman from Indianapolis will be staying in the cabin across the hall from yours. All you have to do is ensure that at some point the boy innocently touches the man's skin."

Valmir looked at Elena then back at Dr. Sutsoff.

"That's it?" Valmir asked.

"That's it."

27

As Lucy Walsh watched the Leekas leave Dr. Auden's office, her breathing quickened. The parts of their conversation with the doctor that she'd overheard confirmed her fears.

For the past several weeks, she'd grown increasingly suspicious that the child-care center was a cover for something illegal.

Something sinister.

Lucy had arrived in the Bahamas from Ireland a year ago after answering an online advertisement for nannies. At the time she thought the center to be a world-class service with humanitarian leanings, secretly aiding families facing difficult adoptions and custody matters.

But she became troubled by Dr. Auden's payments and calls to medical labs and law firms around the world, by her odd dealings with mysterious and scary people, by the cryptic behavior of some of the staff. It led Lucy to believe that the center was involved in illegal adoptions or child smuggling.

Or, Lord above, something worse.

On a recent trip home to Dublin, Lucy confided her worries to a man at her church who worked with a human rights organization. He advised her to covertly gather evidence. When she returned to the Bahamas, she started keeping a journal, collecting files and sending them to her friend in Dublin, who promised to pass them along "through the appropriate channels."

Lucy was typing new notes on the Leekas in her confidential online e-mail account when Dr. Auden suddenly appeared at her desk.

"I need you to arrange an additional flight for me."

"Of course, Doctor. First class and both seats, as usual?"

"Yes, here are the details."

The doctor left her a slip of paper.

After she returned to her office, Dr. Sutsoff closed her door and reread the e-mail she'd just received from her team's African field station.

Our tests confirm we have what is needed. We have a small window to harvest and will make arrangements for your arrival.

Pleased with the information, she picked up a novelty float pen and turned it playfully in her fingers. It was custom-made to her specifications. The barrel showed a sailboat on an azure sea. It floated from one end to the other when the pen was tipped. She unscrewed the cap and slowly emptied the barrel of the liquid, then sterilized it with an antiseptic. She then refilled the barrel with the liquid from the brown bottle in her medical bag, the same liquid she'd tapped into Alek Leeka's juice.

Her latest formula.

She resealed the cap and held the pen up to the light.

It would pass through any security system. She would give it to Elena and Valmir and advise them on how to administer the solution to Alek.

Now it was time to run her test.

Her confidential phone line rang.

"Yes," she said.

"Dr. Auden, this is security."

Upon recognizing Drake Stinson's voice she grew angry.

"I told you to never to call me here."

"Our risks are mounting. Vulnerabilities are emerging out of Dar es Salaam, the U.S. and elsewhere."

"I'm aware."

"Are you aware that aspects of the operation were infiltrated in Brazil? Files were stolen. Countermeasures were taken under the pretense of a drug war but an American wire service reporter is digging deep into our actions. I diverted his attention but take nothing for granted. We must remove him now."

"No. Not yet. You've already removed two journalists. Remove another one and a hundred more will follow. Monitor him but take no action without my authority."

"But think of the risks—"

"Risks? Look at what the Leekas risked in Wyoming for our best specimen. My God, where did you find these people? We needed the best for this operation—now it's too late to replace them."

"I'd warned you that with the large number of operatives you'd demanded we would face a quality issue. And what about the risk you took with your apocalyptic video?"

"We needed to get our message out at a critical time. We did it through the guise of a cult. My identity was masked and the video is untraceable."

"I don't think you understand that our investors are furious at not seeing any tangible results yet. This will be raised at your meeting with the inner group. They want to know how much longer before we launch."

"I've told you, a prototype will be released any day now. I will review the results. Then I will go out in the field to seek the final component. I assure you we will launch the operation on schedule. I will deal with the inner group's worries at our upcoming meeting. Now, I must go."

Sutsoff returned to her computers and her work.

She downloaded an array of data relating to Alek. At the same time Sutsoff watched a large screen linked to a camera monitoring the dimly lit room where Alek had joined some twenty other children watching cartoons.

Everyone was in good health. No indication of any illness.

For the moment.

Dr. Sutsoff adjusted some switches on a control panel and the light in the room faded. Children giggled. Some worried. She put on special glasses and using electromagnetic radiation technology was able to see everything and everyone that Alek Leeka had touched. It was because of the liquid she'd administered. Blue hand prints, smears and smudges radiated as if something had run rampant in the darkness.

Even on the skin of the other children.

Good.

She began manipulating the computer, entering commands and passwords. As the computer screens displayed a response with color bar levels and digitized monitoring, Sutsoff watched Alek.

Within thirty seconds of Sutsoff's commands, Alek released a small tickle cough. Sutsoff's keyboard clicked as the camera zoomed in on Alek.

Within one minute, Alek coughed a bit harder. Sutsoff watched the large flat screen that captured glowing droplets spraying from Alek's mouth and traveling in the air. Some were inhaled by the other children. Some landed on hands that were then dragged over faces and eyes.

Sutsoff made another adjustment, increasing her level, and within thirty seconds, Alek sneezed. The magnification camera showed the spray of droplets traveling throughout the room and bombarding the other children.

Within ten minutes, all of them were coughing and sneezing. The levels on the computers monitoring them showed that they had each started presenting symptoms of a common cold.

It was astounding.

Sutsoff's pulse quickened.

But she was not done. She typed more commands, inputting passwords and codes. Within five minutes the sneezing and coughing subsided.

Within ten minutes it ceased.

Sutsoff studied the computer monitoring the children's levels. Everything had returned to normal.

It was over.

Sutsoff cupped her hands to her face.

Another trial had worked.

Like the others before it.

Sutsoff pressed her intercom and requested to see Alek. She made notes while waiting for the staff member to return Alek to her office for a follow-up examination. Alek was placed on the table while the doctor checked all of his signs again.

Perfect health. Not a problem

Alone, Sutsoff savored what she had dreamed of for years.

Everything she had been working for, everything she'd been struggling to achieve was now within her grasp.

She possessed the power at her fingertips to control who got sick. With the right synthetic biological agent, with the right microbe, she could determine who lived and who died.

Anywhere. Anytime.

She was poised to take the world into a new age.

She glanced up at the TV monitors. One was showing a report on the upcoming Human World Conference in New York. It was going to be one of the largest gatherings in history. As she watched footage of the preparations for crowds that would be in the millions, she reflected on Oppenheimer's breakthrough and his invocation of Vishnu. It was now more applicable to her achievement, she thought, as she considered the scale of the conference.

"Now I have become death, the destroyer of worlds."

Let's get things started.

Dr. Sutsoff went to another computer and entered commands on the keyboard until a head shot of a man appeared alongside some biographical information.

Name: Roger Timothy Tippert. Age: forty-one. Nationality: American. Residence: Indianapolis, Indiana. Occupation: teacher. Marital Status: married. Spouse: Catherine.

Sutsoff stared at Roger's face. Then at Catherine's face.

The Tipperts were cruise-ship passengers.

She'd selected them randomly for the next experiment.

If it worked, only one of them would be returning to Indianapolis alive.

28

Near Bimini

The Spanish luxury liner, *Salida del Sol,* steamed toward the Florida coast and the end of a seven-day cruise of the eastern Caribbean islands.

Before leaving his cabin, Roger Tippert, the schoolteacher from Indianapolis, took one final look in the mirror, approving the shorts and flowered shirt he'd bought in Nassau.

He was headed to Twisters Cocktail Lounge high up on deck 14. Cathy, his wife of ten years, was somewhere on deck 11 with her new friends, enjoying the ship's power-walking club.

He whistled softly as he strolled to the elevator and waited a moment. It chimed and the doors opened to that young couple in the cabin across the hall, the family with the cute baby. They'd come aboard in Nassau. Roger had greeted them a few times and by their accents guessed they were Russian or something.

The little boy had one arm extended over his head, holding his mother's hand. She smiled. "Alek, say hello to the nice man."

The toddler broke from her grip—or did she nudge him?—and made a teetering beeline for Roger, stumbling into him.

"Hey there, cowboy." Roger felt the boy's little hands

slapping at his legs as he squatted down and helped him back to his mother.

"Thank you."

Roger caught something under the woman's smile. Was it the hint of a come-on? Whatever, Roger dismissed it.

"No problem."

He stepped by her husband, who had the warmth of a zombie. The man eyed him while the doors closed. Alone in the elevator, he shook his head. Man, it was yesterday when his kids were that size. As he strolled into Twisters, he thought happily of his wife. Waiting for her in the lounge had become their predinner ritual during the trip.

He took in the ocean view, knowing he was one lucky son-of-a-gun.

Cathy, a dental hygienist, had survived a recent battle with breast cancer. Their two beautiful children, Simon, who was nine, and Melissa, who was seven, were treasures.

At times he thought that he didn't deserve this family.

About three years back, Rosita, a thirty-year-old, divorced ex-beauty queen and substitute teacher had run her hand inside his thigh under the table at a school district lunch and offered to "rock his world."

Roger was going to accept Rosita's offer but on his way to meet her at a motel, he turned around. He knew it was wrong. He was happily married.

He never told Cathy about it.

Seven months later, she found a malignant lump.

But she beat it and in the process became his hero as her strength made him realize that she was too good for him. So it was while they were in the grip of an unrelenting winter that he surprised her with this tropical cruise for an anniversary present.

She cried.

It was something she had always dreamed of doing.

Now, as he sipped a Dutch beer alone at the bar, he reflected on all the places they'd seen—St. Thomas, St. Maarten,

Nassau—and how much Cathy had loved every minute of the cruise so far.

This had been one of the best times of their lives.

"So we meet again, Tippert."

A rugged-faced man in his mid-sixties took the stool next to him.

"Hey there, captain."

Jimmy Stokes, a retired car dealer from Fort Worth, Texas, had been joining him at the bar around the same time every day. Roger liked their conversations on sports, politics, history and life in general. Jimmy was vacationing alone. His wife had died of a stroke five years back. They never had any children and Jimmy was genuinely happy for Roger's situation.

"Sounds like you got things set just right on the home front, son."

Stokes was also a Vietnam vet, who did two tours over forty years ago. After he started into a beer, he opened up to Roger about his time there. "Funny," Stokes said. "For years I couldn't tell anybody about the god-awful things I'd seen when I was in the shit."

Stokes would gaze out at the sea as if something evil waited at the far side of the ocean. Today, Jimmy wanted to talk about 1968. Roger hadn't even been born then.

"Do you know about the battle of Khe Sanh, son?"

Tippert only knew what he'd seen on the History Channel.

"Well I was there." Stokes pulled on his beer then started his story. "We was in Quang Tri Province…"

Roger spasmed.

He dropped his beer and the glass shattered on the floor. His fingertips tingled. Gooseflesh rose on his skin.

"What's the matter, son?"

It felt like a switch had been thrown, his brain pulsated and his tongue started to swell. It wouldn't stop swelling.

Oh, God—can't breathe!

"Is everything all right?" a bartender asked.

"Call the ship's doctor!" Stokes said. "My friend's going into some kind of shock or seizure!"

Clawing at his throat, Roger fell to the floor.

"Son, take it easy!"

Roger didn't notice the alarmed people who'd gathered around him. His insides were on fire. He was burning up. His breathing was tortured. His vision blurred. His hearing felt like he was underwater. His panicked heartbeat was deafening.

Oh, Christ! Somebody help me!

The pressure was increasing as if something was trying to explode from him.

He convulsed.

Something hot oozed from his mouth, his nose, his ears.

He touched it.

Blood.

Jesus!

The pressure. No, please—stop the pressure! His brain was expanding. His head was swelling.

"Dammit! Is anybody here a doctor?" Stokes shouted.

Stokes was holding Roger just as he'd held his Marine friends in the mud at Khe Sanh, and he watched in disbelief as Roger Tippert's blood-laced face contorted.

"What the good goddamn?"

In all his time in Vietnam, Stokes had never witnessed anything like this. Tippert screamed as his eyes melted into bloody pools that overflowed down the sides of his face. His abdomen gurgled as if his organs were boiling in his stomach.

Then his heart stopped.

Two decks below the spot where he died, Roger Tippert's wife, Cathy, was exchanging e-mail addresses with a friendly woman she'd met from Indianapolis, whose husband worked for the Colts' administration.

"I can get you a deal on tickets for your husband," the woman said.

"His birthday's coming up," Cathy said. "Roger's going to love this."

29

Rio de Janeiro, Brazil

Sarah Kirby moaned coming out of sedation.

"You're lucky," the doctor said.

Death had missed her by a sixteenth of an inch.

The doctor flipped through her chart, telling her that the bullet had grazed her neck, and other than the loss of blood and a scar, she would be fine. He poured water in her cup and waited for her grogginess to pass. Then he asked if she was ready for a visitor and turned slightly to the door.

Gannon was waiting in the hall.

"Jack." Her voice was weak.

The doctor left them alone.

Gannon sat beside her. His face was bruised.

"Thank you for saving my life, Sarah."

She smiled at him.

"You have to get the story, Jack. Expose the truth. For Maria, your friends, Gabriela, Marcelo—and to keep your word to the Blue Brigade."

"Three of their gang members were killed. The youngest was thirteen. Dragon escaped."

"He'll be incensed." She coughed. "He'll suspect that you brought police to his favela. Take his threat seriously. You must uncover the truth behind the bombing."

"I need more information."

Sarah drank some water then said, "We'll get Maria's

documents to you quickly and our contacts around the world will have more on this."

A nurse came in to tend to Sarah.

Gannon put his card in Sarah's hand.

"I have to go," he said. "I'll never forget what you did." She reached up, cupped her hand to his face.

"We're counting on you, Jack."

Their eyes met and the strength he saw in hers filled him with resolve.

He bent down, kissed her cheek and left.

On his way out of the hospital, Gannon switched on his cell phone.

He now had messages from Globo TV, *O Dia, Jornal do Brasil,* AP, Reuters, Estralla, the WPA desk in New York, Luiz, Frank Archer, George Wilson and Melody Lyon.

He hadn't had time to return any calls to elaborate on what had transpired. Within minutes of the shootout in the favela, he'd used his phone's camera to take several exclusive pictures of the carnage and police bending over bodies in the street. He sent them to WPA headquarters in New York for the global wire. Then he called, dictated a quick bare-bones story about his hostage-taking and the gun battle. He was advised to call back with updates, just as police had taken him into custody.

After paramedics treated him at the scene, detectives questioned him. He was careful not to reveal too much. While describing his ordeal, Gannon thought it strange that he never saw Roberto Estralla among the cops questioning him. When he was released, Gannon had hurried to the hospital to check on Sarah.

Now, as he reached the hospital's main doors, he stopped to sit down and absorb what he'd just been through.

A gun to his head. A shoot-out.

Think of Maria, Gabriela, Marcelo. Suck it up, Gannon. Get back to work.

He called Melody Lyon's cell-phone number, to alert her to his new lead: the café bombing could be linked to a bigger story.

"Gannon!"

Roberto Estralla caught up to him from behind. Gannon abandoned his call to Lyon.

"I've been looking for you." Estralla pointed to an empty section of the reception area where they found chairs and privacy. "My colleagues shared your statement with me. I have a few questions."

"First, how did you and your SWAT team know I was there?"

"Luiz at your bureau was concerned when he could not reach you. He called, telling us of your interest in going to Céu sobre Rio. Then our sources in the favela confirmed an American might have been taken by the Blue Brigade. So we moved fast, for your safety."

Gannon took his time assessing Estralla's account.

"Jack, what you did was very foolish. You're lucky you are not in a body bag at this moment."

"The Blue Brigade insists they are not behind the café bombing, that they did not kill the Colombian's daughter."

"The narco vendetta was always speculation by the press."

"The Brigade insists Rio police planted the story to trigger a gang war."

"We've always stated that we're investigating all aspects."

"The WPA will move a story with the Blue Brigade's denial of involvement in the bombing of the café."

"A denial made with a gun to your head?"

"You carry guns, too."

"But we're sworn to uphold the law, not deal in death. Jack, it wouldn't be wise for you to be seen siding with murdering narco dealers."

"It wouldn't be wise for me to be seen siding with police, either. I am only interested in the truth."

"Then we're on the same side."

"Tell me then, what more do you have on the bombing? Did you find anything in those documents you took from me?"

"We're still investigating. However, I am curious to know what you found when you went to Maria Santo's home in the favela?"

"I found myself with a gun to my head."

Estralla nodded, glanced around to collect a thought, scratched his chin then reached into his pocket and produced Gannon's passport, turning it over in his hands.

"You should leave Brazil now, while you can fly home upright." Estralla placed Gannon's passport in his hands. "That is a little friendly advice, from one Buffalo Bills fan to another."

Estralla's phone rang. Before taking his call, he shook Gannon's hand then left. Gannon sat alone for several minutes, pondering his passport when he heard his name being cursed.

"Goddammit, Gannon, what the hell is wrong with you? You don't answer your phone?" Frank Archer had entered the hospital with an older man in a light suit, a man Gannon didn't recognize. "Police told us at the scene that you had come here."

"Hello, Frank."

"Lawrence Chapin," the older man introduced himself. "With the U.S. consulate. State Department. You got some nasty bruises there. Are you all right, son?"

"I'm fine."

"Physically, maybe." Archer snorted. "I get back from Gabriela's funeral in Miami and New York's screaming that Gannon's been taken hostage by drug dealers in a favela! There's been a shoot-out! People are dead! I've been unable to reach you. Jesus, Gannon!"

"I said in my note to New York that I was fine, Frank."

"Well George doesn't think so." Archer pulled out an envelope and gave it to Gannon. "You're done here. This is your ticket."

"What do you mean? I'm still on the story."

"Not anymore. You've been a disaster. You're being called back to New York. A flight to JFK leaves in five hours. So check out of your hotel and bon voyage, pal."

"What does Melody say?"

"Doesn't matter—Beland backs George. You're done in Brazil."

"Excuse me," Chapin said, "I need a moment with you, Jack. You see whenever a U.S. citizen is a victim of crime—"

"You know, Jack—" Archer shook his head "—we're going through a tough time down here. It's not easy burying friends. Everyone's emotionally pushed to the breaking point. And while her intentions were good, I think Melody Lyon made a huge mistake sending us someone like you, a person who clearly is not ready to handle a major story of any kind."

Gannon looked long and hard at Archer, standing there, oozing Ivy League arrogance through his designer polo shirt.

"You know, Frank, I think you're right."

"Of course, I'm right. And another thing, you might want to consider going back to Buffalo. Do they still have a newspaper there?"

"That's a thought. And I was going to give you a point to consider but I'm sure you'll figure it out." Gannon turned to Chapin. "We can talk in the taxi to my hotel."

Along the drive, Gannon summarized his ordeal for Chapin, a seasoned diplomat, who'd been involved in many tight situations around the world.

As the car approached the hotel, Chapin offered Gannon his assistance.

"Can I ask you a confidential question?" Gannon said.

"Certainly."

"Do you know of a Drake Stinson, an American with Worldwide Rio Advogados? He used to work in Washington, D.C."

"Yes. I've got friends in the Justice Department and I asked them about Stinson when he arrived in Rio de Janeiro. Seems he used to be a lawyer for the CIA."

"The CIA?"

"You could look him up in old obscure legal bulletins and newsletters. But you won't find much. Stinson handled legal work on critical cases that were usually classified, secret proceedings due to national security."

"Really?"

Gannon turned to the window letting the revelation sink in all the way to the Nine Palms Hotel.

30

Rio de Janeiro, Brazil

At Rio's Galeão International Airport Gannon sat in pre-boarding, turned on his laptop and began drafting a news story.

He had less than forty-five minutes before his flight departed for JFK.

He tried again to reach Melody Lyon.

No luck.

As time ticked by, he worked on his story that would say that mystery continued to shroud the identity of those behind the attack that had killed ten people at the Café Amaldo. He quoted Dragon's denial of gang involvement and his accusation that police had fostered rumors of a blood vendetta to trigger a war among competing drug networks.

As Gannon wrote the final paragraphs, the first preboarding advisory for his flight was announced over the PA system. After a quick rereading, he filed his raw copy to the WPA in New York. Once they'd edited his story, it would be translated and offered to WPA's international subscribers, which included virtually every news organization in Brazil. His story would be posted to online sites and would run in print editions the next day. Gannon was hopeful his article would satisfy the Blue Brigade and they would remove their threat to WPA staff.

This should save Frank Archer's arrogant ass.

Gannon waited until New York confirmed receipt of his file in an e-mail.

Got it. Thanks, Jack.

In his article Gannon had made no mention of Maria Santo's meeting with Gabriela or the bigger story because he was still a long way from nailing it.

This is what he knew: Maria Santo was about to give the WPA secret documents alleging that the law firm where she worked was involved in the illegal adoption and trafficking of stolen children. The documents were marked for destruction. The firm's staff included a former CIA lawyer experienced in highly classified cases. Santo was killed at the café when she'd met Gabriela.

Another preboarding call piped through the air.

Gannon had a story here. Every instinct told him he was on the right track. He had to keep digging but he needed help. He searched his e-mails for anything from Sarah Kirby's organization. He needed to see the complete set of documents Maria Santo had obtained. He needed them now because he would have no Internet access on his nine-hour flight.

But nothing had arrived.

He checked his spam.

Nothing.

He checked his cell phone for any messages.

Nothing.

Again he called Melody Lyon's cell phone. He didn't want to leave a message. It was crucial that he talk to her confidentially about where they go next on this story.

As it rang, people lined up and started boarding.

One woman did a double take at Gannon's bruised face, staring like he was familiar. Her attention bordered on rude and he turned away keeping his phone pressed to his ear.

Gannon did not notice that, in the preboarding line, a man reading a newspaper had also been watching him. Gannon didn't know that the stranger had followed him into the airport, watched him check in, then bought a ticket for the same flight.

Gannon cursed under his breath.

He'd failed to reach Lyon and hung up.

The line of passengers boarding was shrinking and just as he was about to take his place, he checked his e-mail a final time.

He froze.

A new one had arrived.

He didn't know the sender. The attachment was labeled One of Ten. Gannon sat down, opened it and recognized the scanned page bearing the letterhead of Worldwide Rio Advogados. The attachment included a second page of text. It had been translated into English for him.

Must've been why they'd taken so long.

Checking his e-mail, Gannon saw that attachments two and three had arrived. This was going to take time. He neared the end of the line and checked his laptop's battery, it was at half-strength.

The line was getting shorter.

The attendants collecting boarding passes shot glances at him, cradling his laptop. By now, as attachments six and seven arrived, Gannon fumbled in his pocket to get his passport and boarding pass ready.

He was near the desk when eight and nine arrived.

The problem came with attachment ten.

It had downloaded to 50 percent then stopped.

Gannon cursed to himself and didn't move another step.

"Right this way, sir," the attendant said, repeating it in Portuguese.

"Yes, sorry, one moment."

The tenth attachment completed downloading. Now that he had them all, he moved quickly to a seat near the desk.

"Sir, you must board."

"Please, bear with me."

The attendant at the desk was glaring at him. No one else was waiting at preboarding.

"Sir, you cannot delay this flight."

He moved the documents quickly en masse onto his hard drive, put them into one folder and e-mailed that folder to Melody Lyon's home e-mail, labeling the document Confidential from JG in Rio.

"Sir, we have to leave now!"

Once his e-mail was sent, Gannon shut his laptop and boarded.

The flight taxied into position but its departure was delayed for an excruciating hour. Some thirty minutes after the jetliner finally roared from Rio de Janeiro, it leveled off.

The elderly lady in the window seat beside Gannon had fallen asleep.

He turned on his laptop and resumed his work.

He scrutinized every attachment two or three times trying to determine what he had. He saw the unsigned note demanding that files, hardcopy and electronic, be destroyed, and that "no record exists in the firm that makes mention of their existence, including this one which should be destroyed after these instructions are carried out."

From that point, most of the ten pages seemed to be a catalogue of files, and cross-referenced file numbers. All the pages looked similar. Again, he studied the entries on the first few, trying to make sense of them.

LA #212005 to New York67
LA #907864 to Texas908
LA #376274 to Minnesota9087
LA #181975 to Wyoming847

LN #77-487 to Bristol26
LN #F8-787 to Manchester98

LN #FF-879 to Dublin948
LN #00-977 to GlasgowS93...

And so on, and so on. While he could not decipher them, Gannon was convinced they were significant because a handwritten notation on the last page said "Security breach, have alerted E.D., action required."

Who was E.D., he wondered, and what type of action was required?

Below the note he saw the separate message posted to the document that was addressed specifically to him from Sarah Kirby's group.

"To Jack, on behalf of Sarah: We have contacted our friends in London, who have more information and have agreed to help you based upon Sarah's assurance that you can be trusted. See the contact e-mail below. Your contact's name is Oliver. Good luck."

Gannon contemplated the airphone installed in the backrest of the seat before him. He thought most airlines had taken the phones out because passengers complained.

He needed to reach Melody Lyon.

"Excuse me," he asked the attendant who was making her way by, pushing a beverage cart. "Are these working? Can I make a call?"

"Yes." She glanced around. "We're about two-thirds full. If you use one in the empty back rows you'll have more privacy."

"Can I just move my stuff to a seat back there?"

"Sure."

After Gannon settled in at the back, he inserted the WPA credit card into the mechanism, then called Lyon's cell phone, estimating that it had been over two hours since his last attempt.

It was answered on the third ring.

"Melody, it's Gannon."

"Jack, I've been trying to call you. I just got back from Miami. George told me what happened, are you all right?"

"I'm fine. Just a little bruised."

"Where are you?"

"On the plane back to New York, we just left Rio."

"How the hell did you get taken hostage by a drug gang?"

"It was a misunderstanding. I'm fine as long as we run the story I just filed. It's critical that the desk doesn't cut the Blue Brigade stuff."

"I'll tell them."

"Turns out the hostage thing was the price I paid for a strong lead into the bombing. Did you read the material I sent you, the ten attachments of the secret files?"

"I did."

"This is shaping up to be a major story."

"Bring me up to speed."

Gannon related everything he'd learned on Maria Santo, the law firm, Sarah Kirby and the human rights network, and how Marcelo's incredible photos of Maria and the bombing helped advance the story.

Lyon listened, asked an occasional question, then concluded the call.

"Jack, the first thing you're going to do when you get to New York is your laundry. Then pack again. I'll authorize and clear the way. I want you to follow this story to London and wherever else it leads us."

31

Laramie, Wyoming

Emma sat at the big polished oak table in the conference room at the Wyoming Division of Criminal Investigation.

Shadows on the wall drawn by the midday light bled through the blinds. As Emma studied them she blinked back tears, trying not to scream.

Nearly two agonizing days had passed since she'd received the mysterious nighttime call, and police were still no closer to telling her who had made it.

For two days Emma had repeated the circumstances of the call to every official she was referred to. She recounted every detail and answered every question while they took notes. But she soon realized that their concern was just pretense.

Because they don't believe me.

She'd do better to search for answers in the shadows on the wall.

"Emma?"

She shifted her focus to the people around the table, who, at her insistence, had convened this meeting here in Laramie to report back to her on their "investigation" into the call.

She looked into the faces of Aunt Marsha, Uncle Ned, Darnell Horn with the county sheriff's office, his supervisor, Reed Cobb, Henry Sanders, the coroner, Dan Farraday with the highway patrol; and Dr. Kendrix, the psychiatrist from the hospital.

Jay Hubbard, special agent with the Wyoming Division of Criminal Investigation who was running the meeting, repeated his question.

"Would you like a tissue or some water?"

"No, thank you."

"As I was saying," Hubbard continued, "we've responded to the request to assist in this inquiry from the Big Cloud County Sheriff's Office."

She knew this. Was Hubbard being officious for her benefit?

"And, we've used all the records and information you volunteered. Working with authorities in California we have confirmed that you did receive a call at the time you reported."

Emma inhaled.

"The call originated from a public phone in Santa Ana, California, in Orange County," Hubbard read from his notebook.

"It must have something to do with the clinic," she said.

"No, we don't think that's the case."

"Then something to do with Dr. Durbin's letter. Did you talk to him?"

"We're coming to that," Hubbard said. "The phone is located near a Burger King outlet some thirty-five miles south of West Olympic Boulevard, in Los Angeles, the location of the Golden Dawn Fertility Corporation. So we've ruled out that it was a call from the clinic."

Emma said nothing.

"With your permission and using your volunteered material we spoke with Dr. Durbin and with officials at the clinic in Los Angeles."

"What did they tell you?"

"They acknowledged receiving delivery of Dr. Durbin's letter confirming Tyler Lane's death. But they've closed their file. They also stressed that no one at the clinic called you or would have reason to call you."

"That's it?"

"The clinic expressed its sympathies," Hubbard said.

Looking into the faces studying her, Emma felt like she was falling.

"But how do you explain a woman calling me, telling me Tyler is alive?"

"We can only surmise what happened."

"And what is that?"

"That you got a wrong number call from California and in your semiconsciousness, in your grief, and with Dr. Durbin's letter fresh in your mind, you got confused about what you heard."

"Confused? No!"

"Emma." Her aunt tried to calm her.

"It was crystalline. The woman on the phone knew exactly who she was calling and exactly what she was saying. You're wrong!"

"Emma." Dr. Kendrix had been tapping the tip of his pen to his chin. "It is not uncommon for bereaved people under stress, traumatized by an unbearable event like yours, to experience what you've experienced."

"A phone call like that?"

Kendrix removed his glasses. "I'm talking about a post-tragic phenomenon whereby you see or hear deceased loved ones. It happens in dreams. You may hear them or see them in a room. And, yes, people have reported receiving phone calls or messages from those who have passed away suddenly. Usually they say, 'I'm all right, don't worry,' or 'I forgive you,' or something to alleviate guilty feelings or fears. It's not a supernatural event—it's simply a coping mechanism."

Emma shook her head.

"My case is different."

"Of course," Kendrix said. "Each case is. For you, you're

hearing what you need to hear, that your baby did not suffer in the fire while you lay a few feet away unable to help him."

Emma stifled a great sob.

"This call, this phenomenon," Kendrix said, "is your mind working at helping you cope, so you can live, so you can move forward."

"It's not true," Emma said.

"Sweetheart," Aunt Marsha said, "maybe this is because you haven't been taking the pills the doctor prescribed for you when you were released from the hospital?"

Kendrix arched an eyebrow.

"You're all wrong," Emma said. "I know what I heard. I know what I feel. Tyler's not dead."

"You need to rest, Emma," Uncle Ned said.

Kendrix was scribbling on a pad.

"We need to call the FBI," Emma said. "Why didn't you call the FBI?"

"Emma," Kendrix said. "You should take your medication. I'm writing you a new prescription, a stronger one. Now, I've spoken with Dr. Durbin and with Dr. Sanders. We all agree you need to talk to someone, get counseling. Dr. Allan Pierce at Big Sky Memorial Hospital in Cheyenne is excellent. I've called ahead—"

"No, thank you." Emma stood.

"Excuse me." Kendrix looked at Emma, then the others.

"I'm sorry," she said. "I need to think. I'm sorry."

Emma left the room with her worried aunt following after her until Emma turned.

"Aunt Marsha, please, I need to be alone. I just need some air."

Emma left the building for the small patch of lawn at the side and the shade tree that framed the mountains. She stood there, searching the snow-capped peaks, knowing the whole world thought she was crazy.

Insane with grief.

But she didn't care, for in her heart she knew, she felt, that Tyler was alive.

Emma replayed the night call in her mind a million times. Never wavering because she knew with certainty that what she'd heard was no dream, no hallucination, no "coping mechanism."

"Emma Lane in Big Cloud, Wyoming? Listen to me. Your baby is not dead! Your baby is alive. That's all I can tell you."

She cupped her hands to her face thinking of Joe, touching him as he died, remembering what he'd said to her that day.

"You're one of the most fearless people I know. Woe to anyone or anything that comes between you and Tyler."

She felt Joe with her now and she knew.

Emma reached into her bag, saw two tiny eyes looking up at her and caressed Tyler's stuffed bear.

She'd reached a decision on what she had to do.

She would find her son.

32

Fort Lauderdale, Florida

*T*his one was disturbing.

Dr. Wayne Marcott, chief medical examiner for Broward County, stroked his chin in his office on Thirty-first Avenue.

Again he read over his notes for Autopsy No. 10-92787. The decedent's name: Roger Timothy Tippert, a white male, age forty-one from Indianapolis, Indiana.

Was this an outbreak? This case was unlike anything he'd ever seen.

Marcott checked on the status of his request to accelerate additional tests from the autopsy. He'd grown concerned over his findings.

Tippert was a cruise ship passenger on the Spanish liner, *Salida del Sol.* According to the report from Dr. Estevan Perez, the ship's chief medical officer, the ship was returning to Florida from a seven-day cruise of eastern Caribbean islands when Tippert, a teacher, experienced a sudden seizure, collapsed and died while drinking a beer at an upper deck lounge.

The remarkable aspects are owing to his internal organs expanding and bursting. Was it an allergic reaction? Was it viral? It is uncertain at this stage. The subject was in good health. He was not taking medication and he had no known allergies or pre-existing medical conditions. He had not reported any illness. Seems the beer was fine. He was a healthy forty-one-year-old male.

Perez said all procedures were followed for a death in international water. Tippert's body was held in the ship's morgue for return to the U.S., and his widow was offered the counseling services of the clergy.

Perez alerted Florida officials and the ship's medical staff immediately and took precautions should Tippert's death be the result of an outbreak. Tippert's toiletries were tested, his beverage was tested, all of the ship's water and food were tested, as well as the pools and showers.

Nothing was found to be wrong.

All passengers exhibiting any flu-like symptoms were swabbed and tested as were all members of the crew. Nothing of concern had emerged.

This was puzzling because if Tippert's death was the result of a virus, that virus should thrive in the ship's confined environment.

They'd expect to find some further evidence of it.

Perez noted that the passengers in the adjoining cabin were tested and a female child did exhibit cold symptoms so mild as to be insignificant.

Early indications were that a quarantine of the ship was not necessary.

The cruise line intended to initiate a complete scrub down after the ship docked and all the passengers disembarked.

Marcott paged through his notes.

This case made him uneasy because it was baffling.

The external hemorrhaging from orifices was characteristic of the Ebola virus. But there were no other symptoms. It was as if something were mimicking Ebola. And if that wasn't bad enough, there was the speed at which this thing moved.

Marcott shook his head and cursed to himself.

He punched an extension on his phone line.

Once the connection was made, he activated his speaker phone.

"Yes, Wayne?"

"Isabel, have you got the samples from 92787 ready to ship to Atlanta?"

"We're good to go. I called ahead. They're standing by."

"Thanks."

Marcott reviewed his notes again.

His office had followed procedure and alerted the U.S. Centers for Disease Control.

Those hotshots need to take a good hard look at this case fast, because as far-fetched as it sounds, it looks to me like we may have a new killer on our hands.

33

In an airy, secured section of a subterranean floor of the National Anti-Threat Center, intelligence analysts hunted for ex-CIA scientist Gretchen Sutsoff.

They focused on monitors and keyboards, processing data at a configuration of desks that suggested the bridge of a spacecraft.

The Information Command Unit: what insiders called the ICU, where the nature of the work was top-secret cyber sleuthing.

ICU analysts had diverted some of their resources from other classified assignments to accommodate Robert Lancer's request for a "full-court press" to find Gretchen Sutsoff.

He needed to interview her about Project Crucible.

The room was taut with quiet pressure, underscored by the clicking of keys. In a process known as data mining, experts searched secure government archives, property records, court records, news articles, obituaries, Web sites, chat rooms, blogs and social networks—just about everything available online.

They also searched law enforcement databases, drivers' records, criminal records, death records, obits, tax records, corporate records and fee-based sources. And through international agreements, they were able to scour government holdings from foreign countries.

Sandra Deller, the chief analyst handling Lancer's request, had her eyes fixed to her monitor when Lancer arrived at her desk.

"Anything?" he asked.

"Nothing," she said. "In some smaller, developing island countries, they haven't transferred files to computerized databases. It's Dickensian. We have to request manual searches of paper files—it takes forever. There are cases where departments have lost records in hurricanes or earthquakes."

"What about our sources? Like the IRS? Does she receive a pension?"

"Nothing's been found."

"She may have changed her name."

"We're looking into that, too."

"Let me know if you get a hit."

Back at his desk, Lancer loosened his tie and resumed writing his latest report on the CIA file to his supervisor. He'd revisited his list of sources from around the world. No one had gotten back to him with anything on his requests for help. He needed to close the loop on Foster Winfield's concerns about Crucible.

Lancer also noted the separate case he was pursuing out of Dar es Salaam, the claim of an imminent attack. He looked at his calendar. Time was ticking down on the Human World Conference in New York.

Was it a target?

There were so many other events and potential soft targets: airports, malls, amusement parks. It was overwhelming, but Lancer knew he was not alone in assessing threats. Other agencies were doing similar work.

His phone rang.

It was Martin Weller at the East Africa section. Reaching for the handset, Lancer glanced at his watch. He had fifteen minutes to finish his report before the meeting.

"Lancer."

"Bob, we may have something coming to advance Said Salelee's information. We're picking it up from police sources in Africa."

"Can you give me a summary, Marty? I've got to finish reports before the E-3."

"Just some chatter. Something major in the works."

"Where? When? Who? What? I need more, Marty."

"Our analysts are still working on it. No details yet, I'll keep you posted."

The E-3 was a regular meeting within the U.S. intelligence community, held every three days, regardless of the day of the week. It included Homeland Security, the Central Intelligence Agency, the Federal Bureau of Investigation, and the U.S. State Department's Bureau of Intelligence, the Defense Intelligence Agency, the National Security Agency and other intelligence agencies.

Representatives provided updated analysis of threats arising from their areas of responsibility. Their reports were debated and ultimately distilled by the team representing the national intelligence director, who was the intelligence advisor to the president and presented the Oval Office with the president's daily brief.

Today's meeting began with a summary of threats and reports.

Lancer, who was with the National Anti-Threat Center team, did his homework and was aware of most of the threats. A few new ones, like the updated report from the State Department, got his attention.

"Foreign government intelligence and press reports indicate the recent bombing of a café in Rio de Janeiro, Brazil, was not a result of narco gang wars, as first reported. The attack is suspected to be tied to another criminal network."

There was another one from his old section, the Joint Terrorism Task Force.

"East African sources report chatter of operatives preparing to mount a 'large action.' Target and method of attack unknown."

Lancer reflected on that one as the meeting continued with other reports, including an intriguing one from the FBI.

"A forty-one-year-old male U.S. national died mysteriously aboard a Spanish passenger ship returning to Fort Lauderdale, FL, from a Caribbean cruise. Cause and manner unknown. The Broward County medical examiner conducted an autopsy then alerted the CDC. CDC now investigating and accelerating testing. No other signs of illness among other passengers, nor any indication of foul play at this time. Cruise liner scrubbing entire vessel as a precaution."

Near the meeting's end, the U.S. Secret Service reiterated that there was a fifty-fifty chance that the president and first lady would be attending the Human World Conference in New York City. All advance work was continuing. It was processing some sixty individuals on its watch list and analyzing ninety-four threats, everything from a letter to the White House stating the president will die if he comes to NYC, to boasts by fringe extremists groups that they will have "martyrs" in Central Park "for the day of reckoning." The Secret Service had the security lead and was working with federal, state and local agencies.

As the meeting finished, Lancer stayed to make notes when he was approached by two CIA officials he knew: Raymond Roth and Nick Webb.

They were not smiling.

"Isn't Canada nice this time of year, Bob?" Webb asked.

Lancer knew that they were aware he'd been poking around in the CIA's backyard and had expected this.

"I'm curious," Lancer said. "Why didn't you raise Crucible at the meeting?"

"We're still working on it. There's nothing to report."

"Did you find Gretchen?"

"Stay out of the way, Bob," Roth said. "We've got this."

"I'll take that as a no."

"All we have is a few dedicated aging scientists expressing some concerns. We're looking into it," Webb said.

"I can understand why the CIA wouldn't want this little embarrassment getting out of hand—rogue former scientist, lethal top-secret experiments. It's the stuff of thrillers, movies, congressional hearings and the death of many careers."

Roth stepped into Lancer's space.

"We're on this, Bob. I think we know what constitutes a threat."

Lancer's jaw line pulsed. Roth had hit a nerve in sacred territory.

"You know, Ray, the last time I heard talk like that my wife and daughter came home to me in coffins."

"Bob, you'd be wise to stay out of our way."

He stared at Roth and Webb, the tension rising, then his cell phone vibrated and flashed with a call, cuing Roth and Webb's departure.

Lancer had a security-encrypted text. He entered his password to read the message from one of his new sources overseas.

Got new data linked to SS in D es S. Need to meet U in North Africa. Advise.

Lancer responded.

When & where?

34

Benghazi, Libya

Time was ticking down on Dr. Gretchen Sutsoff.

After launching her experiment against the cruise ship passenger, she flew to Libya to confront the angry leaders of her inner group.

The secret meeting was at the new National General People's University. Drake Stinson had arranged it with the help of Professor Ibrahim Jehaimi, one of her inner circle. Jehaimi had worked with Sutsoff on some sensitive projects while he'd studied in the United States. Since then, he'd remained a believer in her cause.

The university's campus featured a vast palm-lined water mall that was deserted today, for Jehaimi had scheduled the meeting on Saturday evening when few students were present. Stinson's private security teams were positioned throughout the building. The meeting took place in a room within the engineering department where Sutsoff sat patiently at a boardroom table.

As Stinson and Jehaimi ushered the members of her inner circle to their seats, Sutsoff surveyed their faces: General Dimitri, who once led the corrupt intelligence agency of a former Soviet Republic; then Goran, the unshaven man in torn jeans, who operated a global human trafficking network out of Istanbul. There was Reich, the man in the tailored suit who headed a web of criminal corporations out of Zurich;

and Downey, the well-built man who was an international arms dealer from Newark.

"You know, Doctor—" Goran, the trafficker, scratched his whiskers then studied his fingertips "—there are people who want you dead for failing to deliver on your promises."

"Such a shortsighted view," Sutsoff said. "It will guarantee our failure when all I require is a little more time to ensure our success."

She put up with this unholy alliance because each member provided resources she needed for her work.

"How much time before we see results?" Reich asked.

"Soon."

"You've been saying that for weeks," Downey said.

"We've been pouring money into your secret tests that we know nothing about. When are we going to see a return?" Reich asked.

"Stinson told you of security breaches in Brazil, Dar es Salaam and other places," General Dimitri said.

"It's your job to take care of them," Sutsoff said.

"We have, but the longer this takes, the greater our vulnerability."

Goran the trafficker scowled at Sutsoff. "I don't like what I'm hearing, Doctor. My people don't like it. We want results now!"

"I've told you, the prototype's been launched," she said. "Watch for news reports. Watch how they'll scramble. Every indication points to a successful outcome. All that remains is for me to obtain the key component to strengthen our formula, then initiate the last stages to activation. I leave tomorrow to personally oversee the final part of the operation."

"You haven't told us what the ultimate target is," the general said.

"The Human World Conference in New York City."

"That's just over a week away. Will you be ready?" Downey asked.

"Yes," Sutsoff said. "That's when E.D. will demonstrate its power to reshape human destiny. The return on your investment will exceed anything you could ever imagine."

Goran smiled.

"Now, Drake, if you will." Sutsoff nodded and Stinson began removing the cork from a dark bottle and pouring its contents into six glasses. "My apologies to our host for violating local custom with this wine, but I picked up a lovely red in Paris and I believe we must toast destiny."

Jehaimi checked his cell phone then excused himself from the room, making Sutsoff curious as to why he was leaving just as all the men joined her in raising their glasses. Each of them drank; however, Sutsoff's glass held wine from a different bottle.

As each of the men swallowed his wine, Sutsoff smiled.

"Now, if you'll allow me to say good evening, I'd like to head back to my hotel. I have an early flight."

Sutsoff had started down the corridor but was halted by the sound of footfalls of several people approaching. It appeared to be an entourage. Jehaimi was among them, walking beside a large man in a white suit. "Doctor," Jehaimi said, "allow me to introduce Shokri Kusa, senior science advisor to the colonel, he flew up from Tripoli."

"I was in Surt, actually." Kusa's bored eyes fell on her. "Jehaimi speaks highly of you." Sutsoff had been promised privacy. She shot Jehaimi a look of betrayal as Kusa continued. "I've been on the phone to the colonel telling him about your research. He'd like to meet you and invites you to be his dinner guest in Surt tomorrow."

Sutsoff stretched her neck to see something behind Kusa, beyond his entourage. Her attention was drawn to a man in his late twenties wearing a wrinkled navy suit. He had his eyes fixed on them from far across the hall, watching as Stinson and the others exited the meeting room to join them. The man in the suit aimed something at them, then hurried off.

"Sorry, that man there—" Sutsoff said "—he took our

picture!" Kusa, Jehaimi and Stinson looked to where she was pointing. "The young man in the blue suit heading down the hall! Ibrahim, do you see him?"

Jehaimi shouted something to two university security guards among the entourage who spoke into their walkie-talkies.

"Drake," Sutsoff said into his ear, "do something!"

"I'm on it. We've got our people here." Stinson fished into his pocket for his cell phone. "Clay? Yes, did you see that? White male, late twenties, dark blue suit. He was headed to the west doors."

"Excuse me, everyone, but I must leave," Sutsoff said. "I have an early flight in the morning. Ibrahim, thank you. Mr. Kusa, please pass my regrets to the colonel. I have to decline the honor. I have pressing matters I must take care of. Ibrahim, can you show me another exit and have my driver meet me there now?"

"By all means. I don't know how this happened."

Sutsoff leaned to Stinson's ear.

"Find that fucker and deal with him, Drake."

35

Benghazi, Libya

Adam Corley knew he was being followed.

Voices echoed behind him as he headed down an empty hall and into an elevator, relieved he was alone.

Six floors to the lobby and the exit—he had to work fast.

He turned on his camera to check the images he'd captured of Drake Stinson, ex-CIA, and Dr. Auden, the scientist, along with other players.

Jesus, it was true. This was huge.

The information Corley's group had received from their friends in Rio de Janeiro and the Bahamas was dead on. It was another critical piece that brought them closer to putting this file together.

He had to alert headquarters.

He stopped the elevator on the third floor, stepped into an empty classroom and pressed his director's cell phone number, praying that the call would work. After several moments of static, the line crackled and his call was answered in London.

"Pritchett."

"Oliver, it's Corley in Benghazi."

"How did it go?"

"Fantastic." Corley heard the distant slam of doors, voices. "I don't have much time. I'll back things up the usual way."

"Can you give me a quick summary?"

"Our Brazilian links are definitely tied to other tentacles of the trafficking ring. Our university source here passed me tons of new data out of Tanzania, the U.S., everywhere. It's incredible. I've got too much to send you now. I'll go through it and send you my report when I get to Rabat."

Corley heard voices getting nearer and hurried his call.

"Oliver, children are being stolen around the world, but there's a rumor that it's all linked to—"

Corley stopped.

"I have to go. I'll start writing my report on the plane. I'll probably need a new cell phone and camera after this."

"Good work, Adam, be careful."

Corley dropped the phone, ground it to pieces, scooped them up and returned to the hall and elevator.

Voices called to him but he got back on the elevator, quickly dropping the fragments of his cell phone down the shaft through the small gap in the floor. As the car descended to the main lobby he double-checked his digital camera then adjusted his tie.

The doors opened to several grim-faced men in suits. One of the men had a small scar on his cheek and confronted Corley in Arabic.

"Excuse me, sir, did you just come from upstairs?"

"Yes," Corley said.

"Your identification, please?"

Corley handed him his cards and passport.

The men passed them to each other. Some of them took notes, while others spoke quietly into cell phones and radios.

"You were born in Dublin, Ireland, and reside in Morocco. What is your business there and here in Benghazi, sir?"

"I'm an international student at Mohammed V University in Rabat. I'm a doctoral candidate, completing my PhD. I was invited by professors here at the university to attend the Clean Water Symposium."

Corley tapped a folded letter of invitation tucked in his passport. The other men who were still scrutinizing his identification and talking into their cell phones eyed Corley coldly.

"We have reports that a man matching your description took unauthorized photographs," said the man with the scarred cheek.

"Yes. It was me. I was unaware of any restrictions."

"It is a serious matter."

"Look, what I did is harmless. I have a small internal newsletter for international students studying global warming. I was taking photos for it."

"Whose photo?"

"I saw an entourage and thought that it was the colonel."

"May we see your camera?"

Corley passed it to the man, who asked him to display the pictures. Corley clicked through them.

"We'll have to confiscate your camera."

"Confiscate it? Are you joking? That camera was a gift."

"We are keeping it, sir. Do you have a cell or mobile phone?"

"No."

"Then you don't mind if we search you?"

"Search me?" Corley hoped he conveyed the right amount of indignation. "This is outrageous."

"Sir, may we have your jacket?"

Corley scowled and slid it off.

He watched them place his personal items on a desk—keys, hotel key card, cash, air ticket back to Morocco. They looked through his wallet at everything, checking and double-checking, as others patted him down.

"This is insulting. I'm going to write to the secretary, the ministry of education and call my embassy."

When the security men were satisfied, they allowed Corley to collect his items and leave, but without his camera. He inhaled deeply as he stepped into the clear evening air, catching breezes rolling in from the Mediterranean Sea.

He hailed a taxi, trying to focus on getting the hell out of Libya and getting all of his new information to London. He needed to check out of his hotel and get to the airport. He had a long flight across the top of Africa. He'd start writing his full report on the plane.

Christ, it was true. This was huge.

Children were being stolen around the world by a global trafficking ring and he had more information and now pictures of the key players. Corley inspected the back of his tie, checking the tiny memory card, the backup he'd affixed to his tie clip.

It was all there.

He was free and clear, he thought, as the lights of Benghazi flowed by.

36

Los Angeles, California

Emma Lane looked at the woman in the mirror.

She stared into her red-rimmed eyes, at the tiny ridges on her cheeks and hair that needed to be brushed.

Was she crazy for what she was about to do?

Emma searched her room. She was in the same hotel that she and Joe had used when they came to the fertility clinic two years ago, *after making the biggest decision of their lives.*

She was terrified then.

"Why are you afraid?" Joe had asked her.

"What if it doesn't work? What if we never have a baby?"

"It's going to work out."

He took her in his arms and her fear melted because she believed him.

It was going to work out. It had to work out.

And it did.

It worked out beautifully, until the day her world exploded.

Emma sat on the bed.

She ached for Joe. She needed him now, because here she was, back where their dream began, fighting her way alone through a nightmare. *Your baby is not dead!* the mystery caller from California had said. *Your baby is alive.* Emma had replayed that call a million times as her determination battled her doubt.

"Am I doing the right thing, Joe? Will I find Tyler? God, I miss you both so much it hurts."

As Emma looked around her empty room, a wave of encouragement passed through her. She ran her hands over her face, collected herself, and considered her situation since leaving Wyoming.

She'd left a note for her aunt and uncle on the kitchen table at her house in Big Cloud. "Don't worry. I'll be all right. This is something I have to do." She'd taken out several thousand dollars in cash from the bank, left her phone and credit cards behind. She did not want anyone to find her.

Or stop her.

She stood, went back to the mirror and summoned the will to apply a little eye shadow and a bit of cover-up. After she finished getting dressed, she called a cab.

The Golden Dawn Fertility Corporation was on West Olympic Boulevard, about a mile from the Staples Center. It occupied the third floor of a three-story rectangle of dark green glass that reflected the McDonald's and 7-Eleven across the street. The reception area was finished with a soft pink-blue-and-yellow floral pattern. Emma thought she detected a hint of baby powder in the air.

"May I help you?" said the young woman at the desk.

"Yes, I'm a client, Emma Lane. I'm here for Christine Eckhardt."

"Do you have an appointment?"

"No, I'm in the city on business but this is an urgent matter. Christine was our advisor. She helped us with our baby boy. I brought my files and I need to see her."

"Please, have a seat. I'll see if she's free."

The waiting area had white cushioned chairs. Family magazines with laughing babies on the covers were fanned out on the table. It had been over two years since she and Joe were here. Emma was glad she'd called earlier today to confirm that Christine Eckhardt was still at the clinic and on duty today.

"Excuse me," the receptionist said, "Chris just stepped out of a meeting. This way please."

They went down the hall to a corner office where Christine pulled her attention away from her computer monitor, closed a file and got up from her desk. Her metal bracelets clinked as she hugged Emma.

"Goodness, Emma!"

"Hello, Chris."

Christine was in her late thirties. Her hair was a bit longer but her smile was as bright as Emma remembered.

"I am so sorry about what happened, Emma," she said. "When word got to us, I didn't know what to do. My condolences, I am so sorry." Christine indicated the small sofa. "Forgive my rudeness—please wait here. It'll take me five minutes to finish up a meeting. Would you like coffee, tea, anything?"

"No, thank you."

Christine stepped into the hall. Emma overheard her telling the receptionist that she had to leave by 3:00 p.m. that day for a meeting in Pasadena. Christine's office was orderly, just as it had been when Emma was here with Joe. Christine had been so sensitive, so patient. Emma never forgot her compassion and sincerity in answering all of their questions, including the one Joe had about Christine's car.

"Is that a '68 Beetle?"

Emma almost smiled because it was still there in the same framed photo on her desk, a restored blue VW. Christine and her husband were leaning on it at the beach. "It is a '68. What can I say? I'm a child of hippie parents."

A faint chime of bracelets announced Christine's return. She closed the door and hugged Emma again before sitting on the sofa next to her.

"I am so sorry. Is there anything I can do, Emma?"

"I need your help."

"I'll do whatever I can."

"I'm not sure how much you know about what happened."

"There was a terrible accident back home in Wyoming and your husband and baby were—" Christine couldn't say *killed.*

"Yes," Emma swallowed and squeezed the tissue in her hand. "I was thrown from the car and before it caught fire I saw someone rescue Tyler from the wreckage."

A question began to take shape on Christine's face.

"But you told police? They looked into it, right?"

"They don't believe me. No one does. But it's true. I was there."

Christine hesitated. "I know."

"Besides, they never found any evidence of Tyler's re—" Emma paused. "They found no trace of him in the crash. They say he was incinerated."

"Oh, Emma."

"I don't believe it. I know what I saw that day." She stared into a crumpled tissue. "And not long ago, after I got Dr. Durbin's letter saying that he'd notified the clinic here about Tyler's death, I got a phone call in the middle of the night from a stranger, a woman. She said, 'Your baby is not dead. Your baby is alive. That's all I can tell you.' The call came from the Los Angeles area. The police looked into it, but they don't know who made it. They told me it was a wrong number and that I'd imagined the conversation, but I know what I heard and in my heart I think it has something to do with the clinic."

Emma searched Christine's eyes.

"Can you help me find out who made that call?"

"Emma, I'm sorry, I don't think I can."

"You don't know anything about it?"

Christine didn't say anything, but in her silence Emma saw unease and a flicker of knowledge, as Christine took Emma's hands and held them.

"Emma, you've been through so much. You're being

forced to bear the unbearable. It's possible that the call happened the way police have suggested, that it was a wrong number and—"

Emma pulled away. "You know more than you're telling me."

Christine cleared her throat. "I'm aware that police talked to people here about the call. We told them it couldn't have had anything to do with our business. That it did not come from the clinic. We would have no reason to make such a call."

Emma turned away, her shoulders sagging with disappointment.

"You've been under so much strain from this horrible accident that it's likely the call was a wrong number, and you thought you heard something that was never said."

Emma shook her head and bit back on her tears.

"Is there someone I can call for you?" Christine asked.

"No." Emma found her composure, straightened her shoulders. "I just thought you could help me. I'm sorry to have taken up your time."

"Emma."

She left the building and walked, block after block without a destination, struggling not to think as her sense of defeat grew, until it was nearly crushing her. Somewhere near the Staples Center she waved down a cab.

"Just drive me to a beach, please. Any beach."

What was she going to do now?

Dark clouds were gathering.

As she sat on the beach for the rest of the morning and early afternoon, watching waves roll over the sand, she realized there was no turning back. She had to see this through. *Trust your gut feelings,* she told herself, as she kept returning to that telling moment when Christine's eyes had betrayed her deception.

She knows, dammit. She knows more about the call.

Maybe she knows where my baby is?

Thunder grumbled in the distance as Emma left the beach, walking to a strip mall where she got another taxi and headed back to West Olympic and the clinic. It was 2:40 p.m. Christine had said she needed to leave by three today. Emma didn't enter the building. Instead, she walked to the rear and inventoried the parking lot for a blue VW bug just as thunder crashed and the sky released a downpour.

As she ran to the side of the building, she glimpsed Christine dashing to her car with her briefcase over her head. Emma ran after her through the lot. She was drenched when she tapped on the driver's side window.

Christine lowered it, concerned.

"You scared me!"

"I know you lied to me today."

"Come on, get in out of the rain."

She hurried to the passenger door and climbed inside. The motor idled and the wipers snapped back and forth.

"You, of all people, should tell me the truth. I deserve to know."

"I understand your pain. You're suffering post-traumatic—"

Emma slammed her palms on the dash.

"Stop it!"

Christine flinched.

"I just want the truth!"

Christine stared at the rain bleeding on her windshield for a full minute then killed the motor. She gripped the wheel, inhaled and turned to Emma.

"I've worked at this clinic for ten years. I believe we do good work. You know we do."

"Chris, I'm begging you!"

"For a long time, one of our lab workers had been overwhelmed with personal problems. Recently she became unstable. We had to let her go."

"Did she make the call?"

"I don't know. She's called a few people late at night, crying, making no sense. But I doubt she called clients. We have no proof whatsoever—that's why we didn't tell police. Because she's not employed by the lab anymore, we didn't want it to reflect on the lab, and it has nothing, absolutely nothing to do with our clinic."

"I want to talk to her."

"I don't think that will help you. You need to go home to Wyoming."

"I need to talk to her."

"Emma, she's going through all kinds of trouble."

"Did she have access to all the client files?"

Christine said nothing.

"Chris! Did she have access to all the files when she worked here?"

"Yes."

"Do you want me to start a civil action against the clinic?"

"Emma."

"Chris, I'm begging you to help me! I need to hear her voice to decide if she made the call."

Christine bit her bottom lip and stared through her windshield.

"Chris, my husband died beside me! I saw someone take our son! *For Christ's sake, will you help me?*"

"Her name is Polly Larenski. She lives in Santa Ana."

37

Gannon gazed out upon the silver wing against blue sky as his jetliner sailed over the Atlantic, bound for London at 550 miles an hour.

It felt as if his life was moving at the same speed.

When he'd returned to the WPA headquarters in Manhattan two days ago, he'd landed in the middle of high-level crossfire. Melody Lyon had ordered him to her office, where she was advising George Wilson that she was dispatching Gannon to London.

"London?" Wilson said. "The guy was a disaster in Brazil—he's not ready for international assignments. And you want to send him to London based on a flimsy lead? Let our people over there check it out."

"It has to be Jack. His source will only meet with him because of the people he met in Rio," Lyon said.

"Look." Wilson turned to Gannon. "You got lucky and I'm glad you're still alive—the last thing we needed was another staff funeral—but you need more domestic experience. Keep him here on desk duty, Mel. Sending him to England, or anywhere right now, is a mistake."

"He's on to something that may be tied to the bombing," Lyon said. "I want him on this. And, I want the support of our London bureau, George, even if it means staying out of his way."

Wilson took stock of Gannon, shaking his head at the bruises on his face as if they were badges of incompetence.

"You're the boss, Mel. I'll warn Ian and Miranda at the bureau. Gannon, try not get arrested, beaten up or taken hostage. Try being a reporter like you were in Buffalo. Only better."

After Wilson left, Lyon said, "Don't mind him. We're still raw after losing Marcelo and Gabriela."

"I know."

"How are you holding up, Jack? Are you sure you're up to this?"

"I'll be okay."

She gave him a large brown envelope.

"Now, it's not a requirement for Americans entering Britain," she said, "but get over to our travel doctor on Broadway and get your main shots. Rachel has set it up. I want you prepared for anything. This envelope has money and other things for you. Rachel's got you on an early flight out of JFK to Heathrow tomorrow."

"Okay."

"Ever been to London?"

"Nope."

Gannon turned from the plane's window. His arm still aching from his shots, he lowered the metal tray, switched on his laptop and reviewed his files. Maria Santo's friend, Sarah Kirby, had put him in touch with Oliver Pritchett in London. He headed Equal Globe International, the human rights group they had been working with. Pritchett knew more about the human trafficking situation. He'd agreed to share information, but his responses to Gannon's e-mailed questions were clear.

I will only meet you alone and face-to-face in London. It will be completely off the record, but I assure you it will be significant. I give you my word you are the only journalist who knows of this case and I will not speak to any other news organization.

Gannon studied the notes on his laptop until metropolitan London sprawled below. He recognized the Thames just as the landing gear lowered and locked into position. At Heathrow, a young British Customs officer, curious about Gannon's bruises, accepted his explanation about his ordeal in Brazil.

"I trust you won't have any similar problems in the U.K."

It took Gannon's taxi a little under an hour to slice through traffic and get him to the WPA's London bureau on Norwich Street.

It was situated in a six-story stone building built on the site of a bakery destroyed by Nazi bombs during the Second World War. It was a five-minute walk from Fleet Street, now the address of more law and business offices than newspapers. But the Associated Press and other foreign wire services were nearby, reminding Gannon that the risk of losing the story increased as time ticked by. The bureau was on the first floor and the reception desk was empty. A man in a suit came from an office to place a folder on it.

"Excuse me." Gannon set his luggage aside. "Jack Gannon from WPA New York. I'm looking for Ian Shelton?"

"You've found him." Shelton shook Gannon's hand. He was a tall, gaunt man in his thirties. "Welcome to London. George Wilson advised us that you were coming to work on your Brazil story."

"That's right."

"I take it you had quite a drama in Rio's slums, judging from your face."

"A little bit."

"Dangerous stuff, given what happened to our friends there. Why don't you let us help you here, Jack? We do know something about the U.K., enough to ensure you aren't taken hostage."

"Thank you. I'm good right now."

"I see. George called you a lone wolf, or some such thing."

"I'm sure he did. Ian, what I'd like to do is get a hot shower. New York said that after I checked in here, the bureau would have a hotel for me?"

"Yes." Shelton searched the top of the vacant desk, finding an envelope with Gannon's name on it. "You said you need to be in Kensington. We've got you at the Seven Seas, in Kensington, Earl's Court, on our account. Not as close to the bureau as we'd hoped, sorry."

"Thank you." Gannon tucked the envelope into his bag.

"Call us if there's anything we can do," Shelton said.

During the cab ride Gannon reflected on what Melody Lyon had said when she hired him—how she'd warned him to expect tension, even resentment, if he were sent to help out at the international bureaus.

"They're turf-protectors. They consider anything and anyone from headquarters a challenge to their expertise about their coverage area."

She was right about that, he thought, as he reached his stop. The Seven Seas Inn was a town-house hotel, a four-level building attached to other four-level buildings that, together, resembled wedding-cake layers where Penywern Road led to the gentle curves of Eardley Crescent.

Gannon's room was the equivalent of a cramped closet with frayed carpet. It was on the third floor, overlooking the street. He started his laptop and sent Oliver Pritchett an e-mail telling him he had arrived. Then he showered. He was unpacking when Pritchett called.

"Trust you had a safe trip."

"It was all right."

"Fancy a walk to our office, then?"

Using his map to follow Pritchett's directions, it took Gannon thirty minutes to walk along Earl's Court Road to Kensington and a side street, Stafford Terrace. Equal Globe

International's nameplate was on a battered red door, shoe-horned between Mae's Flower Shop and First-Rate Tuxedo Rentals. Gannon pressed the button for EGI, and the inter-com buzzed. He looked into the small security camera, held up his WPA ID and said, "Jack Gannon, WPA New York."

"Right," Pritchett said and the door clicked.

Gannon climbed the staircase to a second floor, where he could hear music turned low. "I Don't Like Mondays," the old Boomtown Rats song.

"Oliver Pritchett," said the man waiting at the top of the stairs.

Pritchett had a full salt-and-pepper beard, small round wireless glasses and long silver hair tied in a ponytail. He wore sandals, torn faded jeans and a T-shirt with the face of an emaciated child with huge pleading eyes, under the words Don't Let Another One Die.

Gannon followed him into an office that had a hardwood floor and wooden tables cluttered with computers, and tow-ers of newspapers, books and reports alongside walls pa-pered with posters of Live Aid, protests, starving children, children toiling in sweatshops and prisoners facing torment. Pritchett shoved some files into a faded military canvas shoulder bag, then snatched his keys and a cell phone.

"We'll talk in the park."

A few blocks later they arrived at Holland Park, a glori-ous field of tranquil green space. They sat on a bench. Across the pathway a white-haired man was reading a news-paper. Pritchett waited for a couple conversing in German and pushing a stroller to pass before speaking.

"Sarah's team in Rio said we could trust you, Jack."

"I won't run anything based on information your group provides until we're both comfortable with it."

Pritchett considered the situation.

"Why don't you tell me about Equal Globe International and what you think you're on to?"

"Give you my spiel?" Pritchett looked off to the trees.

"Beyond what's on your Web site."

"We're an ideal really. We hold dear the belief that everyone is equal and we strive to make it a reality. EGI is an umbrella of social justice organizations around the planet—church groups, charities, labor groups, student associations. We fight injustice in all its manifestations—poverty, hunger, crime, war. We lobby governments. We are on the front lines. We issue reports and, well, lately we gather intelligence on acts of injustice and all that they entail."

"That's what Maria Santo was doing in Rio de Janeiro?"

Pritchett removed his glasses and pinched the bridge of his nose.

"She was brave. We think she was the target of the café bombing in Brazil because she'd infiltrated the law firm, Worldwide Rio Advogados. You see we had long suspected that firm of illegal activity around the world—money laundering, bribery, police corruption. Their activities seemed to escalate. Maria worked at getting a job inside, then started sending us reports, files."

"And you found a link to something bigger?"

"It's complicated. Very complicated. But some of her files seem tied to what we were getting from another EGI worker, Adam Corley. He thought there was a link to a vast and organized human trafficking network."

"Wait, who is Adam Corley?"

"Adam is Irish, an ex-cop from Dublin who'd worked in the Irish Garda's Special Branch as a low-ranking security and intelligence officer. When his wife died suddenly of a brain tumor, he left his career, devoted himself to his church and pursued a PhD in humanities abroad."

"So how did he come to work with your group?"

"Through his church's global charity network. When Corley learned of us and what we did, he volunteered. He gathers intelligence. He's one of our best people."

"And he thinks Worldwide Rio Advogados is involved in a global child-stealing operation that involves illegal adoptions?"

"Yes, but he thinks there's more. Recently Corley got word of a private meeting of traffickers and their associates in Libya. He managed to observe the players and obtain more intelligence. He now believes the child-stealing network is tied to something bigger."

"What could be bigger than stealing children for illegal adoptions?"

"Corley thinks there's a purpose."

"Money, I would think."

"No, bigger."

"Like what?"

"Not sure, but he hinted that there were scary elements lurking in the shadows. He was pressing his sources and hoping to learn more for a detailed report he's preparing for us. We may take it to a special committee on human trafficking at the United Nations."

"I need to talk to Corley."

"I've arranged it. He's agreed to talk to you."

"Can we do it tonight?"

"No. This is very dangerous. Adam's convinced that the people behind it are vigilant. He insisted on a face-to-face meeting with you."

"Fine, where is he?"

"Rabat, Morocco."

"Morocco? I'll get my bureau to get an airline ticket and a visa for me."

"Contact me when you get there, then Adam will get in touch with you."

When he returned to his hotel, Gannon alerted Lyon in New York about what he'd learned from EGI and that he'd gotten a lead that required him to go to Morocco.

"It's a good thing you got your shots. I'll authorize the travel and get the London bureau to get you a ticket and visa as soon as possible," she said, adding, "We want this story, but I need you to be very careful given all that's happened so far."

"I know."

"That means no more risks, Jack. We've lost too much already."

"Melody, this story was a risk from the get-go."

38

The sound of seat belts unbuckling filled the cabin as Gannon's Air France flight came to a stop at Salé International Airport.

He tried to concentrate on the job ahead but was haunted by what happened in Brazil. He didn't want to go through anything like that again.

Was he losing his nerve? Or should he chalk it up to jet lag?

Exiting the terminal, he jettisoned his doubts and got into a cab to his hotel. Rabat was Morocco's capital, and the World Press Alliance had a one-person bureau here. But the bureau chief was on assignment in Tangier.

Gannon was on his own, which made him a little nervous. Rabat was not as big as Casablanca, but terrorism in this region remained a security concern because extremist groups had taken up the cause of al Qaeda. His face was still bruised and he was still shaky from his ordeal with the Blue Brigade in Rio de Janeiro.

He looked out at the city with its modern buildings, mosques, markets and ancient tombs. Feather duster palms lined the main thoroughfares. His hotel, the Orange Tree, was on Rue Abderrahmanne El Ghafiki, in the district of Agdal, Rabat's center.

Gannon checked in, then, as he had in London, he

e-mailed Oliver Pritchett with his hotel information, confirming he'd arrived and was ready to meet Adam Corley as soon as possible.

Gannon then went online and searched for developments on the café bombing. Reuters and the Associated Press had each moved items reporting that while no arrests had been made, police had all but ruled out narco gangs. These were obvious follow-ups to his WPA story. It meant the competition was inching closer to his trail.

The phone in his room rang.

"Jack Gannon."

"Corley. Got your message from Pritchett. Are you familiar with Rabat?"

"No, it's my first visit."

"We'll meet in the medina, when the call to prayer ends in one hour."

"The medina?"

"It's the market in the old city. We'll meet at a little place called the Sun and Moon. Its on Rue des Consuls. Directions are tricky, get the hotel people to get you a map. Be there in one hour."

"Why not meet here, or at your location?"

"I ran into trouble in Benghazi. I'd prefer to be cautious. I've got your mobile number, here's mine."

Gannon noted Corley's number then asked, "How will I know you?"

"I've got your picture online, so I'll recognize you."

Before going out, Gannon shut down his laptop, tidied his files, then hid them in his room. The concierge was happy to sketch directions for him on a preprinted tourist map. "Very simple. This way, then that way, sir, simple, and you are at the Sun and Moon. Very simple, sir."

To Gannon, Rabat's medina was a step back in time. As he followed a network of cobblestoned streets, he saw a group of boys roasting a goat's head on an open grill. Artisans displayed their handmade wallets, necklaces, lanterns and wood carvings on mats on the ground.

Small cooking fires created haze and seasoned the air. He saw old men bent over antique sewing machines under bare lightbulbs inside storefronts hidden in the market's shaded narrow alleyways. The medina was choked with people, haggling at stalls and shops over jewelry, leather crafts, vegetables, fruit, pottery, baskets and carpets.

The Sun and Moon was a darkened open-front café with six tables and a counter displaying meats, mixed salad and rice dishes, fish and pastries. Gannon ordered a Coke. He pressed the sweating can to his forehead and sipped slowly.

By the time he'd ordered his third Coke, Corley had still not arrived. The calls Gannon had made to his cell phone had not been answered.

He was hungry and ordered a chicken shawarma.

As time passed he was approached by boys offering to give him private tours of the medina, or find him drugs or women. A withered man with an agitated monkey in a cage offered to have his animal perform tricks for him. A one-eyed beggar with rotting teeth put his hands together in an elaborate thankful prayer gesture after Gannon gave him a coin.

Nearly three hours later as the sun sank, Corley was a no-show.

Gannon gave up waiting. He returned to his hotel, where he sent Oliver Pritchett a terse e-mail before reviewing his files in bed.

Gannon did not remember falling asleep.

For a panicked moment he did not remember anything and his torpid brain struggled to give him information as his phone rang.

"Hullo."

"Jack, Oliver Pritchett in London."

Gannon's memory ignited and he recalled his anger.

"Hey!" He sat up, cradling his head with his free hand. "What the hell's going on? Your guy stood me up! The WPA spent a shitload of money to send me to London then here, and Corley doesn't show!"

"I don't know what to tell you. Maybe something came up. This is unlike Adam. I can't reach him."

"So what now?"

"I'm going to do something we never do with our people."

"I'm waiting."

"I'll give you his private address. You can go bang on his door."

"That's a start."

Gannon ordered a small breakfast to his room, showered and shaved. When his breakfast arrived he ate as he dressed, then got a taxi.

According to Pritchett, Corley lived on a tiny side street off of Rue Calcutta, in the district l'Océan, not far from the Kasbah des Oudaias.

The neighborhood was quiet.

Gannon asked his driver to wait, then walked down the narrow zigzagging street. It was a bright, clear morning.

The quarter was deserted; the only sounds gulls overhead. The ancient square houses were small, neat, built of stone. Many had parapets. They were painted white with blues, pinks and greens, their windows covered with wrought-iron bars. Some had flower boxes and planters with palms near the entrance. Others had rooftop gardens or clotheslines laden with garments drying in the sun.

A gull shrieked just as Gannon reached Corley's address: number 104, a small white house trimmed in coral-pink. He knocked on the wooden door, dark and heavy with its ornate design. A full minute passed without a response. He knocked again, harder this time.

Nothing.

He pressed his ear to it.

Nothing.

He tried to look through the windows, but the ironwork

made it difficult. He went around to a small sun-warmed patio. Fragrant from the dozen or so flower boxes, the patio gave him a view over rooftops to the sea.

When Gannon came to the back door he stopped.

It was slightly open.

What the hell?

He blinked, thinking. Then he leaned into the doorway. "Hello!"

The weather-worn door creaked as he pushed it open to a small kitchen. It was clean with a sand-colored linoleum floor, white shelves, white tiled walls and a gas stove.

"Adam!"

The house was silent as Gannon continued to the living room. Two small sofas with print designs faced each other over a coffee table. Everything was bathed in yellow from the sunlight filtered by the closed yellow curtains.

Everything was in place. He checked the bedroom, the single bed, the quilted spread, the desk, dresser, goatskin lampshade. All in order and tinted blue from blue curtains.

"Adam?"

Gannon moved on to the bathroom.

At least that's what he figured the next room to be, given the white door was ajar and he glimpsed a mirror. As he reached out his hand to open the door, he hesitated.

The house was too still.

He swallowed.

As he slowly pushed the door open, a prickly sensation shot up the back of his neck. A shoed foot was hanging over the lip of the bathtub. He then saw a hand, an arm, blood splattered over the white tiles, before he met Adam Corley's eyes.

Staring into him from a wide-eyed death mask.

A sound.

Something moved fast behind Gannon.

39

Somewhere in Morocco

Nearly two hours outside of Rabat a convoy sped along a dirt road, cutting across a vast stretch of forgotten territory.

The sun hit the chrome on the first two cars; both were government-owned Peugeot sedans out of Temara. The last vehicle was a late model Mercedes-Benz G-Wagen that had been dispatched out of Ain Aouda. Only a few of the men involved were members of the DST—Direction de la Sécurité du Territoire—the Moroccan secret police.

No one knew the identities of the others.

Dust clouds billowed from their trail, forming a rising curtain that concealed their destination and intention.

The man lying on the back floor of the G-Wagen, under a canvas tarp, stripped naked, shackled and blindfolded was Jack Gannon. His brain throbbed and his mouth tasted as if it had been stuffed with burlap and he recalled an overwhelming smell.

Chloroform?

The last thing he remembered was discovering Adam Corley's corpse amid a bloodbath in his Rabat home.

Gannon forced himself to cling to the drone of the wheels, to breathe deeply and calmly. He concentrated on the murmur of French coming from his captors at the front of the vehicle. He tried to pick up any information, a tone, a word he might know.

A cell phone rang, and the man who answered spoke in a language Gannon didn't recognize. The vehicle slowed to a halt, and he heard muted shouting through the closed windows. Dread gnawed at the edges of his mind and he tried not to imagine what awaited him.

Had he been able to see through his blindfold he would have discerned the high chain-link fence topped with razor wire securing the low building, which was half-submerged in the earth. It was a secret facility that did not exist. Not officially. In intelligence circles, it was known as a black prison.

For several years, the building had received suspected terrorists transported on ghost flights from countries that denied knowledge of activities conducted within its walls. It was undocumented work performed by contractors expert at obtaining information from any resistant subjects delivered to them. Some of the interrogators had extracted intelligence on the attacks in Casablanca, Madrid, London, Bali and on September 11. They had also thwarted a number of planned attacks that remained unknown to the world beyond its barbed-wire gates.

A sudden blast of 110-degree heat overwhelmed the SUV's air-conditioned interior as the doors were opened.

Gannon was yanked out.

Stones pricked his bare feet and the ground burned his soles as he hobbled with his captors a short distance before they pushed him indoors. The air was cooler but he was nearly overcome by the stench of urine and excrement. The drone of flies was alarming and he feared he was among corpses. As Gannon was shoved along the building's reeking corridors, he found his voice.

"I'm an American citizen. I want to call my embassy."

A sharp pain exploded in his buttocks from the kick of a large steel-toed boot. Gannon's knees buckled and he was dragged into another room.

Distant shouting and screams echoed. The floor was wet

as he was positioned with his feet spread apart. Chains clinked and steel collars were clamped to his ankles.

His plastic handcuffs were replaced with steel ones that were fastened to chains. The cuffs gouged him as his wrists were hoisted over his head. He had to stand on his toes to touch the ground.

"What have I done?"

A fist drove so fast and deep into Gannon's gut he felt his organs squeeze against his spine and reflexively vomited. The hot contents of his stomach flowed over his skin.

He wheezed through tears.

"The question for you," said a voice in English, with an accent Gannon could not identify, "and it is a question you must ask yourself, is, Are you going to cooperate with pain, or without it?"

Gannon continued gasping.

"Because in the end, you will cooperate."

For a moment, Gannon swore he heard a male American raise his voice in another room. The American sounded like he was talking urgently to someone over the phone.

"Yes! Gannon, run his name again! I need everything on him now!"

Gannon's attention shifted back to the accented voice before him.

"No one knows you are here. No one can help you. We will bury you and poof—you will vanish."

There was the snap of a lighter then the smell of a strong cigarette.

"By the time I finish my smoke, you will be broken."

A table rattled with the tinkling sounds of small metal tools on a tray.

"You can save yourself."

Gannon's stomach quaked. His arms burned.

"Did you murder Adam Corley because he knew of the operation?"

"I want," Gannon gasped. "I want to call my embassy."

Gannon's face was slapped.

"Did you murder Adam Corley because he knew of the operation?"

"No."

"What do you know of the Avenging Lions of Africa?"

"Nothing."

"What do you know of Said Salelee of Dar es Salaam?"

"Nothing."

Gannon heard a slight shuffle then felt a point of pressure under his chin. It felt like the tip of a steel blade.

"What do you know of the operation?"

"Nothing."

The blade's point traveled slowly down his throat to the center of his collarbone, tracing a pressure line without breaking the skin.

"Why did you travel to Rabat?"

"You have my passport. I'm an American journalist."

"You are lying."

"Call the World Press Alliance in New York."

"Why did you come to Rabat?"

The blade's tip traveled down Gannon's chest and over his lower stomach to the top of his groin.

"Why were you in Adam Corley's home?"

"To meet him for a story."

"A story on the operation?"

"Yes, he had information."

"What kind of information?"

"I don't know."

The blade slowed as it traveled lower.

Gannon swallowed.

His blindfold was yanked off, light burned into his face and he sensed the silhouettes of several people outlined in the darkness. Standing before him was an unshaven, swarthy, muscular man about six feet four, sweating under a sleeveless T-shirt.

He wore combat pants.

His cigarette, half gone now, sat in the corner of his mouth. He dragged heavily on it, enveloping Gannon in foul smoke. Suddenly large hands reached from behind and gripped Gannon's head. Fingers reached around to his eyes and held his lids open.

"Why were you in Adam Corley's home?"

"He never showed up for our meeting."

"You are lying. What do you know of the operation?"

The man moved his cigarette closer to Gannon's right eye until the glowing tip was all Gannon could see. It burned like the sun as the man held it to within a hair of touching him.

Gannon felt its heat.

"No, please!"

"What do you know of the operation?"

"Corley was going to tell me more. Please!"

"More about what?"

"The connection between his research and a law firm in Rio de Janeiro. The firm may be tied to a global child-smuggling network and the bombing of a café that killed ten people."

"Is it tied to the operation?"

"I don't know."

"You do know!"

"No."

"Who killed Adam Corley?"

"I don't know. He was dead when I arrived."

"You're lying!"

"No, I swear!"

"I'm finished my smoke."

The man stepped back.

"Up!"

Chains clanked.

Racking pain shot through Gannon as he was pulled up by the wrist cuffs until he was suspended inches from the floor.

He struggled to breathe.

"Now you will become intimate with agony."

40

Gannon's tormentor rolled a tray bearing a set of surgeon's instruments before him.

The man put on a blood-stained butcher's apron, a face shield and tugged on white latex gloves. Then he selected a scalpel.

Gannon's breathing quickened.

The blade reflected the light just as a commotion spilled from another room. Someone had entered but remained at the edge of the darkness.

"Major, I respectfully request you release the prisoner now," an American voice said firmly.

"On whose authority?" an older voice said.

"My people have spoken to the ministry. Here is a fax authorizing you to surrender him to me."

In the dim fringes, someone shuffled a few pages of paper.

"As you can see by the summary," the American said, "Rabat police and the pathologist confirm Corley had been deceased prior to the prisoner's arrest at Corley's residence. And witnesses confirm the prisoner's whereabouts in the market and his hotel. He could not have killed Corley."

A long tense moment passed.

"Should we obtain any further information," the American continued, "we'll share it with you."

More time passed before a voice in the darkness muttered a command. Then Gannon's interrogator grunted, the chains jangled and Gannon dropped to the floor.

He did not know how much time had passed before he was unshackled and taken to a bright, clean room. It appeared to be a medical examination room. He was left alone to take a hot shower. His body shook and he had to stop several times to lean against the wall and breathe.

He could not stop his tears.

When he finished he wrapped himself in a towel and sat on the only furniture available, a padded examination table.

What was happening?

He struggled to think.

Afterward, a doctor with white hair and a kind face under a few days of salt-and-pepper growth entered the room. Without speaking, he tended to Gannon's wounds then returned his belongings, his passport, wallet and his clothes. While the doctor watched, Gannon was allowed to dress, as if the nightmare had never happened.

Everything was intact.

Except Gannon.

He couldn't stop shaking. Tears filled his eyes.

"This will occur for some time," the doctor said in accented English. "You will experience some bad nights, bad dreams. But you will be fine, I assure you. I have seen worse." The doctor patted Gannon's shoulder compassionately before starting to leave. "Return to America immediately, if you can. Say nothing of your experience."

"Doctor?"

The older man stopped at the door.

"Where are we and who controls this place?"

"I don't know."

"Who was the man who intervened—he sounded American."

"I don't know and I don't wish to know." He removed his glasses. "I don't know anyone here. I do as I'm told since they took me from my home in Kurdistan six months ago."

After the doctor left, Gannon stared at the white cinder block walls and battled to understand what had befallen him. His emotions swirled. He was angry at the violation but thankful someone had saved him from the horror that was coming from his captor.

Don't dwell on what he was going to do with that scalpel.

Now, as Gannon tried to recover, he faced question after question.

Why was Corley murdered? What was the information Corley had about this story? Who was the American who'd intervened? What the hell is going on? Is any story worth my life?

Gannon gripped the edges of the examination table.

He would never give up. He would never surrender, being a reporter was all he was. He had nothing else in his life.

The door opened and a stranger entered: a man in his early fifties with short brown hair. His eyes were black ball bearings. They glared with an intensity that bordered on fury, above a grimace chiseled into a face of stone. He was just under six feet and wore khaki slacks and a blue golf shirt over his solid build. He held a slim binder with a file folder tucked inside. After assessing Gannon, he said: "Are you good to walk out of here?"

Gannon recognized the voice of the American who'd saved him.

"Walk to where?"

"My car. I'm taking you to your hotel so you can leave the country."

"And who are you?"

"Who I am is not important. Let's go."

The man slid on sunglasses.

His car was a white Mercedes and neither of them spoke as it rolled soothingly along the unpaved road over a sun-scorched stretch of flatland for nearly half an hour before they came to a modern highway. Gannon noticed tiny scars on the man's chin and an expression void of emotion behind his dark glasses.

"So, who are you and who are you with?" Gannon asked.

Robert Lancer looked straight ahead, considered the question and said, "I'm a U.S. agent."

"Are you FBI?"

He said nothing.

"CIA? Military?"

"It doesn't matter. What matters is you came close to serious harm."

"*Oh, you think?* Now I know firsthand what you and your ilk really do to people."

"It's not pretty but it saves lives."

"It also ruins innocent ones. I don't see how it can do any good."

The man's jaw muscles pulsed.

"Tell that to the families standing at the graves of innocent people murdered in attacks."

"What your pals did to me back there was medieval! Threaten a man with castration and he'll confess to anything."

"Let me give you some context, Jack. You're a foreign national who trespassed in the apartment of a murdered man, who happened to be a source for about six different intelligence agencies. The locals had every right to suspect you. They were just getting warmed up with you."

"By violating my human rights?"

"Look around, this is not the U.S."

"What your friends did was confirm that I've got a huge story."

"Forget your story. You have no idea how dangerous this is for you."

"Is that a threat?"

"That's advice, or did you forget I was the one who got you out of there. The situation is complicated, but let me make one thing clear. You get back to the States and you forget this. Tell your editor your story fell through."

"Fuck you!"

"Are you that stupid?"

"After what I've been through, do you really think I'm going to curl up and forget my profession? A lot of people have died for this story. Now, I'm going to report every iota of what I know and what I went through to know it, including meeting you. It seems to me that maybe a few governments have a hand in some kind of illegal crap."

"Is that what you think you have?"

"You heard it all when your pals were torturing me."

Lancer said nothing.

"Was Corley your source? Did he have information for you?"

Lancer said nothing.

Both men retreated to their thoughts as the countryside evolved into the outskirts of the capital. Gannon took note of how well this guy knew his way around the streets of Rabat. Traffic slowed them up as they entered the district of Agdal.

"When do you plan to run your story?"

"As soon as I put something together."

When they turned on to Rue Abderrahmanne El Ghafiki, Gannon began to recognize the area.

"What's your story going to say about the Rio connection to Corley?"

"What do you think?"

Lancer parked at the entrance of Gannon's hotel, the Orange Tree, shut off the motor and turned to Gannon.

"Cards on the table, Gannon?"

"Fine."

"Corley was going to help me on an investigation. Listen, it's too soon for a story. Give me your word you'll wait until we've got this thing nailed, and I'll give you mine that you will have the full story. I'll help you."

"What's the full story?"

"We've got raw intelligence of a planned attack."

"Where, when? What kind of attack?"

"We don't know yet."

"On what scale, how big?"

"Don't know that, either. That's why any premature revelations would jeopardize our investigation. A lot of people are working on this. Corley was a source and he had a thread of something with African links."

Gannon thought.

"Jack, we know you were in Rio de Janeiro and London."

"Figures. What do you know about Drake Stinson with the Rio law firm, Worldwide Rio Advogados?"

"We know that his firm is involved. That was emerging through Corley's reports and his sources in Brazil. At one time Stinson worked for the Central Intelligence Agency. We think the Rio firm and the café bombing might, stress *might,* have an African connection. Corley uncovered more about it recently."

"That's all you know?"

"It's all I can tell you."

"Who the hell are you?"

"Not important."

"I want to keep in touch."

"I have your word you'll hold off?"

"I have yours you'll help me?"

"You have it."

"And no other press are sniffing at this?"

"Is that your biggest worry?"

"No other press?"

"Just you."

"I want some ID."

The man pulled out his wallet, produced a blank card and wrote on it.

"Here's my protected number. It's good for anywhere, anytime."

"There's no name. Who are you?"

"We'll keep in touch."

"You better hope so." Gannon got out of the car.

"Jack, I'm sorry about what you went through. It was out of our control."

Gannon nodded, waved, then entered the hotel's lobby. He went to the front desk to check for messages. The clerk kept his eyes on the computer monitor and nodded. Gannon had something.

"Excuse me, sir, I'll retrieve it from storage."

Probably something from New York or London, Gannon thought. As he waited he reviewed a mental to-do list. He'd have to arrange a flight to New York, then he'd have to give Melody an update.

Should I tell her about my abduction and torture?

The clerk returned with a small brown package.

"This came for you while you were out, sir. A messenger boy brought it around the time you left the hotel."

The package bore a handwritten note.

To: Guest J. Gannon c/o the Orange Tree.
From: Adam Corley.

41

Over Africa

A lightning bolt of pain tore into Dr. Sutsoff's skull as her Alitalia airbus climbed over the Mediterranean.

Her condition had triggered an attack.

It was brought on by the throngs of passengers queued in the security lines at Tripoli International Airport where she'd boarded her connection.

People everywhere—nudging her, bumping her, intruding into her space, looking at her, talking to her, breathing on her, their skin touching hers.

She wanted to scream.

Her mouth had dried, her heartbeat soared, cutting her breath short. Talons of pain clawed down her spine to her toes, forcing her to clench her jaw, mash her knees together and grip her armrests.

She didn't need this now.

Not when she was about to commence the decisive phase of her work.

She reached for her pills, put two in her palm, swallowed them and set her head into her headrest, thankful no one was beside her. She always paid for the seat next to her, to keep anyone from getting too close.

As the plane leveled her discomfort ebbed.

Agoraphobia. Demophobia. Enochlophobia. Ochlophobia.

She knew the terms but refused to label her condition a

phobia. Her fear and loathing of crowds was not irrational. It was grounded in reality, in the old horror that was reaching for her…pulling her back….

"Gretchen! Help me! Gretchen!"

She shut her eyes, gained control of her breathing and directed her thoughts back to the time of joy in her life.

She was a happy little girl again flying above old London at night.

Flying like Peter Pan and Wendy, and dreaming of living in London with her mother, her father and little brother, Will.

But her family had to leave England. It broke her heart. Of all the cities in the world that they'd lived in, Gretchen had loved London best. On the day they packed, she cried. Her father crouched beside her and dried her tears.

"In a few years when my work is finished, we'll come back to London and we'll live here," he said.

"Promise?"

"Promise."

He'd told her that they would live in Kensington, her favorite part of the city, and later that night Gretchen had dreamed she was flying over it with her little brother.

"We're going to live here forever, Willy."

But her dream died.

Gretchen Rosamunde Sutsoff was born in Virginia where her father, Cornelius, was a scientist who'd become an American diplomat. He was a science attaché who worked with U.S. military and intelligence officials at U.S. embassies. His job meant they'd moved around the world. Every two years it seemed. They'd lived in Moscow, Tokyo, Cairo, Buenos Aires, Nairobi, London, Panama and Vridekistan.

Gretchen's mother, Katherine, was a pianist who gave lessons to students who would come to their home. "Music is the universal language. It makes words unnecessary," her mother liked to say.

Gretchen's parents loved her and Will, but they were

self-absorbed precise people whose displays of affection toward them were as rare as falling stars. The family's constant moving meant they were continually severing ties in one country while establishing new ones in another.

Gretchen and Will had no connection to any place or anybody.

Except each other.

Forever the new, strange child with the accent, Gretchen was often confused about where she belonged. She seldom made friends. Will was her best friend and she was protective of him as she sought refuge in her books, particularly books about science and the nature of life and death.

Wherever they lived, Gretchen always had the highest grades in her class. She astounded her teachers. "Your daughter is a prodigy," her instructor in Moscow said. Another teacher in London said, "We feel the term genius is appropriate. She actually pointed out two errors in the mathematics textbook."

Gretchen was ten years old when she started conducting her own research with Will as her assistant. Her parents allowed her to have a dozen white mice. While botched piano concertos sounded through their home, Gretchen tracked the life cycle of her mice, making exhaustive notes on their development, on which pairs mated, then tracing and noting characteristics of their offspring.

"Pretty cool, huh, Will?"

"Cool."

Will was in charge of naming them and would have funerals when one of them died. He cried when they buried them. Gretchen would roll her eyes. She was more concerned with her new scientific discoveries.

They were living in Africa when she experienced a prophetic incident.

At the edge of the diplomatic quarter in Nairobi, there was a dense forest. Venomous snakes were sighted there by locals. One man was bitten and died. People were warned to keep out of the woods. But Gretchen needed butterflies for one of her many studies, so one day she left school early and slipped into the forest.

She had entered a darkened section. As birds screeched, she began searching. It was not long before she came upon a rare Taita blue-banded swallowtail on a broad leaf. Withdrawing a wide-mouth jar from her satchel, she inched it into position when she heard a moan.

She turned and saw a muddied stream flowing over a boulder.

That's what it looked like.

She gasped. Gooseflesh rose on her arms.

The stream was a moving river of ants: millions, maybe billions of them. The ant-covered lump—judging from the single fear-filled eye staring from it and the protruding tongue—was a dog, panting in the throes of death.

The ants had attacked en masse. Devouring the dog alive.

Horrified, Gretchen was transfixed.

She was fascinated by the idea of the sheer terror of knowing that you could be helpless to battle the consuming force that is slowly killing you.

She ran home with the image seared in her mind.

"Gretchen! Help me! Gretchen!"

The flight attendant touched her shoulder.

"Please move your seat forward. We're landing in Casablanca."

Relief.

Casablanca's Mohammed V International was not busy when Dr. Sutsoff arrived. She had time for a light lunch, a salad, cheese and tea. She checked her encrypted e-mail for a status report from her support team.

"All is ready. We await your arrival, Doctor."

Good, she thought, boarding her connection, a 737 operated by Royal Air Maroc. During the six-hour flight, she read over her files and napped until images of her brother, her mother and father drove her from sleep.

When she was fourteen, her parents had sent her to boarding school in Lucerne, Switzerland.

"It will be hard," her father said, "but the Lucerne boarding school is one of the best. It'll give you a solid foundation for any college."

Gretchen's perfect grades had attracted the attention of Harvard, Berkeley, Oxford and La Sorbonne in Paris. The only thing she loved more than her studies was getting letters from Will. She often traced her fingers over his cheerful handwriting. She could hear his voice, see his smile.

Hi Gretchie,
Have you discovered the cure for everything yet? Guess what!? Since we moved to Vridekistan, football, or what they call soccer in America, is my new passion. It's the biggest sport in the world, you know! Dad takes me to games. Vridekistan's team could qualify for the World Cup. They have a match coming up against the powerhouse team from Iran. It's going to be historic! Dad's got tickets and says we can all go when you come home to visit next week. Say you will come! It will be loads of fun!
Love,
Will

He made her laugh.

Of course she would go to the game. But she doubted her mother would go. Gretchen could understand her father's interest in football. He enjoyed sports. But she could not envision her mother, the refined pianist, among the hordes of sports fanatics. That's why Gretchen's jaw dropped when she agreed to go.

"It will be exciting. A chance for a family outing," her mother said.

The match was held at the national stadium, a monstrous multitiered facility with a capacity for 102,000 spectators. The game was critical to the country's spirit, according to the president, who declared a national holiday. The newspapers reported that officials were expecting huge overflow crowds and Gretchen's father insisted they leave hours before the start.

Traffic jammed the streets to the stadium, so the family abandoned their cab, joined the crowds walking to the stadium and managed to get to their seats ninety minutes before the match started.

The colorful pregame events energized the fans. Emotion electrified the air. Thunder exploded when the national team took to the field. A few seconds passed before Gretchen realized it was fanatical cheering. Flags waved everywhere amid the oceans of people, and battle hymns were sung in unison while the Iranian players were jeered and bombarded with rotting fruit. The mass of humanity roared with such intensity the entire stadium trembled. Gretchen saw unease cloud her mother's face.

Will was enraptured and he joined the chanting, which did not relent, even when the match started.

The first half of the game was controlled by Iran, which had scored two goals. A man sitting near Gretchen and her father was also listening to the game on his radio and said there were reports of huge crowds, maybe another 250,000 people, surrounding the stadium. They were angry the national team was losing and were demanding entry to the game.

Police had locked all the gates.

"It's madness."

Inside, the disappointed stadium crowd tossed trash onto the field, forcing stadium crews to turn hoses on the unruly sections.

Gretchen heard her mother shout into her father's ear.

"I have a bad feeling," she said. "I think we should leave now."

"I was thinking the same," he said, then shouted to Will and Gretchen. "This place is getting dicey. We're going to make our way to the exit, now."

"But, Dad!" Will protested.

"Now, Will!"

The family threaded their way toward their gate. It was difficult because every inch of the stadium was crammed. They were about halfway to their exit, south gate 48, when the national team scored its first goal, igniting an ear split-ting frenzy and the stadium shook. Will joined the celebra-tion, jumping up and down.

The goal detonated waves of jubilation among the crowds outside the stadium. Enthralled, they began surging toward the locked gate, pressing at every point while security peo-ple tried to repel them. At west gate 56, the crowds broke through and desperate police began firing tear gas at the crowds outside the gates, but winds blew it back into the jammed walkways.

Confusing police radio signals were misunderstood and officers at every gate began firing tear gas into the crowds, filling the walkways at every gate, including south gate 48, where Gretchen and her family were stuck in their struggle to get out of the stadium.

Billowing clouds of tear gas were thought to be smoke from a fire, alarming the people seated inside who feared the stadium was ablaze. Fans panicked and rushed to the walk-ways, crushing those already immobilized by locked exit gates. Ammonia from the tear gas made people cough, gasp and vomit.

It blurred their vision.

"Oh, God!" Gretchen's mother screamed. "Will! Corne-lius! Gretchen!"

The crush forced Gretchen's family tight against the crowds choking the walkway. Gretchen felt her mother's hand seize hers, as Gretchen grabbed Will's hand. Her fa-ther had Gretchen's shoulder and Will's hand.

"Hang on, kids! Don't let go!"

The pressure was enormous as people began jumping from the upper tiers. Gretchen turned and saw others stampeding toward them from across the playing field!

No. Please. No more.

Now, as Gretchen's plane began its descent, she swallowed hard.

She knew what was coming. She could not stop it. She glanced at the sky and clamped her eyes shut and bit her bottom lip as the horrible images swirled around her.

The stadium had become a cauldron of hell.

People screaming. Whistles bleating. A foot on her father's shoulder. Waves of men scrambling above the paralyzed crowds. A sharp kick to her head. Blood trickling. Her mother collapsing under two men, then three more stamping her, then more bodies stamping on her from above.

Wake up from this nightmare! Wake up!

"*Nooo!*"

Shoes, boots, fists smashing on her father. Her father falling to his knees. More bodies raining down from the upper levels. Thudding, cracking on them, forcing people down.

"*Daddy!*"

Gretchen struggling to keep on her feet. Her mother's grip loosening. Her mother's fingers slipping from hers.

"*Mom!*"

Her mother vanishing. The light above blotted by wave after wave of frantic bodies. Crawling above them, falling from above, wedging into the immobile mass.

Smells of body odor, sweat, tobacco breath.

Fear.

And death.

Blood flowing everywhere.

"*Nooooooo!*"

A boot grazing her mother's skull, tearing a chunk of her scalp clean off.

"Mom!"

Her father being trampled to the ground, his body lost in a pulpy blur of stamping.

"Daddy!"

She felt Will's hand tight in hers, his warm little hand.

"Gretchen! Help me! Gretchen!"

She did not let go of his hand, but she couldn't see him anymore.

"Nooo!"

One of Will's arms disappeared into a crush of solid bodies. Compressed so tight people were suffocating.

Bones snapping, organs compressing like accordions.

A heart-wrenching squeal.

Will.

"Gretch—help meee!"

His hand went limp.

Lifeless, it protruded from the tangle of corpses.

The death of innocence. The death of reason before her eyes.

"Will!"

Her baby brother was dead.

Her mother was dead.

Her father was dead.

Gretchen fell into a dream-trance. Helpless to battle the consuming force that was slowly killing her, she prayed.

God, I beg you to let me live.

She felt an overwhelming force slowly ending her life.

And the ants devour their prey.

She felt her blood pressure slipping, slipping. Her life slipping, slipping...away. God, I beg you....

The 737 shuddered.

The flaps adjusted the jet's approach with hydraulic groans.

The landing gear grumbled down into position and locked.

Dr. Sutsoff blinked her troubled memories away, inhaled

and took in the outskirts of Yaoundé and the dark forests beyond. She'd come to Cameroon to complete the most critical—most dangerous—aspect of her work.

God had let her live.

She'd come to avenge her family's death by correcting the error of human evolution.

For here she would find the last key to her ultimate goal.

To exterminate the ants.

42

The Devil's Tail River, Cameroon, Africa

The diesel-powered barge chugged along the river that coiled its way through the forests of Cameroon's remote northern region.

The boat was laden with equipment for Dr. Sutsoff's expedition.

After spending the night in Yaoundé, she'd chartered a float plane to an abandoned riverside outpost. It was as far as the Cessna could travel to land safely before the river narrowed. There, four trusted members of her research team awaited her arrival.

They'd arranged for the boat to take them upriver to their field station.

And the discovery.

They had to work fast. Time was running out.

Sutsoff sat alone at the bow in a director's chair, drinking in the solitude. The isolation offered relief from the episode she'd endured on her long flight. The water rushing under her was mesmerizing, gently pulling her back over her life.

The aftermath of the stampede was a blur of images and moments.

The toll was 249 dead.

Gretchen had survived because she'd been pressed into an air pocket. But she'd suffered a serious concussion. Her head throbbed as if it would crack open.

Vridekistan declared three days of national mourning. They'd used a school gymnasium as the morgue. Embassy staff accompanied her to identify the battered bodies of her brother, mother and father. They looked like bloodied broken mannequins.

"Get up!" she screamed at them before she collapsed.

Orphaned at fourteen.

The embassy staff contacted her mother's cousin in Paris. He got her the best medical care. She'd sustained major head trauma. Her skull had been fractured in six places. "A miracle she survived," one specialist said. Her disturbing brain activity concerned doctors who had warned that over time it could degenerate into a psychopathic condition, an inability to feel empathy or remorse or, at worst, a loss of connection with reality. Medication could offset the effects of her injury but she was at risk of painful seizures and potential dissociative episodes for the rest of her life.

After a year of therapy, her uncle helped her return to school in Switzerland and over the years she excelled with near perfect grades, completing degrees in science, medicine, chemistry and cellular engineering at Berkeley, Harvard, Oxford and MIT.

On her own time, she conducted research on the psychology of mass hysteria, mob mentality and population control. As she developed a pathological loathing of crowds, she began forging a personal ideology, a near fanatical belief, that there were too many people in the world.

Too many ants.

Her outstanding academic achievements led to her being recruited by Foster Winfield, the CIA's chief scientist, to join a secret team to conduct work on a range of subjects under a new program.

Project Crucible.

The top-secret program encompassed cutting-edge research on synthetic biological agents, theoretical nanotechnology and state-of-the-art genetic manipulation. Some of it was triggered by File 91, flawed work by North Korea. When she advocated that her similar research on DNA manipulation under Project Crucible required secret live trials on a civilian population, her colleagues accused her of wanting to violate the Nuremberg Code.

They were fools.

Winfield and the others failed to see her logic, her need for live trials. She left the program and ultimately left the United States, changed her name and became a citizen of the Bahamas. She took pains not to be found, ensuring her personal information was removed from most databanks as she continued refining her ideology in solitude.

Through her confidential sources in the intelligence and science communities she quietly sought out those who shared her belief that time was running out on civilization. They created a secret organization and explored ways of transforming their beliefs into action. She named her inner circle Extremus Deus, for she was convinced that her life was spared on the day her family died because she was fated to rescue humanity.

From the day she'd encountered the ants eating the dog, to the horrific moments she'd spent in the stadium, she was destined to reach this point. All of her life's work had led to it, led her to this country, to this river and, soon, to the final component of her formula.

The barge's engine thudded and Gretchen felt Will's hand in hers.

Returning spirits of the dead.

Staring into the water flowing by, she considered an old African legend. It held that when the first white explorers arrived, the masts of their ships on the horizon were the first things seen by Africans, who deemed them to be the dead who'd risen from the bottom of the sea. As the barge churned around a bend she saw a cluster of thatched-roof huts pressed from the forest to the muddy riverbank.

It was a deserted village.

She thought of the old tales of cannibals and leper colonies, but as they glided by the huts so deathly still, she thought of the real nightmare that waited ahead.

They made camp that night.

As the barge's diesel slept, the small group sat around their campfire coated with DEET, listening to the throb of cicadas, the bellow of bullfrogs and the shrieks of things unseen. Flames licked at the night and Sutsoff studied the faces of her team.

Fiona was a brilliant microbiologist from India. Pauline was a doctor from New Zealand who'd worked with aid groups around the globe. Colin was the former science advisor to Britain's health secretary. Juan had been a surgeon with Argentina's military.

All were followers of E.D. All had left their positions to join her. They were the best of her organization, her disciples.

They revered her.

They knew her as Dr. Auden and they adhered to her rules.

They did not sit near her, or speak to her unless she initiated conversation, as she did now.

"Give me the outline for tomorrow, Colin."

"At daybreak the contractor will arrive with men to carry our equipment overland. It's rough terrain and should take us half a day to reach the field station. We can proceed in the morning."

"Anyone else care to add anything?"

"Well—" Juan cleared his throat "—we can't stress enough how dangerous this operation is. No one has ever seen anything like this before."

"Do you wish to withdraw?" Sutsoff said. "Would you prefer to wait here while the others bravely make their mark in history?"

"No."

"Your point then?"

"Thank you for the honor to be part of your team."

They retired to their tents, one for Sutsoff, one for the guys and one for Fiona and Pauline. As the fire died, Sutsoff sensed something breathing, brooding, waiting in the darkness.

And she smiled.

43

At dawn, columns of mist curled from the river, enshrouding the camp and the spectral forms floating in the water.

Four dugouts, each with half a dozen figures waiting. A bird shrieked as Juan poked his head from his tent, fumbled for his glasses, waved to the group then roused the others.

"Our help has arrived."

Sutsoff approached the group and offered a respectful greeting, using some of the dialect she'd learned from tapes Pauline had sent her.

Yes, they knew of the new discovery, said one man who had a command of English. It was frightening, he said, but other than the river people, no one knew what was happening.

"Have the white doctors come to help?" the man asked.

"Yes, we are here to help."

Sutsoff's team washed, dressed, rekindled the fire for breakfast and broke camp. Juan and Pauline saw to the men whom they'd hired to carry the research team's equipment overland to the field station.

Payment was fifty U.S. dollars for each man, a fortune by regional standards. Juan instructed them on the equipment, while Pauline distributed ropes and straps, ensuring each man carried a reasonable load. Heavier items were secured to carrying poles and two men were tasked to carry either end.

The trek began in good time.

Sutsoff took her place near the head of the line behind Juan and two of the older local men, regarded as expert guides. The dark forests appeared impassable. But the locals knew the way, following paths made by elephant herds that had come to water at the banks of the river.

The woods came alive with the buzzing of insects. The pungent smells of mud, decay and the fragrance of the flora challenged her senses. Trees rose like skyscrapers, their branches forming a natural roof pierced by shafts of light. While birds and monkeys screamed, the vegetation rioted with creeping crimson vines and giant purple, blue, orange and yellow flowers.

The load bearers carried items on their head or on their shoulders or strapped to their backs. Sweat glistened on their bodies.

When the expedition stopped for breaks, the locals expertly helped themselves to bananas, oranges or pineapple that were abundant. Their sharp knives sliced with swift surgical precision and they slurped the sweet juices. To the side, Juan crouched and used a stick to draw a crude map in the earth. The elder guides consulted it, then spoke with Juan and Sutsoff.

"We should be at the field station in two hours. That's late morning—earlier than we'd hoped," Juan said.

"Good. We'll start work immediately," Sutsoff said.

The group had gained its second wind as the terrain sloped downward, and in a little over an hour they had reached the field station. It was a crude wooden shack, no bigger than a garden shed, where Juan had spent the past three months conducting research.

"We must move quickly," Sutsoff said. "We must finish our work today. We'll camp here tonight and leave in the morning for the barge and my rendezvous with the float plane. I need to get a flight from Yaoundé and get back to my lab as soon as possible."

Everyone moved with military swiftness and order.

Equipment was uncrated and positioned. Sutsoff's pulse quickened as Juan and two of the elders led her down a path beyond the shack. They'd gone about one hundred yards when the elders stopped.

"They're frightened," Juan said.

"What is it?" Sutsoff asked.

"They refuse to go farther. They say the area is cursed, that we're coming to 'the hole with no end'—what they say is a gate to hell."

Barely able to contain her impatience, Sutsoff said, "We'll go on without them."

She and Juan continued, then paused. The forest seemed subdued, waiting, the quiet punctuated with the rattle of a palm frond falling from high above. They walked for another hundred yards, came to a twist, then arrived at their destination.

The yawning mouth of a cave.

"They're in there, about two hundred to three hundred feet," Juan said.

While working here, he'd been tipped off by a source conducting studies in the region on African witchcraft about a disturbing development: the emergence of a new and powerful lethal agent.

Juan had immediately alerted Sutsoff.

Now, as she stood here considering the cave, the reality of the discovery was palpable. The key to her success lay deep within the darkness—this so-called *gate to hell*. She'd memorized Juan's reports and knew that soon international health experts would descend on this site to neutralize what was inside.

Her job was to isolate and collect what she needed now.

"Good work. We'll suit up and collect our specimens."

At the field station Sutsoff, Juan, Colin, Pauline and Fiona got into protective encapsulated biochemical suits. Nervous tension seeped into the air. Sutsoff saw it in their eyes as they checked and double-checked their equipment, their breathing masks, two-layer face shields, three-layer gloves, special night-vision goggles, specially modified air-conditioned respirators, radio intercom and hazmat boots.

As awkward as it was, it was safer to suit up at the station. In their reflective suits, they resembled alien beings as they walked to the cave. It was unmapped, unidentified and estimated to contain about three million clustered bats, not fruit bats, but a rare new species known as the pariah bat.

The pariah was discovered in the region in the 1980s. But it was thought to have been wiped out after the tragic carbon dioxide explosion at Lake Nyos.

In his attempt to supply Sutsoff with samples of the Marburg virus and its relative, the Ebola virus, which she required for her work, Juan had learned that his source had encountered a farmer upriver who feared he'd been the victim of witchcraft, thinking someone had empowered bats with a powerful poison to bite his cattle at night and kill his entire herd.

Tissue samples obtained by Juan confirmed the presence of a new and alarmingly powerful lethal agent.

The farmer helped Juan track the bats to this cave.

At that time Juan was joined by Pauline at the field station. Both knew the risks but took what precautions they could. They designated a corner of the station to be a lab. Then they secured the structure with layers of heavy plastic sheeting coated with antiseptic. Finally, they donned military biochem suits obtained from a South African lab and began analysis.

Their work determined that the virus, which they'd christened Pariah Variant 1 (PV1), was present only in female bats. It was common for bats to feed on insects from swamps where the virus likely emerged. Sutsoff's review of their testing confirmed that PV1 was one hundred to two hundred times more lethal than Marburg or Ebola. They observed that it would have a fatality rate in humans of 95% to 97%.

Based on the results on the cows and on their initial

study, infection from PV1 could cause death in humans in less than ten minutes, making it the world's deadliest pathogen.

Sutsoff had already created an unprecedented delivery and manipulation system back at her island lab. She'd been in the final phase of developing a potent synthetic pathogen from a spectrum of known biological agents. But Juan's discovery of PV1 meant her model would be far more lethal than she could have imagined. All that she required was a sufficient supply of PV1 to complete her work and initiate her operation.

As they arrived back at the cave, Juan held up a gloved hand.

"Do not use your white light unless it's an emergency. They have an aversion to light, it will agitate them. Use your night vision."

They exercised supreme caution as they entered the mouth of the cave, taking time to allow their senses to adjust as the daylight at the entrance gave way to abject darkness. The cave floor was uneven and jagged; a wrong turn, a fall, could mean a tear in the suit.

According to Juan and Pauline's study, this was the optimum time to collect samples. For a brief period of a few weeks, the females would be sedentary, docile and incapable of flying because at this stage they were lactating. This was the time to manually extract samples of the virus.

"Okay, let's start." Juan's static voice came over his radio.

They each switched on their night vision and waited again for their senses to adjust before proceeding.

"Be mindful of sinkholes," Juan said. "Stay close to formations you can grab if the ground beneath you gives way."

Fiona released a small scream as a lone bat darted by squeaking.

"Just a male checking us out," Juan said.

"Stay calm, everyone," Sutsoff said.

Colin sensed the cave floor was actually soft like padded carpet.

"Kind of cushy," he said.

"Bat droppings," Sutsoff said.

"Eww," Fiona said.

"Stop, everyone," Sutsoff said. "Fiona, behave as a professional scientist or withdraw now."

"Sorry, Doctor."

As they progressed, about a dozen more male bats strafed them, brushing against their helmets and suits.

"The gear has been tested," Sutsoff said. "Stay calm. It will protect you."

Fiona muted her disgust.

"Careful, a steep step down," Juan said.

After a few hundred feet, they came to a mammoth chamber that was dwarfed by a magnificent cathedral with groves of stalactites, stalagmites and dozens of pillars.

It took a moment to realize that the structures were trembling with life—clusters upon clusters of roosting bats.

My beauties. Sutsoff was awed. *My glorious beauties.*

"Let's get started." She set out her kit. "You know the procedure."

Sutsoff demonstrated by plucking a roosting female from a cluster and turning its docile rat-faced head toward her. Using a dentist's pick, she pried the tiny mouth open, inserted a small cotton tip past its fangs, swabbed the oral cavity, then put the specimen in a bottle of diluent.

"Like that," she said. "We need as much as we can get."

While male bats flitted about, nicking and bumping into the scientists, the team worked smoothly.

They had been at it for more than thirty minutes, collecting specimens, when they were distracted by an odd sound.

Click-tap.

"What's that?" Colin asked.

They looked toward the mouth of the cave.

Nothing but darkness.

Click-tap. Click-tap.

Then a muffled cry.

That's not human.

"What is that?" Fiona asked.

They followed a furious thrashing and kicking as if some violent force were charging toward them.

"I have to see!" Fiona switched on her white light.

"Fiona, no," Juan called out too late.

A misshapen deer had staggered into the cave, rearing and swaying its neck. The group quickly realized it was not deformed but instead trapped within the writhing coils of a massive python. The snake's jaws were extended over the deer's muzzle in a hideous death hold.

Pauline screamed and switched on her white light. "I want out!"

A cloud of bats enveloped the deer, which dropped to its knees. Another cloud swarmed the scientists, pinging and nicking at their suits. The air filled with squeaks.

"Everyone keep calm," Sutsoff said. "Get those lights off now! Use night vision and pack up. Juan, take us out. Let's go!"

As the deer and snake thrashed, the team made its way to the mouth of the cave.

"Christ!" Colin shouted. "I'm getting hit harder."

The plunk-plunk of bats strafing the team intensified.

"Keep moving!" Sutsoff said. "We're almost out."

Daylight painted the air as the group hurried from the cave.

There was a collective sigh of relief as they cleared the cave and retreated toward the field station.

"That was a nightmare," Fiona said.

"Incredible!" Colin said. "Absolutely incredible!"

Juan started to take off his suit.

"Why don't you wait until we get to the station?" Colin asked.

"I'm just so hot," Juan said, tugging at his hood.

He had unzipped his foiled outer layer and was working on his lime-yellow layer by the time the group arrived at the field station.

Once Sutsoff placed all the samples in a protective case, the locals began helping her and the others out of their gear. Their faces were moist with sweat and the glow of accomplishing a deadly challenge.

"I need some DEET," Juan said, "got a mosquito bite."

Juan slapped the back of his neck but felt something larger than an insect.

It was furry.

On his fingertips was a bleeding bat.

"Juan!" Pauline's voice filled with fear. "Oh, God!"

"Oh, Jesus, no! I've been bitten!"

One of the local men pointed at a small tear at the back of Juan's suit.

Blood dripped down Juan's neck.

He stared at the quivering bat in his hand.

"In here, Juan!" Sutsoff held out a plastic container. "Drop it in here!"

She snapped it shut, then observed Juan as he spasmed.

"Help him!" Fiona screamed at Sutsoff.

Juan collapsed, writhing in agony.

Colin held him. Sutsoff rushed to get something and Pauline scrambled for her medical bag.

Juan's eyes widened and he screamed at the sky.

"Oh, God!" Fiona screamed. "Look at his eyes!"

His eyes liquefied, melted in their sockets, rivulets of blood oozing from his ears, his mouth as he spasmed. The air cracked with the sounds of breaking bones as Juan's back curved into a humped spine as he died.

"Oh, no," Fiona sobbed.

The others looked to Sutsoff and were stunned by what they saw.

She'd recorded the entire episode with her camcorder.

44

Sparks sprayed from the orbital sander in the open garage of a decaying duplex on Third Street, near the old Civic Center Barrio.

Emma Lane stopped her rented Ford Escort out front.

She checked the address she'd extracted from Christine Eckhardt at the clinic. Polly Larenski lived here. Emma approached the man working in the cluttered garage. Music throbbed with the grinding whirr of the sander.

"Excuse me."

The man's T-shirt complemented the muscles stretching his tattoos. He didn't hear her until she'd interrupted him a second time. The sanding stopped. He reached inside the car, killed the music, then let his eyes take a walk all over her.

"Excuse me, I'm looking for Polly Larenski."

"The new neighbor?"

"Polly Larenski," Emma repeated.

The toothpick in his mouth shifted. "Next door, baby."

"Thank you."

"She's a little psycho. If she scares you, you come see me."

As Emma went around to the door of the adjoining house, the hip-hop music resumed hammering the air. She rang the doorbell and knocked on the door. Peeling paint ravaged the exterior walls. The picture window was cracked.

No one responded, so she rang and knocked again.

Emma peered into the house. She could see down a hall to a kitchen, right through sliding glass doors to the back. She noticed a shadow moving on the rear deck and started for the back, thinking that whoever was there could not hear her at the door.

The music thumped as she went around the side and opened a gate. Flies swarmed the garbage overflowing from plastic bags and boxes leaning against the house. Emma noticed unopened envelopes that looked like bills addressed to P. Larenski in Los Angeles and remembered that Christine told her Polly had recently moved and that when Polly had called Christine asking about her severance check Polly demanded she not reveal her new address because she feared collection agencies were stalking her.

Polly's address change might explain why police saw no link to the clinic in L.A. and the call coming from a public phone here in Santa Ana.

Was this her only hope for finding Tyler?

The hip-hop music thudded away like a distant drum of dread.

As Emma went around the corner to the back of the house, she froze.

A woman sat alone in a deck chair wearing a bathrobe and shawl over her shoulders. Her face was tilted skyward as if she were showering in sunlight.

Emma didn't make a sound, yet without warning, the woman turned sharply and her wide-eyed attention shot toward Emma. Sudden breezes lifted the woman's hair in medusan strands. Her eyes fixed on Emma, the woman stood and calmly went into the house, leaving the sliding glass door open. Breezes made the curtains sway, as if inviting Emma to follow her.

Was this the mystery woman who'd called her?

As Emma entered the house, she heard music playing inside—the old hymn, "Shall We Gather at the River?" The place reeked of cigarettes. It had an open kitchen–living room layout. The living room was littered with cardboard moving boxes erupting with clothes, pictures, boxes and files.

The small table in the eating area was buried under newspapers, more files and shoe boxes containing bills and invoices. An assortment of pill bottles stood next to several liquor bottles, empty glasses and overflowing ashtrays.

"I have no money, if that's what you're here for."

Emma caught her breath.

She recognized that raw voice.

Your baby is not dead. Your baby is alive.

It belonged to the woman who'd called her in the middle of the night, the woman who was now standing at the kitchen sink and had popped two pills in her mouth. The woman snapped her head back, chasing the pills with whatever was in the glass she was holding.

"Are you Polly Larenski?"

"Unfortunately." Hair covered Polly's face as she dropped her head to stare down into the sink filled with unwashed dishes, cups, pots and so much sadness. "Who are you, and why are you standing in my house?"

"My name is Emma Lane. I've come from Big Cloud, Wyoming."

Polly stared at her in glassy-eyed confusion.

"You're not from a collection agency?"

"No."

"What do you want?"

"You called me a few days ago, Polly."

"I called you?"

"Yes."

"In Wyoming?"

"Yes."

"Why would I call you? I don't know you. Or anybody in Wyoming. I don't know what you're talking about."

"You asked for me, specifically. You had my name, my address. You'd called to tell me that my baby was still alive."

"What? Who's still alive? No, I don't know anything about a call."

"Yes, I recognize your voice. The call came from a public phone near the Burger King on Civic Center Drive here in Santa Ana."

"I don't know what you're talking about."

Polly massaged her temples.

"We were clients of Golden Dawn where you worked."

"What?"

"We had our baby, Tyler, through a donor there. My husband, Joe, Tyler and I were in an accident in Wyoming. My husband—" Emma paused "—my husband, Joe, was killed. I was thrown clear and police said our baby, Tyler, died when our car caught fire."

"Why are you telling me this?"

"I saw someone rescue Tyler. Then, after my doctor informed the clinic about Tyler, you called me in the night."

"You're crazy!"

"You called me and told me my baby was not dead!"

Polly shook her head.

"No, I don't remember anything like that."

"I need you to help me find my baby."

Polly flashed her palms at Emma.

"You should leave right now."

"Not until you help me." Emma opened her bag and withdrew a file folder. "I've made a copy of my files from the clinic for you. I'll help you remember—we can work together. I've attached the card of my hotel where I'm staying. It's near the clinic. Maybe we could call them and—"

Polly smacked the folder and the papers flew from Emma's hands and fluttered to the floor. "Stop it! I cannot take it anymore!"

The ferocity in Polly's voice rooted Emma where she stood.

Polly collapsed on the sofa, sobbing, trembling, as she poured a glass of whiskey, downed it, then covered her face with her hands.

"My husband—" she sniffed "—my ex-husband, Brad, committed suicide a few nights ago in a Las Vegas motel after running up a forty-three-thousand-dollar gambling debt."

Emma sat beside her.

"Oh, my God. I'm so sorry, Polly."

"The maid found him in the tub with our family picture on his chest. He'd slashed his wrists."

"I am so sorry."

"I'm being punished for my sins."

"What sins?"

"I'm responsible for the death of our only child."

Emma took Polly's hands.

"No, that can't be."

"Five years ago we were at the beach. Brad was building a sand castle with Crystal, our two-year-old. He was a district bank manager. He got a call on his phone and told me to watch her. He thought I'd heard him but I was sleeping under my sunglasses. He turned and walked away. Crystal followed the seagulls out into the water and a wave took her."

Polly poured another glass of whiskey.

"We went into therapy. I blamed him—he blamed me. We withdrew into ourselves and accepted the fact it didn't matter who was to blame."

"It was a terrible accident," Emma said.

"We were both guilty. I tried to cope by working long hours in the lab at Golden Dawn, becoming a workaholic and making other families happy. Brad drank and would disappear for days. A couple of times I bailed him out of the L.A. county jail. He lost his job, ran up gambling debts. We had a home in Santa Monica but lost it. Brad ran up more debts."

Polly stared into space.

"You know, he told me that when he gambled he'd live in hope of a big payoff so we could get our house back, get our lives back and maybe try for another baby. That adrenaline rush kept him alive, but I told him he was chasing a mirage and had to stop because the bill collectors were not letting up. It was horrible. We moved around constantly until I divorced him. I did everything I could. I got bank loans, lines of credit, juggled credit cards, but they kept coming after me. The pressure took its toll and I lost my job at Golden Dawn."

Polly stared into her glass, took a big swallow, then followed Emma's attention to a box of files that had the Golden Dawn Fertility Corporation insignia.

"What're you looking at?"

"I'm sorry, Polly." Emma nodded to the files. "I just thought maybe you could help me."

"What the—?" Polly's face contorted.

She stood. Woozy and dazed, she pointed to the door.

"Get out!"

"I'm sorry."

"You come into my home and accuse me of all kinds of crap. I don't know who the hell you are!" Polly slurred. "You could be a cop, a bill collector. Get the hell out of my house now!"

"Polly, please. I know you're in pain and I understand, I do, but—"

"Get out!"

Emma left, stepping into the assault of the neighbor's hip-hop music, hammering home the fact she had failed. The blue-white-orange flare of the welding torch blazed in her rearview mirror.

Was it over? Did it end here?

As she headed for the interstate, she glimpsed the dark sedan with dark windows behind her. It had departed Polly's neighborhood at the same time from half a block away. Now it was several car lengths back on the freeway, but she dismissed any notion someone was following her when traffic picked up.

With each passing mile, worry gnawed at her. Blood pounded in her ears. She could not bear to think that the only thread of hope she had of finding Tyler had unraveled and snapped in Polly Larenski's living room.

What now? she asked herself, as she reached her hotel, shifting her thoughts when she saw a dark sedan with dark windows creep by her.

Again, she dismissed it being anything sinister.

Must be a thousand cars just like that in Southern California.

Emma retreated to her room.

What do I do now?

She repeated that question over the next several hours as she lay on her hotel bed staring at the muted TV. She bit back tears and surfed through the channels, struggling to divine an answer from them until she drifted off. She did not know how long she'd been asleep before the hotel phone in her room woke her.

"Hello."

"Emma Lane?"

"Yes."

"It's Polly. I apologize. I'm going through a rough time."

"I understand."

"Pills, whiskey, Brad and—" she exhaled "—everything, you know?"

"I know."

"I called you that night about your baby."

"Will you help me?"

"Yes, but it has to be confidential."

"Okay."

"Let me get myself and my files together. Can you come back tomorrow, say around ten in the morning?"

"Yes, but will you tell me one thing right now? Is my son alive?"

A long, tense moment passed.

"Yes, I think he is."

"Why?"

"Because he was chosen."

45

"What do you mean, my son was *chosen?*" Emma asked Polly.

A strained silence passed over Emma's hotel telephone line until it was broken by Polly's sniffling.

"I've done something terribly, terribly wrong," Polly said.

"What was Tyler chosen for?"

"I'm being punished for all the bad things I've done."

"What bad things? Where's my son? Who has my son?"

"It hurts so much. I have to sleep now."

"Polly, please answer me!"

"I'll tell you more when you come back tomorrow."

"I'll come tonight!"

"No."

"Please let me come tonight!"

"No, tomorrow I'll be better. I'll find files for you."

"Polly! Wait!"

Emma stood, squeezing the receiver as if it were a life-line.

She could not lose Polly again.

Emma's heart was beating wildly. What if this was as close as she ever got to knowing what happened to Tyler that day on the highway near Big Cloud?

Emma wanted the truth.

She'd paid for it, suffered for it, bled for it. If she had to reach through Polly Larenski's psychotic fog and into her tortured soul to get it, then that's what she would do. Emma's grip on the phone was so powerful she swore she heard the handset crack.

"Polly," Emma softened her taut tone, "please, just talk to me. I need you to tell me what happened."

Emma heard Polly's measured breathing, heard her thinking.

"Polly, you are the only person who can help me. Start at the beginning and tell me what happened."

Emma heard the faint rattle of a pill bottle being uncapped, heard Polly swallow then exhale.

"I already told you that Brad's gambling was out of control," Polly said. "He owed a lot of money to a lot of bad people. I was using new credit cards to pay off old ones but it was not going to work forever. I had to do something, don't you see?"

"Yes."

"Some time ago, the company sent me to be its rep at a big international conference for lab technicians in Mexico."

"Mexico?"

"Mexico City. When I was there, I overheard some delegates talking about rumors of new cutting-edge genetic research. It sounded interesting. Later, a woman from that group approached me privately in the lounge. She saw my delegate badge and that I was with Golden Dawn Fertility and asked for my card. Then she asked if I'd be interested in 'confidentially contributing to an important study.' She said I'd be well paid."

"What sort of study?"

Polly coughed and Emma heard her light a cigarette then draw on it.

"She was vague, but something to do with genetics."

"Who was she with?"

"I don't know. I think it was a corporation on an island

somewhere in the Indian Ocean or Caribbean. She took my card and told me to think it over."

"Did you tell your bosses about this?"

"No. Because later I got a follow-up call from a stranger, who told me that if I confidentially supplied them information, I would be extremely well paid. We needed the money, so I agreed."

"How much did they pay you?"

"Five thousand dollars for the first batch of data."

"What was the data for?"

"They said it would lead to a cure for major diseases."

"Why did they have to be so secretive?"

"They said other corporations were trying to duplicate their work. They said they didn't have time to comply with international rules and regulations. They had to take steps now to protect their research."

"What did you have to do?"

"At first I just provided generic information. You see, Golden Dawn collects DNA from all donors and all clients, to ensure quality and avoid the rare chance of well, inbreeding—you wouldn't want to be using your long lost brother's sperm, that sort of thing."

Polly exhaled.

"We have a complex screening process, one of the world's best. It eliminates abnormal DNA, bacteria, infections and viruses from the samples. At first, the 'researchers' asked for general information on our clients. It involved no privacy concerns, so I ran a computer scan and gave them generic information. I thought it was for statistical analysis, demographic tables."

"How did you give them information?"

"They would tell me to go to a branch of the L.A. Public Library at a specific time and leave a memory card in a certain book. I would get an envelope of cash the same way."

"So you never saw anyone?"

"No. I was called at home by different people from 'the study team.' I never knew who or where they were based. They had accents, they said they were contractors. The numbers were blocked. I figured the calls came from all over the world."

"How did this involve Tyler?"

"They started to ask for specific DNA sequences, profiles. I got nervous. This was crossing a line, but they offered more money, so I agreed."

"What did you give them?"

"Samples of your baby's DNA, your DNA, the donor's DNA, your husband's, too. They got very interested in Tyler's DNA, they said it was exactly what they needed. They asked for all of your private information—names, address, and your complete files."

"What did you do?"

"I told them I was uneasy and they offered me fifteen thousand dollars."

"You took it?"

"I thought this was a start at clearing some of Brad's debts and rebuilding our lives, so I took the money and I gave them everything. I kept working with them until your tragedy."

"What happened?"

Polly pulled on her cigarette.

"I was getting so scared. I knew I was acting in denial, that I didn't want to know what was going on because I needed the money. But my conscience ate at me. Finally, I demanded to know what was happening. They said their 'research' was going on around the world, that it was part of a 'major operation' and that I couldn't tell anyone because I was implicated and there would be consequences."

"What did you do?"

"I started freaking out, asking, What did I get myself into?"

"Did you go to the police?"

"I was afraid. I was sure I was being followed, the house was being watched. I started making errors at work. But I thought I was okay when the clinic got your notification."

"My notification?"

"We monitor and update all of our client files, like whenever there's a miscarriage, a stillbirth or a crib death we update the file. When your doctor alerted us to your terrible crash, your husband's death and Tyler's death, I was sad. But also—and oh, God forgive me—I was relieved because I thought that this would end my dealings with the study group."

"What do you mean?"

"At that time they'd called demanding more DNA information on Tyler's file. I told them I was finished with them because Tyler had just died in a car accident. They said, 'Oh we know about that. Your information is incorrect. We've recovered that case.' And I said, 'What do you mean you've recovered that case?' and they said, 'That child is actually alive. Our work continues.'"

"What!"

"I was so terrified, so overcome with guilt. I called you to somehow let you know that your baby is alive."

"Who are these people, Polly?"

"I'm so sorry. Come back tomorrow, I'll give you my files. I'm so messed up with Brad and everything. I need to sleep."

"Wait! Polly, what is this 'operation'? What are they talking about?"

"I don't know." She started to sob. "I'm so scared. All they said was that it was going to change everything and there was nothing anyone could do to stop it."

46

A stern-faced police officer stood before Emma's car and pointed at her then at the curb, commanding her to park.

What was going on?

Traffic clogged Third Street. Emma was still a block from Polly Larenski's duplex when she got out and started walking toward the emergency lights splashing red and blue on the neighborhood. Excited children on bicycles and worried adults hurrying behind them gathered at a cluster of police cars, fire trucks and news crews that ringed a spectacle down the street.

The smell of charred wood permeated the air.

Emma heard the roar of a pumper truck, the bursts of radio chatter. The pavement was wet from water leaking from the lines of fire hoses. As she got to the yellow plastic tape that cordoned the site, she stopped.

Polly's duplex had burned.

Firefighters hosed the ruins. Spears of scorched walls rose from smoldering heaps of rubble and ash. Emma's heart raced.

Where was Polly?

The boy beside her was sitting on his bicycle and talking to the boy standing next to him.

"I heard the fire guy say that a lady died."

"Do you know who it was?" Emma's intensity startled the boys.

"I think it was the lady that lived there."

Emma cast around the area and rushed toward a fire-fighter carrying a hose to a truck.

"Excuse me. This is my—my friend's house. I'm supposed to see her. Was anyone hurt?"

The firefighter's face was smudged with soot.

"There was a female fatality. Better talk to the captain. He's in his van over there."

Emma spotted the fire van and hurried toward it, the ramifications of what happened enveloping her with each step. She felt something fracture, felt something break off and slip away.

She couldn't believe this was happening.

The captain's window was down. He sat behind the wheel reading from a clipboard, ending a conversation on his radio.

"That's right—get back to me. Ten-four." He clicked his handheld microphone.

"Can you help me, please?" Emma said. "My friend lives here. We're supposed to meet today. What happened?"

"Your name?"

"Emma Lane."

He glanced at his clipboard. "Well, Emma, unfortunately a fire started in the garage. We suspect the cause was faulty welding equipment belonging to a neighbor, a male resident working on his car."

"Was someone hurt?"

"Yes, I'm sorry. One fatality, likely due to smoke inhalation, a female resident. Everyone else got out, both homes were destroyed. We estimate damage at—"

"Polly Larenski? Did she get out? I need to see her."

The captain checked his clipboard, flipped a page, his chin tensed. Before he flipped it back, Emma glimpsed *Larenski* on his sheet.

"I can't confirm anything until next of kin are notified."

"It *is* Polly! Oh, my God!"

The earth shifted under Emma; the world swirled around her.

"My baby's files are in there. My baby was saved from a fire!"

Concern registered on the captain's face.

"Your baby's in there?"

The captain seized his microphone, called for assistance then got out.

"Ma'am, are you aware of other people in the residence?"

"No, no! I've come here from Wyoming. My husband was killed. My baby was rescued from a fire. Polly knew! Are you sure she's dead?"

Incomprehension flooded the captain's eyes.

"Ma'am, you're losing me. Are you all right?"

"What am I going to do now? She knew about my baby, she knew everything!"

Emma covered her mouth with her hands and gazed at the remnants of Polly Larenski's home as a circle of faces emerged around her—firefighters, police officers and paramedics. An officer with the Santa Ana police touched her shoulder.

"Do you have any identification, ma'am?"

Emma fumbled in her bag. The officer studied her Wyoming driver's license. "Will you come this way, please? These folks just want to make sure you're okay."

Emma sat in the back of an ambulance.

While paramedics observed her, she told the officer her story. He listened, then went to his patrol car beside the ambulance. The door was open. Emma saw him checking her name through the car's small dash-mounted computer and talking on his radio.

At one point she heard him say, "Not a relative, a bystander. Wyoming DL. Right. Seems disoriented, overcome. Then it goes to OCSD?"

Some fifteen minutes later, a black-and-white cruiser with a six-point gold star on the door arrived. The new officer took Emma's license from the Santa Ana officer, then they both approached her.

"Emma, I'm Deputy Holbrooke with the Orange County Sheriff's Department," the new officer said. "I'm going to take your information."

Emma sat in the deputy's car. Again, she told her story while he entered information into his computer. Then he left the car to make a call on his cell phone, pacing near the trunk where she overheard him say, "Right, not ours. Thanks, Lou."

In the time since she'd arrived at the fire, Emma had pinballed from the fire department to the Santa Ana Police Department to the Orange County Sheriff's Department, and through a maze of police bureaucracy until she landed in the jurisdiction of the Federal Bureau of Investigation.

Now here she was in the office of the FBI's Santa Ana Resident Agency on the top floor of the bronze three-story building on Civic Center Drive. For nearly forty-five minutes, special agent Randy Sikes had listened to her. Occasionally, he'd excused himself to take a phone call on the status of an ongoing identity theft investigation.

Before Emma had arrived at Sikes's desk, he'd been briefed on the phone by the Santa Ana Police and Orange County.

Sikes was a quiet, cerebral agent in his mid-forties. He wore a suit with a white shirt, conservative tie, and his hair was combed neatly. He said little as Emma spoke, but from time to time he paused to study his computer monitor and the results of his query to the National Crime Information Center, the FBI's major database known as NCIC.

It contained records on a range of files submitted by every law enforcement agency across the country. NCIC contained records on subjects such as guns, fugitives, warrants, stolen vehicles, sex offenders, license plates, gangs, terrorist organizations and missing persons.

After Emma had left her home in Big Cloud, her worried aunt and uncle went to the County Sheriff's Office to report her missing. The sheriff's office submitted a report to NCIC that contained all the background about the accident: Emma's reaction, her claims about the phone call. The Big Cloud County Sheriff's Office had characterized Emma as a traumatized, grief-stricken accident victim who'd refused to accept the deaths of her husband and son.

NCIC security forbade police from sharing the file with unauthorized people. Emma never saw it. After Sikes read it, he said, "You've been through a lot lately, haven't you, Emma?"

"Yes."

"There are people in Big Cloud worried about you. Why don't you think about going home?"

"But what about everything I've told you about my baby? What about what I told you about Polly, that she said my baby was 'chosen'? She said someone was planning some kind of action and they chose my baby! Please help me!"

"Yes, it's quite a story," Sikes said. "And I understand you've been under tremendous stress lately. The tragedy of the house fire today must have subjected you to more anguish."

"What about what I told you about Polly?"

"We'll follow that up with authorities here in California and Wyoming, but our first concern is your well-being and getting you home. It might be the best thing, don't you think?"

She stared at the wall.

"I could call someone for you, if you like," Sikes said.

Emma shook her head.

He thinks I'm crazy. They all think I'm crazy.

Emma collected her things and left.

47

A smoky haze rose from the blackened remains of Polly Larenski's house.

Two men in blue coveralls, wearing gloves and surgical masks, used shovels and crowbars to probe the debris. Another man stepped carefully through the aftermath, accompanied by a German shepherd that sniffed the bits and pieces.

It was late afternoon and Emma watched from the yellow plastic tape protecting the site. Much of the commotion had subsided; nearly all of the fire, police and other emergency vehicles were gone. The street was still sealed. A funereal calm had descended upon the scene, scored by the crack-twist-tear of the investigators shifting and lifting pieces.

And there was the eager chink of the panting dog's collar.

Somewhere in that charred heap was the key to Emma's search for her baby and she prayed that somehow she'd find it. She noticed one of the men in blue coveralls walking to a van marked Arson Unit.

She followed him.

"Can you help me? Was this arson? I thought this was an accident."

He shoved his mask down.

"Are you with the press?"

"My name is Emma Lane. My friend died in the fire."

"Sorry to hear that," he said. "It's no secret what we do. Whenever there's a fatality fire, Arson investigates. The dog is sniffing for accelerants."

"Accelerants?"

"To tell us if someone used gas or anything to purposely start it."

"Do you think it was an accident?"

He assessed her before giving her a guarded answer.

"We're not done." He rummaged in his truck. "Do you have information about this fire?"

"No. It's just that Polly had papers she was going to give me today."

"What kind of papers?"

"Personal records."

He looked at her for a moment.

"Tell you what, why don't you show me some identification and I'll let you know if we find anything."

Emma showed him her Wyoming driver's license and a card for her hotel. "Well, you've come a long way, haven't you?" he said as he jotted everything on the back of the card and slid it in his notebook. "Unfortunately, everything in that house is gone." He dropped some tools into a bucket. "Now, if you'll excuse me."

He ducked under the tape and returned to the scene, where his partner hefted a chunk of wall with a crackling twist that released a small flare.

The dog yelped.

The other investigator doused the fire with an extinguisher. Smoke rose over the site and a gust blew clouds toward Emma, burning her eyes, swirling over everything.

Ashes to ashes.

Death was winning.

Emma's only hope was gone. Tentacles of smoke pulled her back through the horror that had descended upon her.

Back to the crash, back to Joe and Tyler.

She could not succumb to her pain.

She had to keep moving.

Just over twenty minutes later and a few blocks away, Emma cupped her hands around a hot tea while sitting alone at the Burger King that was near Polly Larenski's house.

There was a pay phone out front. Emma had stopped to consider it on her way into the restaurant and jotted down the number. Now, she compared it to the one that had been used for the late-night call she'd received at home.

It was identical.

This was the phone Polly had used that night to tell her Tyler was still alive. Emma had come full circle.

Your son was chosen.

Polly Larenski's files were lost in the fire.

Emma had come so close to the truth. But now it was gone. Now she had nothing.

Don't give up, she thought, as she got into her car. *Do something.*

She concentrated.

There was one last thing she could try.

A horn honked behind her.

The blast yanked her from her brooding, reminding her that she was stopped in slow-moving traffic on the freeway, northbound from Santa Ana. If she could get downtown in time, she might have a shot, she thought. But traffic all around her was at a standstill.

She arrived at the Golden Dawn Fertility Corporation before closing and went to the reception desk. "Emma Lane," she said. "I need to see Christine Eckhardt. Please, it's urgent."

"I don't think she's available to see you." The receptionist, appearing slightly flustered, ran a polished fingernail down an appointment sheet when Christine Eckhardt emerged with her briefcase on her way out.

"Emma?" Christine was surprised.

"We need to talk about Polly Larenski."

"We just heard. It's terrible. One of the doctors saw it on KCAL and we got a call from police looking for family. They traced the parking sticker on Polly's car to us."

"I need to talk to you about what she told me."

Christine's face reddened. She started shaking her head and glanced at the receptionist.

"I really can't; I'm sorry. It's a terrible time for everyone. I'm so sorry but I just can't talk to you, Emma. I really have to go."

Christine headed for the door, giving her a compassionate but awkward smile that vanished when Emma seized her arm.

"Emma!"

"I just came from the fire, and I need to talk to you, Chris. I am your client, remember?"

Christine stared at her for a tense moment, then nodded to the sofa in the waiting area, keeping things within view of the receptionist, who was braced to call security.

"I talked to Polly about my baby and she told me she sold private information from your files, our DNA—"

"Stop, Emma."

"Why?"

Christine swallowed hard and dropped her voice.

"You've threatened to sue the company. I'm a partner and I was legally bound to report your threat to the board. I've been advised by our legal department not to talk to you as anything I say could potentially be used in your case against us."

"No, Chris, you don't understand."

"I'm so sorry."

"I was upset then."

Christine stood.

"You have to go, Emma. Go home, get some rest. Get some help."

"No. I need *your* help. Please, I'm begging you."

"It's all very, very tragic."

"I'm begging you, please."

"I can't talk to you, I'm so sorry."

"No, please just listen to me!" Emma reached for Christine's wrist.

"Larissa, can you call Mac in security to help Emma to her car?"

Emma released Christine's wrist, her voice breaking when she said, "That won't be necessary." She stood, touching her fingertips to the corners of her eyes. "You were an angel when Joe and I first came to you for help."

"I'm so sorry, Emma."

"Not sorry enough to help me."

By the time Emma had returned to her hotel room she was numb.

Smelling the smoke on her clothes, seeing her disheveled reflection in the mirror, she realized she needed a shower.

As steam clouds rose around her, she sobbed in great heaving waves. Overwhelmed by anguish she slammed her back against the wall and slid down to the shower floor, letting the water rush over her as she hugged herself in vain.

She'd already come apart.

Emma was exhausted when she stepped from the shower. As she pulled on a robe, the phone in her room rang and she answered it.

"Emma?"

"Yes."

"Oh, thank goodness, it's Aunt Marsha in Big Cloud."

"Hi."

"Emma, are you all right, dear?"

"I'm so tired."

"We were so worried. You gave us a scare, leaving like you did. We didn't know where you were. A concerned FBI agent gave us your hotel number. Emma, you've been through too much. Please, come home."

Emma didn't answer because she didn't know where home was anymore.

"Emma?"

She remained silent.

"Sweetheart, do you want us to fly there and get you?"

A long silence passed, Emma felt warm tears flow.

"No. I'll come back."

The next morning, Emma's jet lifted off from LAX to Denver with a connection to Cheyenne. As she gazed down at the eternal urban sprawl she felt so small.

So lost.

And so alone.

She reached into her bag and touched Tyler's stuffed bear. As the plane climbed into the sky she was suddenly lying on the road again in Wyoming, reaching for her husband's hand.

I don't know if I can do this alone, Joe. Help me find him.

48

I*'ve been sent a package from a dead man.*

The thought raced through Jack Gannon's mind as he locked his hotel-room door, then tore open the yellow padded envelope from Adam Corley.

What he found inside was a small camel.

It was a beautiful object a bit larger than Gannon's palm. According to the tag affixed with a gold tassel to its neck, it had been carved from walnut wood by an artist in Essaouira, a town along the Atlantic coast.

Gannon also found a handwritten note in the envelope. "Jack: a gift to help you remember Morocco —Adam C."

Nothing else.

Gannon sat at the desk, puzzled.

Why did Corley send him this and when? He turned it over, running his fingers along its smooth surface. It was almost blood red with nice, overlapping grain. Its meaning was a mystery that Gannon was pondering when his phone rang. He placed the carving in his computer bag then answered.

"Mr. Gannon, this is the concierge. As you requested, we've looked into flights. You can depart Rabat early tomorrow morning on an Air France flight to Paris's Charles de Gaulle, where you will connect to New York for arrival at JFK late in the evening."

"I'll take it."

"Would you like us to confirm it on your credit card, sir?"

"Yes, thank you."

"Very well, we'll slide the ticket under your door later and arrange for a taxi for 6:45 a.m."

After hanging up, Gannon turned on his laptop. Among his e-mails were several from Oliver Pritchett in London and Melody Lyon in New York. Her most recent one asked, Haven't heard from you—what's happening?

It gave him pause.

How could he begin to answer her?

Well, other than being abducted, stripped and tortured, not bad.

Gannon decided it best to call Melody but when he reached for his phone, he started shaking. He ran his hand over his face.

Somehow the world felt different.

He felt different.

Now he understood why some assault victims refused to talk. The humiliation of the violation was overwhelming and it brought back images of Rio de Janeiro and the drug gang drilling a gun into his mouth, pulling the trigger on an empty chamber.

This sort of thing doesn't happen to guys like me. I'm a blue-collar nobody who grew up in Buffalo. I don't need this crap. Maybe I should find a job at some safe suburban weekly.

Maybe I don't have what it takes.

Shut up! Suck it up. You asked for this, Gannon. You yearned to work for the WPA. Well, you got your wish, pal. Don't forget, Gabriela Rosa and Marcelo Verde paid with their lives for this story. So did Maria Santo, and now Adam Corley. Remember what Melody said—Find the truth, no matter where it leads. This is how we will honor the dead.

Gannon collected himself and started an e-mail to Melody Lyon.

A source was murdered before we met. I was questioned by police. I'm now on my way back to NYC with more crucial information. I'm okay. I'll discuss it with you in New York.

After he sent the e-mail his body shook again.

Maybe if he just talked to somebody, somebody he trusted. He pulled out his wallet for a Buffalo number. It took a few seconds for the overseas connection to go through.

"Clark Investigations. Please leave a message and I'll get back to you."

In that moment, Gannon pictured his friend Adell Clark, a divorced former FBI agent who ran a one-woman private detective agency out of her modest Parkview home in Lackawanna where she lived with her daughter. A few years back, Clark had been shot in an armored-car heist at a strip mall in Lewiston Heights. He'd profiled her, and they'd become friends and had many heart-to-hearts. Adell knew him better than he knew himself.

Could he bear to tell her what happened?

The message cue beeped.

No. Not now.

He hung up and dragged his hands across his face, then started packing. He was nearly done when his phone rang again.

"Jack, Pritchett in London. Are you all right?"

"I'm fine," he lied.

"You know what happened to Adam?"

"Yes."

"It's bloody horrible, the British Embassy called his father and he called us. Did you see him before he was killed?"

"No, but I was at his house after it happened. The police questioned me."

"Do they know who's behind it? Did they arrest anybody?"

"I don't think so."

"Christ, this has to be linked to the intelligence he was gathering. You have to be careful, Jack. This is terrible."

Gannon glanced toward his computer bag.

"Oliver, something odd happened. I got a package from Corley at my hotel."

"What?"

"Obviously he sent it before our meeting. It's a small hand-carved camel."

"Did he send a note with it?"

"A small one, it said, 'Jack: a gift to help you remember Morocco —Adam C.' What do you think it means, given we hadn't even met?"

"Knowing Adam, it's more than a gift. I can't tell you what, exactly. Hang on to it. Were there any documents with it, anything like that?"

"No."

"Adam was supposed to send me a full report on what he'd learned from his sources and from his trip to Libya, but I haven't received anything."

"Maybe he dropped it in the snail mail to you?"

"I don't know. This whole thing is very bad. Jack, get out of there. It's too dangerous for you. Equal Globe International has lost two people. Your news agency has lost two people. Get out of Morocco before it's too late."

The next day Gannon peered at the Atlantic from the starboard window seat of an Air France jetliner.

He had the row to himself and tried to relax as he studied the carved camel in his hands. He turned it over and over, recalling how Pritchett had said that Corley's act of sending him the figure must have a deeper meaning.

Like what?

Caressing its smooth surface, Gannon noticed a tiny square indentation in the camel's belly. He'd missed it at first because it ran along the grain line. Holding the camel closer for inspection, he noticed the grain line was, in fact, a seam. It ran along the length of the carving, dividing it in half.

He tried wedging his thumbnail into the seam. The indentation was smaller than a grain of rice. No luck. He took stock of his surroundings, then withdrew a pen from his pocket and managed to insert the tip into the tiny slot. After wiggling the pen's tip, the two halves of the carving shifted. With careful, controlled effort, Gannon pulled the camel apart into two equal pieces. They'd been hollowed out and opened to a memory card, hidden inside.

How did the airport scanner miss this?

Gannon shrugged, pulled out his laptop, switched it on and inserted the card. Dozens of file folders appeared on his screen. The first was labeled Note to Jack Gannon.

His pulse quickened when he opened it.

Jack: This is rushed. I hope to see you soon but wanted to get this down first. Since my return from Benghazi I have obtained significant new data that relates to what Maria Santo discovered in Brazil and to your investigation. However, since I don't trust everyone in the intelligence community, I've passed this to you. I know I am being watched by people connected to this operation. Now, they could be watching you, too. I don't know who they are or how far this goes. I therefore have taken precautions to give you a copy of all my files, all the intelligence I have gathered. I include my notes for the report I am drafting on our investigation into a worldwide child-stealing operation that involves illegal adoptions. We've discovered that this operation seems to involve more than child stealing and illegal adoptions. An objective or purpose is emerging. No one knows, or has, what you now have. I've made arrangements for a local messenger boy I trust to deliver my "gift" to your hotel, as a precaution should something untoward happen before our meeting.

If you're reading this, he has succeeded.

The problem is, if we have not met, you will not have the benefit of my explaining what I've provided and the context. But one thing is certain: Some sort of operation, an attack of some sort, appears to be imminent. Read through this material, see where it fits. Good luck, Jack.

Adam Corley

Gannon began surveying Corley's files. It was a long flight, and he would have time to read, but for now he'd scroll through the files quickly and randomly to see what he had.

Here was something on Drake Stinson, the ex-CIA attorney with the Brazilian law firm Worldwide Rio Advogados. Here was something about him in Benghazi at a meeting with some shady-looking types and an American scientist, who used several aliases.

Who was she?

He came to another labeled Extremus Deus.

Never heard of that term—sounds Latin.

As he paged quickly through the files, he caught something that twigged a memory, a reference to LA #181975 to Wyoming847.

Wyoming?

Gannon recalled some reference to Wyoming from files passed to him by Sarah Kirby, Maria Santo's friend from the Human Rights Center in Rio.

Only Corley's file seemed larger and more detailed.

He came to a document labeled Big Cloud, Wyoming— Golden Dawn Fertility Corp.

Big Cloud, Wyoming? What was that about?

49

Cheyenne, Wyoming

Dr. Allan Pierce gave Emma hope.

He understood her and today he'd promised to explain how he would help her. This morning she saw the words of her file reflected in his glasses as he studied his patient assessment, profile and notes.

He actually listened.

The fatal fire and her futile battle with the clinic in California were devastating setbacks in her search for Tyler. The police in Big Cloud were dismissive of her claims of a conspiracy behind Tyler's disappearance. These disasters had thrust her into a pit of self-doubt and despair.

But Dr. Pierce had told her that something extraordinary had happened to her at the crash.

Optimism about Tyler now flickered in the darkest corner of her heart as she sat in Dr. Pierce's office, watching as he reviewed her case.

Pierce had graduated from UCLA and USC and had held the second-highest psychiatric post at Big Sky Memorial Hospital since arriving last year from Los Angeles. In the few sessions Emma had had with him at the hospital, he'd run a number of tests. He was thorough, but more important, he was warm, kind and paid attention to her.

He missed nothing.

What Emma didn't know was that he was still grappling with the toll exacted on him by his former job where he'd been saddled with an impossible caseload and had grown bitter about his life. When his marriage ended in divorce, he'd come to Wyoming.

As he uncapped his pen he concluded Emma Lane had a severe case of post-traumatic stress, coupled with a profound grief reaction. And she had a fixed delusional system going, too.

Treatment orders showed regular blood work, chest X-ray and E.E.G., and neurology showed zip.

Pierce closed her file and pushed his glasses atop his head.

"Emma, what you're experiencing is an acute case of grief reaction. It's early in the process, so there's no way to predict when it will wane, but it will. However, your case is somewhat unusual, given the circumstances and the intensity of your reaction. And you have other things at work."

Emma was listening.

"We'll try to help you understand that, while it is normal to yearn as you are doing, you must accept that you can't bring your family back."

"No, wait, I told you that I do accept that Joe is gone, but Tyler did not die in the fire. He was rescued and someone has him."

Pierce nodded.

"We'll get you on a healing track by first helping you forgive yourself."

"Forgive myself?"

"You are showing signs of survivor's guilt among other symptoms."

"I don't understand."

"Your preoccupation with finding and recovering your dead son is normal. And, Emma, this sense of presence you're experiencing does occur as part of the grieving process. The hallucination of seeing Tyler rescued, the phone call, things that are even characteristic of spiritual or metaphysical phenomenon—the profound conviction that Tyler is alive in another time and space—this is all part of the grieving process."

"It is? Is someone calling you to tell you your son is alive part of the grieving process?"

Pierce let a long silent moment pass.

"Emma, your leaving home to search for Tyler at the clinic in California, the symbolic place of his origin, is extreme, but it is still part of the mourning process. As is your anxiety, your disbelief, even your self-recrimination. As you said, you were the one who suggested the picnic, which resulted in the drive and accident. You said that had you not gone on that drive the tragedy never would have happened. This is survivor's guilt. Essentially all of these symptoms have converged to form your yearning, and at the same time, deceive you into believing Tyler is alive. It's a protective mechanism."

"Wait!" Emma held up her hands. "I don't understand."

"I know it's difficult to absorb what I've identified."

"No. Not that. I thought you believed that Tyler was alive, that the phone call, the information I obtained from Polly Larenski—who admitted she sold Tyler's files, admitted someone somewhere has Tyler—all pointed to the fact that there is some sort of plan, plot or conspiracy going on."

"No, Emma, I'm sorry if I gave you that impression."

"I thought with you being from L.A., that you had contacts with police, authorities, that you were going to help me follow up on Polly's information. It was all very real. I did not hallucinate any of that."

"Emma, I understand—" he cleared his throat "—but I also agree with the earlier observation by Dr. Kendrix that you were hearing and searching out what you needed to hear to counter your disbelief. You need to be assured that Tyler did not suffer in the fire while you lay a few feet away unable to go to him."

"No!" She clenched her hands into fists. "You are my only hope."

Pierce said nothing as a long awkward silence passed.

"Emma. I understand that you believe deeply that what you've experienced is reality, that it has in fact happened. I promised at the last session that once I had your test results, I would explain how I would help you confront what is real. And that's what I've done."

All the blood drained from Emma's face as he reached for a pad.

"I'm going to give you a strong prescription and I want you to follow it."

As his pen scraped across the pad, Emma shut her eyes. Her faint light of hope had gone out.

Pierce tore the page from his pad. It was the sound of betrayal as Emma felt the last measure of hope being ripped from her heart.

Pierce was like all the others.

He didn't believe her.

No one believed her.

She sat motionless in the chair as Pierce went around his desk and opened his office door to where Emma's aunt Marsha and uncle Ned had been waiting.

"She'll need this prescription." Pierce gave it to Emma's aunt. "You can get it filled at the hospital pharmacy on your way out. Emma—" Pierce put his hand on her shoulder "—I'll see you Friday at the same time?"

She said nothing.

"We'll have her here," Uncle Ned said.

"Thank you, Doctor," said Aunt Marsha.

No one spoke in the car. Emma sat with Aunt Marsha in the back. Uncle Ned drove and fiddled with the radio, finding a classical music station. He kept the sound low.

Emma loved them. Their devotion to her was unyielding, never giving way to their own pain. She could not have survived this far without them. They were halfway across town, stopped at a red light, when Emma made a decision.

"Can you please take me to the cemetery?"

Uncle Ned looked in the rearview mirror where he found Aunt Marsha's face and the answer.

"Of course, dear," Emma's aunt said.

When they reached the entrance to the Sun View Park Cemetery, Emma asked her uncle to stop.

"I'd like to go the rest of the way alone. I'll walk home later."

"But, dear?" Aunt Marsha was worried.

"I need some time alone out here, a long time."

"We can wait, or come back," Uncle Ned said.

"I'll be fine. I'll walk home. I just need to be alone, to think."

The anxiety in her aunt's eyes was clear.

"Don't worry, Aunt Marsha."

"Try telling the rain not to fall."

Both women released a laugh.

"What happened is nobody's fault," her aunt said.

"I know."

"We love you, Emma," her aunt said.

They drove off, leaving Emma alone to walk along the high prairie that disappeared into the mountains. She made her way around the headstones to the gravesite that was marked by a white wooden cross and a mound of dark earth.

The stone wasn't ready yet.

The small plate affixed to the cross read Joseph Lane and Tyler Lane.

Emma sat on the grass.

No one else was in the cemetery.

Birds twittered.

Am I wrong? Is everyone else right? Have I lost you forever?

She was so tired. She didn't know what to do.

I want to be with you. I need to be with you.

A breeze rolled down from the Rockies and lifted her hair, tugging her down a river of memories as moments of their lives together rained upon her like falling stars.

I feel your hand, Joe. I really do. I feel that shirt, that stupid faded denim shirt, softened by a thousand washings. I feel your skin. I smell you. I taste your cheek on my lips.

Oh, Tyler, Mommy sees you laughing in the sun.

I see you, Mom and Dad.

I see the fires that took you all.

I see you together.

Don't leave me here.

Can you hear me?

Please, take me with you.

I want to be with you.... I can't bear to be alone.

I can't be without you. I can't. I can't live without you.

I can't fight anymore.

Was I wrong about it all?

Was the phone call really about Dr. Durbin's letter? Was Polly Larenski crazy with grief, too? Was she not in her right mind when she called me and said Tyler was alive?

Help me!

Joe, help me! Tell me what to do. Tell me what is real because I don't know anymore. Send me a sign, show me the way, please. It hurts so much.

Time slipped away as Emma struggled with half-dreamed fears, listening and searching. But no one spoke to her and no signs emerged.

Reality descended upon her with the sinking sun.

She was alone.

Defeated.

She had come to another decision.

As she walked home from the cemetery, the truth emerged at every turn and every corner where she was met by the ghosts of her happiness.

There was the Wagon Wheel Diner where she first saw

Joe. And there was the Branding Bar where she met him again a month later. And there were two houses that Joe and his crew built. And down the way, in the distance, she saw her school and, near it, the hospital where she had Tyler. There was the park where he liked to play.

I can't live without you.

Reality had arrived with the night, and the truth was as dark as the starless sky. She walked into Yancy's Drugs, went to the cold remedy aisle and snatched a large bottle of extra-strong sleeping pills.

The store was deserted.

Mindy, the teenaged clerk, picked up the bottle from the counter. She hesitated to slide it over the scanner next to the cash, giving Emma a look that telegraphed her knowledge. Like when boys bought condoms or Mindy's girlfriends paid for birth control or Rudy, the furniture salesman, bought hair dye. If you wanted to know what was really going on in Big Cloud, talk to the checkout girl at Yancy's Drugs.

"How are you doing, Emma?" Mindy turned the bottle to find the barcode.

"I'm having trouble sleeping, Mindy. How's your mom?"

"Good. We're so sorry about what happened and everything."

The scanner beeped.

"Will that be cash or charge?"

Emma set a ten on the counter then gathered up her change, her pills and left. When she put the bottle in her purse, it sounded like a baby's rattle.

Aunt Marsha was relieved when Emma arrived home. Uncle Ned woke from napping in front of the TV and an old John Wayne movie.

The Searchers. Joe's favorite. Was that a sign?

"Do you want something to eat, dear?" Aunt Marsha asked. "I can fix you a chicken sandwich and we have potato salad."

"No. I'm not hungry. I'm going to bed. I'm very tired."

"Oh, before I forget, I have your new prescription in my purse and Dr. Pierce said you were to take two pills before bed. I'll get them."

After Emma swallowed the pills with a glass of water, she hugged her aunt, a bone-cracking, passionate hug that lasted more than a moment.

"Goodness, dear!"

Then Emma hugged her uncle the same way.

"Thank you both for everything. I love you."

"We love you, too, Em." Uncle Ned, rubbed his eyes. "Sleep well."

"Emma?" her aunt asked. "Is there anything you want to talk about?"

Emma stopped, swallowed, blinked back a few tears and forced a weak smile before shaking her head.

"I'm just tired."

Alone in her bedroom she shut the door.

She got a cup of cold water from her bathroom and set it and the bottle on her nightstand under the glow of the reading lamp.

In the dim light, she undressed and wrapped herself in one of Joe's old flannel shirts. She pulled out Tyler's stuffed teddy bear from her bag as well as her wallet, which held a worn snapshot of the three of them at the park.

She loved this picture.

I want to be with you. When I sleep, I dream. In my dreams we are together. I need to be with you.

She could hear crickets in the night. See the darkness from her window.

Warm joy flowed through her heart, carrying her to every tender memory, every sweet second of their lives together.

Help me find my way back to you.

Please.

It hurts.

The bottle rattled slightly when she reached for it.

It was hard to see because of her tears, but she managed to read a few words on the label: One hundred extra-strength capsules. The recommended dosage for adults was two before bed.

She unscrewed the cap, stared at the foil seal.

She caught her breath, then using her thumbnail, punctured the foil.

She peeled it back, removed the cotton and peered inside.

50

New York City

*W*yoming.

There's a link to Wyoming, Jack Gannon thought, working late at his desk at the World Press Alliance.

But what is it? And there's a link to Brazil, Africa, human traffickers, an ex-CIA player and something called Extremus Deus. Man, this story shoots in a thousand directions but I have no way of knowing how the threads connect.

A planned attack was feared.

Gannon sensed time was hammering against him.

People have died. People have been murdered. I've got to nail this story.

He had to settle down, he had to focus.

Reaching for his mug to take a hit of coffee, his hand shook. He set the mug down. *Jet lag,* he told himself, *it's jet lag.*

He'd returned from Africa late yesterday.

Or was it the day before?

He'd lost track of time.

He glanced out the window. Dusk had fallen on Manhattan and the Empire State Building ascended from a galaxy of light. His body was sore from stress, from tension. He'd arrived at the office that afternoon and worked with a sense of urgency, propelled by caffeine and adrenaline. The midlevel editors had left him alone. He was working for Melody Lyon.

For her part, Lyon had yet to get a face-to-face debriefing from him. She'd been in Montreal, then in Boston on company business. She was due back at headquarters at any moment and she'd ordered him to wait at the office no matter how late she was.

All right, Gannon, focus.

He tried the coffee again, managed a decent gulp and got back to work.

He had so many files open that he risked freezing up his computer. He'd scanned in the pages he'd found near the café bombing in Rio and was reviewing them. He'd also downloaded and opened everything from Maria Santo and Sarah Kirby's group in Rio. He had Adam Corley's massive file open, and he had his own notes on what he suspected were the major veins of the story.

What was connected to what?

It was overwhelming. He had to pick an angle, see where it led, then pick another.

All right, the human traffickers were linked to illegal adoptions, which usually involved young children, even babies, which could be tied to—where was that now? He clicked on several files. There—fertility.

There—the Golden Dawn Fertility Corp. What was that? Where was it?

A quick online search confirmed that the Golden Dawn Fertility Corp. was in Los Angeles, California. Had they been in the news lately? Gannon searched WPA's news databases. All that came up for the last five years were features on infertile couples.

Wait, what was this item from the *Orange County Register?*

Santa Ana Woman Dies in House Fire
Polly Marie Larenski died from smoke inhalation in a blaze that destroyed her town house in the Civic Center area. Larenski, 37, was living alone and had recently worked as a lab manager at the Golden Dawn

Fertility Corporation in Los Angeles. Cause of the
fire, which resulted in $500,000 damage, remains
under investigation by the Arson Unit.

Gannon highlighted the phrase "Golden Dawn Fertility
Corporation in Los Angeles."

It called to mind something he'd seen in Maria Santo
and Sarah Kirby's files—a reference to LA #181975 to
Wyoming847.

Right.

Wyoming again. Adam Corley had something on Wyoming, as well.

He searched Corley's files until he found it again: a
document among dozens of others. There was the file
again: Big Cloud, Wyoming—Golden Dawn Fertility Corp.
He opened it.

There was a list of names and nothing else.

Joseph Lane, Emma Lane and Tyler Lane.

What was this about?

"Jack?" Rachel, the news assistant, stood before him.
"Melody's back—she's meeting with George and Al in the
conference room now."

"Thanks."

"Because it's late, they've ordered in some Chinese."

Gannon smelled the stir-fried food before he entered.

Melody Lyon and her two senior editors, George Wilson
and Al Delaney, were loading their paper plates and opening soda cans.

"Nothing Jack tells us is to leave this room until we clear
it. George, get the door, please?" Lyon said. Then she turned
to Gannon: "Help yourself to some food. You look tired.
How bad was it in Morocco?"

Gannon recounted the history of his research but with-
held details about his torture.

"After I found Adam Corley's body, they took me in for
questioning."

"Who took you in?" Lyon asked.

"Moroccan police, security types."

"And what have you got now?"

"I have a lead from Brazil that the café bombing may be linked to a larger group, possibly a conspiracy involving human trafficking, illegal adoptions and maybe even a feared attack against the U.S."

"That's quite a tale, Jack," George Wilson said, "and held together with maybes and a lot of possible links. Is any of it verifiable?"

Gannon knew Wilson disliked him for what happened in Rio de Janeiro. He also knew the point of these meetings was for the editors to challenge Gannon's findings, to ensure that every iota of research was solid, backed up with sources or documents; that it had no holes. Because ultimately the news organization, editors and reporters were like mountain climbers roped together on a story.

A weak link anywhere could bring them all down.

"I've got some files and documents I'm going over," Gannon said.

"What are the sources of the documents?" Wilson asked.

"International aid and human-rights groups—mainly Corley's group, Equal Globe International."

"Groups with political agendas," Wilson said.

"Groups that the United Nations relies on for frontline information."

"Right. Don't get me started on the UN," Wilson said. "I'm a little skeptical about fears of an attack. How many times have we heard this kind of talk before and nothing comes of it? You have anything else?"

"I met a U.S. intelligence agent in Morocco. He was present at my questioning."

"That so? And how did you verify that he, or she, was an intelligence agent?" Wilson asked.

He saved my fucking life, Wilson, was what Gannon wanted to say. Instead, he said, "It was clear by his actions.

He intervened. Later he told me that Corley may have had information related to a planned attack against the U.S."

"This is what he wanted you to believe?" Wilson asked.

"You're twisting things," Gannon said.

The editors exchanged glances.

"What's the agent's name?" Lyon asked.

"All he gave me was contact information."

"Of course," Wilson said.

"In any event," Lyon said, "Jack's on to something substantial here."

"I'm not convinced." Wilson was reading from his Black-Berry. "See, when we learned Jack was going to Morocco, I had Taz, our bureau chief in Rabat, do some checking. His Moroccan police sources told him that Adam Corley, the Irish ex-cop who also volunteered with Equal Globe International, was tied up with drug dealers who likely murdered him."

"That's bullshit," Gannon said.

"Jack, Taz has lived in Morocco for twelve years. You were there for what, three days?"

"So? He didn't see what I saw. He doesn't know what I know."

"Take it easy, Jack," Lyon said.

"That drug crap is just a cover story for whoever really killed Corley," Gannon said.

"Jack—" Lyon searched his face "—have you told us everything that happened to you in Morocco?"

"Yes." He cleared his throat. "The café bombing is linked to Corley's murder in Rabat and human traffickers and this ex-CIA guy, Drake Stinson, and some shadowy group or think tank called Extremus Deus, a scientist, and all of it is tied to some plot against the U.S."

While Lyon made a few notes, Delaney said, "Jack, you seem to have a lot going on there. Mel, maybe we should put more people on this story."

"Why waste our resources?" Wilson said. "All I see is a lot of disparate pieces to a conspiracy theory."

Lyon swiveled her chair to the window and the view of Madison Square Garden. The banner announcing the upcoming Human World Conference was illuminated.

"Tell me something, George. What have Frank Archer and our people in Rio learned about the café bombing?"

"That it's still under investigation."

"Then Jack's got the only substantial follow-up story on it, directly from the narco dealers. And that kind of confirmation goes a long way in my book. He's got us leads on something significant. During my recent business flights, I've read through most of the files Jack's sent me. Granted they do seem disparate, as you say, but my gut tells me he's got something. And for what it's worth, this morning I learned on the grapevine that the *Washington Post* has caught wind of a story about national security concerns over long-buried, secret U.S. military experiments falling into criminal hands. Maybe it's related to this, maybe it's not. In any event, we're not going to get beat on what happened in Brazil. The bottom line is two of our people were among those murdered in Rio de Janeiro. I assigned Jack to find out who is responsible, to pursue the truth no matter where it leads. That's what he's been doing. We are not going to let someone else write the ending for us. Not after what we lost. This is our goddamn story. So, I'm going to demand all of our bureaus keep digging for anything related to the bombing. George and Al, I'm counting on you to watch your story lists and alert me personally to anything remotely connected to what Jack has discovered. It that clear? I'm going to leave Jack on this story to keep doing what he's been doing. And we're putting the full support of this news agency behind him. Do you have any questions?"

No one spoke.

Wilson picked through the wontons.

"All right," Lyon said. "We're done. It's late, go home."

"Hold up," Delaney said, consulting his BlackBerry. "I just got something interesting from Nan in Miami who is checking with Butler in Atlanta. Seems a passenger on a cruise ship became violently ill and died, a forty-one-year-old man from Indianapolis. The medical examiner for Broward County alerted the Centers for Disease Control who, according to our sources, alerted Homeland Security. Seems they don't know what caused his death, but sources say it was like something from a horror movie."

"Stay on that, get it all confirmed. Track down the ship's passenger list, the ship's medical crew," Lyon said. "Jack, I want you to go home, rest. Tomorrow we'll talk about our next steps."

"Sure, I just want to finish up what I was working on."

Gannon got fresh coffee, returned to his desk and went back to examining the documents concerning Big Cloud, Wyoming, the Golden Dawn Fertility Corporation in Los Angeles and the fire in Santa Ana that killed a former lab manager. There were some names… Yes, here they were— Joseph Lane, Emma Lane and Tyler Lane.

Gannon rubbed his chin, thinking.

Using the paper's Internet services, he found public telephone listings for nearly 400 Joseph Lanes in the U.S., and nearly 250 Joe Lanes. They were listed by state. He scrolled through them, pleased when he came to a phone listing for Joe and Emma Lane in Big Cloud, Wyoming.

He jotted down the number, starting with the 307 area code, then the rest, thinking he'd made a mistake because the last three numbers, 847 were familiar to him.

Why was he repeating those three numbers? Was it fatigue?

Gannon clicked on Maria Santo and Sarah Kirby's files. He went to the listing, a reference to LA #181975 to Wyoming847.

There it was. The last three numbers of the file and the Lane's home phone number matched. All right, he'd check one more thing.

He then went online for the newspaper for Big Cloud. The *Big Cloud Gazette.* The WPA subscribed to it electronically. He searched the paper's archives for anything on Joe, Emma and Tyler Lane and got several hits.

Gannon froze.

The most recent was an obituary.

Then he found a news story about a tragic car accident that killed a Big Cloud father and his infant son—*Joe and Tyler Lane.*

The sole survivor was Emma Lane, Tyler's mother and Joe's widow.

Gannon clicked on to a family picture and was drawn to Emma Lane's bright smile and beautiful eyes.

Something told him to call.

He didn't know why but something in his gut was insisting he call the number he had for Joe and Emma Lane.

Call right now!

Gannon double-checked the time difference, then dialed.

51

Emma tilted the bottle to shake the sleeping pills into her palm when the phone next to her bed rang.

Startled, she didn't move.

It did not ring a second time because it was answered by the extension in the living room. Through her bedroom door, she heard Uncle Ned's muffled voice involved in a conversation that included Aunt Marsha. Then someone approached her door and rapped on it softly.

"Emma?" Aunt Marsha said.

Emma poured all of the pills back into the bottle, capped it and put it under her pillow.

The door cracked open.

"Dear, I'm sorry to disturb you but there's a call for you. It's a reporter. I told him you were asleep but he insisted I get you."

"A reporter? Is it that guy from the *Gazette?*"

"No, it's a man from New York."

"New York? Did he say why he was calling?"

"No, only that it was important that he speak to you. Do you want to talk to him? Or we could tell him to call back another time?"

Is this my sign? Emma wondered.

"No, I'll take it here. Thanks."

She swept her hair back and picked up the handset.

"Hello?"

"Hi, is this Emma Lane?"

"Yes."

"Emma, my name is Jack Gannon. I'm a reporter with the World Press Alliance in New York. I'm sorry to impose on you at this time but I need to speak to you briefly. It's important. Do you have a moment?"

"Yes, what's this about?"

"Thanks, I'll get to that, but first I need to confirm that I've reached the right person. Again, my apologies, but I have to ask this. Are you the Emma Lane whose husband Joe and son Tyler were in a recent car accident?"

Emma took a breath.

"Yes."

"And have you had any dealings whatsoever with the Golden Dawn Fertility Corporation in Los Angeles California?"

A shiver rattled up Emma's spine. She stifled a sob, covering her mouth with her free hand, feeling tears cascading over her fingers.

"We were clients."

She glanced at Joe and Tyler's picture on her nightstand.

"Please, tell me what this is about?"

"Your case at the clinic surfaced in a story I'm working on."

"Our case? How? What kind of story?"

"It's complex, Emma. I need to talk to you. I think you might be able to help me. Would you talk to me if I came to Wyoming to see you?"

Emma was overwhelmed by what was happening. After all she'd been through, was this call real? Before she answered Gannon, he asked another question.

"Emma, have any other reporters contacted you, anyone from the *Washington Post* or the *L.A. Times?*"

Gannon's sobering tone cut through the haze that had nearly swallowed her. She felt Joe's shirt, felt Tyler's stuffed bear, felt a hand pulling her out of the abyss, felt her breathing quicken as she squeezed the handset.

"No. You're the only one who's called. I'll meet with you if you answer my questions," she said.

"I'll try."

"If I help you, will I find out what happened to my son?"

"I'm not sure I know what you mean."

"I don't think he was killed in the crash, I think he was stolen from it. Now, given what you know, is it possible someone took him? Or am I crazy?"

She waited for his answer. Everything depended upon it.

"Given what I know, anything is possible."

"I have one more question," she said.

"All right."

"How fast can you get here?"

52

"Six miles south, you got the ruins of the old wooden fort where the Eighth U.S. Cavalry was posted for a time." Ned Fuller nodded to the sweep of flat land that reached to the sky and mountains. "Big Cloud's just up ahead."

Fuller had become Jack Gannon's tour guide after picking him up at the airport in Cheyenne where he'd held up a small sign bearing Gannon's name in block letters. He had a firm handshake and gunmetal eyes that drilled into Gannon's when they met.

"This had better be for real because my niece has been through hell."

"It is, sir," Gannon assured him before they left the terminal.

Now as they drove, he listened to Fuller point out landmarks. The mid-nineteenth-century storefronts and the municipal buildings evoked the frontier. As they cut through town, Gannon reminded himself of what he was pursuing, of what he'd endured and how far he'd traveled since Melody Lyon had first put him on this story.

Last night, after telling her that his call to Emma Lane was a strong lead, Lyon had urged him to fly to Wyoming and follow up. "We've just learned Reuters is sniffing around Adam Corley's murder in Morocco."

The pressure for Gannon to break the full story was mounting.

"Want me to drop you at your hotel, or do you want to go straight to the house?"

"I'd like to get started," Gannon said.

After they parked in the driveway of Emma's bungalow, Gannon grabbed his computer bag and approached the house with Fuller. Aunt Marsha met them at the door. Gannon smelled freshly brewed coffee and a faint hint of soap as he entered.

"Welcome, Mr. Gannon. I'm Marsha Fuller, Emma's aunt." She shook his hand and gestured to the sofa. "We hope you had a good trip—all that way from New York, goodness! Would you like some coffee?"

"That would be fine."

"How do you take it?"

"Milk and sugar, thanks."

He set his bag near the sofa and before sitting, turned to a woman about his age who'd entered the room.

"I'm Emma Lane." She held out her hand. "Thank you for coming."

"Thanks for seeing me," he said, "and please accept my belated condolences."

Emma sat in the sofa chair opposite him. While she took stock of his face, the fading cuts, he noticed hers, how the anguish manifested by her stress lines and reddened eyes failed to disguise the fact she was pretty.

"After you called," she said, "I'd thought of having my doctor and some of the local police join us. But for now, I think only my aunt and uncle need to be here."

"I understand."

"Tell me what you know."

He began with the bombing in Brazil, his murdered colleagues, Maria Santo's discovery and the ex-CIA player's link to the law firm suspected of illegal adoptions. Then he went on to tell her about the link to the London human-rights group and human trafficking, and finished with Morocco and the murder of Adam Corley and Gannon's encounter with a U.S. agent.

Emma took it all in slowly, while every few minutes her aunt and uncle questioned how such things could happen.

"It's almost too fantastic to believe," Uncle Ned said.

It was Emma's turn.

She allowed Gannon to set out a recorder and she started by recounting the details of the crash.

"I know Joe died out there, I felt it, but I swear other people were present—that they took Tyler. The investigators here told me Tyler was consumed by the intensity of the fire. All they found were his shoes. But during our drive, I had removed them and set them aside. In my heart, I know he is alive."

Emma explained how she and Joe had gone to an L.A. fertility clinic, and she told Gannon about Polly Larenski's disturbing call, how everyone had dismissed it. How she felt compelled to go to California. How she'd learned Larenski was a lab manager at the clinic and was fired. How she'd tracked her down in Santa Ana, and how, before Larenski died in the fire, she'd admitted to selling Tyler's DNA to some shadowy corporation.

"What corporation?"

"I don't know, but Polly told me that the people she was dealing with had boasted to her after the crash that Tyler was alive, that Tyler was 'chosen.'"

"Chosen for what?" Gannon asked.

"I don't know."

"And you told police everything?"

"Yes. I went to the authorities in California, the FBI. I told police here. Nobody believes me. They think I've lost touch with reality. The doctors say I'm delusional, that I'm hallucinating as part of my grieving to help me cope with post-traumatic stress and survivor's guilt."

Emma touched the corners of her eyes.

"Jack," she said, "do you believe it's possible I'm not crazy? Do you believe Tyler may have been taken from the crash, that he may be alive?"

Looking into her eyes Gannon found pain, fear, helplessness and hope, and then he told her the truth.

"Yes, I believe he could still be alive."

Emma's hands flew to her face. She gulped air and took a moment to maintain her composure.

"Then help me find my son. Oh, God, please, before it's too late!"

"Let's get started."

Gannon set up his laptop and turned it on. Emma went to her bedroom and returned with a collection of file folders bound by a thick rubber band. Aunt Marsha made more coffee while Uncle Ned shook his head and quietly cursed to himself before turning to his niece.

"Honey," he said softly. "I'm so damned sorry for not believing you. We couldn't have known. We just—"

Emma pressed her fingers to his mouth and hugged him.

"At times I didn't believe it myself," she said.

Hours passed and Gannon and Emma examined file after file, page after page of the information they each had.

"Do you have any more details on who Polly Larenski was dealing with, or how she had contact with them?"

"No. She told me they called her at home, or at a pay phone. She said she had files she was going to give me, but they were lost in the fire."

"Which is still under investigation by the Arson Unit."

"Are you thinking someone killed her?"

"It's possible, since someone murdered ten people in Rio de Janeiro, and someone murdered Adam Corley in Morocco." Gannon rubbed the back of his neck then shifted his thoughts. "When Polly Larenski called you the first time and said Tyler was alive, you said police here traced the number to a pay phone in Santa Ana?"

"Yes." Emma flipped through her files for a document. "Here's the number and address."

"And do you have Polly's home address and phone number?"

Emma passed him the information. As he jotted notes in his book, she pointed to one of Gannon's computer files labeled E.D.—Extremus Deus?

"What's that?"

"I'm not sure, some shadowy group. I need to follow up on that one," he said while yawning and rubbing his eyes. There were so many files they had not yet reviewed. It was nearly 3:00 a.m., 5:00 a.m. New York time, and he was struggling to stay awake.

Uncle Ned drove Gannon to his motel, the Blue Sage Motor Court, dropping him off under the big wagon-wheel arch entrance.

"I'll pick you up around nine in the morning," he said.

Emma planned to take Gannon to the crash site in the morning.

In his room Gannon took a hot shower to clear his mind. After he got into bed, he flipped through the notes he'd written in his notebook, reflecting on everything he'd learned.

Emma Lane's baby was "chosen."

Was he plucked from a fiery crash?

Who stole him?

Polly Larenski was the key here, and now she was dead.

Who was she selling the DNA to?

Polly Larenski's phone numbers—her home number and the one for the pay phone near her house—they were the thread to the answer.

Gannon studied them.

He knew what to do.

He was closer now, closer than he'd ever been.

53

Dr. Sutsoff's island lay among a chain of uninhabited cays stretching for a few hundred miles southeast of Nassau.

It was a square quarter mile, ringed by white beachfront that slid into warm turquoise water and was lush with palm trees hissing in the breezes.

Aided by her investors, Sutsoff had purchased Deus Island from a Dutch drug dealer for eight million dollars in U.S. cash. Legend held that the island's name originated with Spanish pirates who, after a storm, thought they'd died and arrived at God's doorstep.

Geographically, it was within the Commonwealth of the Bahamas. But through forgotten treaties between Spain, France and Portugal, it had disappeared into a legal nether-world, giving the island's owner the unique ability to claim citizenship with the Bahamas and the other countries.

Sutsoff held a number of counterfeit passports under aliases.

Nearly two dozen people lived in the huddle of houses on the northern side. Sutsoff employed them to maintain her home and research facilities on the southern side, which included several dishes linked to advanced satellite systems, and a small biosafety containment lab.

Dr. Sutsoff had the lab constructed in an isolated area. Through her trusted intelligence connections, she'd bought components from Malaysia, Indonesia and India, and hired experts to build it.

The structure was made with specialized ceilings, walls and floors that formed a sealed internal shell within the facility. It had airlocks and airtight double-door containment entrances, dunk tanks, showers and fumigation chambers. It also had sophisticated ventilation, exhaust and decontamination systems.

The lab had its own energy sources, powered by long-life batteries, in addition to wind, solar and diesel generators, whose mechanisms were reinforced to withstand hurricanes.

Sutsoff had trained her island staff on the safe handling, storage and testing of sample materials. Because they worked with agents for which there was no known cure, they had to be skilled at decontamination, containing spills, proper immunization and reducing the risk of infection.

Sutsoff reminded them that she'd lost a member of her African research team and that even the world's best microbiologists had been infected during their experiments. A top Russian military scientist working with the Marburg virus had died hours after a lab accident.

Sutsoff's staff wore the newest positive pressure suits and had been well trained in decontamination showers and the removal and disposal of all clothing after working in the lab. They respected procedures for decontaminating materials such as tubes, scalpels, syringes and slides.

In the days since Sutsoff had returned from Africa with her samples, she and her staff had been working around the clock.

Now, hunched over her table where she was checking the results of refining her agent with the new material from the pariah bats Sutsoff knew success was within her grasp.

She had monitored news reports concerning cruise ship passenger Roger Tippert. Elena and Valmir, who had offended her with their mistakes and insolence, managed to do their job. Investigators had failed to identify the mystery illness that had killed Tippert.

And they never will.

Looking through her microscope, Sutsoff imagined how the linear-thinking eggheads at the CDC and in the labs in Maryland must be crapping in their knickers wondering, *What the hell is this?*

Just a teeny harbinger of the shape of things to come.

Sutsoff took pride in what she'd achieved. Her mind raced through the images from her years of struggle to accomplish the impossible.

She thought back to the crude work of Project Crucible.

The truth was, she had carried the other CIA scientists on that entire assignment. They'd gotten petty and had invoked Nuremberg when she told them what they all knew had to be done, but were too afraid to admit.

Those fools will be an asterisk in the history books.

Her work on Project Crucible was merely a first step. Sutsoff had corrected and advanced North Korea's misguided assumptions on File 91. Her cutting-edge research on molecular manipulation led to her discovery of a new pathway. Her work on remote-controlled nanotechnology was theoretically implausible, but if applied properly in the field, would work.

And it did work.

Very well.

Ask Roger Tippert's widow.

And Sutsoff's experiments on pathogens, which were aimed at developing the most effective lethal agent known, had progressed. She'd created a concoction using characteristics of Ebola and Marburg. Her study had shown a fatality rate in humans of 70 to 75 percent.

It worked beautifully in the Tippert trial.

But that rate soared after her team discovered Pariah Variant 1 in the African pariah bats of Cameroon. Sutsoff determined that the new lethal microbe must have arisen out of the deadly carbon dioxide explosion at Lake Nyos. Her team had first observed that Pariah Variant 1 would have a fatality rate in humans of 95 to 97 percent. Now, after a little more work her in the lab, Sutsoff had pushed that rate to 100 percent.

One hundred.

Behold the most lethal agent the world will ever know: Extremus Deus Variant 1.

The perfect killer.

Unstoppable. And completely under her control.

The delivery mechanism had always been the tricky aspect. Sutsoff had grappled with it until she decided to refine nature's delivery system, human-to-human transmission.

But with a twist.

Subjects with certain DNA characteristics would be the perfect vessels for initial delivery—the younger the better. She'd worked out the calculations, factoring in failures and unforeseen challenges. A successful operation would require seventy subjects who met the criteria, a support system to nurture the operation and a security system to protect its covert development.

Sutsoff had known Drake Stinson through old agency connections and he'd shared her fears, her philosophy regarding Extremus Deus and her desire to see the operation to its successful conclusion.

Stinson had connections to human traffickers, illegal adoption rings, fertility clinics and various underworld networks around the globe. These resources would fulfill her requirement of finding seventy children with the DNA coding she'd required.

Money and methods were not a concern.

The only criteria were secrecy and invisibility.

The criminal networks used bribery, abductions and even murder to obtain the seventy children whose DNA was tested and retested. The children were held by others posing as adoptive parents while they awaited Sutsoff's instructions.

When the time came, the new lethal agent would be introduced easily into the children's systems. The children would experience absolutely no symptoms ever and never be at risk. They were the mode of delivery. Their DNA coding made them ideal delivery vessels. If left inactivated, the agent would pass harmlessly through their systems. But once Sutsoff activated the agent, each person a child touched was at risk.

Using her advanced work on remote-controlled nanotechnology and low-frequency GPS technology, Sutsoff could use her computer and track and pinpoint the location of those who had been exposed. Then, by submitting the parameters for the targets, Sutsoff could determine who would succumb to the microbe.

If she chose to limit the parameter to certain DNA types with certain variables, then her target pool would be reduced. If she chose to broaden it, the number of victims would increase.

She could target it to all subjects with blue eyes, or only those with red hair, or people whose genetic codes were characteristic of males from the Mediterranean region, or females who possessed Asian DNA signatures.

By entering a few commands on her laptop, she could determine who lived and who died.

Extremus Deus.

A sudden pain jabbed her, her knees buckled and she had to steady herself at the lab table.

The onset of an attack.

"Doctor!" Her alarmed lab assistant approached her. "Do you require evacuation from the lab?"

"No. We're nearly finished."

She wanted to scream.

Not now. She couldn't battle this now.

Her pills were in the outer chamber. She couldn't leave now.

There was no time to lose. They were so close. She seated herself on her lab stool and took deep, measured breaths.

Slowly her agony subsided.

As she struggled to anchor herself, she focused on the reason she needed to complete her work.

It was her little brother, Will…reaching for her…pulling her back…

"Gretchen! Help me! Gretchen!"

The memory replayed in her mind, bleeding into the horror to come.

Her motivation for why she had to do this went beyond vengeance against a world that saw her brother, mother and father trampled to death before her eyes in Vridekistan—although it was the life-shattering event that had forged her destiny to change the course of civilization.

Like Oppenheimer, Sutsoff knew that in order to save something, you had to destroy something. It was the underlying philosophy of her inner circle, Extremus Deus.

Humanity was doomed unless corrective action was taken.

By her tragedy and through the power of her intellect and will, fate had equipped her to be the architect of that action.

That was what was at play here, she realized as she resumed her work, filling novelty float pens with the new lethal agent. It was like loading a plane with bombs. The pens themselves were not dangerous. A few more steps had to be followed: the introduction of the agent into the delivery vessel, then remote activation.

When their work was finished in the containment lab, Sutsoff's team followed the exit protocol, clean-up and decontamination procedures. Then they met on the lab's outdoor patio.

Sutsoff looked upon the novelty pens in the plastic tub. She played with one, watched the sailboat float from one end to the other as her staff awaited instructions.

She gazed out to the seaplane tethered to the dock at the island's leeward bay.

"Add the pens to the kits and alert the pilot that we have to get these to Nassau and expedited by courier to the seventy addresses."

"Yes, Doctor."

"No mistakes can be made. We have no time left."

"Yes, Doctor."

"Once they've been delivered, we'll embark on the final stages."

54

Vancouver, Canada

Brakes creaked as the Zoom It Courier van stopped in front of the apartment house on East Pender.

The driver confirmed the address on his package, hustled to the door and pressed the buzzer. While waiting he took in the filthy porch, bordered with empty beer bottles and fly-covered takeout food containers. He wasn't fond of deliveries on the east side.

"What is it?" a female voice crackled through the intercom.

"Zoom It Courier—package for Chenoweth in Unit B."

"Just leave it at the door."

"Need a signature."

Minutes passed.

A woman emerged on the other side of the door's wrought-iron security bars. Locks clicked before the door opened. The driver thought she was Asian, like the little boy at her side, who looked to be about three or four. The woman said something to the boy in Chinese, he stepped back and she signed for the delivery, Joy Lee Chenoweth.

The small package was from the Blue Tortoise Kids' Hideaway at the resort in the Bahamas where she and her boyfriend, Wex, had stayed.

She had an idea what this was.

Joy Lee took it to the kitchen. Before she opened it, she got a cookie for the little boy. The kid loved sweet things.

The package contained a letter thanking them for their recent business. It included a float pen as a small gift and instructions to go to a Web site and enter the unique barcode on the side of the pen.

Oh, yeah, Joy Lee knew what this was about.

She immediately went to their laptop, found the site, entered the security barcode, then went to another secure page where she was stopped. In order to proceed, she had to provide the first part of a password assigned to her at the outset of her job.

Her laptop beeped its approval.

She was given access to another secure site, which required the second part of the password. As she waited, Joy Lee glanced at the boy sitting on his chair eating his cookie.

He was a sweet boy who cried in his sleep for his mother. Sure, it broke Joy Lee's heart, but beyond that she didn't care. She couldn't care. Because watching over him was just a job.

A very lucrative one.

Less risky than her previous profession as a drug courier, at least that was the lie she'd been telling herself lately.

Twenty-five years old and what was she doing with her life?

Joy Lee had been an international student at Simon Fraser University. But her parents in Hong Kong had disowned her when she succumbed to partying and drugs and dropped out.

She'd met Wex at a party, a good-looking drug dealer who got her work delivering drugs. She earned ten thousand dollars U.S. per trip smuggling drugs from Bangkok, Jakarta, Mexico City, Amsterdam and Jamaica.

The smugglers trained her, paid for her airfare and the best hotels. It was like a vacation. She'd been saving to buy a flower stand, but her addictions inevitably eroded her profits.

Joy Lee wanted out of the life she was living and seized her chance in a hotel in Kingston, Jamaica, when Wex introduced her to an ice-cold, old white dude. He offered them the job of a lifetime. Wex half joked that the old dude was old-school CIA, or something.

Anyway, the old dude said he had a wealthy client who needed them to pose as a married couple adopting a Chinese boy, then watch over him for a few months. They would be paid two thousand dollars a day U.S. for as long as the job lasted, which he estimated could be four months.

Joy Lee and Wex agreed and the old dude arranged to get them counterfeit passports, credit cards, legal documents and cash. He warned them that the job required absolute secrecy and obedience, that any violation would result in immediate and unpleasant consequences.

Joy Lee and Wex flew to Malaysia and picked up the boy in a law office in Kuala Lumpur. The boy cried a lot and Joy Lee soothed him by telling him she was his aunt and would take care of him for a while. They returned to Vancouver without any problems. Nor were there problems when their employer paid to send "the family" on a fantastic Caribbean cruise.

It was all cool except for when they met the doctor at the Hideaway in the resort at the Bahamas.

Dr. Auden. That woman gave her the creeps.

The doctor checked over the boy like he was some kind of amazing specimen, asking if they'd been adhering to all their medical instructions while watching over him: diet, exercise, medicine, all that crap. Then the doctor told them to be ready to follow the "next step in the operation."

Whatever, weirdo, she thought, now willing her computer to speed up. *Just keep that delivery dude coming every week with an envelope of cash.*

Finally, Joy Lee's computer had loaded and she entered the updated secure pages.

She was instructed that they would be receiving a new mobile satellite phone, and that they were going on an all-expense-paid trip to attend the Human World Conference in

New York City. Their air tickets were online, the hotel was reserved and all tickets to events and further instructions would be waiting for them in the hotel room.

"Wow!" Joy Lee was thrilled and turned to the little boy. "We're going to see the best bands in the world, even the monster show at Central Park!"

Joy Lee reread every online instruction twice. The last one directed her to view a short video. When it commenced, she groaned as she recognized creepy Dr. Auden.

The old girl's smile seemed so insincere, Joy Lee thought as the video played.

"Hello to our friends around the world. The fact that you are watching me now means that you have received your kits and your instructions. Please follow them carefully. Thank you for your cooperation. By attending this event you are about to embark on the experience of a lifetime. Your small group will change history. Follow the written instructions, then make certain you spread goodwill to everyone at the conference by shaking hands and having your little ones shake hands. Reach out and touch everyone you can. It is imperative that you do this. Your participation will take humanity into a new era. Believe me, it will happen before your eyes, a transformation unlike the world has ever known."

The message ended.

Was she some kind of religious cult nut?

Whatever. Joy Lee shrugged, reviewing instructions on how to give the boy a few drops of medicine contained in the liquid of the float pen. Looked easy. More important to Joy Lee was the lineup of bands performing at the five-day event.

This was so great. Wex was not going to believe this.

She ran up the stairs to wake him up.

Alone, the little boy picked up the float pen.

He watched the little sailboat float from one end to the other while above him, Wex and Joy Lee began packing for New York City.

55

McLean, Virginia

Ensconced in the wooded countryside near the Potomac River west of Washington, D.C., stood the white concrete-and-glass structure that served as headquarters for the Central Intelligence Agency.

As he entered, Robert Lancer knew time was working against him.

He cleared security and strode to one of the building's vaulted rooms for his early morning meeting, mentally reviewing his concerns.

Nothing had emerged yet from the Moroccans on the murder of his source, Adam Corley.

Then there was the reporter—Jack Gannon.

Gannon was going to meet Corley to learn more about a link to a law firm in Brazil and its suspected ties to a global human-smuggling network and the bombing of a café in Rio de Janeiro that killed ten people. Drake Stinson, ex-CIA, who'd played on Black Ops, was a member of that firm.

Stinson had vanished.

Now a new threat had emerged out of Florida—a mystery death on a cruise ship—the CDC's alert to Homeland was that whatever killed the man from Indianapolis was engineered by somebody.

Was this part of an attack or something else?

Lancer could not dismiss Foster Winfield's fears that someone was attempting to replicate Project Crucible's abandoned experiments. How Winfield and his colleague Phil Kenyon were so uneasy about Gretchen Sutsoff, who had led most of the research. While they regarded her as a brilliant scientist, her extreme views troubled them.

And me, too, because I can't find her, Lancer thought. *Could any of this stuff be connected?*

He exhaled as he entered the meeting room. He nodded to the people he knew, helped himself to coffee and took his place. The conversations were muted, the mood was tense.

Everybody was at the table.

The agency had people from Intelligence, Clandestine, Science and Tech and Support. Homeland was there, as were the FBI, Secret Service, the National Security Agency, Defense Intelligence Agency, U.S. State Department's Bureau of Intelligence, the National Joint Terrorism Task Force and an array of others from the intelligence community.

The meeting commenced when Lincoln Hunter, assistant to the National Intelligence director—the president's advisor on intelligence—slapped his report on the tabletop.

"What do we have?"

The woman from the Centers for Disease Control summarized the gruesome case of Roger Timothy Tippert, a forty-one-year-old high school teacher from Indianapolis, who died while on a Caribbean cruise. Aspects of the autopsy troubled the Broward County M.E. who alerted the CDC.

"We've observed that it appears—I mean—" she cleared her throat "—there are strong indications that the pathogen that killed Mr. Tippert was manufactured."

"Do we know who's behind it and if there are other victims?"

"No," she said. "We alerted Homeland."

"And we've alerted Fort Detrick," the Homeland analyst said.

"We're in the process of flying samples from Atlanta to the U.S. Army Medical Research Institute of Infectious Diseases at Detrick," said the colonel from the Defense Intelligence Agency. "But our people are extremely concerned about the early indications."

"What do they show you?" Hunter asked.

"Based on our teleconferencing with CDC, we concur, there are signs of genetic, or DNA, manipulation. It's very complex but it seems similar to or evocative of, classified research conducted by U.S. scientists years ago."

"What? Is this a domestic? What do we know about this research?" Hunter was taking notes.

Lancer watched Raymond Roth, Nick Webb and a few of the CIA people shifting uncomfortably in their chairs.

Roth leaned forward to respond.

"It was called Project Crucible," he said. "It emerged in the years following the end of the Cold War. Through covert operations we obtained access to advances in military, chemical, biological and genetic research made by enemy and rogue states."

"What was the objective of Crucible?" Hunter asked.

"The project's scientists were tasked to first defend, then dismantle, the work. But in many cases, they had to replicate it."

"Replicate it? And you think someone is using the technology gleaned from Crucible against us?"

Lancer was waiting for his CIA colleagues to reveal the full story.

"We won't know that until the people at Fort Detrick conclude their testing," Roth said.

"Who ran Crucible?" Hunter asked.

"We did, sir," Roth said. "And when this Florida case came to light we endeavored to locate former personnel who had been assigned to Crucible to determine if it was a factor."

"Excuse me," Lancer said to Roth, "but I understand

concerns surfaced long before this Florida case. I believe that approximately one month ago, Crucible's lead scientist contacted the agency expressing anxiety about someone attempting to replicate the project's research."

"I don't believe that's entirely accurate." Roth did not look at Lancer.

"I have a copy of Foster Winfield's letter and the agency's response," Lancer said.

"Could I see that?" Hunter asked. "I'll attach it to my report to the director for his brief to the Oval Office." Hunter then took stock of the room and shook his head.

Roth refrained from looking at Lancer.

"Sir," Roth continued, "since we've been investigating we've discovered that files and material from Crucible are missing, dating back to the time the project was abandoned."

"Christ." Hunter clicked his poised pen. "What's missing?"

"Samples of Marburg and anthrax."

"Christ," Hunter said. "What else?"

"A number of other materials and files."

"And no one knew?"

"It first appeared to be an inventory error. Dangerous material was to have been destroyed or locked away years ago. But our further investigation, prompted by Winfield's letter, confirms material was never destroyed and has, in fact, been missing since Crucible was phased out."

"And you've accounted for and interviewed all former personnel?"

"We're in the process."

"Listen up." Hunter's jaw was pulsating. "You find every scientist who worked on this nightmare and get them to Detrick ASAP to, first, help us determine who's behind the missing material and, second, help our people there analyze the tissue to determine what we're dealing with."

"Yes, sir."

"And you hold them until we determine what the hell

we've got and who's responsible. And to the rest of you—
don't let your guard down or rule out other sources."

Hunter stood, gathered his material and glared in
Roth's direction.

"You get those scientists to Fort Detrick—now," Hunter
said.

As the meeting broke up, Lancer went to Roth and Webb.

"Marburg and anthrax? That's a witch's brew—how do
you lose that right from under your own noses?"

Roth and Webb glared at Lancer without speaking.

"Would you guys like some help?" Lancer asked. "I
could use some help locating Sutsoff."

The agents began walking away.

"We're supposed to work together to connect the dots,
break down these compartmentalized barriers."

"Stay out of our way, Lancer."

Lancer left the room and the building, and hurried to his
car.

*Dammit, is this all connected? Is something big coming
down?*

A million scenarios shot through Lancer's mind as he
drove across Fairfax County to the Anti-Threat Center.
When he came to a red light, his cell phone rang. He pulled
over to answer it.

"This is Jack Gannon with the World Press Alliance."

"Yes."

"Are you the agent who was with me in Libya?"

"Yes."

"I have to be sure. What was the name of the man I was
supposed to meet?"

"Corley."

"I have information that might be critical to both of us."

"I'm listening."

"Before I go ahead, I want a name. I want to know who
I'm dealing with."

Lancer hesitated. "None of this ever goes in print, you swear."

"You've seen what I've gone through for this story."

"Lancer, Robert Lancer, FBI, tasked to Anti-Threat Operations."

Gannon explained Emma Lane's case, the accident that killed her husband, her conviction that her baby was alive and the connection to the clinic and Polly Larenski.

"What sort of information was this Polly selling?"

"DNA."

A car horn sounded behind Lancer and he realized he was blocking a lane.

"Hold on."

He wheeled his car around to a strip-mall parking lot and continued his conversation with Gannon.

"Lancer, I have two phone numbers. You have to search the phone records and see who was buying DNA from Polly Larenski. It could lead us to whoever is behind the child trafficking."

"I'd need to get warrants. You should call the local police."

"No. She tried that, there's no time. These numbers are critical."

"I need to know how you got your information."

Gannon hesitated.

"Jack, what led you to Emma Lane and the DNA angle?"

Gannon was deciding on how much to share with Lancer.

"Come on, Gannon!"

"Corley sent me his files."

"What?"

"Before I was supposed to meet him, he'd made arrangements to send me a memory card. He thought he was being watched. The card came to the hotel before I left and I read the files on the plane home."

This changed everything.

"Are you withholding evidence? You'd better turn those files over to us."

"I'm sharing the information. Listen, Emma Lane's file was in Corley's information. There's some sort of connection to her baby's DNA. Lancer, you have to search the call history of these two numbers, look for a similar number on both. One is Polly Larenski's home, and one is a pay phone near her home."

"I want that memory card, Gannon."

"We can't waste time!"

"Give me the numbers and let's go over everything one more time."

56

Big Cloud, Wyoming

Swirls of scorched pavement marked the spot where Emma Lane had lost her husband and baby boy.

Today under the morning sun, she knelt near it, where the gravel shoulder met the grass, and placed a memorial wreath of roses against a small white cross that Joe's friends had erected.

Jack Gannon was watching with Emma's aunt and uncle a short distance away. Seeing Emma mourning on the high plains before the majestic mountains resurrected what he'd lost. He thought of his mother and father, killed in a car crash in Buffalo. They'd been on their way to meet a priest who had information on the whereabouts of his sister, Cora. Years earlier, she'd run off with a loser who'd gotten her hooked on drugs.

In the time that had followed, Gannon's parents tried to find her. There were a few long-distance calls from her, an occasional letter with no return address, but ultimately, they never saw her again.

Gannon searched the peaks.

In his loneliest times, when he missed having a family, he thought of finding Cora. He thought of confronting her with all he was carrying: anger for leaving them and hurting everyone. He hated her for what she had done, yet loved her for what she had meant to him.

She was his sister.

As Emma returned to the car, his cell phone vibrated. It was his editor calling from New York. He answered and strolled away.

"Gannon."

"It's Melody, how is it going?"

"Major pieces have emerged. Emma Lane believes her son was abducted from a crash that killed her husband. Get this—she says it's tied to a California fertility clinic she'd used where someone in the lab was selling DNA to some shady corporation. I've got some phone numbers we're trying to trace. I think this could be tied to the café bombing, that Rio law firm, illegal adoptions and child trafficking."

"Is it the clinic Golden Dawn Fertility Corp. in L.A.?"

"Yes, how did you know?"

"The *Los Angeles Times* just reported that a woman who died in a suspicious fire was a former lab worker suspected of selling the clinic's files to an unknown research group."

"Oh, man."

"People are gaining on us, Jack. We need to hide Emma Lane. We've invested too much in this story to get beat now. Ask her if she'll come to New York today, for further interviews on the story. The World Press Alliance will pay her expenses. Try to get back here as soon as possible."

After Gannon told Emma what the WPA wanted, she contemplated the request then consulted her aunt and uncle.

A moment later she gave Gannon her answer.

"I'll do anything if it brings me closer to my son."

57

Robert Lancer entered his section chief's office at FBI Headquarters and set a folder before him.

Hal Weldon slid on his bifocals and loosened his tie. As he reviewed the file, Lancer glanced out the window overlooking the National Mall and the White House.

Since Jack Gannon called him yesterday, Lancer had worked on warrants to obtain the phone records of Polly Larenski and the pay phone in Santa Ana, California.

He'd called the FBI's Los Angeles field office and FBI's Santa Ana Resident Agency. He prepared a summary of all the facts, including his sworn oath and belief that the information was linked to a suspected imminent attack. The rest had to be processed up the chain for sign-off before it went to a judge.

"Looks good, Bob. I'll take it from here." Weldon removed his glasses. "I just got off the phone with Charley. We're still trying to locate Drake Stinson and Gretchen Sutsoff."

"Are we going to go public?"

"It's being considered."

"And the others?"

"Defense and the CIA have located the other scientists who worked on Crucible, and they've volunteered to cooperate. They've been taken to military bases to be flown to Detrick, but the CIA will give them a rough reception."

"Why?"

"They're suspects, too," Weldon said.

"What? Foster Winfield's the one who first alerted them to this. The guy's got a terminal condition."

"They're covering their asses," Weldon said. "Look, we'll flag our warrant application as an expedited request. How fast we make it through the lawyers to a judge is anybody's guess. I'll keep you posted."

As he navigated D.C.'s traffic back to the Anti-Threat Center in Virginia, doubt gnawed at Lancer.

In the warrant application, he'd failed to specifically detail that Jack Gannon claimed to possess Adam Corley's computer files on the case, because he knew Weldon would have demanded he go after Gannon for the files with a warrant, or even an arrest.

Am I a fool to allow Gannon, a reporter, free rein with what could be a significant piece of evidence in a threat to national security?

Lancer was on a tightrope.

He needed time to cultivate Gannon as a source. The guy was good at digging up information. Maybe he could strengthen their uneasy alliance with some quid pro quo? As for the warrant, well, that was a roll of the dice at best. They could take days or hours.

Even then, would it yield anything?

At his office at the center, Lancer scrutinized everything he had that was related to the case. He made calls and followed leads. The sun had set by the time he got a call from Weldon.

"We got our pitch to a judge who granted the warrant. Our people are banging on doors in California. We should have the phone records by morning, Bob. I hope to hell we get some mileage out of this."

58

Rapid keyboard tapping underscored the intensity with which Sandra Deller attacked the data yielded by the new warrants.

Deller, the chief analyst at the Anti-Threat Center's Information Command Unit, had made Robert Lancer's case her priority. Pages of call logs going back several months for Polly Larenski's landline number appeared on Deller's monitor.

"According to my source—" Lancer came and stood next to her "—Larenski is believed to have received and made calls concerning our subject from her home phone and the pay phone near her home on Civic."

Deller clicked and a second set of call logs appeared.

"This one?" she said.

"Correct."

"We're looking for a number or numbers that will appear in both logs." Deller issued a few commands for a merge. "Voilà." She highlighted the number that appeared: 242-555-1212.

"Where is that?"

Deller entered the number in another database.

"Bahamas. Nassau. Actually, it's Paradise Island. That's a resort area. Hang on." Deller continued her swift searches. "Look, it's for the Grand Blue Tortoise Resort." Deller went to a Web site for the resort and clicked through pages. "Nice. Let's see if we can be more specific with the number." She continued searching and said, "The number is for the Blue Tortoise Kids' Hideaway. Let's check it out." She went to the Hideaway's Web page. "It's a child-care center, Bob."

Lancer raised his eyebrows as his instincts hammered at him.

"I think we have something. Thank you, Sandy. Let me know if you find anything more."

At his desk, Lancer searched for the FBI's legal attaché at the U.S. Embassy in Nassau. The whole time he questioned whether they should put the child-care center under surveillance or hit it with the Bahamian police?

There were risks to both, he thought, as he dialed a number. If you took your time and watched your subject, you built a stronger case for prosecution. But if an attack happened during that time, if something got by you, you'd be accused of not taking action.

So many signs pointed to an imminent attack.

He couldn't take anything for granted.

The call connected to Nassau.

"Paul Worden, FBI."

"Bob Lancer, FBI at the Anti-Threat Center. Paul, you're our Legat in Nassau, right?"

"That's what they tell me."

"Going to need your help. It's urgent."

For the next twenty minutes as they reviewed the file over the phone, Lancer brought Worden up to speed.

"I'll get in touch with our senior people at the embassy," Worden said, "then with my sources at the Bahamian Attorney General and the Royal Bahamas Police Force. I'll use the wording from your warrant to get the wheels turning here. We'll run every record we can on the Kids' Hideaway. We'll request surveillance or get warrants to swoop down on the place, whatever you want. We'll keep each other posted."

Lancer hung up and his line rang. It was Sandra Deller.

"There's a second number," she said. "It has an 841 area code."

"What's that one?"

"It's an area code for a satellite phone with world service."

"Anything on an owner?"

"A numbered company with a post office box on Cable Beach, Nassau."

Lancer called Worden back with the new information, then exhaled and dragged both hands over his face.

Now what?

He glanced at his small desk calendar and the red Xs marking the Human World Conference in New York.

Was it the target? Was the president attending? There were too many unknowns.

Then there was Jack Gannon, who had Adam Corley's files.

Were there answers on Corley's memory card?

Lancer had to move on this.

His digital clock rolled into a new hour.

59

The World Press Alliance had a contract with a hotel near the Empire State Building to put up out-of-town editors and reporters.

The WPA had arranged for Emma Lane to stay in a twentieth-floor room. Gannon and Emma's flight had arrived late at LaGuardia. He got her checked in to the hotel and met her there the next morning.

Sirens and traffic noises filled the sunny morning air.

As they walked to WPA headquarters, Emma took in the buildings and searched the stream of faces, wondering if she would ever see Tyler again, hoping Jack Gannon and his global news service were the answer to her prayers.

It did not take long to travel the few blocks beyond Madison Square Garden and Penn Station. Melody Lyon met them in her office.

"Thank you for coming, Emma." Lyon shook her hand. "On behalf of the WPA, please accept our belated condolences for your loss."

Once Emma was seated, Lyon got down to business.

"You're obviously contending with more than anyone should have to bear," she said. "Jack told us of the extraordinary steps you've already taken. Are you certain you're up to this?"

"I'm certain because I need to find my son."

"As you know, we've lost two of our people recently and we think their deaths are linked to your case. In our pursuit of the truth we'll be sharing confidential information with you. Emma, as crass as it sounds, we need to know that your cooperation remains exclusive to the WPA."

"Yes," Emma said. "No one else believed me or would help me. Before we left, my aunt and uncle promised not to speak to any other reporters."

"I'll update you," Lyon said. "Jack, we've just learned that the *New York Times* is going to report that the CIA wants to question former scientists about a canceled top-secret program that may be at play somewhere in all of this. This could be related to our story. A number of news organizations are chasing pieces of it, but we've got most of them. Jack, is there anything new on your other angles?"

"I'm still waiting to hear back from Lancer on Polly Larenski's phone numbers. I have files to review and sources to check."

"Good, we've put more WPA people on this story, quietly digging. I did some checking with my sources in Washington. I've just sent you some new data we've put together. I want you both to review it. Jack, you will remain our lead reporter on this file. Start a running draft of all we know as soon as possible."

The first thing Gannon and Emma did was go to the WPA cafeteria for two strong coffees. Alone in the elevator, Emma turned to Gannon.

"Will I find my son?"

"I don't know. But a lot of people are pushing hard to get to the truth behind what happened to you, Adam Corley and the people murdered in Rio de Janeiro," he said. "We've both come a long way and neither one of us is giving up."

At his desk in the newsroom, Gannon got a second chair for Emma, then set up his laptop for her to read over files. While he worked on his PC, Emma paged through older files and notes from his sources. Her concerns grew as she realized the magnitude of what could be looming.

She looked at Gannon's monitor and her breathing quickened as she read what was on it: the detailed note from Melody Lyon.

Jack, I called in a few favors with my sources in the intelligence community and this is what I've put together on Extremus Deus. The group's origins flow from the following:

In the Cold-War era, various White House administrations and Western governments expressed alarm over the population explosion. There were fears the earth's population would double, even triple, in a short time, deplete the planet's resources and result in chaos and the collapse of civilization.

At that time, some officials were consumed by these fears and over a few decades, various strategies for slowing growth were secretly discussed. Some included chilling military options involving the creation of new lethal agents that could attack certain segments of the population.

By the late 1970s, fears about population had subsided, but the years that followed saw a combination of key events, namely, the collapse of Communism in Eastern Europe and the emergence of the new threat of global warming. New democratized nations joined materialistic Western societies in a wanton depletion of the earth's resources in a time of out-of-control greenhouse-gas emissions.

In some darker corners of the world, this served to rekindle the belief that the world was racing headlong to ruin and that action was needed.

Some conspiracy theorists hold that a select number of scientists, intellectuals and various rogue political, military and intelligence players created a secret organization known as Extremus Deus, from the Latin meaning "Extreme God," to formulate policies, strategies and action.

According to the theories, the most effective way to reduce the strain on the planet and the threat to humanity is to reduce population.

The conspiracy theorists hold that Extremus Deus has been secretly developing chemical and biological options gleaned from military experiments, such as a genetic attack through the manipulation of DNA…

Emma's face was a mask of fear. She'd dropped her coffee. Gannon reached for a box of tissue as she tapped his monitor and the note.

"This group, this Extremus Deus—this can't be serious."

"There's no evidence this group exists, but the theories are based on facts."

"Are you telling me some freakish doomsday cult stole my baby for his DNA? Oh, God, they've killed Joe and now they'll kill Tyler."

"Take it easy, Emma. We don't know if there's a connection. This is just one possible piece of a story that has many pieces. We don't know what's real, speculation or fiction."

The phone next to his computer rang.

"WPA, Jack Gannon."

"It's Lancer."

"Did you process those phone numbers I gave you?"

"I'll tell you something, but think hard before you answer."

"All right."

"I want Corley's memory card. I need to see those files."

"I already told you what I found."

"You don't have a clue as to what's relevant. Now, I can invoke national security, get warrants, jam up your life, even have you arrested."

"Don't threaten me, Lancer! After you witnessed me

being—" Gannon caught himself. "You know what I went through, so don't threaten me."

"You forget that I'm the guy who got you out of that mess."

"What do you want?"

"Send me electronic copies of Corley's material now—all of it—and I'll give you new information."

Gannon looked around, knowing where news organizations stood when it came to sharing information with police. He was walking a fine ethical line.

"What have you got for me, Lancer?"

"Possibly the next phase of this case."

Gannon had to decide this on his own. No one but Lancer knew what he went through in the Moroccan prison. And it was true: Lancer was the one who got him out.

"Send me an e-mail address," Gannon said, "then give me a few minutes. It's a large file."

Gannon worked fast copying everything from Corley's files into special folders he sent via e-mail to Lancer. Ten minutes went by, then twenty, thirty, nearly forty when Gannon's line rang again.

"Listen up," Lancer said. "We're going to execute warrants on a subject in Nassau, Bahamas, tomorrow. It's a three-hour flight from New York. Check in to the Grand Blue Tortoise Resort and wait for my call."

"Wait! Give me some idea of the target."

"When you get there."

"No, I need to alert my desk."

"A child-care center."

"A child-care center?"

Emma's eyes widened.

"Okay, Lancer, I'll be there, but I'll have another person, a reporter, with me and maybe a photographer."

"Just get there, stay out of the way and wait for my call."

60

Less than twenty minutes after Foster Winfield was helped into a waiting plane, it accelerated down the runway and lifted off.

Hours earlier, a caravan of vehicles carrying two plain-clothes RCMP officers, two Canadian military officers and three U.S. military personnel, one of them an army doctor, arrived at his cottage in Canada.

Winfield was instructed to give them his passport and to pack a bag.

His escorts provided no details. Their classified assignment was to deliver the CIA's former chief scientist to a specified location. It concerned a matter of U.S. national security. Few words were spoken as they sped through the tranquil countryside, but Winfield had deduced that it was about Project Crucible. He hoped that there was still time to do something.

The caravan crossed into the United States without a hitch at the Thousand Islands border crossing, then rolled toward Watertown, New York, and Fort Drum, where a plane stood by to rush Winfield to Maryland.

The short flight ended when his escorts handed him off to a team from U.S. Army Intelligence and the CIA. They put Winfield into a black SUV and drove him to Fort Detrick and the army's biodefense lab, located northwest of

Washington. During the drive, Winfield considered all the scenarios that could arise from Crucible and hoped that Lancer, the FBI agent, was still working on the case.

The vehicle arrived at the fort's checkpoints, where they were cleared by armed guards before driving to a remote building. In silence, Winfield was led down hallways equipped with security cameras, electronic sensors and a series of secure doors passable via keypad-coded entry systems.

He was taken to a small, barren room with white cinder-block walls. It had a hard-back chair on either side of a table with a wood veneer finish.

The door opened and two men in suits entered.

One sat opposite Winfield. The other stood.

"Dr. Winfield, this concerns our investigation into your letter."

Winfield had assumed as much.

"We have reason to believe the subject is related to an on-going threat to national security."

Winfield nodded.

"Before we proceed," the man said, "I'll remind you that as a retiree you must still adhere to agency standards and agree to undergo a polygraph examination."

Periodic polygraphs were fairly common when he'd worked on Crucible.

"Of course."

A few minutes later, a young man with prematurely gray hair entered the room carrying polygraph equipment in a hard-shell case.

"It'll take a moment to set up," the polygraphist said.

He explained that his new machine was a five-pen ana-log. The man connected instruments to Winfield's heart and fingertips to electronically measure breathing, perspiration, respiratory activity, galvanic skin reflex, blood and pulse rate. Then he began posing questions.

"Are you Dr. Foster Winfield?"

"Yes."

"Did you oversee Project Crucible?"

"Yes."

"Was the program abandoned?"

"Yes."

"Are you currently involved in using material from Project Crucible for any means?"

"No."

"Do you have factual information on anyone currently attempting to use research from Project Crucible for any means?"

"No."

"Do you have information on the whereabouts of Dr. Gretchen Sutsoff?"

"No."

"Are you currently in contact with Gretchen Sutsoff?"

"No."

"Are you aware of anyone who may have information on her whereabouts?"

"No."

"Do you think Dr. Sutsoff currently could pose a risk to the security of the United States and other nations?"

Winfield hesitated.

"Sir, your response? Do you think Dr. Sutsoff currently could pose a risk to the security of the United States and other nations?"

Winfield swallowed.

"Yes."

The exam continued with similar questions asked different ways for nearly an hour before it ended. Winfield was given a few old copies of *Newsweek* and *Time* and left alone in the room. Thirty minutes later he was taken to another room where he saw three men his age.

They were familiar.

"Foster?" One of them stood. "We figured they'd grab you, too."

It took a few seconds before he recognized what time had done to Andrew Tolkman, Lester Weeks and Phil Kenyon, his old team from Project Crucible.

"Hello. Good to see you." Winfield touched each of them on the shoulder then glanced around. "Although, not ideal circumstances."

"They can't find Gretchen," Tolkman said.

"No one can," Kenyon said. "I told them she's the one they need."

A door opened and a man in his forties, wearing jeans and a golf shirt, entered and handed each of them a slim file folder.

"Gentlemen, my name is Powell, Army Intel. Biochem. We have little time. As you may have gathered, this concerns your work on Project Crucible. In a nutshell, we think some of your classified work is being applied to launch a strike. In fact, it may already be under way."

Kenyon muttered a curse.

"No one else is better qualified to help us at this stage than you. I'll give you time to read the material, then we'll suit you up to work with our people on the sample we have in the lab. We hope you can tell us what we're up against."

The file contained information on the deceased cruise-line passenger from Indiana, based on reports provided by the Broward County M.E., the CDC and the army's experts. The aging scientists read it all carefully.

"How is it possible?" Andrew Tolkman whispered more to himself than to the others as Powell returned.

"Gentlemen," Powell said, holding the door. "We'll head to the lab."

Cutting across the compound to the lab, he led the scientists through several secure doors to areas flagged with signs warning of danger. They passed through a series of sealed rooms before coming to a changeroom with lockers and other lab staff. The lab staff helped the men into blue containment suits, taping their socks and wrists after they tugged on latex gloves.

Next they entered a sealed chamber that featured a disinfectant shower. After they each showered with their suits on, they put on rubber boots and another set of heavy rubber gloves and proceeded down a corridor where they each reached for a hose from the ceiling and connected it to their suits.

They then passed through another air lock, waiting until it was safe to enter the lab where a team of army scientists was at work. The Crucible experts joined their teams, analyzing, processing and running tests on the tissue samples from the cruise-ship victim. Each team worked on different aspects of the sample. During this time, Powell remained in a remote room watching the work on closed-circuit TV while communicating with them.

"What do you think?" Powell asked.

"It is definitely evocative of the work we did on Crucible," Winfield said into his radio-intercom.

"You mean the work Gretchen did," Kenyon added.

After some three hours, the scientists exited the lab, moving carefully through the various chambers. They each stayed in their suits and took another decontamination shower before moving along to the locker room where they were helped out of their suits.

Powell was waiting for the four men again in the same room where he had originally briefed them.

"Your assessment?"

Winfield looked at his colleagues.

"We would not have believed it had we not seen it," he said. "Theoretically, it should be impossible."

"What do you mean?"

"It's definitely a manufactured agent," Winfield said. "It's totally new and has characteristics of Ebola, Marburg and anthrax. We can't really identify it. But there's more."

"More?"

"Its foundation is in File 91 and some of the other agents developed by some enemy states. But we cannot fully understand the delivery system, the control system and how it seems to be manipulated."

"I'm not sure I follow you."

"It's extremely sophisticated. I don't think we can defend against it."

"What about an antidote or vaccine?"

"Well, while it encompasses a manufactured lethal agent, it's less characteristic of a virus, more like a controllable agent. Its engineering is very advanced."

"Isn't there anything we can do?"

"It's like a weapon with no off switch. I don't think there's much we can do to stop it."

61

Paradise Island, Bahamas

As their cab from the airport climbed the bridge over the crystal water of Nassau Harbor, Emma looked at the hotels rising from the island.

"It's funny," she told Gannon. "I was a travel writer before I became a teacher, and I have been to a lot of places but never here. Joe and I were planning a trip to the Bahamas. We were going to bring Tyler but now, to come here as a widow, wondering if my baby's alive…" Emma reached under her sunglasses and touched the corner of her eye. "I'm sorry."

"Don't be," Gannon said. "We need to know the truth."

Gannon paid the driver after they arrived at the massive main building of the Grand Blue Tortoise Resort. Tourists, guests and staff crowded the lobby, which was as chaotic as an airport terminal. Live parrots cawed in a four-story aviary and calypso music filled the air. The reservation for two rooms next to each other was under Gannon's name. He used the WPA's credit card.

"Are there any messages?" Gannon asked as he collected their keys.

The clerk consulted the computer.

"No, sir."

"I'm looking for my friend Robert Lancer—he should be registered here."

The clerk checked.

"Yes, room 2322 Blue Reef Tower D. That's the next building west from you, sir. Do you wish to send Mr. Lancer a message?"

"Yes, tell him I've arrived and to please call my room."

When Gannon got to his room there was still no message from Lancer. He set up his laptop and sent Lancer an e-mail telling him that he'd arrived at the hotel and was standing by. Then he sent a text message.

No response.

Gannon called the WPA's Nassau Bureau. Prior to his Bahamas assignment, the Nassau chief had run the Amsterdam Bureau.

"WPA, Peter DeGroote."

"Jack Gannon. I just arrived."

"Ah, yes, Jack. New York advised us to expect your call. We'll support you in every way possible. I trust you had a good flight?"

"Yes, thanks. Are you hearing anything at all related to a police action on a day-care center anywhere?"

"No, but we are monitoring police emergency radio chatter on our scanners and we'll alert you on your mobile phone."

"Do you have a photographer ready?"

"We have two. One is a freelancer. Both are in Nassau waiting to be dispatched."

After the call, Gannon went to the next building to find Lancer.

Alone in her room, Emma studied her color photograph of Tyler and Joe, taken a week before the crash. She'd downloaded it to her cell phone. She traced her finger over their faces, smiling back at them before starting to unpack. That's when she noticed the resort's leather-bound directory of services on the desk. Paging through it she saw that the resort offered child-care service at the Blue Tortoise Kids' Hideaway.

Gannon's source had said police were going to get warrants for a child-care center and had advised Gannon to come to this specific hotel. She hurried to Gannon's room and knocked hard on his door.

No answer.

She'd go alone.

At her desk in the offices of the Blue Tortoise Kids' Hideaway, Lucy Walsh quickly read over the letter she was leaving for her employer.

"It is with the great regret that I must inform you that I am resigning from my position as chief executive assistant to Dr. Auden…"

The truth was Lucy had to leave the Bahamas because she was afraid.

When she finished with the letter, she printed a copy, signed it, put it in an envelope and slid it under Dr. Sutsoff's door. The office was always locked when the doctor was away. It was just as well Lucy did it this way; she never felt totally comfortable in the doctor's presence.

She returned to her desk and resumed packing her personal items.

Her growing fears that this company was a front for something evil had deepened. Last night she'd received stunning news from her church friend in Ireland, who had been forwarding her secret reports to an ex-cop who was working with a human rights organization.

"My contact on this case has been killed. I got word from London he may have been murdered in Morocco. It's dangerous for you. Take precautions, Lucy."

Something was horribly wrong at this place.

Lucy glanced at her computer from which she'd duplicated every file she could to a private online folder. She had also copied them to a blue memory card, no bigger than a stick of gum. Maybe she would send the information anonymously to the *Irish Times?* Somehow she had to alert the outside world.

As the computer beeped and lights flashed, she noticed through the glass walls that a woman was standing in the playroom staring at the children. The other staff members had not seen her.

Lucy went to her.

"May I help you?"

The woman turned, telegraphing an intense unease behind faded bruises and desperate eyes that failed to brighten as she tried to smile.

"Yes. My name is Emma Lane and I'm looking for my son."

"Lane?"

"Yes, my son is Tyler Lane."

"Lane, that name's familiar but we have about 104 children currently registered. Some are out on excursions. Follow me." Lucy led Emma to her office and sat before her computer monitor and started typing. "L-A-N-E?"

"Yes." Emma twisted the straps of her purse. "Tyler is spelled T-Y-L-E-R. He's a year old."

"When did you bring him in?"

"I didn't."

"Oh, his father brought him in?"

"His father's dead. I think my son was abducted and brought here."

All the blood drained from Lucy's face.

"Please," Emma whispered. "Please help me."

After knocking on Lancer's door in vain, Gannon called Lancer's cell-phone number.

It was futile.

Dammit. Where was he?

Walking from Blue Reef Tower D across the complex,

Gannon froze. Almost hidden at the base of a grove of coconut palms, he glimpsed a shoulder flash, dark military overalls and a leather holster.

A cop. A SWAT member in tactical gear.

As Gannon's eyes adjusted, he noticed a second cop in the grove.

Then, through the courtyard in the distance, he saw a cube van, obviously a police equipment truck. Next to it, he saw an ambulance.

They were setting up for a takedown somewhere.

Was this Lancer's target? It had to be near.

Walking quickly through the vast courtyard, Gannon looked in every direction for any sign of Lancer, for any clue. Guests lounged around the pool, oblivious to what was coming. Gannon knew from his crime reporting days how police would soon seal the area with inner and outer perimeters as they prepared to move in.

Where were they going?

Gannon scanned everything until he saw the entrance of a low-roofed building almost hidden by tropical vegetation. He strained to read the wooden sign amid a garden of flowers: Blue Tortoise Kids' Hideaway.

Yes, it all fit.

Lancer's information

We're going to execute warrants…Grand Blue Tortoise Resort…a child-care center.

Gannon started trotting to the building.

Lucy Walsh stared at Emma not knowing what to say.

"Please," Emma said, "I know it's crazy, sometimes I think it's all a bad dream, but it's real. Please, I'm begging for your help."

Lucy said nothing and Emma continued.

"I sense you're a good person and by your reaction, I think you know something. Please." Emma struggled as she cued up the photo of Joe and Tyler on her cell phone and showed it to Lucy, her voice soft. "My husband died beside me and my son is missing—please!"

Maybe it was fate, maybe it was the timing, but Lucy did not have to search Emma's eyes long before she found a reason to follow her convictions.

She got up, glanced around to be sure they were alone, then locked her door and returned to her computer.

"Where are you from, Emma?"

"Wyoming."

Lucy entered her database of secret files she'd been copying.

"Emma, are you from Big Cloud?"

"Yes!"

Lucy caught her bottom lip between her teeth, then continued checking files. Her concentration sharpened as she pulled up more information.

"You have to swear that you'll never tell anyone you got this from me."

"Yes, yes! Please, do you have something?"

Lucy jotted information on a slip of paper.

"Your son is here."

Emma's hands flew to her face. Her body started shaking.

"Here? Oh, God! Where? Do you have him?"

"No, he's not here at the center."

"Where? Who has him? Tell me!"

"Listen carefully. Two people, their names are Valmir and Elena Leeka, are traveling on Albanian passports or U.S passports. Tyler is identified as their son Alek on an Albanian passport. They will say that they adopted him through an international agency and are staying here on vacation."

"How do you know all this? What's going on?"

"Just listen. I've just learned that they're supposed to leave for New York City today, at any moment. They are registered here, at the resort in Main Sail Tower A, Room 1658."

Lucy thrust the paper with the information into Emma's hand. "You have to swear not to say how you found out."

"Yes. Room 1658, Main Sail Tower A."

"Go before it's too late."

"Thank you."

"It could be dangerous. Don't go alone."

"God bless you, thank you!"

"Wait! Wait, there's something else!" Lucy snatched the tiny blue memory card from her desk and handed it to Emma. "Don't lose this."

"What is it?"

"Information. Don't say where you got it, just look at it later. It'll help explain everything."

Emma stared at the memory card, then jammed it into her bag.

"One more thing."

Emma waited.

"I had no part in this."

"Thank you for helping me."

Emma hurried from the center. Once outside, she began running across the courtyard when she spotted Gannon heading in her direction.

"Jack!" Emma held up the slip of paper like it was a winning lottery ticket. "He's here. Tyler's here!"

"What? How did you find out?"

Emma updated him as they hurried through the complex, following the direction signs to Main Sail Tower A. They found a private corner in the busy lobby to come up with a strategy. To confirm if the Leekas and Tyler were in the room and to gauge what they might be facing, Gannon would knock on the door alone in case the couple had Emma's picture. If they were there, then Gannon and Emma would summon police.

"What do we do if they're not there?" Emma asked as they stepped into the elevator.

"I've got a plan," Gannon said.

On the sixteenth floor, Emma stayed down the hall out of sight while Gannon knocked at room 1658. He tried for thirty seconds. He placed his ear to the door but heard nothing, then signaled to Emma.

"Follow my lead on this," he said as they walked down the hall and around a corner until they found a chambermaid's cart parked outside a room.

"Excuse us," Gannon said.

An older slender Bahamian woman emerged from the bathroom wearing rubber gloves.

"I am so sorry to trouble you but we just stepped out of our room and realized we left our room keys and camera inside."

The woman eyed them both.

"We're running a little late—we don't have time to go to the desk in the main lobby. Is there a chance you could let us in?" Gannon reached for his wallet and produced an American twenty-dollar bill.

The woman sighed and waved off the money.

"This happens all the time, which room?"

"Thank you. This way." Emma pointed and started ahead of them, smiling at Gannon, then checking the woman's tag, "Oh, thank you, Matilda."

"No need to thank me. All the time people are forgettin' this and forgettin' that."

Matilda inserted her plastic keycard in the key slot, a small light winked green, the locks clicked and she cracked the door a few inches for Gannon.

"Please, Matilda, we insist." He pushed the twenty in her hand.

"Well, with all my grandchildren I have to get a birthday present every other week. Thank you." She smiled and returned to her work humming.

Gannon allowed her to get a safe distance away before they entered.

Nothing prepared them for what was waiting.

Blood.

The room was drenched in blood.

On the ceiling, walls, curtains, the floor, the lamps, the mirror, the furniture and the bed, where two meaty mounds rested on the blood-soaked sheets. It was as if something had exploded, leaving two sets of adult arms and legs reaching out from the visceral matter.

Emma's groan morphed into a stifled scream.

She cupped one hand over her mouth and searched the room, bathroom and closet.

"Tyler!"

There was no sign of her son.

She began rummaging through the documents on the desk.

Gannon stood before the wall over the bed transfixed, for amid the splatter he discerned a message scrawled in the blood: "Erase them all!"

62

Deus Island, Exuma Sound

At that moment, sweat beaded on the upper lip of the American military scientist working in Dr. Sutsoff's secret laboratory.

The biochemistry engineer was part of the elite rapid response team rushed overnight to the island to investigate Sutsoff's clandestine research.

Working in protective pressure suits, team members took painstaking care. The lab housed such material as rabies, small pox and the Marburg and Ebola viruses. They'd come upon glass cases housing snakes—the deadliest snakes on earth. A venom expert identified them as a black mamba, a king cobra, a Russell's viper, a taipan and a krait. All could be milked for their lethal neurotoxins, cardiotoxins and hemotoxins.

They also discovered a large clear container with a cluster of roosting pariah bats, a species thought to be extinct. They found containers of autopsied bats and evidence of newly engineered super-lethal agents. The scientist felt her scalp prickle when a team member's voice crackled over the radio.

He said, "Sutsoff may have booby-trapped this place. Stay calm, be careful."

The female scientist constantly checked the floor and ceiling in case a snake or bat had escaped its hold.

It was like viewing live coverage of a space mission,

Lancer thought, watching via closed-circuit TV in an outer room crowded with U.S. and Bahamian law enforcement agents.

Within the past forty-eight hours, security agencies in the U.S., the Bahamas and around the world had been working full bore. The telephone numbers and information Lancer got from Jack Gannon had broken the case open with several significant leads. Gannon's first number enabled them to obtain warrants on the Blue Tortoise Kids' Hideaway. Lancer glanced at his watch, figuring that that operation should be happening right about now on Paradise Island.

The second number, the satellite phone number, led to a post-office box in the Cable Beach area of Nassau, which led to a numbered company. Some criminal intelligence work by detectives from the Royal Bahamas Police Force confirmed a link to the Blue Tortoise child-care center and Gretchen Sutsoff. Interviews with seaplane pilots confirmed her flights from Deus Island. Other Bahamian government departments helped with property, tax and other records, which prompted calls through Interpol and help from police in France, Spain and Portugal.

It all led to securing emergency warrants to hit Deus Island with support from the Royal Bahamas Defense Force and the U.S. Coast Guard. Overnight, each group had sent ships to the island, while other resources were flown in by seaplane.

They'd failed to find Sutsoff but after questioning her island staff and searching Sutsoff's lab and her residence, Lancer knew they were gaining on her. For in a short time this had become an international investigation with new leads coming nearly every fifteen minutes.

Would they get her in time?

Lancer's attention went back to the slow, meticulous probe of Sutsoff's lab, which was being transmitted live via satellite to the Crucible scientists and other experts at Fort Detrick in Maryland.

Analysis under the microscope in Sutsoff's lab was being

shared with the former CIA scientists via secured U.S. military laptop computers and secured satellite Internet links.

"We can't identify what's been created down here. What does the team at Fort Detrick think?"

"Foster Winfield here. We conclude from our analysis that what you've got there was applied in the death of the cruise passenger."

"Are you certain that was a homicide, Doctor?" Lancer asked.

"Absolutely, and we can also say the lethal agent used has its foundation in material from Crucible."

"Stolen material?" someone from Defense Intelligence asked.

"Yes."

"Would you testify to that in court, Dr. Winfield?" Lancer said.

"If I live long enough, yes, but I'm sure Phil and the others would, as well."

"Then," Lancer said to the others, "we have enough to put out a warrant for Sutsoff's arrest and deem her a fugitive suspect."

"One moment, gentlemen," Winfield said. "You must understand that based upon the new material found in her lab, it is clear that Gretchen has created an even more powerful lethal agent than what was used on the cruise-ship victim. She remains well ahead of us. Again, we stress the critical need for more analysis on this newer agent. We don't know how, or when, or if she intends to introduce it or even if we can stop it."

Frustration rippled among the investigators in the crowded room. A moment later, one of the men nudged Lancer to look out a window at someone pointing at him.

"They need you outside."

Lancer welcomed the fresh air and Caribbean sun as he headed toward a Jeep and the FBI agent waiting behind the wheel.

"Bob, they found something in Sutsoff's residence you should see."

"What is it?"

"I don't know—they told me to get you."

"Any word on how they did with the warrants at the child-care center?"

"We just heard that the operation went well but there may be more victims. Homicides."

"What?"

"It just came in—we don't have anything else."

Lancer climbed in and as the Jeep rumbled down the road, Lancer saw that his phone signal was strong now that he was outside of the sealed lab buildings. He called Hal Weldon, his supervisor at FBI Headquarters in Washington.

"Hal, it's Lancer. Have you heard anything on the take-down at the child-care center?"

"It's sketchy. The operation went well but there could be other victims. It's all hot right now. We're trying to get more. What do you have?"

Lancer updated him and made the urgent request for warrants for Sutsoff's arrest and to prepare her fugitive file.

"We're getting what we can," Lancer said. "The CIA, the Bahamians, Interpol, the French, Portuguese and Spanish police are sending stuff on her passports. We should have recent photos."

"We'll take care of it up here, Bob. Keep me posted and we'll blast something out to Homeland and Customs and Border Protection ASAP to warn them to watch for entry while we track her aliases."

When Lancer arrived at the house, Bahamian and U.S. computer experts were searching Sutsoff's private computer files and e-mails. They'd bypassed encrypted and password-protected files to find a list of some seventy names and addresses around the world.

"Any idea what this means?" one of them asked.

They scrolled through names and locations in Toronto,

London, Shanghai, Berlin, Moscow, Paris, Buenos Aires, Mexico, Tokyo, Hamburg, Chicago, Dallas—and the list went on to include some of the world's largest cities.

"I think it means a strike is imminent."

"But when and where?"

"That's the question," Lancer said as his phone rang.

63

The rotating blades of the ceiling fan offered no relief in the stifling offices of the Central Detective Unit's headquarters on Thompson Boulevard.

"The new air-conditioning unit has quit again." Inspector Franklin opened his window wider, before resuming reading his statement. "Don't worry, Mr. Gannon, we're almost done."

Gannon checked the time.

It had been several hours since he and Emma had discovered the two bodies at the resort and that Emma's baby was alive. During that time, Gannon was permitted to go to the washroom, where he made some secret phone calls. He alerted the WPA's Nassau Bureau to the story, and he tried unsuccessfully to reach Lancer for help.

In the early part of Gannon and Emma's questioning, the Nassau police were suspicious about them. Detectives interviewed them separately and were wary to link the two deaths with the child-care center until more information had emerged from the FBI. From what Gannon could gather, a second police action was unfolding on an island in Exuma Sound, but he was not sure what it was. Finally, Inspector Franklin tapped the collection of papers together, indicating he had finished.

"Here is your passport. Thank you for your cooperation.

You are free to enjoy your stay or return to New York. We will contact you if necessary."

"What about my friend, Emma?"

"She should be joining you in the reception area momentarily."

Gannon stepped from the building and called Lancer's number again.

Come on, come on.

This time the connection clicked.

"Lancer."

"It's Gannon. I need your help."

"Where are you?"

"Nassau. I just finished up with Nassau detectives. You know that Emma Lane and I found two corpses in the hotel where you sent us?"

"You found them?"

"Yes."

"I haven't been fully debriefed, but I will be. I really have to go."

"Wait, you owe me a few minutes. I need your help." Gannon spotted Emma and waved her over to him. They moved to a couple of palm trees, which offered them shade and privacy. "Emma Lane's baby is alive."

"What? How do you know this?"

"When we came upon those dead people, Emma feared for her son. She'd learned at the care center that he was supposed to be with that couple. For as long as we could stand being in that room we looked for her baby, for any sign of him. There was nothing. But we found Albanian passports for Valmir and Elena Leeka and one for Alek Leeka with a new picture of Emma Lane's son. It confirms what she's feared, that her baby was stolen and is alive. We told the detectives everything."

"I haven't been briefed on that aspect yet."

"I'm telling you this now. It proves there's a conspiracy. We want you to help us find her son. If we find him then we could find the answer to everything. Tell us what's going on, Lancer. You owe me that much and you owe her."

Emma nodded.

"Did you give those passports to the Nassau police?"

"Yes, we cooperated fully."

"Is there anything else you can tell me?"

"You know about the message on the wall?"

"What message?"

"Written in blood, 'Erase them all.' What the hell does that mean?"

"It could be related to everything. What about the couple, what else do you know?"

"Only that Emma learned that they were supposed to be leaving for New York City."

"What?"

"She was told by a staff member at the child-care center that they were bound for New York City."

"Do you know where, or why?"

"No."

"Which staff member? You have a name?"

"No."

A long silence passed. It sounded as if Lancer had put his hand over his phone to tell someone else something. Gannon noticed Emma was searching through her bag, as if she'd remembered something.

Gannon thought he'd lost his connection. "Lancer, are you there?"

"Yes."

"Where are you? What's going on?"

"I'm in Exuma Sound at a second search site."

"What's the location? Maybe we should be there with you, or send someone from the WPA Bureau?"

"No, it's not safe now, believe me. And I have to leave."

"Where're you going?"

"Back to the States."

"What's going on?"

"I don't have a lot of time."

"Hold on, it was Emma Lane's case that produced those phone numbers for you, Lancer, and you know it. I flew down here with her and waited for your call, just like you said, but it never came."

"I got tied up."

"You owe us. Tell us what's going on."

"Very soon the FBI will put out an alert for a wanted fugitive. I'll see what I can do to give your wire service the jump."

"Who is it?"

"It's Gretchen Sutsoff."

"Who's that?"

"The scientist Corley mentioned. She's using several aliases. We're still getting everything together. I really have to go."

"Wait, where do you think the next break on this will be?"

"I have no idea, Jack."

"Yes, you do. You said you were heading back to the States. Come on, Lancer, I've bled for this story and I've helped you."

"I would guess New York. That's it."

Gannon hung up and headed for the street, scanning traffic for a cab as Emma hurried with him.

"We have to get the next plane back to New York," he said.

Emma pulled her hand from her bag. She had the blue memory card the woman at the center had given her. "I'd forgotten about this."

"What is it?"

"I don't know, the woman at the child-care center wanted me to have it. It's supposed to help explain what these people are up to."

64

Long after the A330 jetliner from Nassau leveled off, the attendant on duty in first class could no longer resist.

Engaged to be married in two months, she gave in to her maternal stirrings and knelt before the little angel asleep in 3B.

"He's such a sweetheart." She beamed at the woman seated next to him in 3A, reading the screen of her small laptop. The attendant assumed she was his grandmother. "He's such a good flyer. Not a bit of fuss."

The woman closed her computer. "I gave him a little home remedy before we left."

"It's working, you should bottle it. How old is he?"

"He's one."

"What's his name?"

Gretchen Sutsoff had chosen the name of her dead brother for the Wyoming child's counterfeit passport.

"Will."

The attendant caressed his little fingers.

"I bet he's destined for great things."

"I'm confident of that," Sutsoff said.

"You're so blessed. If you need help with anything, let me know."

When the attendant left, Sutsoff looked at the baby.

Yes, this one was destined for great things. He was the

ideal specimen. His DNA made him the perfect vehicle. He was too valuable for her to have entrusted him with Valmir and Elena Leeka for the final stage.

Elena was a whore.

Valmir was an idiot.

By taking stupid risks with that brazen car crash in Wyoming, Valmir could have killed this little treasure. Sutsoff was lucky those two didn't bungle the cruise-ship operation. But when they came back demanding more money, then getting drunk at the casino, their fate was sealed.

Sutsoff erased them.

The world was better without them.

There were too many ants.

But had she jeopardized the operation?

No.

The Bahamian police would never figure it out. Besides, her work was so far advanced now that nothing could stop her. After this operation she had new plans for her prized specimen with the perfect DNA.

Her little Will would shape the new world.

Sutsoff embraced a memory of her brother.

She turned to the clouds, and for several minutes she was a terrified fourteen-year-old girl again in the panicked stadium at Vridekistan, seeing her mother and father trampled, hearing Will's heart-wrenching squeal, feeling his little hand going limp in hers. She gazed at the ocean and took several slow breaths.

She could do this.

She would do this.

The pills she'd taken to help her face crowds were working. She looked at the float pen on her tray and contemplated how she'd survived the horror that killed her family to devote her life to correcting nature's errors with the human race.

She alone had forged the solution.

It was right here, in her laptop and in this novelty pen.

And seventy others like it that would be put to use. She picked it up, raising and lowering the ends, making the tiny sailboat bobble up and down in the barrel filled with her new formula.

About one thousand miles northwest in Washington, D.C., the FBI was working on the fugitive file for Sutsoff.

Information and intelligence from police agencies around the world was flowing into FBI headquarters.

The CIA had provided her Social Security number, date of birth, physical description and fingerprints. Interpol obtained what were thought to be the most recent passport photos and a number of aliases.

Gretchen Rosamunde Sutsoff was characterized as a scientist formerly contracted by the U.S. government, who was wanted for a range of charges including, murder, kidnapping and theft of U.S. government property. When the file was ready, Gretchen Sutsoff would be sought around the world by Interpol and would top the FBI's Ten-Most Wanted list.

As Sutsoff's plane came to a full stop at Newark Liberty International Airport in New Jersey, the Office of Enforcement at U.S. Customs and Border Protection headquarters in Washington, D.C., received an urgent alert from the FBI through Homeland Security.

The alert was for Gretchen Rosamunde Sutsoff, a dangerous murder suspect, believed to be preparing to enter the United States. It was immediately sent to a coordinator for processing.

After studying the details listing Sutsoff's DOB, race, height, weight, eye and hair color, and aliases, and looking at the accompanying photographs, the coordinator called her supervisor for final sign-off before releasing it.

In Newark, Sutsoff gathered Will and her bags and prepared to leave the plane. Smiling attendants helped her get

Will into her umbrella stroller. Just before boarding in Nassau, Sutsoff had it gate-checked; now it was waiting for them on the jetway.

She pushed the stroller along, joining other passengers walking through the terminal toward U.S. Immigration, where she got into the line for non-U.S. citizens. The wait was not as long as she'd expected. Weary security officials had just cleared three 747 charter flights from Europe—*here for the Human World Conference?*—and they were coming to a shift change before a new wave arrived.

Sutsoff's queue moved smoothly. She got her passport and other papers ready. It was not long before she reached the front of the line.

In Washington, after the U.S. Customs and Border Protection enforcement supervisor had read the alert on his monitor, he issued his electronic approval and called his senior coordinator.

"Let's get this out to everyone now," he said.

Back at the airport in Newark, the U.S. Immigration inspector waved Sutsoff to his desk and received her passport, her I-94 card, her B-2 visitor's visa, a notarized letter signed by her "daughter" allowing her to travel with her "grandson," and other papers. She was photographed and fingerprinted on a scanner, after which the inspector studied her documents. All of them were in the name of Mary Anne Conrad, a new alias she'd arranged through a passport forger and people she'd bribed to help her obtain documents. The baby was identified as William John Conrad. The inspector scrutinized Sutsoff, ensuring her photograph matched her face.

"Where were you born?"

"The United States, Virginia."

"How did you become a citizen of the Bahamas?"

"My family moved around quite a bit when I was young."

"Who is the child and why does he have an American passport?"

"He's my grandson. My daughter lives here in the United States."

"What's the purpose of your visit?"

"My daughter will be joining us in New York for a visit to see the city, then taking Will home with her. He stayed with me for a bit while she dealt with a career change."

"And where does your daughter live?"

"Wyoming."

"All right, thank you."

After she cleared Immigration, the inspector's shift ended. He closed his station and directed other passengers to the next desk. Sutsoff went to baggage claim, then lined up for U.S. Customs, handing her information to the female officer who yawned as she processed her entry.

In the half minute after Sutsoff had cleared Customs, the officer's computer beeped with an alert, but she'd already turned from her desk to allow a colleague to take her place for a break.

The relief officer's eyebrows rose when she read the details of the alert, but she had no inkling that a wanted fugitive had just cleared her very post.

Struggling with the stroller and her luggage, Sutsoff made it to the arrivals area, where she'd spotted a man wearing a black chauffeur's cap, a sport coat, white shirt, black tie, black pants and holding up a sign reading M. Conrad NYC.

"Over here," Sutsoff said. "Thank you. Do you have the car seat I reserved?"

"Yes, we're all set, ma'am. Let me get your things."

The driver helped Sutsoff and Will settle into the luxurious Buick. After loading the luggage and stroller, he got behind the wheel and confirmed their destination.

"The Grand Hyatt in Manhattan?"

"Yes."

Sutsoff had requested to be dropped off there, but she planned to walk three blocks to another hotel. As the gleaming black sedan glided along the freeway, she took another pill. The miles clicked by and the span of the magnificent George Washington Bridge ascended in the distance just as they passed a huge billboard announcing the Human World Conference.

Sutsoff felt her stomach lift as she gazed across the Hudson where Manhattan's skyline awaited them.

She turned to the baby, content in his car seat, then she contemplated New York City, then her float pen.

This was the power.

Ahead was the glory.

65

Fort Detrick, Maryland

That night, the ramifications of Gretchen Sutsoff's new creation dawned on Foster Winfield.

He turned to his colleagues Tolkman, Weeks and Kenyon, seated at the table in a small meeting room. They had worked nonstop, analyzing material transported by jet fighter from Sutsoff's secret lab on Deus Island. The four scientists sat in silence, then Kenyon said what everyone was thinking.

"She's insane."

"This defies the science," Tolkman said. "How did she do it?"

"Why did she do it?" Weeks asked.

"I'm responsible," Winfield said. "I brought her in to Project Crucible."

Major Powell entered the room carrying a briefing binder.

"They're all set in Washington." Powell positioned a telephone console and speakers at the center of the table, keyed in several numbers and linked them to an emergency teleconference call with a spectrum of security agencies working on the new threat.

"Who've we got there?" a voice asked.

"Major Powell in Fort Detrick. With me are the four agency scientists who'd worked on Project Crucible."

"Thank you. Everyone, identify yourselves when you speak, please. We'll get started with the chair of the meeting."

"This is Lincoln Hunter, assistant to the National Intelligence director, the president's advisor. Time is an issue here, let's keep things simple and keep it moving. We'll go to the FBI. We have a suspect—a former agency scientist, Sutsoff, developing an attack. Updates, please."

"Robert Lancer, FBI. She's a Bahamian national. We believe she'll attempt to enter the U.S. We've alerted Customs and Border Protection."

"And if she's already here?"

"We're going out with a public fugitive alert as soon as possible."

"And the target city for the strike, Lancer?"

"We have information suggesting it's New York. We suspect it could be the Human World Conference."

"In Central Park?"

"Yes. We strongly urge consideration be given to canceling the event. We're working with the NYPD, the Port Authority and New York State Police."

"Are we even close to this suspect's trail, Lancer?"

"We're working 24/7, assessing information obtained from Sutsoff's island lab, her residence, her staff and from the child-care center on Paradise Island. We believe a number of foreign families with children will be traveling to New York and could be involved in the operation. We're working with police agencies around the world."

"Anything else?"

"We're analyzing new information on other potential players. A person of interest is Drake Stinson, a former employee with the agency, now based in Brazil with a law firm that has ties to the operation through illegal adoptions. Stinson may have knowledge of the bombing of the Café Amaldo in Rio de Janeiro. His last known whereabouts was Europe."

"And the weapon? I understand Sutsoff's stolen something from Project Crucible and will turn it on us, is that correct?"

"Yes." Winfield cleared his throat. "Foster Winfield here. I was the chief scientist on Crucible."

"I've been briefed," Hunter said, "but need you to tell me in simple terms, Dr. Winfield, what we've got, so I can brief the director. I understand Sutsoff's unleashed a new virus?"

"No, not exactly. It's complicated."

"Simplify it, please, Doctor."

"She's created a new super-lethal agent to attack DNA. She can manipulate it to work at a hyper rate to target any specific group, or combination of groups."

"How?"

"We've just completed deeper analysis that shows evidence of molecular electronics and manipulation on a supramolecular nanoscale."

"Which means?"

"She can control her new lethal agent using radio-frequency command via wireless technology, from a cell phone or computer."

"But to do what, exactly? I still don't understand. If I were carrying this super Pariah V1 agent, infected as it were, wouldn't I be dead?"

"No, that's part of the sophisticated, unbelievable aspect of her engineering. The agent acts less like a virus and more like a dormant remote-controlled bomb."

"How?"

"I could carry it and remain in perfect health, then transmit it to you or a thousand people through contact. Those people could continue transmitting it to others and so on, that's the virus-like aspect she's developed. But the agent would remain dormant as it were. Nothing would happen to anyone until Sutsoff activates the agent using remote manipulation. And she could target people with specific DNA characteristics. It would be like creating armies of microscopic lethal time bombs, transmitting them to a large group and then commanding them to detonate in everyone in that group according to the targeted DNA characteristic. Or put another way, targeting everyone in the group who has a 212 area code, or everyone who has a 212 area code with a 555 prefix and so forth."

"Or anyone at all?"

"Yes, she can establish whatever range she likes."

"I've seen the photos from the cruise-ship victim and the two victims in Nassau. They're gruesome. The potential here is apocalyptic."

"Yes."

"Mr. Hunter," Lancer said. "While we do not have irrefutable evidence of a planned attack in New York, we strongly urge cancellation of the Human World event."

"Agent Lancer, this administration does not govern by fear. You know as well as I that it will never allow potential threats to dictate its agenda. As you say, you do not yet have irrefutable evidence of a planned attack. You have not yet confirmed your suspect is in the country, or the city. There are many complications, many considerations," Hunter said. "I need to know, what if Sutsoff succeeds in passing along this lethal agent but never activates it?"

"Nothing happens. The agent passes harmlessly through your system, like a placebo, in about twenty-four hours."

"So how do we stop it?"

"We don't know yet."

"We better find a way and fast. We expect over one million people to gather in less than twenty-four hours for the main event of the conference in Central Park. This morning, the Oval Office said the president and first lady will attend and greet as many people as possible."

66

New York City

It was down to hours.

Robert Lancer checked his watch against the wall clocks.

Long before the sun rose over Manhattan, law enforcement for New York City notched up security for one of the largest peace-time gatherings in the city's history.

No word on the possibility of pulling the plug on the event.

Not far from the Brooklyn Bridge, on the eighth floor of One Police Plaza, Lancer had taken his place at Operational Command. The NYPD was the lead agency for the conference.

Now, it was coordinating with the FBI's Command Center at Federal Plaza and the city's Office of Emergency Management, which was on full alert for a biological attack. Other local, state and federal agencies were also bracing for a possible strike, and the U.S. Secret Service big-footed its role to protect the president. Security had been heightened over concerns arising from Gretchen Sutsoff's emerging threat.

It was 3:50 a.m.

The next security status meeting would start in ten minutes. Lancer was checking e-mails when his cell phone rang.

"Bob, it's Norris at Federal Plaza Command."

"Go ahead."

"Our embassy in Kuwait City says Drake Stinson's just been detained for questioning by Kuwaiti security."

"Did he give them anything on Sutsoff?"

"No, they've had him for twenty minutes and will transmit the interview live. We're setting up to share it with Operational Command."

"Is that it?"

"Yesterday Dutch police arrested a couple at Schipol in Amsterdam bound for New York, traveling with a two-year-old with a forged German passport. Under questioning they said they knew a Dr. Auden."

"One of Sutsoff's aliases. They get anything more from them?"

"They're still in questioning. In France last night, police intercepted a couple with a toddler at de Gaulle. They were bound for New York. Their passports were suspect and the pair admitted knowledge of Auden in the Bahamas. Bob, there's talk she made a video."

"A suicide video?"

"We don't know. But add the most recent couples detained to the others yesterday from Madrid, Hong Kong and Argentina, and we now have twelve couples linked to the doctor."

"That's twelve out of the seventy we found in her computer files. Keep me posted, Norris. I have to go."

The meeting commenced with updates and arguments over the best course of action.

"We have to pull the plug on the Central Park event," a state official said. "If this is a significant threat, we have to shut it down."

"Organizers are dead set against it," said a woman from city hall.

"What about the president?" an NYPD official asked.

"The White House hasn't indicated yet if the president and first lady are pulling out," the Secret Service official said. "We're flowing all updates to the Oval Office. However, it's still a go. To answer the question that was raised at the last meeting, when the Pope celebrated Mass here, we had twenty-three real threats. Four were deemed significant and involved evidence of weapons and explosives. We thwarted all of them and the event went ahead without incident. Nothing made it into the press."

"This is Johnson with Tactical. At our last briefing we were advised that this weapon could be remotely activated by wireless. Do we know what frequency range? Can't we jam it, or shut down towers, block satellites?"

"Captain Tillser, NYPD Comms. We're exploring that option with the NSA and wireless providers. Bottom line, if we go that route, we risk disrupting or disabling all emergency communications for police, fire, ambulance. It would render us useless."

"Where are we on Sutsoff, Lancer?" The NYPD captain shot him a sour look. Lancer was checking the new message he'd received.

"We got her alert out to Customs and Border Protection and Interpol. The public alert goes to media this morning. Ahead of all that, we gave Interpol our intelligence for some seventy suspects we think are linked to Sutsoff and the Human World Conference. Several people around the world have been detained for questioning, including Drake Stinson, who at this moment is being questioned by police in Kuwait. Stinson is known to be a member of Sutsoff's secretive inner circle, a doomsday group known as Extremus Deus. He is a person of interest." Lancer nodded to the large screen at the far end of the room. "I've just been alerted we're receiving video of his questioning in Kuwait, which we'll share with the task force now. Okay, Norris, send it through."

Three seconds passed before Drake Stinson appeared on the screen.

"Is this live, real-time?" someone asked.

"Aside from a five-second delay, it's live," Lancer said.

Stinson was seated at a table in a stark room across from the two men questioning him.

"Mr. Stinson, what can you tell us about Dr. Sutsoff's operation?"

"It's too late. She's crazy, you can't stop—"

Stinson grimaced.

"Mr. Stinson?"

Stinson's chair scraped and his body spasmed.

"Are you all right?"

Stinson wrapped his arms around his stomach and groaned. Agony spread over his face and his skin began to bubble as if corn were popping under the surface. Bloodstains blossomed on his shirt as his abdomen expanded.

"Oh, God!"

Stinson's eyes liquefied and he slid to the floor, bones and spine cracking as his body contorted into a hunched position before he died.

The two Kuwaiti agents stood over him, their mouths agape, before the video signal was switched off.

"What the Christ was that?" an NYPD official asked as others around the room muttered in disbelief.

"This is what we're facing," Lancer said.

"How the hell do we stop that?"

67

Gretchen Sutsoff rose before the sun.

She was rested and ready.

Little Will was sleeping soundly.

Still in her nightdress, Sutsoff went to her laptop computer.

Drake Stinson had betrayed her. She knew that he was now somewhere in the Middle East trying to broker a deal with what he thought was an antidote to Pariah Variant 1.

As she started entering the activation codes for him, she did the same for the other members of her inner circle—General Dimitri, Downey, Goran, Reich and especially Ibrahim Jehaimi for violating her trust.

Before they'd joined her in the toast in Benghazi, she'd worked a veterinarian's hypodermic needle through the wine cork and injected enough lethal agent—a special prolonged-acting version—for all of them.

She took care of Jehaimi with a little gift of sweets later.

Now it was time to tidy things up.

It took five full minutes to complete the activation process, which ended when she tapped the enter key. Wherever they were in the world, they'd just taken their final breaths.

Goodbye.

She'd erased them.

Done.

Sutsoff was hungry.

She showered, then ordered a breakfast of poached eggs and English tea to her room. While the baby slept, she ate quietly and watched the new day break over Manhattan.

When she finished, she switched on the TV to watch the morning news programs. The weather called for a clear day in the low seventies.

Pictures of herself appeared on the TV screen.

A news crawler under the images said the FBI was searching for a former CIA scientist wanted in connection with murder, a conspiracy to commit an act of terrorism and theft of government property. No mention of a target or method of operation. *Do they know?* The news report showed footage of CIA headquarters, Fort Detrick, the resort on Paradise Island, a cruise ship and the face of the passenger from Indiana.

Sutsoff was calm.

She no longer looked like the wanted fugitive—Botox, body padding and a wig had taken care of that. She was Mary Anne Conrad, traveling with her grandson Will.

Her work would continue. She was only a few hours away from full activation. *This just makes things interesting,* she thought, as the baby woke and started to fuss.

Sutsoff changed him.

Then she unscrewed her float pen and mixed the clear liquid from the barrel into his breakfast: fruit, toast and juice from room service.

There we go.

As the baby ate, she checked on progress through her various e-mail accounts. She was disappointed to learn that only a handful of families were now in place in New York hotels.

She returned to the TV news, which was now showing preparations for the gathering in Central Park. The event would start later that morning. Over one million participants were expected for the full slate of music and addresses from global celebrities, including the president.

"Over a million people—my, isn't that perfect?" She smiled at the baby. "It's more than perfect. It's beautiful."

Sutsoff noticed a new e-mail.

One of the couples was having trouble. They'd lost their floater pen. They were at the Tellwood, only four blocks away. Sutsoff had prepared extra pens.

She typed an e-mail to them.

"All finished eating, Will? Let's take a little walk before we head to the park."

She got him dressed, collected her laptop and some other things in a bag and loaded her stroller. Before she left, she took some more medication.

Nothing would stop her now.

68

Nassau, Bahamas

In the predawn darkness, a police car crept through Nassau's Over-the-Hill district.

The faint yelp of a distant dog sounded a warning as a flashlight beam shot from the car's passenger door. Light raked across the dilapidated shops with barred windows, the boarded-up canteens, eviscerated cars and tumbledown houses.

Royal Bahamas Police Detective Colchester Young and his partner Angelo Morgan had worked their street sources. An angry ex-girlfriend had tipped them to their subject, hiding at his aunt's place in Over-the-Hill.

"He said he had to lay low," she'd told them, then added, "he carries a gun all the time."

The car rolled up to a neat home with pretty flower boxes.

In a heartbeat, Young and Morgan, armed with a crowbar, semiautomatic pistols and a warrant, entered the house and found Whitney Wymm struggling to get up from the couch.

Wymm reached for the gun he'd stashed under the couch, but his wrist was crushed under Morgan's boot. Young slammed Wymm to the floor, rolled him on his stomach, put his knee in his back and cuffed him.

Wymm was one of the top document counterfeiters in the West Indies.

Young and Morgan had effective methods of extracting information and within an hour of his arrest, Wymm admitted that he'd created new passports for the woman in the photograph the detectives had shown him.

Gretchen Sutsoff.

Wymm gave them all the photos he'd used to create new passports for her in the name of Mary Anne Conrad and for the baby she had with her, William John Conrad.

By the time the sun rose, the detectives had alerted their supervisor to the vital new information. The supervisor alerted his bosses, who saw that the update was immediately rushed through official channels to the FBI in Washington.

The FBI passed it to the FBI Field Office in Manhattan and the New York Police Department, and it was circulated to every law enforcement officer tasked to find Gretchen Sutsoff.

Early that morning in Manhattan, Art Wolowicz and Clive Hatcher were among the teams of NYPD detectives assigned to that aspect of the case. They were canvassing hotels when the new alert beeped on the mobile computer in their unmarked Chevy Impala.

"A new picture and alias—this one's a freakin' chameleon. Where we goin' next?" Wolowicz asked.

Hatcher pried the lid off his takeout cup, blew on his coffee and said, "LaQuinta, then Comfort Inn, then let's go back to the Tellwood."

69

"We're close to Tyler, I can feel it, Jack." Emma Lane's concentration never strayed from Gannon's computer monitor.

The memory card she'd obtained from the Blue Tortoise Kids' Hideaway held hundreds of files. Gannon and Emma continued studying them now at Gannon's desk in the World Press Alliance headquarters.

They'd first read the files yesterday, during their flight from Nassau.

Tears had rolled down Emma's face when she'd found Tyler's case among them. It contained his health records from his doctor and the clinic in California, Emma and Joe's personal information, their photos, articles on their crash from the *Big Cloud Gazette,* even Joe's obituary. Then separate information about "adoptive parents" Valmir and Elena Leeka, and something about Tyler's birth parents having died in a car accident.

"Why are they doing this?" Emma had asked over and over.

Gannon didn't have the answer

Today, he zeroed in on the data related to seventy couples or families located around the world.

"There seems to be a pattern."

Earlier that morning, after Gannon had brought Melody

Lyon up to speed, she'd assigned other reporters to help. They'd taken the names Gannon had mined from the files and started calling New York hotels to see if any people named in the files were registered.

In studying the files, Gannon had discovered that each case involved a small child, usually under three years old. Each case also seemed to involve an adoption through law firms or agencies in Brazil, South Africa, Eastern Europe, Malaysia, China or India. And each case involved name changes and exhaustive health records.

In the more recent files, Gannon found that names of the "families" or "couples" had been removed or changed. But a few files contained notes about traveling to New York for the Human World Conference. Gannon had managed to pull some of those names from those files. He was reviewing them when he got a call from a WPA reporter who was helping them.

"Jack, it's Linwood."

"You get anything with those names I gave you to check?"

"Zip."

"Keep checking."

Gannon kept poring over the files. His focus sharpened when he found one he'd overlooked. It contained two names: Joy Lee Chenoweth and Wex Taggart out of Vancouver, Canada.

There were photos of the couple with a boy about three years old and recent notes suggesting that they would be going to the Human World Conference and staying at the Tellwood Regency Inn.

Gannon picked up his phone and called the hotel.

"Tellwood Regency, how may I help you?"

"Yes, I'm trying to reach two guests, Joy Lee Chenoweth and Wex Taggart. Did they check in yet?"

"One moment, sir." Keys clicked. "Yes, Wex Taggart from Vancouver, British Columbia."

"That's right."

"We have them. Would you like me to connect you, now?"

"Yes, please."

The line switched and rang twice before a woman answered.

"Hello?"

Gannon hesitated while looking at the file photos. The voice on the line seemed suited to the pretty young Asian woman staring back at him.

"I'm sorry. I think I've got the wrong room."

Gannon hung up and turned to Emma.

"We have a lead at the Tellwood hotel."

70

Gannon updated Lyon.

Two news photographers were dispatched to meet Gannon and Emma at the northwest corner of the intersection closest to the Tellwood.

Lyon then authorized Emma to have a temporary WPA photo ID made for her at Gannon's insistence.

The Tellwood Regency Inn stood in the shadow of the Chrysler Building near Grand Central Station. Gannon and Emma found news photographers, Matt Ridley and Penny Uhnack, waiting at the nearest corner with their cameras tucked away in their shoulder bags.

Both were seen-it-all, shot-it-all pros.

"Matt, get everybody coming in and out of the hotel with a stroller or small kids," Gannon said. "Penny, come with us."

Inside, the gleaming four-star hotel was bustling.

"I'll wait here and do the same as Matt." Uhnack unshouldered her bag. "But I won't be obvious, just a tourist testing my camera."

Gannon cut across the lobby to the desk where a young clerk smiled.

"Yes, can I help you?"

"Sorry, it's been a rough day. I'm a reporter with the World Press Alliance." Gannon showed her his photo ID and unfolded a sheet of paper with the names Taggart and

Chenoweth. "I'm late for an interview with the people in this room, 1414. My desk didn't give me all the information. I think the people moved to another room. Can you please help me?"

The clerk looked at the note then tapped her keyboard.

"We have them, Mr. Gannon. Room 2104."

"Thank you so much."

Gannon and Emma stepped into one of six elevators and rode to the twenty-first floor. On the way up, they exchanged nervous glances. Gannon had decided he would confront Chenoweth and Taggart with the truth and try to persuade them to help.

They stepped off at the floor and headed to room 2104. Gannon knocked on the door.

No response.

Would they find a repeat of the scene in the Bahamas?

Gannon put his ear to the door. No movement inside. Emma looked in vain for cleaning staff.

"Let's go back down," Gannon said.

In the lobby, Uhnack's face was flushed as she approached them.

"I think I got something." She cued up several frames on her digital news camera. "These people just left. I barely got my camera out."

Uhnack had captured images of an Asian woman in her twenties pushing a stroller with an Asian boy who looked about three or four. A Caucasian man in his twenties was with them. Gannon compared the shots to the file photos.

"That's them," Gannon said.

"Definitely," Uhnack said. "I got these pictures, too."

She showed them more images. A white couple in their thirties holding hands with two little girls, then a frame of a young African-American woman with a baby in a stroller and a frame of an older woman pushing a stroller.

"Wait!" Emma drew her face to the camera's viewer. Uhnack enlarged the frame. "Oh, my God, that's Tyler!"

"Who is he with? She's familiar." Gannon recalled the woman's face from that morning's fugitive alert. "It might be Gretchen Sutsoff."

"Which way did she go?" Emma demanded. "Tell me!"

Uhnack shook her head. "I didn't see!"

Gannon's phone rang.

"Jack, it's Ridley outside. I got some stuff, but something's up. Looks like an unmarked just pulled up and two detectives are at the desk."

Gannon went to the desk and got close enough to see a badge flash and hear NYPD detectives Wolowicz and Hatcher say they were looking for a Mary Anne Conrad, traveling with a baby, William John Conrad. The clerk checked registrations, then shook her head.

"We have other names," Hatcher said as the clerk ran through them. Then Gannon heard the investigators say, "alias Gretchen Sutsoff."

"Excuse me," he interrupted. "I overheard you and I think I may have some information."

The detectives turned.

"That right? And who are you?"

Gannon produced his ID, waved Uhnack and Emma over and called Ridley in. They showed the detectives their photographs. Emma struggled with her emotions as Gannon explained everything quickly to Wolowicz and Hatcher. Their stone-faced expressions revealed nothing.

When Gannon had finished briefing them, Hatcher called his captain.

"Which way did you say she was traveling?" Hatcher asked Ridley.

Emma fought back tears, staring at Tyler's photo.

"West on Forty-second," Ridley said.

"—ASAP, that's right," Hatcher said into his phone. "Get all radio cars looking for her from the Tellwood, west on forty-second." Hatcher studied Ridley and Uhnack's photos. "Description—white female, mid-fifties, medium build.

Five-seven, maybe one-twenty, one-thirty. She's wearing a red top and white shorts. She's pushing a blue canvas stroller. The kid is white, about one or so, and is wearing a white 'I heart New York' T-shirt."

Emma wanted to scream.

"I can't stand here. I have to look for Tyler!"

"Hold it. No one goes anywhere." Wolowicz tapped the cameras. "We want those pictures, this is a police investigation."

"These are WPA property," Ridley said. "Work that out with WPA brass." He hit his speed-dial button for the WPA photo editor.

"We will, pal. I'm going to hold you all until we settle this."

"I need to go now!" Emma screamed.

"No one is going anywhere, miss." Wolowicz leveled his finger at her. "There are half a dozen police cars in this area now that are looking for our subject. Stay calm. We're going to find her and the baby."

"We're wasting time!" Emma shouted.

Heads shot around as people watched the exchange. Ridley was on his phone explaining their predicament to the photo editor.

Gannon called Lancer.

"Lancer."

"It's Gannon in New York. She's here. Sutsoff is here."

"Where?"

"Our photographers saw her leaving the Tellwood on Forty-second heading west about fifteen minutes ago. She has Emma Lane's baby with her."

"Are you sure?"

"We've got photos and two NYPD detectives are here."

"Give us the photos."

"It's being sorted out now. Where would Sutsoff go?"

Lancer hesitated.

"Come on, Lancer!"

"She'll likely go to Central Park for the conference."

71

Gretchen Sutsoff heard an old melody on Fifth Avenue.

She stopped the stroller in front of a coffee shop. Its open door was leaking music, a song that her little brother had cherished.

Will.

The memories flooded back. Will was such a good boy.

To hear his song on this day pleased her until she was jerked from her reverie.

"Lady, would you get outta my freakin' way?"

A sweating, grunting delivery man balancing a steel handcart loaded with soda nearly grazed her, forcing her to move. Sutsoff came to another storefront and saw a TV inside broadcasting the fugitive alert.

The report showed the older photos that bore no resemblance to her.

As a precaution, she entered a Fifth Avenue shop, bought a summer dress, a sun hat and dark glasses. She took the baby with her and changed in the washroom of a fast-food restaurant. She also put on a new wig that was a different color and length. She tested her laptop. The signal was strong, she had full battery power and she had spares.

Good.

Finally, she checked the baby. His signs were fine. *He's in perfect health,* she thought, taking a couple more pills to help her contend with the crowds before wheeling the stroller back to the street.

They resumed their long walk on Fifth Avenue.

Sirens wailed and helicopters whomped overhead as they neared Central Park. The traffic and crowds increased and charter buses crawled along, diesels chugging, brakes hissing. Mounted patrols stood by as, even at this hour, vendors hawked pretzels, ice cream, nuts, soda and Human World T-shirts to people streaming toward the park. All were wearing the required orange wrist bands that came with the tickets.

As Sutsoff and the baby disappeared into the crowds, she saw him playfully touching people who brushed against them. She smiled as she watched the people he touched touch others.

Thirty minutes to go and Robert Lancer's stomach knotted.

The size of the crowd was sobering.

The number of people gathering on the Great Lawn, the huge midpark expanse where Pope John Paul II had celebrated Mass, was estimated at 1.3 million.

Is Sutsoff out there? Lancer wondered as he looked through his binoculars from the police command post on West Drive, at the Eighty-third Street level. Other command posts were located around the park.

The air crackled with sound checks from the huge stage flanked by massive video screens. Other giant screens and speaker towers ascended from the tranquil sea of humanity.

Squadrons of emergency vans, ambulances and police trucks were strategically parked in and around the park. NYPD Communications trucks monitored the crowd via video cameras on speaker towers.

So much was in play; there were metal detectors and X-ray machines, K-9 explosives teams and chemical sensors to analyze the air for gases and toxins. The stage and VIP areas had been swept, then triple-checked by the Secret Service. Lancer exhaled. So far paramedics and first-aid stations had reported no unusual or alarming medical problems.

Organizers refused to consider shutting the event down at this stage.

All officials agreed that to make any sort of announcement of a potential threat would create chaos. The White House was clear: the president would attend. The first lady and vice president would remain in Washington. Oval Office staff told the Secret Service that the president would not cower. No group would dictate his agenda through threats. The president's stance was firm: he would be with the people at this major event. Facing threats was part of his job.

The pleas for cancellation by Lancer and other security officials were in vain. That left them few options. Yes, events like these were often subject to threats, but this one had a horrific blood trail that led straight to it.

Teams of undercover police and cadets were threading through the crowd, looking for anyone who matched Sutsoff's photo, the new one obtained by police in the Bahamas.

As the MC took to the stage to start the day's program, Lancer looked hard at the images filling the nearest big screen.

He had an idea.

The show started.

Gannon was with Emma on the east side, near the obelisk behind the Metropolitan Museum of Art. They were patrolling the edges of the crowd, scrutinizing every person they saw who had a child in a stroller. Emma's heart raced each time she spotted someone who looked like Sutsoff or Tyler.

Gannon called the WPA and learned that the WPA's lawyers and NYPD were urgently finalizing use of the WPA's photos. TV news helicopters circled overhead. The *Times, Daily News* and *Post* had reported online that security was heightened at the event because of the president's visit, amid rumors of an increased threat level.

So far, no news organization knew what Gannon and the WPA knew. The wire service had assigned eight reporters and six photographers to the event. As music filled the air, Gannon and Emma scanned the ocean of faces. The size of the crowd was overwhelming.

It was futile.

"I feel so helpless," Emma said. "Did they find them?"

Again, Gannon called the WPA newsroom where Mike Kemp, a seasoned crime reporter, was monitoring emergency scanners.

"Anything happening, Mike?" Gannon asked Kemp, hearing the clatter of the scanners in the background.

"Nothing out of the ordinary for a crowd this size," Kemp said. "Some guy in the southwest sector had an asthma attack, a seventy-two-year-old woman in the north section had a fainting spell and a teenage girl got stung by a bee."

"What about arrests? Does it sound like they found Sutsoff?"

"Two gang bangers were fighting with knives near the Guggenheim and a drunk was exposing himself near the Museum of Natural History. I'll let you know if we pick up anything."

Gannon hung up. "Nothing," he told Emma. "Let's keep moving."

They headed south in the direction of Turtle Pond.

At the west side of the park, at the Eighty-third Street police command post, Lancer had his cell phone pressed to his ear.

"We're all clear?" he asked.

"It's a go, Bob, just ahead in the program."

"Good. Alert every cop out there. This might be our only hope."

* * *

Sutsoff and the baby had been sitting on the grass northeast of the Delacorte Theater.

She had decided enough time had passed.

The program had now been going for over two hours with short concert performances punctuated by brief speeches from celebrities, Nobel laureates and politicians. The weather was ideal—everyone was upbeat.

As she removed her laptop from her bag to run a status check, a long, loud roar rose from the Great Lawn. For an instant, she was pulled back to Vridekistan, but her medication dulled her anxiety as the president started to address the crowd. With his tie loosened and shirtsleeves rolled to his elbows he told the conference how "for every one of us, being human in today's world means bearing enormous responsibility…."

Sutsoff paid little attention to him.

She concentrated on her work. She saw that of her operation's seventy couples, thirty-one had succeeded in administering Extremus Deus Variant 1 to the "delivery vehicles" and were currently present somewhere on the Great Lawn.

That number was in keeping with what she'd anticipated. She was pleased with her rough calculations as to how many people had been touched by the children and how many of those people would have touched someone, who then touched another and so forth.

At least 50 percent of all the people who'd gathered here.

A touch was all it took.

And given the scale of the victim pool, with people coming and going and touching others, the variant would be carried beyond the park and the numbers would grow and grow.

All Sutsoff needed to do was submit the range.

"How about everyone, except for me and little Will?" She smiled to herself.

She entered the parameters, ensuring it excluded her and the baby.

No harm will come our way.

Entering the activation code would require about five minutes.

As Sutsoff was about to start, another loud cheer floated over the crowd and people around her got to their feet. The president had called for everyone to "rise up, show your human side. Reach out to your neighbor." He had formed a human hand-holding chain on the stage. It stretched into the crowd which swayed as people joined a soloist in the chorus of "Give Peace a Chance." Sutsoff declined to hold anyone's hand but encouraged others to hold the baby's hand.

When the song ended, the crowd sat down to wait for the next rock band to perform, leaving Sutsoff enthralled. She had not expected this hand-holding exercise. She estimated that 90 percent of the people here now carried the variant.

All she had to do was submit the activation code and press Enter.

She looked at her keyboard and listened to the sounds of happy families talking and laughing, then lifted her face to the sky and swallowed.

After today, the world will never be the same.

She positioned her laptop to enter the complex code.

"Ladies and gentlemen!" A man's voice boomed through the sound system. "May we have your attention please for a very important announcement?"

Sutsoff stopped typing and stared at the nearest large screen.

It filled with pictures of her and the baby, images showing them exiting the Tellwood hotel. There were several photos that changed every four seconds in a slide show. Crisp head-to-toe color shots credited to the World Press Alliance.

Sutsoff was stunned.

"We have a serious medical situation," the voice boomed, "for Mary Anne Conrad who is traveling with her grandson William John Conrad. We need to locate them immediately.

We believe they may be here, so please look around you. If you see her, please point her out to the nearest security or medical official. Please, do it now."

Waves of mild concern rolled through the park as people looked around them and back at the giant screens displaying Sutsoff's photos, now being enlarged to show details of the stroller and the baby's shoes.

Still wearing her large hat and dark glasses, Sutsoff turned to the group of teenaged boys on the lawn beside her.

"I think she's right over there." Sutsoff pointed to the east.

"What?" a boy with metal rings in his nose said.

"The lady they're looking for—see, by the man with the flag?"

"Big deal, whatever."

Sutsoff paused her work, closed her laptop, gathered the baby and her things then headed west to the nearest exit. She remained calm. All she needed was to find a safe place for five minutes to enter the code. She had to get out of the park now and get as far away as possible.

Gannon and Emma stared at the screen, then each other. "That's pretty good," he said.

In the vicinity of the southwest quadrant, an NYPD detective locked onto the woman pushing a stroller among the crowd. He compared the stroller shown on the big screen to the stroller he saw a short distance away. They were the same blue color, and the same dancing elephant patch and the same wheels. Then he focused on the baby's shoes.

It was them.

He lifted his radio to his mouth.

Gannon and Emma were not far from the Delacorte Theater when Gannon's cell phone rang.

"Jack, it's Mike. We just heard on the scanner that they spotted them near West Drive not far from Seventy-ninth."

"We'll head there now. Alert the photographers."

Gannon and Emma started running.

Lancer and several NYPD officers bolted from the police command point on West Drive, at the Eighty-third Street level. They navigated their way through the park toward Central Park West, while above them a police helicopter rolled into position to offer support. Radios crackled with updates from the breathless detective who was now running.

"She's on foot on Central Park West, north of the museum. She's moving fast, I could lose her if she gets in a cab. Goddammit, am I the only one watching her? Wake up, you guys!"

Gannon and Emma worked their way from the park. Mike Kemp called as a chopper thudded above them.

"Give me your location," Kemp said.

"Uh—" Gannon looked around quickly "—Central Park West, around Eighty-first."

"Okay, go south, Jack. You're close! Keep the line open."

Gannon could hear Kemp crank up the scanner volume.

At that moment, he and Emma saw a CBS news crew running to a parked news van, a reporter with a phone pressed to his ear, just ahead of a camera operator.

Kemp was shouting in Gannon's phone.

"She's crossing from the east to the west side of Central Park West!"

As Gannon and Emma crossed to the west side and ran south, they saw flashing emergency lights several blocks away. Two parked NYPD patrol cars had swung into the street, their tires squealing as they headed north toward them.

Closer to them but a few blocks away, Emma glimpsed a woman pushing a stroller across the traffic lanes of Central Park West.

"I see her! I see Tyler!" Emma screamed.

* * *

Two blocks ahead, Sutsoff, pushing the stroller, heard the sirens and saw the chopper. Her ears were ringing from the blood rush of her racing heart.

Her medication was wearing off.

All she needed was five minutes.

"NYPD, freeze!"

A man behind her was running, gaining on her. She saw the badge on a chain around his neck. Police cars were roaring toward her. She glimpsed a hotel entrance a block ahead. If she could make it, then get up the elevator in time to hide for five minutes.

She just needed five minutes.

"NYPD. Freeze or I'll shoot!"

Gannon and Emma, racing south, were a block away when they saw Sutsoff, who was approaching them, throw a look over her shoulder at the man chasing her.

From her position, Emma saw the stroller, saw the little face of the baby strapped in it and saw the shouting cop behind Sutsoff draw his gun.

"No! Don't shoot!" Emma screamed.

Emma thrust her palms out just as Sutsoff pushed the stroller into the street against the red light and the chrome grill of a ten-ton Brooklyn Gravel Service dump truck catapulted Sutsoff thirty feet, onto the windshield of a Mercedes, before she bounced into the middle of Central Park West.

Her bag with her laptop tumbled down the street.

The impact had clipped the stroller, sending it toddling into Central Park West traffic and into the path of the two pursuing NYPD patrol cars, their sirens wailing and lights flashing.

Jack moved toward the stroller, but Emma, her arms, hands, reaching, was quicker, seeing the fear in the baby's eyes as wig-wag lights and bumpers roared toward him.

"Noooo!"

Emma's fingers clamped the stroller handle and pulled it to her just as the officers braked, skidding to within inches of the baby's foot.

The child was unharmed.

"Tyler!"

Emma thrust her face to his, gasping as his eyes brightened with recognition. She lifted him from the stroller, sat on the street and sobbed.

"Mommy's got you! I'll never let you go, never!"

Adhering to training and using their doors as shields, the officers put their hands on their weapons.

"Don't move, lady! Don't harm the baby. My partner's going to approach you slowly. You give her the baby."

"No!"

"Lady, you have to give us the baby!"

Gannon tried to help. "She's the mother."

"Back off, sir!" one cop said, taking in the gathering crowd. "Back off, everybody!"

Other officers took charge of the scene and one shouted into his shoulder microphone for an ambulance as the smell of burning rubber, the wail of more sirens and the hovering helicopter filled the air.

When Lancer and the other NYPD officers arrived, Gannon pleaded to him.

"Lancer, tell them it's her baby!"

Lancer held up his ID and slowly defused the situation.

Police gathered around Sutsoff, while others rerouted traffic and sealed the scene, clearing the way for the ambulance as spectators and other reporters arrived.

Lancer picked up Sutsoff's bag, pulled out her laptop and took it to a patrol car. Gannon nodded to a WPA photographer to get pictures.

"I didn't see them," the truck driver said. "I swear. I had the green!"

His rig was deep into the intersection. Sutsoff was a few feet away.

Her neck was broken, rib shards had speared her heart and she didn't hear the paramedics working to save her. They slid an oxygen mask over her nose and mouth. Her head lolled and she met the eyes of Emma Lane, rocking her baby.

Emma stared at her.

As Gretchen Rosamunde Sutsoff lay in a growing pool of blood staring at the sky, a warm wave rolled over her.

Project Crucible no longer mattered to her.

Extremus Deus no longer mattered to her.

Gretchen was a happy little girl again flying above old London at night.

Flying like Peter Pan and Wendy and dreaming of living in London forever with her mother, her father and little brother, Will.

Epilogue

Gretchen Sutsoff died before her ambulance reached the hospital.

The first news reports indicated that there had been an attempted abduction of a baby boy at the Human World gathering when the fleeing suspect was killed in a traffic accident.

The unharmed child had been reunited with his mother.

What was not reported at the outset was how Dr. Foster Winfield and the experts from Project Crucible, Fort Detrick and the CDC had examined the files found in Sutsoff's laptop and confirmed that she never activated her lethal agent. The microbe remained harmless and would pass safely through anyone's system within twenty-four hours.

That analysis was supported by the fact that medical staff at the event in Central Park had no reports of any serious or unusual illnesses arising from the gathering.

In the days and weeks that followed, the Royal Bahamas Police, aided by U.S. authorities, began dismantling Sutsoff's lab on Deus Island and the Blue Tortoise Kids' Hideaway on Paradise Island.

Investigations at the Golden Dawn Fertility clinic, and clinics at other locations around the world, helped police uncover the networks used by Sutsoff and her inner circle.

All of the major players—Drake Stinson; General Dimitri, the intelligence chief; Goran, the human trafficker; Reich, the global banker and Downey, the arms dealer—had been found dead, victims of the weapon they'd helped develop.

An autopsy performed on Sutsoff resulted in the discovery of a malignant tumor that was removed from her brain. It exhibited widespread necrosis that could have contributed to her actions.

For all investigators, the priority remained the stolen children. They were all recovered with help from Sutsoff's files. Medical experts examined them closely and monitored their health. Detectives around the world conducted exhaustive interviews and examinations of records, counterfeit and forged passports and illegal adoption files, and they determined that most of the adoptions were processed by Stinson's firm in Rio de Janeiro. Brazilian detectives, including Roberto Estralla, provided information enabling the stolen children to be reunited with their families.

One of those reunions happened in Kunming, China.

Late one night, local police knocked on the door of Sha Shang and Li Chen's home. Sha was fearful of a police action but Li screamed when the officers smiled and little Pan Qin emerged.

Li thought she was dreaming and told her husband to pinch her as she checked her boy for the birthmark on his left ankle shaped like two hearts touching, symbolizing her eternal love for her son.

It was there.

Li fell to her knees and crushed her son in her arms.

Similar scenes were replayed in countries around the world where children were returned safely to their families.

For weeks, the plot to unleash Extremus Deus Variant 1 in Central Park remained the top news story around the world. Any doubt about Jack Gannon's skills vanished as he led the WPA's coverage with exclusive reports that made use of Marcelo Verde's dramatic photos of the explosion at the Café Amaldo.

"I was dead wrong about you, Gannon." George Wilson

removed his glasses and winked. "But you know, you're only as good as your last story."

Gannon wrote about Gretchen Sutsoff's life, her genius and her descent into madness. It was the tale of a brilliant scientist who came within a heartbeat of committing one of the most devastating acts in history.

Sutsoff was buried next to her mother, father and little brother in a small cemetery in the Virginia countryside not far from where she was born. The ceremony was arranged by a distant relative. Gannon was among the few people present. Lancer, Winfield and Kenyon were there. None of Sutsoff's relatives were present when her coffin was lowered into the ground. The woman who wanted to erase the world was not mourned.

Gannon never forgot the people who'd helped him. He thanked Oliver Pritchett and Sarah Kirby and everyone along the way. And in a feature about Gabriela Rosa, Marcelo Verde, Adam Corley and Maria Santo, he honored the dead.

Gannon arranged through Roberto Estralla to send bonus money he'd received to Pedro and Fatima Santo in the Rio favela of Céu sobre Rio to set up a scholarship in the name of their murdered daughter, Maria.

About a month after Emma and Tyler were reunited, Gannon accepted Emma's invitation to visit them in Big Cloud.

The three of them got into Emma's car and headed across Wyoming's high, rolling plains. They went to one of Emma's favorite spots, twenty miles north of town alongside the Grizzly Tooth River. Emma had packed a lunch, and while Tyler threw pebbles into the river, she turned to Gannon.

"The other day I was given a gift, Jack."

Gannon could not begin to guess what it was.

"After we found Tyler, he was examined thoroughly by

so many doctors, goodness. He's perfectly fine, but when they double-checked his DNA they found that he's Joe's biological son."

"Really?" Gannon grinned.

"Yes. Somehow, in all of this, a miracle happened." Emma looked at the sky. "It means Joe is still with us, you know?"

"Sure."

"What about you, Jack?"

"What about me?"

"Ever think of settling down?"

Gannon shrugged. "I almost got married once, to a reporter at the *Cleveland Plain Dealer*."

"What happened?"

"Didn't work out. I guess I've always been a loner."

"Well, you'd better watch yourself." She smiled. "You never know what's coming for you."

"You never know."

He smiled back, watched Tyler toddling after a butterfly, then reflected on Sutsoff and her lonely funeral. That got him thinking about how he really had no one in his life except his sister, Cora.

But he'd lost her long ago.

He looked toward the mountains.

If she wasn't dead, she was out there.

Somewhere.

As he considered the snow-crowned peaks he thought that maybe it was time to find her.

* * * * *

AUTHOR'S NOTE

In crafting *The Panic Zone,* I was inspired in part by the public record and accounts of people subjected to experimentation without their consent. A little online research or, better yet, a pleasant visit to your local public library will yield information on chilling projects conducted, or secretly planned, throughout history. I make no claim to being a scientist or possessing any knowledge in the field and apologize to the experts among you for any technical errors or implausibility in my made-up tale. I ask you to bear in mind that *The Panic Zone* is not a textbook but rather a work of fiction drawn in my imagination after reaching into the darkest corners of historical fact.

ACKNOWLEDGMENTS

I owe a debt of gratitude to a number of people. I would like to thank Valerie Gray, Dianne Moggy, Catherine Burke and the excellent editorial, marketing, sales and PR teams at Harlequin and MIRA Books around the world. As always, I am thankful to Wendy Dudley. I would also like to thank my friends in the news business for their help and support: in particular, Sheldon Alberts, Washington Bureau Chief for Canwest News Service; Juliet Williams, Associated Press, Sacramento, California; Bruce DeSilva and Vinnee Tong, Associated Press, New York. Also, Lou Clancy, Eric Dawson, Jamie Portman, Mike Gillespie, colleagues from the *Calgary Herald, Ottawa Citizen,* Canwest News, Canadian Press, Reuters, the *Toronto Star, Globe & Mail, Los Angeles Times* and so many others.

You know who you are.

Very special thanks to Barbara.

I would also like to thank Milly Marmur in New York, Lorella Belli in London and Ib Lauritzen in Denmark.

A big thanks to Amy and Marianne.

Again, I am indebted to sales representatives, booksellers and librarians for putting my work in your hands. Which brings me to you, the reader; the most critical part of the entire enterprise.

Thank you very much for your time, for without you a book remains an untold tale. I hope you enjoyed the ride and will check out my earlier books while watching for my next one. I welcome your feedback. Write to me at RMofina@gmail.com. Drop by www.rickmofina.com, subscribe to my newsletter and send me a note.

Sneak peek of IN DESPERATION,
coming soon from Rick Mofina

Clair Martin was propped against two pillows in her bed when she heard a faint noise and put her book down.

Was that Tilly, her daughter, asleep down the hall?

No, that sounded as if it came from outside.

Clair listened for half a minute. Everything was quiet. She dismissed the noise as either a bird or the Wilson's darned cat. The clock on Clair's night table showed 12:23 a.m. She returned to her book. After reading two more pages she grew drowsy when she heard another noise.

Like a soft murmur. This time it came from the far side of the house.

What the heck is that?

Clair got up to investigate, groaning because she had to go to work in a few short hours. She needed to get some sleep.

She went down the hall to Tilly's door. It was partially open as usual. Her eleven-year-old daughter was asleep on her stomach. One foot had escaped from the sheet. Clair moved to her bedside, adjusted the blankets then paused to take in the room—Tilly's stuffed toys, posters of teen idols and Clair's favorite: the drawing of two figures holding hands titled *Mommy & Me.*

Clair smiled.

Soft light painted Tilly's face. She was more than a beautiful child to Clair; she was her lifeline, her hope and her dream.

I love you more than you'll ever know, kiddo.

Clair's attention shifted to the soft knock on her front door. Who could be calling at this hour? Moving through her small rented bungalow, Clair looked through the living room window and glimpsed two uniformed police officers standing outside.

She opened the front door.

In the instant Clair absorbed their cheerless expressions, half in shadow under the porch light, she was pricked by an icy twinge of unease. Something was wrong here.

Not the kind of wrong that often accompanies a late-night visit by police, but something darker. Something overwhelming, like a karmic lightning bolt that, in a heartbeat, had Clair considering the mistakes she'd made in her life. She feared for her daughter.

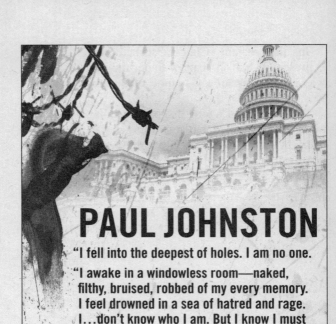

RICK MOFINA

32638	VENGEANCE ROAD	___ $7.99 U.S.	___	$8.99 CAN.
32901	SIX SECONDS	___ $7.99 U.S.	___	$9.99 CAN.

(limited quantities available)

TOTAL AMOUNT	$ _____
POSTAGE & HANDLING	$ _____
($1.00 for 1 book, 50¢ for each additional)	
APPLICABLE TAXES*	$ _____
TOTAL PAYABLE	$ _____

(check or money order—please do not send cash)

To order, complete this form and send it, along with a check or money order for the total above, payable to MIRA Books, to: **In the U.S.:** 3010 Walden Avenue, P.O. Box 9077, Buffalo, NY 14269-9077; **In Canada:** P.O. Box 636, Fort Erie, Ontario, L2A 5X3.

Name: _____

Address: _____ City: _____

State/Prov.: _____ Zip/Postal Code: _____

Account Number (if applicable): _____

075 CSAS

*New York residents remit applicable sales taxes.
*Canadian residents remit applicable GST and provincial taxes.

MIRA®

www.MIRABooks.com

MRM0710BLTALL